Angels

MARIAN KEYES

PENGUIN BOOKS

PENGUIN BOOKS

Published by the Penguin Group

Penguin Books Ltd, 80 Strand, London WC2R 0RL, England

Penguin Group (USA) Inc., 375 Hudson Street, New York, New York 10014, USA

Penguin Group (Canada), 90 Eglinton Avenue East, Suite 700, Toronto, Ontario, Canada M4P 2Y3
(a division of Pearson Penguin Canada Inc.)

Penguin Ireland, 25 St Stephen's Green, Dublin 2, Ireland (a division of Penguin Books Ltd)

Penguin Group (Australia), 250 Camberwell Road, Camberwell, Victoria 3124, Australia
(a division of Pearson Australia Group Pty Ltd)

Penguin Books India Pvt Ltd, 11 Community Centre, Panchsheel Park, New Delhi – 110 017, India

Penguin Group (NZ), 67 Apollo Drive, Rosedale, Auckland 0632, New Zealand
(a division of Pearson New Zealand Ltd)

Penguin Books (South Africa) (Pty) Ltd, Block D, Rosebank Office Park,
181 Jan Smuts Avenue, Parktown North, Gauteng 2193, South Africa

Penguin Books Ltd, Registered Offices: 80 Strand, London WC2R 0RL, England

www.penguin.com

First published by Michael Joseph 2002
Published in Penguin Books 2003
Reissued in Penguin Books 2012

001

Printed in Great Britain by Clays Ltd, St Ives plc

A CIP catalogue record for this book is available from the British Library

B-format ISBN: 978–1–405–91204–4

www.greenpenguin.co.uk

MIX
Paper from
responsible sources
FSC® C018179

Penguin Books is committed to a sustainable
future for our business, our readers and our planet.
This book is made from Forest Stewardship
Council™ certified paper.

ALWAYS LEARNING   **PEARSON**

For Tony

Acknowledgements

I'd like to thank the following people:

My editor Louise Moore for her clever, intuitive input, Harriet Evans for her meticulous work, and all at Penguin.

Everyone at Poolbeg, with special thanks going to Paula Campbell for the snooker story.

Jonathan Lloyd, Tara Wynne and Nick Marston at Curtis Brown.

The wonderful Ricardo Mestres, Danny Davis and Heij at Touchstone Pictures for my first LA adventure.

The equally wonderful Bob Bookman, Sharie Smiley and Jessica Tuchinsky at CAA for my second LA adventure.

And the following, for generously providing information, encouragement and/or confectionery: Guy and Julie Baker, Jenny Boland, Ailish Connelly, Siobhan Coogan, Emily Godson, Gai Griffin, Dr Declan Keane at Holles St Hospital, Caitríona Keyes, Mammy Keyes, Rita-Anne Keyes, Julian Plunkett-Dillon, Deirdre Prendergast, Eileen Prendergast, Suzanne Power, Morag Prunty, Jason Russell, Anne-Marie Scanlon, Emma Stafford, Louise Voss, Amy Welch and Varina Whitener. Thanks to all of you.

Finally, thanks to my beloved Tony, to whom this book is dedicated.

Prologue

'We will shortly be landing at Los Angeles International Airport. Please ensure your seat is in the upright position, that you weigh less than a hundred pounds and that you have excellent teeth.'

1

I'd always lived a fairly blameless life. Up until the day I left my husband and then ran away to Hollywood, I'd hardly ever put a foot wrong. Not one that many people knew about, anyway. So when, out of the blue, everything just disintegrated like wet paper, I couldn't shake a wormy suspicion that this was long overdue. All that clean living simply isn't natural.

Of course, I didn't just wake up one morning and skip the country, leaving my poor sleepy fool of a husband wondering what that envelope on his pillow was. I'm making it sound much more dramatic than it actually was, which is strange because I never used to have a penchant for dramatics. Or a penchant for words like 'penchant', for that matter. But ever since the business with the rabbits, and possibly even before that, things with Garv had been uncomfortable and weird. Then we'd suffered a couple of what we chose to call 'setbacks'. But instead of making our marriage stronger – as always seemed to happen to the other luckier setback souls who popped up in my mother's women's magazines – our particular brand of setbacks did exactly what it said on the tin. They set us back. They wedged themselves between myself and Garv and alien-ated us from one another. Though he never said anything, I knew Garv blamed me.

And that was OK, because I blamed me too.

*

His name is actually Paul Garvan, but when I first got to know him we were both teenagers and nobody called anybody by their proper names. 'Micko' and 'Macker' and 'Toolser' and 'You Big Gobshite' were some of the things our peers were known as. He was Garv, it's all I've ever known him as, and I only call him Paul when I'm extremely pissed off with him.

Likewise, my name is Margaret but he calls me Maggie, except when I borrow his car and scrape the side against the pillar in the multi-storey car park (something that occurs more regularly than you might think).

I was twenty-four and he was twenty-five when we got married. He'd been my first boyfriend, as my poor mother never tires of telling people. She reckons it demonstrates what a nice girl I was, who never did any of that nasty sleeping-around business. (The only one of her five daughters who didn't, who could blame her for parading my suspected virtue?) But what she conveniently omits to mention when she's making her proud boast is that Garv might have been my first boyfriend, but he wasn't my only one.

However.

We'd been married for nine years and it would be hard to say exactly when I'd started to fantasize about it ending. Not, let me tell you, because I wanted it to be over. But because I thought that if I imagined the worst possible scenario, it would somehow be insurance against it actually happening. However, instead of insuring against it, it conjured the whole bloody thing into existence. Which just goes to show.

The end came with surprising suddenness. One minute my marriage was a going concern – even if I was doing strange stuff like drinking my contact lenses – the next minute it was entirely finito. Which caught me badly on the hop, as I'd always

2

thought there was a regulation period of crockery-throwing and name-calling before the white flag could be waved. But everything caved in without a single cross word being exchanged, and I simply wasn't prepared for it.

God knows, I *should* have been. A few nights previously I'd woken in the darkness for a good worry. Something I often did, usually fretting about work and money. You know, the usual. Having too much of one and not enough of the other. But recently – probably longer than recently, actually – I'd been worrying about me and Garv instead. Would things ever get better? Were they better already and I just wasn't seeing it?

Most nights I didn't come to any conclusions and lapsed back into an unreassured sleep. But this time I was afflicted with sudden, unwelcome x-ray vision. I could see straight through the padding of the daily routine, the private language and the shared past, right into the heart of me and Garv, into all that had happened over the last while. Everything was stripped away and I had a horrible, too-clear thought: *We're in big trouble here.*

It literally made me cold. All the little hairs on my skin lifted and a chill settled somewhere between my ribs. Terrified, I tried to cheer myself up by having a little fret about the amount of work I'd have to do the following day, but no dice. So then I reminded myself that my parents were getting older and that I'd be the one who'd end up having to take care of them, and tried to scare myself with that instead.

After a while I went back to sleep, scratched my right arm raw, ground my teeth with gusto, awoke to the familiar sensation of a mouth coated with bits of grit, and carried on as normal.

I was to remember that *We're in big trouble here* when it transpired that we actually were. On the evening in question we were meant to be going out for dinner with Elaine and Liam, friends of Garv's. And who knows, if Liam's new flatscreen television hadn't fallen off the wall and on to his foot, breaking his big toe in the process, so that I'd gone out instead of going home, maybe Garv and I would never have split up.

The irony is, I was *praying* that Elaine and Liam would cancel. The chances were good – the last three times we were supposed to meet up, it hadn't happened. The first time, Garv and I had bowed out because we were getting our new kitchen table delivered. (No, of course it didn't come.) The next time, Elaine – who's some bigwig in pensions – had to drive to Sligo to make a load of people redundant. ('The new Jag arrived just in time!') Then the last time I'd managed to come up with some spurious excuse which Garv had agreed with all too readily. This time it was their call.

Not that I didn't like them. Well, actually I didn't. Like I said, she's a bigwig in pensions and he's a stockbroker. They're good-looking, earn *tons* of money and are unkind to waiters. They're the sort of people who always seem to be getting new cars and going on holiday.

Most of Garv's mates were lovely, but Liam was a glaring exception: the problem was that Garv was one of those types who went around seeing the good in people – most people, anyway. This is a great quality in theory, and I'd no objection to him seeing the good in people I liked myself, but it was a bit of a pain when he persisted with the ones I didn't. Himself and Liam had been friends since junior school, in the days when Liam had been a lot nicer, and, even though Garv had tried very hard for my sake, he'd been unable to shake his residual affection for him.

But even Garv agreed that Elaine was terrifying. Shespokerealfast. Firingquestionsfromamachinemouth. How'swork? Whenareyougettinglisted? Her dynamic glamour reduced me to stammering inadequacy, and by the time I'd cobbled together an answer, she'd have lost interest and moved on.

But even if I had liked Liam and Elaine, I still wouldn't have wanted to go out that particular night – putting on a big, fat, happy head is that much harder if you've an audience. Also there was a pile of scary manila envelopes to be dealt with at home. (Plus two soaps eager to tend to my needs and a couch that couldn't do enough for me.) Time was too precious to waste an entire evening out enjoying myself.

And I was *so* tired. My work – like most people's, I would imagine – was very demanding. I guess the clue is in the name: 'work'. Otherwise they might call it 'flat on your back on a sunlounger' or 'having a deep-tissue massage'. I worked in a legal firm which had a lot of dealings with the US. Specifically, entertainment law. (After we'd got married, Garv, on account of his general fabulousness, had been seconded for five years to his company's Chicago office. I'd worked for one of the big legal firms there, so when we returned to Ireland three years ago I claimed to be well versed in US entertainment law. The kicker was that even though I'd done night classes and got some qualifications in Chicago, I wasn't a proper lawyer. Which meant I got tons of the work, most of the abuse, but only a fraction of the moola. I was more of an interpreter, I suppose; a clause which meant one thing in Ireland could mean something different in the States, so I translated US contracts into Irish law and drafted contracts that should – hopefully – stand in both jurisdictions.)

I lived in vague but constant fear. Sometimes I had dreams where I'd left out a vital clause and my firm got sued for four trillion dollars, which they deducted from my wages at the rate of seven pounds fifty a week, and I had to work there for all eternity paying it back. Sometimes, in those dreams all my teeth fell out as well. Other times, I'm sitting in the office and I look down to find that I'm naked and that I need to get up and use the photocopier.

Anyway, the day the balloon went up, I was very busy. So busy that my new fitness regime had gone by the board. I'd recently realized that biting my nails was the only exercise I was getting so I'd hatched a cunning plan – rather than ring Sandra, my assistant, to come and collect my dictaphone tapes, I'd walk the twenty yards to her office and hand-deliver them instead. But no time for such self-indulgence that particular day. A deal with a film studio was about to fall apart: if the contract wasn't finalized that week, the actor who'd attached himself to the project was going to walk.

For a minute there my job sounded glamorous. Take my word for it, it was as glamorous as a cold sore. Even the business lunches I occasionally had to go to at expensive restaurants weren't all that. You could never truly relax – people always asked a question requiring a long and detailed answer just after I'd put a forkful of food into my mouth, and whenever I laughed I was haunted by an irresistible fear that I had green food stuck in my teeth.

Anyway, the scriptwriter – my client – was desperate to get the contract all sorted out so that he could get his fee and his family could eat. (And so his father might finally be proud of him, but I digress.) The US lawyers had come to work at three in the morning, their time, in order to try and close the deal, and all day e-mails and phone calls zipped back and forth. Late in the day we dotted the final 'i' and crossed the

6

final 't', and even though I was wrecked I felt light and happy.

Then I remembered that we were supposed to be going out with Liam and Elaine and a cloud passed over the sun. It wasn't so bad, I consoled myself; at least I'd get a nice dinner out of it – they were fond of fancy-dan restaurants. But God, I was exhausted. If only it was *our* turn to cancel!

And then, just when it seemed that we were beyond all hope, the call came.

'Liam's broken his toe,' Garv said. 'His new flatscreen telly fell on it.' (Liam and Elaine had every consumer durable known to man – and I stress *man*, not woman. Give me a mobile phone and a hair-curler and I'm happy. But Garv, being a man, yearned after digital this and Bang & Olufsen that.) 'So tonight's off.'

'Great!' I exclaimed. Then I remembered myself; they were his friends. 'Well, not great for him and his toe, but I've had a tough day and –'

'It's OK,' Garv said. 'I didn't want to go either. I was just about to ring them and pretend our house had been burnt down or something.'

'Dandy. Well, see you back at the ranch.'

'What'll we do about food? Will I pick up something?'

'No, you did it last night. I'll do it.'

I had just launched into an orgy of switching stuff off when someone said, 'Going home, Maggie?' It was my boss, Frances, and her *already?* might have been silent but I still heard it.

'That's right.' Lest there be any confusion. 'Going home.' Polite but firm. Trying to keep my prone-to-quaver-under-pressure voice free of tell-tale traces of fear.

'That contract ready for tomorrow morning's meeting?'

'Yes,' I said. No, actually it wasn't. She was talking about a different contract, one I hadn't even started on. There was no point whinging to Frances that all day I'd been frantically sewing up a great deal. She was an über-achiever, well on her way to being made a partner, and she'd made hard work into a performance art. She rarely left the office and popular opinion (not that she *was* popular, of course) had it that she slept under her desk and washed, like a bag lady, in the staff toilets.

'Can I take a quick look?'

'It's not really laid out properly yet,' I said awkwardly. 'I'd rather wait until it's all done before I show you.'

She gave me a watchful, too-long look. 'Make sure it's on my desk by nine-thirty.'

'Right!' But the good spirits engendered by being let off the hook for the evening had all leached away. As she hammered her heels back to her office, I looked appraisingly at the computer I'd just switched off. Should I stay and do a couple of hours on it there and then? But I couldn't. I was all out. Of enthusiasm, of work-ethic, whatever. Instead I'd get up very early and come in and do it then.

I hadn't eaten much all day. At lunch-time, instead of stopping work, I'd foraged in my desk drawer for a half-eaten Mars bar that I'd vaguely remembered abandoning some days earlier. To my delight, I found it. I dashed off the paper clips and the worst of the fluff and, I must say, it was delicious.

So as I drove home I was hungry, and I knew there would be shag-all in the house. Food was a big problem for Garv and me. We subsisted, like most people we knew, on microwaved stuff, takeaways and meals out. Now and again – at least, before things had gone weird on us – when we'd cleared our backlog of ordinary worries, we'd spend a bit of time worrying that we

8

weren't getting enough vitamins. So we'd vow to embrace a new, healthier way and buy a jar of multivitamins, which we'd take for a day or so, then forget about. Or else we'd go on a mad splurge in the supermarket, pulling our arms out of their scurvied sockets lugging home heads of broccoli, suspiciously orange carrots and enough apples to feed a family of eight for a week.

'Our health is our wealth,' we'd say, pleased as punch, because it seemed that *buying* raw foodstuffs was an effective thing to do in itself. It was only when it became clear that the food had to be eaten that the trouble would begin.

Immediately events would set about conspiring to thwart our cooking plans: we'd have to work late or go out for someone's birthday. The ensuing week was usually spent in edgy awareness of all the fresh fruit and vegetables clamouring for our attention. We could hardly bear to go into the kitchen. Visions of cauliflowers and grapes constantly hovered on the corner of our consciousness, so that we were never truly at peace. Slowly, day by day, as the food went off, we'd furtively throw it out, never acknowledging to each other what we were doing. And only when the final kiwi fruit had been bounced off the inside of the bin did the black shadow lift and we could relax again.

Give me a frozen pizza any time, far less stressful.

Which is precisely what I bought for that evening's meal. I mounted the pavement, ran into the Spar and flung a couple of pizzas and some breakfast cereals into a basket. And then Fate intervened.

I can go without chocolate for weeks at a time. OK, days. But once I have a bit I want more, and the fluff-covered, lunch-time Mars bar had roused the hungry beast. So when I saw the boxes of handmade truffles in a chilled compartment I decided in a mad splurge of go-on-you-divil justification to buy myself one.

Who knows what would have happened if I hadn't? Did something as benign as a box of chocolates alter the entire course of my life?

Garv was already home and we greeted each other a little warily. We hadn't expected that this evening would be just the two of us; we'd been kind of depending on Liam and Elaine to dilute the funny atmosphere between us.

'You just missed Donna,' he said. 'She'll call you at work tomorrow.'

'So what's the latest?' Donna had a messy, high-concept love life and, as one of her best friends, it was my duty to provide advice. But she often consulted Garv to get what she called 'the male perspective', and he'd been so helpful that she'd rechristened him Doctor Love.

'Robbie wants her to stop shaving under her arms. Says he thinks it's sexy, but she's afraid she'll look like a gorilla.'

'So what did you advise?'

'That there's nothing wrong with women having hair –'

'Right on, sister.'

'– but that if she really doesn't want it, she should say that she'll stop shaving under her arms if he'll start wearing girls' knickers. Sauce for the goose and all that.'

'You're a genius, you really are.'

'Thanks.'

Garv pulled off his tie, flung it over the back of a chair, then raked his fingers through his hair, shaking away the vestiges of his work persona. For the office his hair was Ivy League neat:

shorn close at the neck and sleeked back off his face, but off-duty, it flopped down over his forehead.

There are some men who are so good-looking that meeting them is like being hit on the head with a mallet. Garv, however, isn't one of them; he's more the sort of man you could see day-in, day-out for twenty years, then just wake up one morning and think, 'God, he's nice, how come I never noticed him before now?'

His most obvious attraction was his height. But I was tall, too, so I'd never gone around saying, 'Ooh, look at how he towers over me!' All the same, I was able to wear heels with him, which I appreciated – my sister Claire had been married to a man who was the same height as her, so she'd had to wear flats in order that he wouldn't feel inadequate. And she really *loves* shoes. But then he had an affair and left her, so everything works out for the best in the end, I suppose.

'How was work?' Garv asked.

'Mostly awful. How was yours?'

'Bad for most of the day. I had a nice ten minutes between four-fifteen and four-twenty-five when I stood on the fire escape and pretended I still smoked.'

Garv works as an actuary, which makes him a cheap target for accusations of being boring – and on first meeting him you might confuse his quietness with dullness. But in my opinion it's a mistake to equate number-crunching with being boring; one of the most boring men I ever met was this gobshite novelist boyfriend of Donna's called John – you couldn't get more creative. We went out for dinner one night and he BORED us into the ground, loudly monologuing about other writers and what overpaid, meretricious bastards they were. Then he began questioning me about how I'd felt about something or other;

probing and delving with the intimacy of a gynaecologist. 'How did you feel? Sad? Can you be more specific? Heartbroken? Now we're getting someplace.' Then he hurried to the gents' and I just *knew* that he was writing everything I'd said into a notebook, to use in his novel.

'You're not to be jealous about Liam's flatscreen telly,' I said to Garv, happy to pretend that his subdued mood was down to his mate having more consumer durables than him. 'Didn't it attack him? It might have to be put down.'

'Ah,' Garv shrugged the way he always does when he's bothered, 'I'm not bothered.' (Though happy to discuss Donna's problems with her, you'll note his reluctance to talk about his own feelings, even when they're only about a telly.) 'But do you know how much it cost?' he blurted.

Of course I knew. Every time I went into town with Garv we had to call into the electrical department in Brown Thomas and stand before said telly, admiring it in all its twelve thousand pounds' worth of glory. Though Garv was well paid, he didn't earn anything like Liam's telephone-number wedge. And what with our high mortgage, the cost of running two cars, Garv's addiction to CDs and my addiction to face creams and handbags, funds just didn't run to flatscreen tellies.

'Cheer up, it probably broke when it fell off the wall. And one day soon you'll be able to afford one of your own.'

'Do you think?'

'Sure I do. As soon as we finish furnishing the house.' This seemed to do the trick. With a slight spring in his step, he helped unload the shopping. And that was when it happened.

He lifted out my box of go-on-you-divil truffles and exclaimed, 'Hey, look!' His eyes were a-sparkle. 'Those sweets again. Are they following us?'

I looked at him, looked at the box, then back at him. I hadn't a clue what he was on about.

'You *know*,' he insisted skittishly. 'The same ones we had when –'

He stopped abruptly and, my brow furrowed with curiosity, I stared at him. He stared back at me and, quite suddenly, several things occurred at once. The playful light in his eyes went out, to be replaced with an expression of fear. Horror, even. And before the thoughts had even formed themselves into any order in my consciousness, I *knew*. He was talking about someone else, an intimate moment shared with a woman other than me. And it had been recently.

I felt as if I was falling, that I would go on falling for ever. Then, abruptly, I made myself stop. And I knew something else: I couldn't do this. I couldn't bear to watch the downward spiral of my marriage begin to catch other people and spin them into the vortex too.

Shocked into stillness, our eyes locked, I silently beseeched him, desperate for him to say something to explain it, to make it all go away. But his face was frozen in horror – the same horror that I felt.

'I –' he managed, then faltered.

A sudden stab of agony shot up into my back tooth and, as though I was dreaming, I left the room.

Garv didn't follow me; he remained in the kitchen. I could hear no sound and I presumed he was still standing where I'd left him. This, in itself, seemed like an admission of guilt. Still in my waking nightmare, I was picking up the remote and switching on the telly. I was waiting to wake up.

2

We didn't exchange a word for the rest of the evening. Perhaps I should have been shrieking for details – who was she? How long? But at the best of times that wasn't my way and after all we'd gone through over the past while, I'd no fight left in me.

If only I was more like my sisters, who were great at expressing pain – experts at slamming doors, crashing phones back into cradles, throwing things at walls, screeching. The whole world got to hear of their anger/disappointment/double-crossing man/chocolate mousse missing from the fridge. But I'd been born without the diva gene, so when devastation hit me I usually kept it inside, turning it over and over, trying to make sense of it. My misery was like an ingrowing hair, curling further and further into me. But what goes in must come out and my pain invariably re-emerged in the form of scaly, flaking, weeping eczema on my right arm – it was a cast-iron barometer of my emotional state and that night it tingled and itched so much that I scratched until it bled.

I went to bed before Garv and, to my surprise, actually managed to fall asleep – the shock, perhaps? Then I awoke at some indeterminate time and lay staring into the blanket of darkness. It was probably four a.m. Four in the morning is the bleakest time, when we're at our lowest ebb. It's when sick people die. It's when people being tortured crack. My mouth tasted gritty and my jaw ached: I'd been grinding my teeth again. No wonder my back tooth was clamouring for attention – making a last desperate plea for help before I ground it into nothingness.

Then, wincing, I faced the repulsive revelation full-on. This truffle woman – was Garv really having a thing with her?

In agony, I admitted that he probably was; the signs were there. Looked at from the outside I'd conclude that he definitely was, but isn't it always different when it's *your* life that's under scrutiny?

I'd been afraid of something like this happening, so much so that I'd half-prepared myself for it. But now that it seemed it had come to pass, I wasn't at all ready. He'd got such a glow on when he'd noticed 'their' chocolates . . . It had been dreadful to witness. He *must* be up to something. But that was too much to take on and I was back to not believing it. I mean, if he'd been messing around, surely I'd have noticed?

The obvious thing would be to ask him straight out and put an end to the speculation, but he was bound to lie like a rug. Worse still, he might tell me the truth. Out of nowhere, lines came to me from some B-movie. *The truth?* (Accompanied by a curled lip.) *You couldn't HANDLE the truth!*

The thoughts kept coming. Could she be someone he worked with? Might I have met her at their Christmas party? I shuffled through my memories of that night, endeavouring to locate a funny look or a loaded comment. But all I could remember was dancing the hora with Jessica Benson, one of his colleagues. Could it be her? But she'd been so nice to me. Mind you, if I'd been having sex with someone's husband, maybe I'd be nice to her, too . . . Apart from the women Garv worked with, there were the girlfriends and wives of his mates – and then there were my friends. I was ashamed even to have that thought, but

I couldn't help myself; suddenly I trusted no one and suspected everyone.

What about Donna? Herself and Garv always had a great laugh *and* she called him Doctor Love. I went cold as I remembered reading somewhere that nicknames were a cast-iron indication that people were up to high jinks.

But then, with a silent sigh, I released Donna without charge: she was one of my best friends, I truly couldn't believe she'd do that to me. Plus, for reasons best known to herself, she was mad about Robbie the flake. Unless he was an elaborate red herring, of course. But there was one thing that convinced me totally that Garv wasn't having an affair with Donna, and that was the fact that she'd told him about her verruca. In fact, she'd pulled off her boot and sock and thrust the sole of her foot at him so that he could see for himself just how gross it was. If you're having a passionate fling with someone, you don't own up to things like verrucas. It's all about mystique and impractical bras and round-the-clock upkeep on hairy legs – or so I'm told.

What about my friend Sinead? Garv was so kind to her. But it was only three months since she'd been given the road by her boyfriend, Dave. Surely she was far too fragile for an affair with her friend's husband – and far too fragile for any normal man to try it on? Unless it was her fragility that Garv liked. But wasn't he getting enough of that from me? Why go out for broken crockery when you've got it in absolute smithereens at home?

Beside me, I realized that Garv was awake too – his fake deep-breathing was the giveaway. So we could talk. Except we couldn't, we'd been trying for months. I didn't hear the intake of breath that precedes speech, so I was startled when the ink-dark silence was violated by Garv's voice. 'Sorry.'

Sorry. The worst thing he could have said. The word hung in the darkness and wouldn't go away. In my head I heard it echo again, then again. Each time fainter, until I wondered if I'd just imagined hearing it. Minutes passed. Without ever replying, I turned my back to him and surprised myself by falling asleep again.

In the morning, we woke late, and there was blood under my nails from scratching my arm. My eczema was back in force – I'd have to start wearing gloves in bed again if this continued. But would it continue? Again I got that falling sensation.

I busied myself with showers and coffee, and when Garv said, 'Maggie,' and tried to stop my incessant motion, I neatly sidestepped him and said, without eye contact, 'I'll be late.' I left, carrying that empty, four-in-the-morning feeling with me.

Despite sidestepping Garv, I was late for work and the contract wasn't on Frances's desk by nine-thirty. She sighed, 'Oh Maggie,' in an I'm-not-angry-with-you-I'm-disappointed way. It's meant to reach the parts a bollocking doesn't and make you feel shitty and ashamed. However, I appreciated not being shouted at. Not the reaction Frances was looking for, I suspect.

I felt entirely lost, but at the same time unnaturally calm – almost as if I'd been waiting for a catastrophe and it was a weird sort of relief that it had finally happened. Because I had no idea how to behave in these circumstances, I decided to mimic everyone else there and immerse myself in work. Wasn't it strange, I thought, that after such a dreadful shock I was still functioning as normal? Then I noticed I kept botching the double-click on my mouse because my hand was trembling.

For seconds, I'd manage to lose myself in a contract clause, but all the time the knowledge surrounded me: *Something is very wrong.* Over the years, like every couple, Garv and I had had our rows, but not even the most vicious of those had ever felt like this. The worst scrap had been one of those odd ones which had started out as a muscular discussion over whether a new skirt of mine was brown or purple, and had unexpectedly disintegrated into a bitter stand-off, with accusations of colour-blindness and hyper-sensitivity flying about.

(*Garv:* 'What's wrong with it being brown?'

Me: 'Everything! But it's not brown, it's purple, you stupid colour-blind fucker.'

Garv: 'Look, it's only a skirt. All I said was I was *surprised* at you buying a brown one.'

Me: 'But I DIDN'T! It's PURPLE!'

Him: 'You're overreacting.'

Me: 'I'm NOT. I would NEVER buy a brown skirt. Do you know the first thing about me?')

At the time I'd thought I'd never forgive him. I'd been wrong. But this time was different, I was horribly sure of it.

At lunch-time, I just couldn't find it in me to care about my urgent piles of work, so I went to Grafton Street, looking for comfort. Which took the form of spending money – again. Unenthusiastically, I bought a scented candle and a cheapish (relatively speaking) copy of a Gucci bag. But neither of them did anything to fill the void. Then I stopped into a chemist to get painkillers for my tooth and got intercepted by a white-coated, orange-faced woman who told me that if I bought two Clarins products – one of which had to be skincare – I'd get a free gift. Listlessly I shrugged, 'Fine.'

She couldn't believe her luck, and when she suggested the dearest stuff – serums in 100 ml bottles – again I lifted and slumped my shoulders. 'Sure.'

I liked the sound of a free gift – I found the idea of a present very consoling. But back at work, when I opened my present, it was a lot less exciting than it had looked on the picture: funny-coloured eyeshadow, a mini-mini-mini tube of foundation, four drops of eye-cream and a thimble of vinegary perfume. Anti-climax set in, and then, in an unexpected reprieve of normality, came guilt, which swelled big and ugly as the afternoon lengthened. *I had to stop spending money.* So as soon as I could reasonably leave, I hurried back to Grafton Street to try to return the handbag – I couldn't return the Clarins stuff because I'd already tried the free gift – but they wouldn't give me a refund, only a credit note. And before I'd made it back to the car, my eye was caught by yellow flowery flip-flops in a shoe-shop window and, like an out-of-body experience, I found myself inside, handing over my card and spending another thirty quid. It wasn't safe to let me out.

That evening I went to a work thing and did something I don't usually do at work things – I got drunk. Messy drunk, so bad that on one of my many trips back from the loo, when I met Stuart Keating, I ended up lunging at him. Stuart worked in another department and he'd always been nice to me; I can still see the surprise on his face as I zoomed in on him. Then we were kissing, but only for a second before I had to disengage. *What was I doing?* 'Sorry,' I exclaimed and, appalled at myself, I returned to the party, picked up my jacket and left without saying goodbye to anyone. From across the room Frances watched me, her expression unreadable.

When I came home, Garv was waiting bolt upright, like an anxious parent. He tried to talk to me, but I mumbled drunkenly that I had to go to sleep and lurched to the bedroom, Garv in hot pursuit. I stripped off my clothes, letting them lie where they fell, and climbed between the sheets. 'Drink some water.' I heard the clatter as Garv put a glass on my bedside table. I ignored it and him, but just before I sank into the merciful oblivion of sleep, I remembered I hadn't taken out my contact lenses. Too tired, drunk, whatever to get on my feet and go to the bathroom, I slipped them out and plopped them into the handily placed glass of water, promising myself I'd rinse them good and proper in their solution in the morning.

But when morning came, my tongue was superglued with dryness to the roof of my mouth. Automatically, I stretched out my hand for my glass of water and gulped it in one go. Only when the last of it was racing down my throat did I remember. My contact lenses. I'd drunk my contact lenses. *Again.* The third time in six weeks. They were only monthly disposables, but all the same.

And the following day, as luck would have it, I lost my job.

I wasn't exactly sacked. But my contract wasn't renewed. It was a six-month contract and since I'd moved back to Dublin from Chicago it had already been renewed five times. I had thought renewing it again was a mere formality.

'When you first started here,' Frances said, 'we were impressed with you. You were hard-working and reliable.'

I nodded. That sounded like me all right. On a good day.

'But in the last six months or so, the standard of your work and commitment has dropped dramatically. You're often late, you leave early . . .'

I listened, almost in surprise. Of course, I'd known that in my *head* stuff hadn't been great, but I'd thought I'd done a pretty good job of presenting a convincing business-as-usual façade to the outside world.

'. . . you've been clearly distracted and you've taken ten days' sick leave.'

I could have leapt to my feet and given a speech telling Frances why I'd been distracted and where I'd been on my ten days' sick leave, but I remained sitting like a plank, my face closed. It was no one's business but mine. Yet, paradoxically, I felt she should have seen that something had been very wrong over the past months and made allowances for me. I've been more rational, I suspect.

'We want people who care about their work –'

I opened my mouth to protest that I did care, until I realized, with a shock, that actually I didn't give a damn.

'– and it's with regret that I have to tell you that we are unable to renew your contract with us.'

It was years since I'd been sacked. In fact, the last time had been when I was seventeen and babysitting for a neighbour. I'd smuggled my boyfriend in when the children had gone to bed, because a house with no adults in had been too much to resist. But the horrible son – appropriately enough called Damian – spotted me smuggling my boyfriend back out. I'll never forget it: Damian was standing at the top of the stairs, and his expression was so malevolent that the Old Spice music began playing spontaneously in my head. I was never asked to babysit there again. (To be honest, it was nearly a relief.)

But since then I had never been fired. I was a pretty good worker – not so good that I was ever in danger of winning the Employee of the Month Award, but fairly reliable and productive.

'You want me to go?' I asked faintly.

'Yes.'

'When?'

'Now would be good.'

Oddly enough, it was losing my job that finally made me decide to leave Garv. I don't really understand why. Because, you know, it's not easy to leave someone. Not in real life. In fiction it's all so cut and dried and clear: if you can see no future together, then of *course* you leave. Simple. Or if he's having an affair, then you'd be a total idiot to stay, right? But in real life it's amazing the things that conspire to keep you together. You might think, OK, so we can't seem to make each other happy any more, but I get on so well with his sister and my friends are so fond of him, and our lives are too interwoven for us to be able to extricate ourselves. And this is our house, and see those lupins in our little back garden? – I planted them. (Well, not planted *planted*, I didn't actually put them in the ground with my own hands, it was a narky old man called Michael who did, but I masterminded the whole thing.)

Leaving someone is a big deal. I was walking away from a lot more than a person, it was an entire life I was saying goodbye to.

But the shock of losing my job had triggered the conviction that everything was falling apart. Once the door to one disaster had opened, the possibilities for catastrophe seemed open-ended and I felt I'd no choice but to go along with my life as it unravelled. Losing a job? Why not go for broke and lose a marriage as well? It had suffered so many body blows during the past months, it was over in all but name anyway.

By the time Garv came home from work, I was in the bedroom, waist-high in a pathetic attempt at packing. How anyone manages to do a midnight flit is beyond me. Most people (if they're anything like me) accumulate so much *stuff*.

He stood and looked at me, and it was like I was dreaming the whole thing.

He seemed surprised. Or maybe not. 'What's going on?'

This was my cue for the dramatic exit lines people always deliver in fiction. *I'm LEAVING you! It's OVER.* Instead, I hung my head and mumbled, 'I think I'd better go. We've tried our best with this and . . .'

'Right,' he swallowed. 'Right.' Then he nodded, and the nod was the worst bit. Such resignation in it. He agreed with me.

'I lost my job today.'

'Christ. What happened?'

'I've been distracted and taken too much sick leave.'

'Bastards.'

'Yeah, well.' I sighed. 'The thing is, I mightn't make this month's mortgage, so I'll give it to you from my Ladies' Nice Things account.'

'Forget it, forget it. I'll take care of it.'

Then we lapsed into silence and it became clear that the mortgage was all he was planning to take care of.

Maybe I should have been angry with him and Truffle Woman. Perhaps I should have despised him for not jumping into the breach and promising me passionately that he wouldn't let me go and that we could work it out.

But the truth was, right then, I *wanted* to go.

3

Maintenance level dysfunctional. That's how I'd like to describe my family, the Walshes. Well, actually, that's not how I'd *like* to describe my family. I'd *like* to describe my family as the proto-type for the Brady Bunch. I'd *like* to describe my family as the Waltons of Waltons' Mountain, only more lickarsey. But alas, maintenance level dysfunctional is as good as it gets.

I have four sisters, and the credo that each of them seems to live by is: The More Dramas the Better. (Sample thereof: Claire's husband left her the day she'd given birth to their first child; Rachel is a (recovered) addict; Anna doesn't really *do* reality; and Helen, the youngest – well, it's kind of hard for me to describe . . .) But I've never been fond of chaos and I couldn't figure out why I was so different. In my lonelier moments I used to entertain a fantasy that I was adopted. Which I could never truly relax into, because it was obvious from my appear-ance that I was *one of them*.

My sisters and I come in two versions: Model A and Model B. Model As are tall, wholesome-looking and, if left unchecked, have brick-shithouse tendencies. I am a textbook Model A. My eldest sister, Claire, and the sister next in line to me, Rachel, are also Model As. Model Bs, on the other hand, are small, kitten-cute and gorgeous looking. With their long, dark hair, slanty green eyes and slender limbs, the two youngest sisters, Anna and Helen, are both clear-cut examples of the genre.

Though Anna is nearly three years older than Helen, they look almost like twins. Sometimes even our mother can't tell them apart – although that's probably as much to do with her not wearing her glasses as their appearance, now that I come to think of it. To make it easy, Anna – a neo-hippy – dresses as though she's been rummaging through the dressing-up box, and Helen is the one with the air of psychosis.

Model As share the common characteristics of being tall and strong. Not necessarily fat. Not *necessarily*. Indeed, Model As have been known to look willowy and slender. If they're in the grip of anorexia, that is – not as unlikely as it sounds. It's certainly happened, although not, sadly, to me. I've never had an eating disorder – apparently I didn't have the imagination, Helen told me.

I mightn't have had an eating disorder, but I suspected I had a mild problem with another form of bulimia – shopping bulimia. It seemed like I was always splurging on stuff, then trying to return it. In fact, it had recently caused a huge row that involved most of my family. Helen had been lamenting on how hard it was to live on what she got paid as a make-up artist, and she suddenly rounded on me and accused, 'You're good with money.' This happened a lot; they referred to me as clean-living and sporty – even though I hadn't played any sport since living in Chicago – and painted a picture of me that was years, probably decades, out of date. My parents were wholly in approval of this sepia-tinted version of me, but my younger sisters – affectionately, mind – treated me as a figure of fun. Most of the time I humoured them, but that particular day I suddenly baulked at being – albeit affectionately – depicted as life-crushingly dull.

'In what way am I good with money?'

'Not living beyond your means. Thinking carefully before you buy stuff, that sort of thing,' Helen said, scathingly. 'Neither a borrower nor a lender be, hahaha.'

'I'm not good with money,' I said sharply.

'You are!' they chorused – my parents with admiration, Helen without.

'She's not,' Garv said.

'Thank you,' I turned briefly to him.

'You are so! I bet you've a huge stash of used fivers in a biscuit tin under your bed.'

'She wouldn't keep it in a biscuit tin,' Dad defended me against Helen. 'You don't get any interest in biscuit tins. She has her savings in a high-interest account.'

'What savings? I don't have any savings!'

'Don't you?' Mum sounded confused. Upset even. 'Didn't you used to have a post-office book? Didn't you pay in 50p a week?'

'Yes, when I was *nine*.'

'But you've a pension fund?' Dad asked anxiously.

'That's different, that's not savings and you don't get it till you're sixty. And I'm *always* buying things I don't need.'

'Then you bring them back.'

'But they don't always give refunds. Sometimes they only give credit notes, so that's the same as spending money.' My voice was rising. 'And sometimes they go out of date before I use them.'

'No!' Mum was appalled.

'Well, I bet you pay your credit card off in full every month,' Helen persisted.

'I DON'T pay my credit card off in full every month.' They were all slightly open-mouthed at my unexpected fury. 'Only SOME MONTHS!'

'Oh, rock'n'*roll*.'

I knew it was a little strange to be having this argument. I knew people argued about money — but usually they were being accused of spending too much and insisting that they didn't, not the other way round. So overwrought was I that eventually Mum made Helen apologize. Then she murmured to me, 'It's nothing to be ashamed of, earning good money and putting some by.'

It was at that point that Garv made me leave, raging that they'd upset me so. (You know the way Garv sees the good in most people? Well, he suspends such altruism around most of my family.)

On the drive home, I said anxiously, 'I know everything is relative and I know I'm not in their league, but I *am* neurotic, aren't I?'

'You are, of course,' he said stoutly. 'Don't mind them!'

However, I'm not dwelling on my family in this manner to provide background colour, there's actually a reason for it: it's because I'm about to resume living with them. I *could* have moved in with Donna, except she'd recently managed to get on-again-off-again-I'll-just-get-my-head-out-of-my-arse-if-you'll-give-me-a-second Robbie to live with her, so I wasn't sure she'd welcome the presence of a third party. Or I could have asked Sinead, except Dave had kicked her out and she was currently even more homeless than me. And I could have tried my best friend Emily, who has *plenty* of room. The only problem is that she lives in Los Angeles. Not exactly handy.

So, cap in hand, I've to return to the bosom of my family. First, though, I have to tell them, and I'm dreading it.

Perhaps it's never easy to disappoint your mum and dad, but in my case it feels extra difficult. I'm the one who married her first boyfriend, and they've been so heartbreakingly proud of me and of the ticks beside almost every item on the checklist: the marriage, the house, the car, the job, the pension plan, the robust mental health.

'You've never given us a moment's worry,' they've often said. 'The only one who hasn't.' Then would follow a baleful look at whichever of my sisters was giving them grief at the time. Now, after successfully avoiding them all those years, it was *my* turn for the baleful looks.

I paused at the front door before letting myself in. Just taking a moment. Filled with a fierce need to run away, leave the country, avoid facing my atrocious failure. Then, with a sigh, I shoved my key in the lock. I couldn't run away – I'm responsible and conscientious. In a family where several black sheep are jockeying for position, being the sole white sheep isn't much fun.

There was a racket coming from the television room and it sounded like all those currently domiciled in the house – Mum, Dad, Helen and Anna – were actually present. Helen, at twenty-five, still lived at home because of her on-off relationship with gainful employment – she's had many career changes. Two or three years were spent wasting time at university, and after a spell of unemployment she'd tried to be an air hostess, but couldn't manage to be pleasant enough. ('Stop ringing that fucking call-bell, I heard you the first time,' was, I believe, the sentence that ended her high-flying career.) More unemployment followed, then she did an expensive course as a make-up artist. She'd hoped to work in theatre and film, but instead ended up doing wedding after wedding after wedding – mostly the daughters of my parents' friends. But Mum's efforts to drum up work for Helen weren't appreciated and, in high dudgeon,

Mum told me that Helen had sworn that if she ever had to make up another six-year-old flower-girl she'd gouge her eyes out with her taupe eyeliner. (It wasn't clear whether she was talking about her own eyes or the flower-girl's.)

Helen's problem is that she's burdened with high intelligence coupled with an unfeasibly short attention span, and she has yet to find her true calling.

Unlike Anna, who has yet to find *any* calling, true or otherwise. She's resisted any encouragement to embark on a career path and has eked out a living waitressing, bartending and reading tarot cards. Never for any sustained period, mind; her CV is probably as long as *War and Peace*. Until she and her ex-boyfriend, Shane, split up they'd lived a hand-to-mouth, free-spirited existence. They were the type who'd pop out for ten minutes to buy a KitKat and the next time you'd hear from them they'd be in Istanbul, working in a tannery. Their motto was 'God will provide,' and even if God wouldn't, the dole did. I'd envied them their devil-may-care existence. Actually, that's a complete lie. I'd have hated it – the insecurity, never knowing if you could eat, buy exfoliator, that sort of thing.

The thing about Anna is that she can be acutely, almost shockingly perceptive, but she's not great on practical things. Like remembering to get dressed before leaving the house. There was a time when we felt her sweet, absent nature was down to her fondness for recreational drugs, but she knocked that on the head about four years ago, around the same time that Rachel did. And although she's possibly a little more lucid than she used to be, I couldn't say for sure.

She'd moved back in with my parents a few months before, when she'd broken up with Shane – though she hadn't been given the same sort of grief as I expected to get. One, because she hadn't been married and two, because they seemed to expect her to be unreliable.

Cautiously, I opened the lounge door. They were clustered on the couch watching *Who Wants to Be a Millionaire?* and pouring scorn on the candidates.

'Any thick knows the answer to that,' Helen threw at the screen.

'What is it, then?' Anna asked.

'I don't know. But I don't HAVE to know. I'm not about to lose ninety-three thousand pounds. Oh, go on then, phone your friend, for all the good it'll do, if he's as thick as you –'

Why did they all have to be in? Why couldn't it just have been, say, Anna? I could have told her, then slunk off to bed like a coward, leaving her to break the news to everyone else.

Then Mum spotted me at the door.

'Margaret!' she exclaimed. For years I've been telling her that my name is Maggie, but she's in denial. 'Come in. Sit down. Have a Cornetto.' She elbowed Dad. 'Get her a Cornetto.'

'Chocolate? Strawberry? Or . . .' Dad paused, before triumphantly delivering his *pièce de résistance.* 'Or M&M? They're new!'

There is always a wonderful selection of confectionery available at my parents' house. Unlike most houses, though, this isn't in addition to the usual foodstuffs, it's *instead* of. It wasn't so much that my mother didn't enjoy cooking meals, it was more that we didn't enjoy eating them. Some time in the early eighties she stopped preparing meals altogether. 'What's the point if you ungrateful brats never eat them?'

'I eat them,' Dad bleated, a voice in the wilderness.

But it made no difference. Convenience foods were ushered

in and it made me sad. I'd always yearned for an Italian-style family who gathered for their evening meal, passing platters and bowls of steaming homemade food along the scrubbed pine table while the roundy mama beamed from the stove.

All the same, unlimited ice-cream was not to be sniffed at. Graciously, I accepted a Cornetto (an M&M one, of course) and watched the end of the programme. I might as well, there was no way I'd get their attention until it was over. Besides, it suited me to defer the moment when I had to spill the words *Garv and I have split up*. I was afraid that saying it out loud would mean that it had actually happened.

And then it was time.

I sighed, swallowed away the nausea and began. 'I've something to tell you all.'

'Lovely!' Mum rearranged her features into her I'm-going-to-be-a-granny-again expression.

'Garv and I have split up.'

'Ah, here!' With a sharp rustle my father promptly disappeared behind his paper. Anna flung herself upon me, even Helen looked startled, but my poor mother . . . She looked as though she'd been hit on the head by a flying brick. Stunned and stricken and shocked beyond belief.

'In a minute you'll tell me you're joking,' she gasped.

'In a minute I won't,' I said stoutly. I hated doing this to her, especially because I was the second of her daughters to have a failed marriage, but it was important not to mislead her. False hope was worse than no hope.

'But,' she struggled for breath, 'but you've always been the good one. Say something,' she angrily urged my father.

He appeared reluctantly from behind the newspaper shield. 'Seven-year itch,' he offered tentatively.

'*Gentlemen Prefer Blondes*,' Helen countered, then elbowed Anna, who thought for a moment, then said, '*The Misfits*.'

'You're describing yourself,' Helen replied scathingly, then curled her lip at the wall of newspaper. 'See, Dad? We can all name Marilyn Monroe films, but how does it help?'

'It's actually *nine* years I've been married,' I quietly told Dad's newspaper. He meant well.

'This has come as an awful shock to me,' Mum reiterated.

'I thought you'd be glad, seeing as you all hate Garv.'

'I know, but –' Abruptly Mum collected herself. 'Stop that nonsense, we don't all hate him.'

But they did – all apart from Claire, who'd got to know him when she had a teenage fling with his big brother (also confusingly known as Garv). She'd always thought *my* Garv was sweet, especially since he'd fixed her tapedeck for her. (You wouldn't want to get her on the subject of the elder Garv, mind.) But despite Claire's stamp of approval, *my* Garv had somehow – through no fault of his own – acquired a reputation for tight-fistedness and old-before-his-time fustiness with the rest of the family.

The stinginess allegation had raised its ugly head the first night I'd ever officially brought him out with my family. He'd been knocking around on the fringes for a good while before that, but I'd realized I was serious about him and that it was time he met my family properly. With a sense of occasion we repaired to Phelan's, the local pub, and the salient fact is that Garv didn't stand his round.

Not Standing Your Round is a mortal sin in my family, and there's always great competition to out-give and out-convivialize all the others. Hand-to-hand combat almost breaks out as people try to be the first to get to the bar.

32

On the night in question, Garv was more than willing to buy drinks for my family, but he was nervous and way too mild-mannered to stand up to them. As soon as anyone's drink had passed the halfway mark, he'd leap to his feet, fumbling for his money, asking, 'Same again?' But each time he did so the table erupted like a dealing-room floor, with everyone yelling at him to sit down and put his money away, that he was insulting us. Even I joined in, getting carried away in the heat of the moment. Beaten back by a hail of words, Garv reluctantly lowered himself back on to his bar stool.

The net result of the evening was that Dad bought a round, Rachel bought a round, I bought a round, Anna bought a round, then Dad bought another round. And Garv gained a reputation as a tight-arse.

Hot on the heels of that miscarriage of justice came the polo-shirt incident. A story that begins happily and ends tragically. One Saturday afternoon, Garv and I were traipsing around town, half-heartedly going in and out of clothes shops. Because Garv was still only a trainee and he'd just bought a car, money was tight, so we were on the lookout for bargains. Free things, preferably. When by pure chance we found a polo shirt in the bottom of a clearance bin. To our great surprise, it had none of the characteristics you normally associate with things found in clearance bins, like three sleeves, no neck-hole or indelible, bile-coloured stains. In fact, it was perfect – the right size, the right price and a pale, icy colour that made his eyes look blue when normally they look grey.

It was only when we got it home that we realized there was a small logo above the breast pocket. A tiny outline of a man swinging a golfclub which, somehow in the euphoria of discovering the garment only had two sleeves, we'd missed.

Naturally enough, we were both dismayed, but concluded that it was so small it was barely visible. Besides, we were too skint for him not to wear it. So he wore it. And the next thing I hear is that Garv wears the same kind of jumpers as Dad. Then a rumour started up that he played golf, which was not only untrue but very, very unfair.

Garv is no fool and he was aware of my family's antipathy. Well, it was hard to be *un*aware, when every time he appeared at the house, Helen would bellow, 'For God's sake, don't let him in!'

While he never responded to their discourtesy with rudeness of his own, nor did he launch a charm offensive to try and win them over either. And he *could* have – he had a nice, easy manner most of the time. Instead, he became very protective of me around them, which they interpreted variously as stand-offishness or downright hostility. And *responded* with stand-offishness or downright hostility. All in all, it hasn't been that easy, especially at Christmas times . . .

'You're just going through a bad patch,' Mum tried valiantly.

Wretchedly, I shook my head. Did she think I hadn't thought of that? Did she think that I hadn't clung on to that, hoping with gritted teeth that that was all that was wrong?

'Was he, ah . . . ?' My father was clearly trying to frame a delicate question. 'Was he dipping his wick where he shouldn't have been?'

'No.' Perhaps he had been, but that wasn't the cause. It was a symptom of what was wrong.

'Things haven't been easy for you, for either of you.' Mum was off again. 'You've had a couple of –'

'– setbacks,' I said quickly, before she used another word.

'Setbacks. Would you not have a holiday?'

'We've had a holiday, remember? It was a disaster, it did more harm than good.'

'What about going for counselling?'

'Counselling? Garv?' If I'd been capable of laughter, this would have been a good opportunity. 'If he won't talk to me, he's hardly likely to talk to a total stranger.'

'But you love each other,' she said, with desperation.

'But we're making each other miserable.'

'Love conquers all,' Mum coaxed, like I was five.

'No. It. Doesn't,' I spelt out, an edge of hysteria to my voice. 'Do you think I'd do something as awful as leave him if it was that easy?'

That plunged her into sulky, that's-no-way-to-talk-to-your-mother silence.

'So you're not going to tell us what's going on?' Helen concluded.

'But you know everything that's happened.' OK, not quite everything, but Truffle Woman was not the cause, she was simply the final nail.

Scornfully, Helen flicked her eyes upwards. 'This is like your driving test all over again.'

I might have known someone would bring that up. The bitterness still ran deep.

When I was twenty-one, I did a course of driving lessons, then sat my test and passed it. Only then did I tell any of my family, but instead of being delighted for me, they were hurt and confused. They felt left out, short-changed, deprived of a drama, and they couldn't understand why I hadn't involved them.

'I could have given you a St Christopher's medal for your test,' Mum had protested.

'But I didn't need it, I passed anyway.'

'I could have taken you out to practise in my car,' Dad had said wistfully. 'I see Maurice Kilfeather takes Angela out.'

'We could have waved you off from the test centre,' Claire had pointed out.

Which was precisely the kind of thing I'd wanted to avoid. Doing my driving test was just something I'd wanted to do on my own. I didn't think it was anyone else's business. And if I was being brutally honest, I'd have to acknowledge the issue of failure – if I'd failed my test I'd never have been let forget about it.

Finally Dad spoke. 'How's work?'

4

I was dreading the first night away from Garv (and all the subsequent nights, but first things first). I was sure I wouldn't sleep, because wasn't that what happened to people in distress? But I needn't have worried: I slept like I was dead and woke up in a bed and a room that I didn't recognize. *Where's this?* For a moment my curiosity was almost pleasant, then reality tumbled down on to me.

That day was one of the most dislocated of my life. With no job to show up at, my time was spent mostly in my bedroom, keeping out of Mum's way. Even though she was very vocal about how this was just a phase I was going through and that I'd be back with Garv in no time, my popularity with her was enjoying an all-time low.

Helen, on the other hand, was treating me like a visiting freak show and dropped by to torment me before she went to work. Anna came too, in an attempt to protect me.

'God, you're still here,' Helen marvelled, marching into the room. 'So you've really left him? But this is all wrong, Maggie, you don't do this sort of thing.'

I was reminded of a conversation I'd had with my sisters the previous Christmas – we were trapped in the house without even a Harrison Ford film to take our minds off things and were driven to wondering what each of us would be if we were food instead of people. It was decided that Claire would be a green curry because they were both fiery, then Helen decreed that Rachel would be a jelly baby, which pleased Rachel no end.

'Because I'm sweet?'

'Because I like to bite your head off.'

Anna – 'this is nearly too easy,' Helen had said – was a Flake. And I was 'plain yoghurt at room temperature'.

OK, so I knew I'd never been in with a shout of being, say, an After Eight ('thin and sophisticated'), or a Ginger Nut biscuit ('hard and interesting'). But I saw nothing wrong with me being a trifle ('has hidden depths'). Instead, I was the dullest thing, the most flavourless thing anyone could think of – plain yoghurt at room temperature. It cut me deep, and even when Claire said that Helen was a human durian fruit because she was offensive and banned in several countries, it wasn't enough to lift my spirits.

Back in the present, Helen continued jibing me. 'You're just not the type to leave her husband.'

'No, having a broken marriage isn't the sort of thing that plain yoghurt at room temperature does, does it?'

'What?' Helen sounded confused.

'I *said*, having a broken marriage isn't the sort of thing that plain yoghurt at room temperature does, does it?'

She gave me a funny look, muttered something about brides-maids who looked like the elephant man and what was she supposed to do about it, then finally left.

Anna got into bed beside me and linked her arm through mine. 'Plain yoghurt can be delicious,' she said quietly. 'It's perfect with curry. And . . .' After a long, searching pause, she added, 'And they say it's very good for thrush.'

*

I languished in the house, with no real idea of what I was doing there. I let telly programmes wash over me: 'Smokin' crack ain't so all that'; 'Girlfrien', your butt is bigger than my car'. Whenever they finished, I'd find myself looking around, confused to find myself no longer in the Chicago projects, but in a flowery-curtained, befigurine'd, suburban Dublin house. And not just any flowery-curtained, befigurine'd, suburban Dublin house. *How have I ended up back here? What happened?*

I felt like such a failure that I was afraid to leave the house. And I thought about Garv and the girl – a lot. So much that I had to go back to using my much-hated steroid cream on my unbearably itchy arm. I was tormented by her identity. Who was she, anyway? How long had it been going on? And – God forbid – was it serious? The questions scurried incessantly; even as I watched two obese girls punching each other and Jerry Springer pretending to be appalled, another part of my brain was panning over the past few months with a magnifying glass, searching for clues and discovering nothing.

But I felt I'd no right to mind about the girl and that it didn't make any difference anyway. With or without her, the game was up.

I'd been back at my parents' about twenty-four hours when the reaction set in. As I listlessly watched telly, my temperature abruptly plummeted. Though the room was warm (far *too* warm), the skin on my arms had contracted like cling-wrap before heat, and the hairs were standing to attention from goosepimpled follicles. I blinked, only to discover that my eyes hurt. Then I noticed that my head was packed tight with cotton wool and my bones ached, and I was unable to find enough energy even to pick up the remote control. Muzzy and spaced,

I watched *Animal Hospital*, wishing I could do something to make it stop. What was wrong with me?

'What's wrong with you?' Mum had come into the room. 'Lord above! What are they doing to that poor Alsatian?'

'He's got piles.' My tongue belonged to someone else, someone with a much bigger mouth. 'And I think I've got the flu.'

'Are you sure?'

'I'm cold and everything hurts.' Me, hardy Maggie, who never got sick.

'I didn't know dogs could even *get* piles.' She was still glued to the screen.

'Maybe he sat on a cold step. I think I've got the flu,' I repeated, slightly louder this time.

Finally I had her attention. 'You don't look the best,' she agreed. She looked concerned. Almost as concerned as she had been about the aller. She placed her hand on my forehead. 'I wonder if you've a temperature.'

'Course I have,' I croaked. 'I've the flu.'

She located a thermometer and gave it several of those violent flicks that people always do before they take someone's temperature. An energetic throw, as if they're about to fling the glass stick across the room, but change their mind at the last minute. But despite her adherence to protocol, my temperature was normal.

'Though it's hard to be sure,' she added, casting a jaundiced eye at the thermometer. 'Thirty years we've had it and that yoke has never worked.'

I went to bed at nine-thirty and didn't come round until two the following afternoon. I was lying in exactly the same position I'd been in before I went to sleep, as though I hadn't moved once in any of that time. Instead of feeling better I actually felt worse: lethargic and hopeless. And I continued to feel wretched.

I'd never believed it was possible to become sick from sadness. I'd thought that was a nonsense concept confined to melodramatic Victorian novels. But sometime over the course of the following week I understood that there was nothing wrong with me – nothing physical, in any case. My temperature was normal, and how come no one else had caught my flu? Whatever was wrong with me, it was emotional. Mourning sickness. My body was fighting my separation from Garv as though it was a hostile organism.

I couldn't stop sleeping. Deep, druggy sleeps from which I never fully woke up. Once conscious, I could barely manage the smallest things. I knew I was supposed to be getting on with stuff. Getting another job. Tidying up the loose ends of my old life. Sorting out my new one. But I felt as though I was walking underwater. Moving too slowly through an unwieldy world.

When I got beneath the shower, the water felt like a hail of sharp gravel being hurled at my tender skin. The house was too noisy – every time a door slammed my heart pumped too hard. When Dad dropped a saucepan with a clatter on the floor, I got such a fright my eyes filled with tears. I carried a permanent oppression, as though a dirty grey sky had been nailed in place two inches above my head.

I continued to perform poorly in the opinion polls. Mum was still vacillating between sharper-than-a-serpent's-tooth-it-is-to-have-a-thankless-child chilliness and would-you-not-cop-on-and-go-home-to-your-husband cajolery. I wasn't getting the same degree of grief from Dad, but then again I've always been his pet. What with once having played in team

41

sports and going to the snooker championship with him, he's nearly managed to convince himself that I'm his son.

Outside of my immediate family, I spoke to no one. People were keen to speak to me, however. Nothing like a disaster to get those phone lines a-hopping. Close friends like Donna and Sinead rang, but I mumbled, 'Tell her I'll call her back,' and never managed it. Coffin-chasers like Elaine also called. (Mum thought she sounded like 'a lovely girl'.) Claire rang from London and begged me to go and stay with her. Rachel rang from New York and we had much the same conversation. But there wasn't a hope of me visiting either of them – walking from the telly to the kettle was about the only journey I could manage.

I didn't call Garv – and to the great disappointment and confusion of my parents, he didn't call me either. In a way it was a relief, but a relief that somehow managed to be an unpleasant one.

Anna was also in the house a lot – she was devastated about Shane. We hung out furtively, because when Mum saw us together her mouth would squinch like a cat's bottom and she'd enquire, 'Is it a rest home for fallen women I'm running here?' As best we could, we talked about our respective break-ups. What had happened for her was that Shane had set up a computer business making on-line music, and out of nowhere he became a bread-head. 'He got his hair cut. At a hairdresser's. He bought styling wax, then I knew it was all over. I suppose,' Anna sighed, 'he wants to grow up and I don't. So what about you and Garv?'

'Oh, you know . . .' I couldn't tell her about Truffle Woman. Whatever energy would have been required to pull those words out of my gut and into the open just wasn't there. 'Mostly I feel

42

nothing,' I managed. 'It's a horrible sort of nothing, but . . . you know . . . that can't be right. Shouldn't I be roaring crying?'

Shouldn't I be breaking into Truffle Woman's house and planting grass in her carpets and prawns in her curtain rails? Shouldn't I be making plans to cut the arms and legs off all Garv's clothes?

'I haven't even rung Garv to say I miss him.' Even though a spasm of longing for him jack-knifed me roughly once every waking hour. 'My life is ruined and all I feel is nothing.' My future was a roped-off area – I managed occasional fleeting glimpses of the sadness, but they didn't stay. It was as if a door into a noisy room opened and immediately slammed shut again.

'You're depressed,' Anna said. 'You're very depressed. Is it any surprise, after all you've been through?'

But that didn't sit comfortably. 'I'm not a depressive.' (I know because I did a quiz in *Cosmopolitan*.)

'You are now. And Garv probably is too.'

She'd said something interesting, maybe even important, but I couldn't hold the thought. I was too weary.

Unlike me, Anna couldn't sleep. At least, not in her own bed, so she wandered the house at night, moving from bed to bed. She often got in beside me, but was usually gone when I woke, leaving the faint residue of a wraith-like creature who sighed a lot and smelt of Bacardi Breezers. It was like being haunted by a benign ghost.

Occasionally she was still there when I woke. One morning I came to to find one of her feet resting on my ear and the other in my mouth; for reasons best known to herself, Anna had decided to get into bed upside-down.

Another night I emerged from sleep feeling absurdly happy: warm, safe, cherished. Then, going into hollow freefall, I realized what it was – Anna was snuggling into me, nuzzling and mewing, 'Oh Shane.' Deep in sleep, her arm tight around me, I'd thought she was Garv.

Sometimes Anna and I could provide comfort for each other. She developed a theory that our lives were so awful because our guardian angels had gone on sabbaticals, and that currently we were being minded by temps who took no pride in their work.

'They do the bare minimum. We won't get our hands caught in a mincing machine, but that's all they'll do for us.'

'What's my real angel called?'

'Basil.'

'Basil?'

'Henry, then.'

'Henry?'

'How about Clive?'

'He's a boy angel?'

'Oh no, they're neutral.'

'What's he like?'

'He smells of Turkish Delight and he's pink.'

'Pink?'

'With green spots.'

'You're not taking this seriously.'

'Sorry. What's mine called?'

'Penelope.'

'Favourite food?'

'Carrots and parsnips mashed together.'

'Best bit about being a guardian angel?'

'Helping people find the right dress and shoes for their Christmas party. What's Clive's best bit?'

'Finding lost earrings.'

. . . And sometimes we couldn't provide comfort for each other.

One bad morning, Anna got in beside me and we both lay on our backs, staring miserably at the ceiling. After some time she said, 'I think we're making each other worse.'

'I think we are,' I agreed.

'I'll go back to my own bed, will I?'

'OK.'

Unlike me, Anna occasionally left the house – if only in response to a request from Shane.

'He says he wants "to talk".'

'And what's wrong with that?'

'He really means he wants to have sex. That's what's happened the last three times. It gets my hopes up, then leaves me feeling even worse.'

'Maybe you shouldn't sleep with him any more,' I suggested.

'Maybe,' she said vaguely, unconvinced.

'Maybe you shouldn't even meet him.'

But the next time he rang and said he wanted to see her, she agreed. 'Don't worry,' she promised me. 'I'm not going to sleep with him.'

But as I went to bed that night she wasn't back. Mind you, it was barely nine-fifteen and she'd only been gone half an hour.

Some unknown time that night, I woke into darkness. I wondered what had disturbed me – and then I heard it, a noise I remembered well from my teenage years: a scraping and scratching from the front door. One of my sisters – Anna in this case – was having trouble getting her key in the lock. It went on for so long that I was just about to get up and let her in when the door was finally pushed open, then I heard the reassuring crash as she bumped into and knocked over the hall table, followed, a few minutes later, by the disgusting smell of baked beans heating in a saucepan. Just like the old days, I thought dreamily, as I sank back into sleep. It's yesterday once more . . .

Some time later I jumped awake again. The fire alarm was beeping in a fussy frenzy and Dad was hopping about the landing in a wild-eyed, pyjama'd panic. 'How do I turn this shagging thing off?' Grey smoke was swirling around the hall, the beans and saucepan were burnt to a crisp and Anna was slumped over the kitchen table, deep in sweet slumber.

We put her to bed, but sometime later she got in beside me, reeking so strongly of drink that if I'd been awake, I'd have passed out. As it was, her incendiary breath had the effect of smelling salts, and woke me up.

Later that same night, the whole house was once again woken – this time by an almighty thump; it sounded like a ceiling had fallen in. Closer investigation revealed that it was nothing quite so exciting. All that had happened was that Anna had tried to get into bed beside Helen, and Helen, who objected to sleeping with 'a one-woman brewery', had pushed her out on to the floor.

'But at least I didn't sleep with him,' Anna said the following morning, as she inspected her bruises. 'OK, I drank myself into a coma and nearly burnt the house down, but at least I didn't sleep with him.'

'It's progress,' I agreed.

At some stage during the second dreadful week, I needed *something*, but there were so few options open to me.

'Go for a walk,' Dad suggested. 'Get some fresh air.'

I've never really understood the concept of Going for a Walk. And not even at my sportiest did I get the appeal of Going for a Walk in suburbia. But I was bad enough to give it a try.

'Take a coat,' he advised. 'It might rain.'

'It's June.'

'It's Ireland.'

'I haven't got a coat.' Well, I had, but it was in my house, Garv's house, you know the one I mean. I was afraid to go there in case he'd moved the girl in. Perhaps that sounds like a wild overreaction, but my instinct was warning me that anything was possible.

'Take mine.' Dad's anorak was red, nylon, awful, but I longed for affection and I couldn't resist letting him help me into it.

Off I went. Nothing too ambitious. I walked a couple of hundred yards to the green and sat on a wall, watching some kids do whatever kids do on greens: surreptitious smoking; trading inaccurate information on sex; whatever. I felt horrible. The sky was mushroom grey and stagnant, even the bits that weren't directly over me. After a while, when I didn't feel any better, I decided I might as well go home again. It was bound to be time for some version of 'Girlfrien', you ain't so all that.' No point in missing it.

I was traipsing back down the hill when someone flickered across my vision and vaguely alerted me. I looked properly. It was a man about fifty yards away, lifting things out of a car boot. Oh my . . . God. Shay Delaney. Well, for a second I thought it was him, then it was clear that it wasn't. There was just something about the man that reminded me slightly of Shay and even that was enough to unsteady me.

But as I continued, with a whoosh of dizziness I saw that it *was* him. Different, but still the same. The change was that he looked older and this gave me some pleasure, until it dawned on me that if he looked older, then so would I.

He was lifting stuff from the boot of a car and stacking it at the gate of his mother's house. How could I not have instantly known it was him? He was outside his own house. Well, the house he'd lived in until he'd left to go away to college fifteen years ago. *Fifteen years.* How? I'm young now and I was grown-up then, there isn't *room* for fifteen years. Dizzy again.

I *couldn't* meet him. Not now, not with all this shame. A powerful impulse almost had me marching away in the direction I'd just come from and, after a frantic, weighing-up session, only the fear that he might notice stopped me.

But of all the times to bump into him, I thought wildly. Of all the times to have to play the game of How Did Your Life Turn Out? Why couldn't I have met him when I'd had a marriage I was proud of, when I'd been happy? Of course, I didn't have to tell him how wrong everything had gone. But wouldn't he guess, wasn't it obvious. . . ?

My hollow legs continued leading me down the hill, straight into his path.

For years I used to fantasize about meeting him again. Time after time I comforted myself with meticulous plans. I'd be thin, beautiful, trendily dressed, expertly lit. I'd be poised, confident, on top of my game. And he'd have lost his appeal. Somehow he'd have shrunk to about five five, his dark-blond hair would have fallen out and he'd have put on a ton of weight.

But from what I could see, he still had his hair and his height, and if he'd bulked out a bit, it had the unfortunate effect of suiting him. Meanwhile, look at me – the trackie bottoms, the air of failure, the way my face had gone a bit funny and immobile. It was nearly laughable. The only thing I had going for me were the floodlights in my hair – I'd been uncertain when the 'dresser first suggested it, but now it was clear it was a godsend.

Closer I got. Closer. He'd no interest in me, not at all. It seemed as if I could escape with my raw, white face, my dad's anorak, my air of recently separated bleakness. Then I was right up beside him, passing him by and still he wasn't looking. And with a strange defiance I decided that if he wasn't going to speak, then I would.

'Shay?'

He looked, I have to say, gratifyingly shocked.

'Maggie?' He froze in the act of lifting something from the boot, then stood up. 'Maggie Walsh?'

'Garvan,' I corrected shyly. 'Maggie Garvan now, but yeah.'

'That's right,' he agreed warmly. 'I heard you got married. So, ah, how's Garv?'

'Fine.' A little defensively.

All was still – and mildly uncomfortable. Then he rolled his eyes playfully to indicate shock. 'Wooh, Maggie Walsh. Long time. So!' Before he even asked it, I knew he was going to. 'Any kids?'

'No. You?'

'Three. Little monkeys.' He made a face.

'I bet. Hahaha.'

'You look fantastic!' he declared. He was either blind or insane, but such was his enthusiasm that I tentatively began to half-believe him.

'How's your mum?' As if he was genuinely interested. 'How's the cooking?'

'Ah, she gave up on it.'

'She's some gal,' he said admiringly. 'And your dad? Still driven mad by the lot of you?'

'Oh, yes.'

'And what are you up to these days?'

'Paralegal stuff.'

'Yeah? Great.'

'Yeah, great. You?'

'Working for Dark Star Productions.'

'I've heard of them.' I'd read something about them in the paper, but couldn't remember what exactly, so I said, 'Yeah, great,' a bit more.

And then he said, 'Well, *great* to see you,' and stuck out his hand. I looked dumbly at it – only for a second: he was expecting me to shake it. Like we were business colleagues. As I rubbed my palm against his, I remembered that he used to hold that hand over my mouth. To muffle the sounds I was making. When we were having sex.

How weird life is.

Already he was moving off. 'Tell your mum and dad I was asking for them.'

'And Garv?' I couldn't help it.

'Sure. And Garv.'

As I walked away I was fine. I couldn't believe it. I'd finally met him, and spoken to him, and I was fine. All those years wondering about it and I was fine. *Fine.* On a huge high, I danced towards home.

The minute I was inside the house I started to shake. So badly I couldn't get my fingers to undo the zip of the anorak. Too late, I remembered that I shouldn't have been nice to him. I should have been cold and unpleasant, after the way he'd treated me.

Mum appeared in the hall. 'Did you meet anyone?' she asked, her antipathy to me wrestling with her social curiosity.

'No.'

'No one at all?'

'No.'

She'd loved Shay Delaney. He'd been a mother's dream, already manly looking and with a golden-stubbled jaw while the other youths were still raw and unformed. This she put down to the fact that Shay's father had left them, and Shay had to be the man of the house. The other lads in the gang – Micko, Macker, Toolser, even Garv – were sullen around adults; they found it impossible to maintain eye contact with anyone more than a year older than them. But Shay, the only one of his contemporaries to be called by his real name, as I recall, was perpetually good-humoured. Almost, at times, flirtatious. Claire, who was a couple of years older than him, used to say wryly, 'I'm Shay Delaney and I always get what I want.'

But I was too busy for one of Mum's avid interrogation sessions. ('Had he a big car?' 'I believe his wife's very glamorous?' 'Did the father ever leave the floozie and come home?') I had to lie on my bed and tremble and think about Shay.

He'd been in the same year in school as Micko, Macker, Toolser and Garv, but he wasn't fully part of their gang; his choice, not theirs, they'd have been delighted to be first best friends with him. He'd seemed to float between several factions and was welcomed by all. He was just one of those people who had – although I wouldn't have known the word for it in those days – charisma. Claire had articulated it best by saying, 'If Shay Delaney fell into a pit of shite he'd come out smelling of Chanel No. 5.'

Not only was he noticeably good-looking, but he had the

51

decency not to rub people's noses in it, so he got a rep as a nice person into the bargain. And of course, the tragedy of his father having walked out on the family generated a lot of sympathy for him. Because he looked older and had the confidence and charm to blag his way past doormen, he went places that we didn't and inhabited different worlds to ours. But he chose to return to us, and he managed never to sound like he was boasting when he regaled us with stories of drinking crème de menthe in a nurses' residential or going to some horsey girl's twenty-first party in Meath. Of course, he'd always had lots of girlfriends; they'd usually left school and were either working or in college, which impressed the other lads no end.

Anyway, I'd been going out with Garv for about six months and I was perfectly happy with him – then Shay Delaney began to pay me attention. Giving me warm smiles and one-on-one conversations so low they excluded everyone else. And it seemed like he was always *watching* me. We'd all be there, hanging around a wall, smoking, pushing each other – the usual messing – and I'd look up to find his gaze upon me. If he'd been anyone else I'd have assumed that he was flirting, but this was Shay Delaney, he was way out of my price range. And then, after a week when he'd cranked up the intensity of his smiles and intimate conversations, there was a party. A fluttering in my gut let me know that something was going to happen and sure enough, when Garv had been sent out to buy more drink, Shay headed me off as I emerged from the kitchen, then pulled me into the cupboard under the stairs. I protested breathlessly but he laughed and shut the door behind us and, after some half-teasing compliments about how I was driving him mad, tried to kiss me. Squashed up against his bigness in the dark, confined space, finally knowing that I hadn't imagined his interest in me, I felt him move his face down to mine, and it was like every dream I'd ever had had come true.

'I can't,' I said, turning my head away.

'Why not?'

'Because of Garv.'

'If you weren't with Garv would you let me?'

I couldn't answer. Surely it was obvious?

'Why me?' I asked. 'Why are you bothered with me?'

'Because I am. Big time,' he said, pulling his thumb along my mouth and making me dizzy.

I never really got to the bottom of why he wanted me. I was nothing like as good-looking as his other girlfriends, or as sophisticated. The best I could come up with myself was that as his father had left them and his home-life was a bit chaotic, I represented stability. That my normalness was the most attractive thing about me.

So, shallow cow that I was, I broke it off with poor Garv. We kind of pretended that it was a mutual thing and insisted that we'd stay friends and all that other crap you talk when you're a teenager, but the truth of the matter was that I dumped Garv for Shay. Garv knew it as much as I did. From the moment Shay had decided he wanted me, Garv hadn't stood a chance.

Later that evening, Dad sidled into my room, a brown paper bag under his arm.

'McDonald's!' he declared. 'Your favourite.'

When I'd been eleven, perhaps, but I welcomed the company. 'Chicken nuggets,' he announced proudly. 'With two different dips.'

'What's this in aid of?'

'You have to eat. And your mother . . .' he paused and sighed, his expression wistful, '. . . well, she tries her best.'

Since the night I'd left Garv, the mere thought of food had been anathema – it didn't make me feel sick, just amazed. But this evening I was going to have to try, because as well as the chicken nuggets, Dad had also got me a large fries and a coke and, by the look of things, a Happy Meal for himself. It came with a free robot.

'Eat a fry yoke,' he tempted. (He feels silly calling them 'fries'. The real name, he feels, is 'chips'.)

I'd almost have preferred to eat the robot, but because I felt sorry for him, I tried. The chip (or fry, if you prefer) sat in my mouth like a foreign body. He watched me anxiously and I attempted to choke it down my closed throat.

'Do you want a drink?' he asked. 'Brandy, vodka, cider?'

I was stunned. That was one of the strangest questions I'd ever been asked in my entire life, bar none. The only time my parents ever have drink with their meals is on Christmas Day, when the bottle of warm Blue Nun is wheeled out – always assuming that it hasn't been discovered and drunk the night before. Besides, there wasn't any – what had he suggested? – brandy, vodka or cider in the house. Then I realized Dad wasn't *offering* me a drink. He was simply curious, trying to gauge how bad I was.

I shook my head. 'I don't want a drink.' That would be a huge mistake. When I was depressed, alcohol never cheered me up. In fact, it probably made me worse – maudlin and self-pitying. 'If I got drunk I'd probably kill myself.'

'Good then. Marvellous.' Suddenly he was as happy as his meal. He ate with relieved gusto, attempted to play with his robot – 'What does this yoke do?' – then departed.

A few minutes later he was back. 'Emily's on the phone.'

5

Emily is my best friend. Best *girl*friend, that is, and actually, since Garv and I have gone weird on each other, probably best friend.

Gawky twelve-year-olds, we met at secondary school and instantly recognized in each other a kindred spirit. We were outsiders. Not total pariahs, but we were a long way from being the most popular girls in the class. Part of the problem was that we were both good at sport: genuinely cool girls smoked and faked letters from their parents saying they had verrucas. Another black mark against us was that we'd no interest in the usual teenage experimentation with cigarettes and alcohol. I was too terrified of getting into trouble and Emily said it was a waste of money. Together we pronounced it 'stupid'.

At school, Emily was small, skinny and looked like ET with a bad perm. A far cry from how she looks today. She's still small and skinny, which we now know to be a Good Thing, right? Especially the skinny bit. But the bad perm (which wasn't a perm at all, but the real thing) is just a distant memory. Her hair is now swishy and glossy – very, very impressive, even though she says that in its natural state she could still double for a member of the Jackson Five and that to get her hair fully frizz-free, her hairdresser sometimes has to put his foot on her chest and tug hard.

Her look is very pulled together and confident. When a

certain style is in vogue, I usually buy something from the 'new-look' and team it with the rest of my 'old-look' wardrobe and think I'm doing pretty well. But not Emily. For instance, remember when the rock-chick look was in? I bought a T-shirt that said 'Rock Chick' in pink, shiny letters and I thought I was it. Emily, however, appeared in bandage-tight snakeskin jeans, purple stiletto-heeled cowboy boots and a pink leather stetson. But instead of looking preposterous – and she could have done, that pink leather stetson was borderline – I wanted to applaud. She's also a woman who knows how to accessorize. Coloured shoes (a colour other than black, that is), handbags shaped like flower-pots, kooky barettes in her hair if the occasion demands it.

I'm not a total klutz. I read magazines, I'm an enthusiastic shopper and I take a keen interest in skirt lengths, heel shapes and the light-diffusing qualities of foundation. But you only have to look at my single friends to see that they're all thinner and more glamorous than me and their make-up bags are cornucopias of breaking-news wondrousness. While I'm still reading about something, they're already wearing it. (Do you know how long it took me to realize that blue shimmer shadow was back in? Honestly, I'd be too ashamed to tell you, and even though it's a cliché, it *is* something to do with having a man and not being 'out there'.)

Despite our divergent lifestyles and living several thousand miles apart, my friendship with Emily has endured. We'd e-mail each other twice or three times a week. She'd tell me about all her disastrous relationships, then she'd debrief me on my dull, married life, then we'd both go home happy.

It was a great source of sadness to me that we couldn't seem to manage to live on the same continent. Garv and I had only been married a few months before we moved to Chicago for five years. Then less than four weeks before we returned to Ireland, Emily departed for Los Angeles.

What happened was, Emily had always wanted to be a writer. She'd tried her hand at short stories and novels and got nowhere. Her stuff always seemed good to me, but what would I know? Like Helen says, I've no imagination.

Then, five or so years ago, Emily wrote a short film called *A Perfect Day* which was picked up by an Irish production company and got shown on RTE. It was whimsical and charming, but what normally happens with a 'short' is that it gets shown once, then disappears. It's regarded as a type of practice run for wannabe film-makers. But something unprecedented happened with *A Perfect Day*, because it was a very odd length: fourteen and a half minutes. Whenever Ireland had some sort of corruption scandal (every other week), the nine o'clock news would run over and a 'filler' item would be needed to occupy the airwaves until ten o'clock, when things could get back on schedule. Three times over a four-month period *A Perfect Day* was that filler, and it began to work its way beneath the skin of the nation. Suddenly at water-coolers and photocopying machines and bus-stops throughout the land people were asking each other, 'Did you see that lovely thing that was on after the news last night?'

Overnight, in Ireland at least, Emily became a householdish name – people didn't exactly know who she was, but they knew that they'd heard of her, and they had definitely heard of her film. She could have made a decent enough living in Ireland, if she'd been prepared to be flexible, and do sit-coms, plays, ads – apparently they pay very handsomely – as well as films. But she decided to go for broke, left her dreary day-job and departed for Los Angeles.

Time passed, then news came back that she'd been taken on by one of the big Hollywood agencies. Not long after that came the announcement that she'd sold a full-length script to Dreamworks. Or was it Miramax? One of the big ones, anyway. The film was called *Hostage* (or it might be *Hostage!*), and was about a tiny, honeymooners' island in the South Pacific, which is invaded by terrorists who kill the few locals and take several of the honeymooners hostage. Others escape into the undergrowth, survive castaway-style on twigs etc., and plot a rescue mission. It was described as 'an action movie, with a love story and comic overtones'.

The *Sunday Independent* did a feature about the deal, RTE ran *A Perfect Day* again, and Emily's mother bought a long, navy, spangledy dress for the première. (She got it in the sales, at 40 per cent off, but it was still fairly pricey.)

More time passed, and not much happened. No one got cast and whenever I asked what stage they were at, Emily said tersely, 'We're still fine-tuning the script.' I stopped asking about it.

Eventually, Emily's mother rang and asked Emily would she mind if she wore the long, navy, spangledy dress to Mr Emily's Christmas work do? Only it was nearly a year since she'd bought it, and though it had been in the sales, at 40 per cent off, it had still been fairly pricey. She'd like to get some use out of it.

Work away, Emily advised.

Then, lo and behold, a rival studio brought out a film. It was about a group of eight couples who go on a golfing holiday on a tiny island off Fiji. The island is invaded by terrorists, who kill the few locals and take several of the golfers hostage. Some escape into the undergrowth, survive castaway-style on twigs etc., and plot a rescue mission. It was an action movie, with – you'll never guess – a love story. And even, would you believe, one or two laughs. I'd worked on the fringes of the film business long enough not to be surprised when news filtered back that the studio had decided to 'pass' on making Emily's movie. 'Pass' was Hollywood-speak for 'turn down', 'reject' or 'want nothing further to do with'. I rang Emily to tell her how sorry I was. She was crying. 'But I'm working on a new script,' she told me. 'You win some, you lose some, right?'

That was a year and a half ago. Soon afterwards, she came home to Ireland for Christmas and persuaded me to go out on the town with her, just the two of us.

Garv begged to be allowed to come, but sorrowfully Emily told him it was a girls' night out and he wouldn't be able for it. And she was right – at the best of times, she was a dangerous person to go out with, and when she was feeling raw, humiliated and disinclined to talk about it, she was even worse.

It was the pink stetson night: the rock-chick look was reaching critical mass and was about to collapse under the weight of its own silliness. But it hadn't yet happened and she looked sensational.

I jumped all over her, so happy to see her, but despite our delight in each other's company, it was a strange night. At the time I thought I was having the time of my life, but in retrospect I'm not so sure. Emily drank an awful lot at high speed – since she'd started drinking she'd become very good at it. Normally I didn't even attempt to keep up, but on this particular night I did. Obviously I got very drunk, but strangely I didn't realize it. I felt perfectly sober. The only indication that anything was amiss was the fact that everyone I came into contact with seemed to do something to insult or annoy me. It never occurred to me that the fault might be mine.

We were in a bar in the Hayman, a new fancy-dan hotel,

where everything from the roof tiles right down to the ashtrays had been 'created' by some celebrated New York designer. I'd heard about the place – it had been all over the papers, not least because most of its *objets* were for sale – but had never been there, whereas Emily had only been home three days and had already been there twice.

We settled down at a corner table, ordered a bottle of wine, and Emily launched into the story of her life since we'd last seen each other. She refused to talk about her writing – 'Don't mention the war,' she'd groaned, and instead told me about her love life. The dates she'd gone on with the gay man who insisted he wasn't and the straight man who insisted he was gay. She was a great raconteur, with impeccable attention to detail. No broad brushstrokes. Gripping stuff.

She always seemed to do a lot more talking than me. But then again she had a lot more to talk about. By the time we were finally up to speed on her life we'd almost finished our second bottle of wine.

'Now you,' she ordered. 'What's the story with the rabbits?' She frowned. 'And what does a girl have to do to get a drink around here?'

I sighed and began my sorry tale, then through the throng spotted my sister Claire.

'What are you doing here?' she exclaimed. Then she saw Emily and understood. She spent a bit of time chatting to us, then noticed the people she was meant to be meeting, so off she went. No sooner was she out of earshot than Emily muttered darkly, 'Oh yeah? You go on off and have a nice time with the people at the BIGGER table.'

She looked at me levelly – or so I thought at the time, but clearly we were just swaying in time with each other. 'I've taken agin your sister . . . And,' she appended grandly, 'her friends.'

I looked over at the table that Claire had just joined. At her arrival it had blown up with laughter and talk. I was pierced with a peculiar sense of exclusion. 'I've taken against them too!'

'You haven't taken against them.'

Hadn't I?

Emily leant her head back and tipped the last of her wine down her throat. 'You've taken *agin* them.'

Fair enough. I'd taken agin them.

We managed to procure another bottle of wine, then decided to go somewhere else, where the people weren't quite so annoying. As we beat our way out, we passed Claire and her friends.

'We're leaving now,' Emily said haughtily. 'No thanks to you.'

Cryptic, I know, but at the time it made perfect sense.

In the hotel lobby, by the front door, we decided to have a little dance before we left. I'm not sure whose idea it was, but we were both agreed that it was a good one. We actually put our handbags down and had a brief dance around them before cackling off into the night. To this day I can still see the astonished expressions of the three considerably more sober men standing near us.

Outside, we hailed a taxi and asked – demanded, more likely – to be taken to Grafton Street. Within seconds we'd taken agin the driver, paranoid that he was taking the long and lucrative way round.

'You can't turn right on that bridge,' he defended himself.

'Sure,' Emily scorned. 'You can't swizz me, I live here,' she lied aggressively. 'I'm not a tourist.'

Then she poked me with her small, sharp elbow and giggled hoarsely, 'Maggie, look.' She opened wide her handbag – like a dentist trying to reach the furthest molars – where, in amongst

61

her LV wallet (fake) and Prada make-up bag (real), nestled one of the ashtrays from the hotel. If I remembered correctly it had carried a price tag of thirty pounds.

'Where did you get that?!'

A rhetorical question. When Emily is under stress she nicks things and I hate it. Why can't she be more like me? My way of dealing with stress is to get an outbreak of eczema on my right arm. I'm not saying it's pleasant but at least you can't get arrested for it.

'Stop stealing things,' I scowled, low and fierce. 'Sometime you'll get caught and you'll be in terrible trouble!'

But answer came there none, because she was berating the driver again.

We went to a nightclub that we were really far too old for and had a great time taking agin more people – the doorman, who didn't summon us to the top of the queue quickly enough for Emily's liking, barmen who didn't serve us instantly, sundry merry-makers who didn't leap to their feet and give us their seats as soon as they saw us.

Basically, we had a blast, and the following day Garv was not unsympathetic. He speedily vacated the bathroom when I had to vomit, and stood patiently on the landing, his face covered in shaving cream, his razor in his hand.

By six that evening I was well enough to talk, so I rang Emily. I was quite giddy – almost proud of our wild behaviour the night before, but Emily sounded subdued.

'Did we dance around our handbags in the Hayman?' she asked.

'We did.'

'Do you know?' she said fake-casually. 'I have a horrible feeling there was no dance-floor.'

'Never mind no dance-floor,' I exclaimed. 'There was no music. And wasn't it great the way we took agin all those people?'

Emily made a funny noise. A whimper crossed with a groan. 'Don't tell me I was taking against people.'

'Agin,' I corrected. 'We took *agin* people. It was great.'

'Oh God.'

I picked up the phone. 'Emily?'

'Are you OK?'

'I'm fine,' I croaked. 'I just think I've a touch of the flu.'

'Your mum says you've split up with Garv.'

'Oh . . . yeah.'

'And that you've lost your job.'

'Yes,' I sighed, 'I have.'

'But . . .' She sounded both astonished and helpless, 'I've been e-mailing you at work. Whoever has taken over from you will have got the finer details of Brett and his penis enlargement.'

I managed to say, 'Sorry. I haven't really been in touch with anyone.'

A silence while static hopped and blew on the line. I knew she was dying to ask questions, but she satisfied herself with, 'Are you sure you're OK?'

'I'm fine.'

More static. 'Look,' she said slowly, 'if you're not working and . . . stuff, why don't you just hop on a plane and come out here for a while?'

'What's out there?'

'Sunshine,' she cajoled. 'Fat-free Pringles, *me*.'

It was a measure of how far gone I was that I suspected she didn't mean it. That she was only saying it because she felt she

63

had to, that it was what a good friend *should* say. But all the same, something sparked in my deadness. Los Angeles. City of Angels. I wanted to go.

6

We were spending an alarming amount of time flying over the suburbs of Los Angeles. They just kept unscrolling beneath me, grid after grid of dusty, single-level houses, the neat squares occasionally interrupted by a huge concrete freeway snaking violently through them. From far away in the distance came the diamond glint of the ocean.

It was barely a week since the phone call from Emily and I could hardly believe I was here. *Almost* here – were we ever going to land?

There had been strong opposition to me making the journey. Especially from my mother. 'Los Angeles? *What* Los Angeles?' she had demanded. 'Didn't Rachel say you could stay with her in New York? And didn't Claire say you could go to London and live with her for as long as you wanted? And what if there's an earthquake in that Los Angeles place?' She turned on Dad. 'Say something!'

'I've two tickets for the Hurling semi-final,' Dad said sadly. 'Now who'll come with me?'

Then Mum remembered something and addressed Dad. 'Isn't Los Angeles the place where you hurt your neck?'

About twenty years ago, Dad had gone with a load of other accountants on some junket to Los Angeles, and had come back with a gammy neck from the Log Flume at Disneyland.

'It was my own fault,' he insisted. 'There were signs saying I shouldn't stand up. And it wasn't just me, the whole seven of our necks got dislocated.'

'Oh, mother of God!' Mum clapped a hand over her mouth. 'She's taken off her wedding ring!'

I'd been kind of experimenting, to see what it felt like. The missing rings (the engagement ring went too) left a very obvious indent and a circle of white skin like uncooked dough. I don't think in the nine years I'd been married I'd ever taken them off: being without them felt strange and bad. But so did wearing them. At least this way was more honest.

Next to register his displeasure at my departure was Garv. I'd phoned to tell him I was off for a month or so and he'd come hot-footing it round. Mum ushered him into the sitting-room. 'Now!' she declared triumphantly, her entire demeanour saying, 'Time for this nonsense to stop, young lady.'

Garv said hello, and we both looked at each other for far too long. Maybe that's what you do when you split up with someone: try to remember what once welded you together. He'd gone slightly bitty and unkempt. Even though he was in his work clothes, he was wearing his off-duty hair and his expression was grim – unless it was always grim? Maybe I was reading more into this than I should.

Indeed, he didn't look like he was fading away through sorrow; he was still, to use a phrase of my mother's (except she never said it about Garv), 'a fine figure of a man'. Hazily, I suspected that these weren't the right thoughts to be thinking in the circumstances; they didn't seem weighty enough. But they were all I could manage. Why? Shock, maybe? Or could it be that Anna was right and *Cosmopolitan* was wrong – perhaps I *was* depressed.

'Why LA?' Garv asked stiffly.

'Why not? Emily's there.'

He gave me a look which I didn't understand.

'I've no job and . . . you know . . .' I explained. 'I might as well. I know we've a lot of stuff to sort out, but . . .'

'When will you be back?'

'Don't know exactly, I've an open-ended ticket. In about a month.'

'A month.' He sounded weary. 'Well, when you come back, we'll talk.'

'That'd make a change.' I hadn't meant to sound so bitter.

Rancour mushroomed between us, like a cloud of poison. Then – poof! – it was gone again and we were back to being polite adults.

'We do need to talk,' he stressed.

'If I'm not back in a month you can come and get me.' I strove to sound pleasant. 'Then we'll get solicitors and all that.'

'Yes.'

'Don't you go jumping the gun and getting one before me.' It was meant to sound light-hearted, but instead emerged sounding spiteful.

He looked at me, without expression. 'Don't worry, I'll wait until you're back.'

'I won't be working so I'll pay the mortgage from my Ladies' Nice Things account.'

I had a separate bank account from my joint one with Garv, into which I put a small amount every month – just enough to cover impractical sandals and unnecessary lip-glosses without feeling riddled with guilt at spending our mortgage money. Some of my friends – specifically Donna – wondered how I'd conned Garv into agreeing to it, but in fact it had been his idea and he was the one who'd come up with the jokey name.

'Forget the mortgage,' he sighed. 'I'll cover it. You'll need your Ladies' Nice Things money to buy ladies' nice things.'

'I'll pay you back.' I was relieved to have a bit more money for Los Angeles. 'Is it OK for me to go to the house to get some of my stuff?'

'Why wouldn't it be?' Something guilty and defensive flickered. He knew exactly what I was talking about, but he pretended not to. And I didn't bother to elucidate. There was a funny complicity between us, and an awful lot not being said. It was the way I wanted it: if he had someone else I *so* did not want to know. 'It's your house,' he said. 'You own half of it.'

It was then that I had the first normal thought that a person whose marriage has just broken up should have – we'd have to sell the house. The mist cleared and my future unspooled like a film. Selling the house, having nowhere to live, searching for somewhere else, trying to make a new life, being alone. *And who would I be?* So much of my sense of self was tied up in my marriage that, without it, I hadn't a clue who I was.

I felt dislocated from everything, floating in empty time and space, but I couldn't think about it now.

'All in all, how are you? Are you OK?' Garv asked.

'Yeah. Considering. You?'

'Yeah.' A breathless little laugh. 'Considering. Keep in touch,' he said, and made a funny move towards me. It began as a hug, but ended up being a pat on my shoulder.

'Sure.' I slid away from his heat and familiar smell. I didn't want to get too near to him. We said goodbye like strangers.

Through the window I watched him leave. That's my husband, I told myself, marvelling at how unreal it seemed. Soon to be *ex*-husband, and more than a decade of my life is going with him. As he walked out of the short drive and became hidden by the hedge, I was ambushed by an inferno of white-hot fury. *Go on*, I wanted to empty my lungs and bellow, *fuck off back to Truffle Woman*. As quickly as it had appeared, the rush of rage receded, and once again I felt heavy and kind of dead.

Helen was the only one who approved of me going to LA.

'Smart work,' she said. 'Just think of the men. Lovely ridey surfey types.' She groaned. '*Christ*. Tanned, sun-bleached hair all tangled and salty, six-pack stomachs, muscly thighs from staying up on the surfboards –' She paused and announced, 'Jesus, I might come with you!'

And then it hit me: I was single. I was a single woman in my thirties. I'd spent my twenties in the safe cocoon of marriage and I had no idea what it was like to be on my own. Of course I knew about singletons, about the culture of the thirty-something single person. I'd heard the statistics: a thirty-something woman had a better chance of being abducted by aliens (I think) than receiving a proposal of marriage. I had watched my single sisters and friends pursue true love, and had joined in wondering where all the good men were when things didn't work out. But the interest I'd taken had been purely theoretical. I'd *wondered* where all the good men were, but I hadn't really cared. I hadn't been smug – at least, not consciously – but there's no doubt that pride comes before a fall.

I had no man now. I was no different from Emily or Sinead or anyone. Although, in fairness, I didn't want a man. I no longer wanted to be with Garv, but I was blocked. I couldn't make the necessary leap of imagination to being with anyone else.

It was then that I had my second normal thought: *My life is over*. That was the only thing I was sure of, the one fixed fact in an uncertain world. I clung on to this knowledge because, strangely, it gave me comfort.

Immigration took for ever. Finally, it was my turn to hand my passport over to the big, unpleasant guy at the desk. (And it made no difference which desk you picked: somewhere there must be a factory where they manufacture these men.) As he ran a disgusted eye over me, I found myself wondering if he was married or divorced. Not – let me hasten to add – because I fancied him. I'd wondered it about the woman I was sitting next to on the plane, too, and I'm fairly sure I didn't fancy her. I just didn't want to be the only one . . .

My speculation came to an abrupt halt when he barked, 'Reason for visiting the United States?'

'Vacation.'

'Where are you staying?'

'With a friend in Santa Monica.'

'And your friend in Santa Monica? What does he do?'

'*She* is a scriptwriter.'

And I swear to God, Mr Narky changed before my eyes. He sat up straight, stopped narrowing his eyes contemptuously, and suddenly he was as sweet as candy.

'Oh yeah? Someone buy her script?'

'Universal.' Or was it Paramount? But then they'd sidelined it . . .

'So is there a part for me in this movie?' he joked. Only thing is, I'm not sure he was joking.

'Dunno,' I said nervously.

'You dunno,' he sighed, reaching for his stamp and giving my passport a good thump with it.

I was in!

*

And there was Emily, tapping her (beautiful, Japanese-style besandalled) foot impatiently. God, it was so good to see her.

'How are you? Psychotic with jet lag?' she asked sympathetically.

'Certifiable. I believe I watched three films on the plane and I couldn't tell you the first thing about any of them. One of them might have been about a dog.'

'Gimme that.' Emily positioned herself at the helm of my trolley – or should I say 'cart'? – and pushed it briskly towards the airport car park.

The heat hit like God had opened a huge oven door. 'Lord,' I reeled.

'Not far,' she encouraged.

'Hey, look!' I was distracted from the faint-making heat by a bunch of holy-roller, culty types, clustered on a patch of grass, wearing turquoise robes, shaking tambourines and chanting away goodoh. I half-suspected they'd been laid on specially for me – Welcome to LA – the way in Hawaii they get some girl to put one of those garlands of flowers around your neck.

Emily was unimpressed. 'Plenty more where they came from. Get in.' She opened the car door. 'The air-con will be on in a minute.'

I'd never been to Los Angeles before, but I'd have known it anywhere. It was all so familiar – the sixteen-lane freeways, the tall, skinny palm trees, the adobe-style houses. The skyline was low and extended for ever – it was nothing *at all* like Chicago.

Every few blocks we passed mini-malls which advertised pet-grooming, nail salons, gun shops, surveillance equipment, dentists, tanning salons, more pet-grooming . . .

'You could groom a lot of pets in this town,' I remarked dreamily. It was the jet lag. I was gone a bit mental from it.

Emily had no time for such nonsense. There was a story and she wanted to hear it. 'So what's up with you and Garv?'

I had a very real urge to jump from the speeding car. I plumped for, 'We were making each other miserable, so we've called it a day.'

'Yeah, but –' I could hear fear in her voice. 'You haven't actually *split up*? You're just taking a break from each other? 'Cos of everything?'

What was this conspiracy? Why would nobody accept it was finished?

'We *have* split up.' My right arm began to tingle. 'It's all over.'

'God.' She sounded terribly upset. 'But you're not going to . . . get divorced?'

A wash of shame hit me. 'What else would we do?'

'Have you actually started proceedings?'

'Not yet. We're waiting until I get back.' With those words, a fact I'd known intellectually transformed itself into something personal. 'I'll be a divorcee!'

'Um . . . if you get divorced, you probably will.' Emily threw me an anxious glance. 'Is that a shock?'

'No, it's just . . . It's just hit home.' All the same, it had hardly been part of my life plan. 'A divorcee.' I tried out the word again and my ever-present sense of failure intensified. Striving for humour, I said, 'You know what that means? I'll have brassy blonde hair and make a show of myself at family parties, drinking too much and dancing provocatively with younger men.'

'That's me now,' Emily said. 'And, you know, it's not so bad.'

Silence descended, and I could almost hear the turning of the cogs in her overtaxed brain.

'But I still can't believe it,' she breathed. 'Like, what *happened*? Did he end it or did you . . . ?'

I didn't want to discuss it. I wanted to forget it and enjoy myself. 'Neither of us. Both of us, I mean.' Then, like a grenade, I lobbed into the conversation, 'I think he's met someone else.'

'Who? *Garv!*' she shrieked, nearly so high-pitched that only bats could hear her.

'He's an attractive man.' I felt oddly defensive.

'That's not what I meant.' With a volley of well-targeted questions she extracted the story of Truffle Woman, and she took it almost worse than I had done. Driving into the sun, she muttered, 'I thought the decent behaviour of Garv Garvan was the one thing I could depend on. I thought he was one of the few good ones out there. Maggie, I'm devastated.'

'I'm not exactly jumping for joy myself.'

'And who is this girl?'

'Could be anyone. Someone he works with. Could be . . .' I made myself say it. 'Could be Donna. Or Sinead. He gets on well with both of them.'

'It's not Donna or Sinead. They wouldn't do that. And if they did I'd have heard. Men,' she said bitterly, 'they're all the same. The few brains they have are in their mickeys. How much do you hate him?'

'Lots. When I have the energy.' The thing was that even though I was raging with Garv, in a way I didn't blame him.

Emily gave me a sharp look. She knows me very well, I have no secrets from her. But before she could explore further I tried to head her off at the pass.

'It could be worse,' I said with grisly cheer. 'At least it's amicable . . . Amicable*ish*,' I added, less certainly. 'The money and house will be sorted out properly.'

'Of course they will. Garv is nothing if not decent. At least you don't have –' She stopped, aghast.

'Children,' I finished for her.

'I'm sorry,' she whispered.

'It's OK,' I reassured. It wasn't really, but I wasn't going to think about it.

'Do you –' she started, at the same time as I said, '*Any*way! So what road is this we're on?'

Emily ignored my attempt to change the conversation. Instead she warned, 'Amicable or not, you're going to have to talk about you and Garv.'

I sagged with reluctance, and all of a sudden I knew what this reminded me of. When I was sixteen I'd slipped coming down the stairs and my knee accidentally went through the glass front door. I'd ended up with hundreds of slivers of glass embedded in my knee, each one having to be removed individually with tweezers. Pain relief hadn't been on the agenda, and I'd been rigid and sweating with pain and the anticipation of more to come. Every word about me and Garv was like another sliver being picked from my raw flesh. 'I will talk about it,' I said. 'But not now. Please.'

'OK.'

Eventually, the character of the roads began to change until we were in a modest residential area. All the houses looked like one-offs – some adobe style, some New England, some deco, painted in low-key pastel shades. There was a general air of kemptness. Everywhere there were flowers.

'We're nearly there. Nice, isn't it?'

'Lovely.' It was just that I'd expected something a little edgier from Emily.

'When I first moved to LA I had to live in a rotting – literally, it was rotting in the heat – apartment building in East LA, and people kept getting shot and killed outside my window.'

OK, maybe edgy wasn't so great.

'The murder rate in Santa Monica is way low,' she reassured.

Marvellous!

We pulled up outside a white clapboard bungalow, with a small lawn on to the pavement. Water sprinklers worked like searchlights back and forth on the grass.

'Keep an eye out for them fecking sprinklers,' Emily advised. 'They're on a timer, and they're always surprising me and destroying my hair. And keep an eye out for the neighbours on that side, they're the kind of people who give LA a bad name.'

'Serial killers?'

'New Agers; they'd read your aura as soon as look at you. The neighbours on the other side aren't much better. Boys. College students, doing computer programming or something. They're handy if ever you want to buy drugs, not that you'd want to, I know.'

This gave me a little breathing space of relief; I didn't want to be surrounded by married couples. Drug-dealing students were far preferable.

Flowers blazed shocking pink against the dazzling white of Emily's house. It was all very pretty. Then I noticed the 'Armed Response' sign in the front garden and my delight with my surroundings dimmed somewhat. What happened around here that an armed response was necessary?

We hoicked my stuff into the cool, shady house. While I oohed and aahed over the hardwood floors, white blinds and pretty back garden, Emily made straight for her answering machine. 'Gaaaaaargh,' she groaned. 'Ring, you bastard.'

'A man?' I asked, with as much compassion as I could muster.

'I wish.'

'Oh?'

'Maggie,' she slumped on to a chair. 'I'm officially Down on My Luck.'

'Are you?' I asked faintly, suddenly aware that I wasn't the only person in the world who was mid-crisis.

'I'm so glad you're here.'

'Are you?' How had I suddenly mutated from comfortee to comforter?

Emily sighed, then her whole sorry story unravelled.

After the studio had passed on *Hostage* (or was it *Hostage!*?) her agent had fired her, which was nothing less than catastrophic. Studios never, but *never* looked at work which hadn't been submitted by an agent; and it was almost impossible to get an agent, she explained. Every day, literally thousands of screenplays arrived at the mail rooms of the big agencies and had to go through a savage screening process. If the mail-room kids didn't like it, it was out. If it made it past them, it had to pass muster with a reader. In the unlikely event of that happening, it got read by an agent's assistant. And only if they raved about it would an agent deign to look at it.

Emily had spent the past year and a half writing several new scripts, and every time she tried to get an agent, she got knocked back.

'But you've a name.'

'I've a *bad* name,' she corrected. 'Everyone remembers that the studio passed on *Hostage*. I'm in a worse position than a total newcomer. It's an unforgiving town.'

'Why didn't you tell me?'

'Dunno. Too ashamed. Me, the big success story. And I kept hoping things would improve. You know?'

I did, as it happened.

Only ten days ago, Emily had managed to place her most recent script with a new agent. But he was with a much smaller agency which didn't carry the same clout with the studios.

'His name is David Crowe. He's gone out with my script. He's trying to get a buzz going and see if he can kickstart a bidding war. And I've heard nothing.'

'But he's only just gone out with it.'

'Things happen very fast in this town, or they don't happen at all. It's working my last nerve,' she said. 'If this doesn't take off, it's over for me.'

'Don't be mad. You'll just pick yourself up and try again.'

'I fucking won't, you know,' she said grimly. 'I'm burnt out. This city has me in shreds. The casualties are everywhere. You'll see . . . And I'm skint,' she added.

'How?' I was shocked. She'd got a huge fee for *Hostage*, which she didn't have to return when the studio passed on making the film.

'I got paid nearly three years ago and two hundred grand, after taxes and agents' commission, doesn't last so long. And don't think I was too high and mighty to look for commissions writing B-movie, straight-to-video crap. I even pitched for a porn film!'

'To be *in* it?' Were things really that bad?

'No, to write it. But now that you mention it, I'd probably have had more luck if I'd auditioned to star in it. Even they turned me and my studio pedigree down. I couldn't get arrested.'

'Oh, my God.'

'It's been a horrible eighteen months,' she admitted. 'The day that Beam Me Up Productions –'

'Who?'

'Exactly. Some C-list, outer-space merchants operating out of a Portakabin in Pasadena. The day they passed on my pitch to do the fourth sequel to *Squelch Beings from Gamma 9* was my blackest day so far.'

I was crippled by the magnitude of her problems. It was too hot, I was too tired, and I wanted to go home. But home no longer existed.

'Oh Christ, Christ, Christ.' She looked suddenly stricken. 'I'm sorry, Maggie. I'm terribly sorry . . . What a thing to be doing to you! Let me make you something to eat.'

She flung together a salad and opened a bottle of white wine. Mercifully, she seemed to cheer up.

'Things aren't so bad. I can always go back to Ireland and get some film work there, now that I have a lot of contacts,' she chattered.

She paused. 'Do you know who I see the odd time in the course of work?'

Something in her tone alerted me.

'Who?'

A beat. 'Shay Delaney.' It was clear that she'd been waiting for the right time to tell me.

'How?'

'He's a producer with Dark Star Productions. An –'

'– independent film company,' I finished for her. I'd suddenly remembered what the name had meant to me when he'd told me who he worked for.

'He has to spend a lot of time over here.' She sounded almost defensive.

'I suppose he does. People who work in movie-production companies tend to.' She looked puzzled and I said, 'I met him. Last week.'

'No way!' As Emily marvelled at what a coincidence that was, I hunched over my salad. Was that why I'd been so keen to come to Los Angeles?

7

I awoke in darkness to the rattle of machine-gun fire. My blood was pounding. I listened for more sounds – shouts, moans, police sirens – but nothing.

We're not in Kansas any more, Toto.

Lying in the blackness, I admitted the bitter truth. I was sorry I'd come. I'd expected to feel magically better, but how could I when I'd brought myself and my failed life with me? And living in someone else's house – even a good friend's – was tougher than I'd expected. Despite the eight-hour time difference, I hadn't got to sleep for ages because Emily had the telly on so loud. I'd seethed in my bedroom (which was actually her office), wishing she'd turn it down. But there was nothing I could do – it wasn't my house. When a raucous blast of canned laughter had exploded through the thin walls, I'd experienced a violent longing for my life with Garv. I couldn't live like this. All at once, I was ready to admit that splitting up had been a terrible mistake and that business as usual could resume with immediate effect. I was used to harmony and being able to turn off the telly whenever it suited me.

But was that a good enough reason to try again? Probably not, I decided reluctantly.

I did eventually go to sleep, but now I was awake.

Another crackle of machine-gun fire caused my heart to burst against my ribs. What was going *on* out there?

If only I could go home, I yearned. But I suspected I had to stick it out. Everyone would think I'd cracked up if it came out that I went to Los Angeles and only stayed a day. And this wasn't just about me – it was clear that Emily needed someone around. Christ, maybe we'd be going home together, a duo of failures. We'd have to sit in a special cordoned-off area on the plane in case we infected the other passengers.

A noise at the window made me jerk about three feet off the bed. What was it? The branch of a tree banging against the glass? Or a roaming madman on the lookout for a girl to torture and murder? My money was on the roaming madman. After all, this was Los Angeles, full, by all accounts, of pathological killers. I'd read one or two Jackie Collins novels in my time and I knew all about psychos who think in italics.

Not long now. Not long before revenge would be his. And then they'd be sorry they'd laughed at him and refused to return his calls. He was strong now. He'd never been stronger. And he had his knife. The knife that would do his deft bidding. First he'd cut off her hair, then he'd cut off her jewellery, then he'd start opening her skin. She'd beg, she'd plead for mercy, for the agony to stop. But it wouldn't stop, because this time it was her turn for the pain, this time it was her turn . . .

I began to sweat. These clapboard Californian houses were so flimsy and I felt the vulnerability of being on the ground floor very keenly.

Slick with fear, I had to turn on the lamp and look on Emily's bookcase for something to read. Preferably something light, to take my mind off my imminent dismemberment. But because I was in her office, all I could find were textbooks on the art of scriptwriting. Then I saw the bundle of pages on the desk. *Plastic Money*, her new screenplay. That'd do.

Two pages in, I was gripped, the roaming madman forgotten. The story was about two women who pull off a jewellery heist to pay for plastic surgery for their daughters, so that they'll have better luck with men than they did. It was a comedy, a thriller, a love story and, most importantly for Hollywood, it had the requisite schmaltzy bit. ('But I love you, Mom. You don't have to buy me new boobs.')

Just before I fell back to sleep, I thought fuzzily, *I'd option it* . . .

When I woke up again, I got the fright of my life – the sun was shining, pouring lemon light into the room. With a pounding heart I wondered, *Where the hell am I?* The last nine months galloped towards me, gathering up awful memories and whooshing them at me, until I remembered why I was in this strange sunny place. Oh yeah . . .

Emily was in the kitchen, clicking away at her laptop.

'Morning,' I said. 'Are you working?'

'Yes, on a new script.'

'A *new* new one?'

'Yeah.' She laughed, then got up and began making herself what I would later come to know as a protein shake. 'I don't know if it's any good, but I've got to keep pressing on with it just in case *Plastic Money* doesn't work out.'

What a nightmare, I thought. To cheer us both up, I said, 'Isn't it a gorgeous day?'

'Yes, I suppose.' She sounded surprised. 'But they're all like this. So did you hear the fireworks last night?'

'Fireworks?'

'Yeah, for the Santa Monica festival. But you were probably out for the count.'

'No, I heard them.' Then in a mortified rush I blurted, 'But I thought they were machine guns.'

'Why would you think they were *machine* guns? Christ in the marketplace!' Her face was stamped with distress and concern. 'You *are* in a bad way.'

She was behind the table and wrapping her wiry little Emily body around mine, and I was so touched by the contact that for the first time since I'd left him, I was able to cry. All my tears had been packed tight inside me, frozen and out of reach until now.

'I'm so sad,' I choked. 'I'm so sad. I'm just so sa-aa-aaad.'

'I know, I know, I know.' On a loop.

The grief that, until then, I'd only caught out-of-the-corner-of-my-eye glimpses of suddenly revealed itself to me, and I felt the full weight of all our blunted hopes. The end of a marriage is the saddest thing in the whole world. Surely no one gets married thinking that theirs mightn't make it? I had an image of a twenty-four-year-old me and a twenty-five-year-old Garv and our innocent trust in the future, and it was killing me.

'All the hope we had and it did us no good.' I pressed a lump of kitchen paper to my leaking face. 'I had to go, Emily, I didn't have any choice, it was so awful. He would have left if I hadn't. But now it's all go-onnnne.'

'I know, I know, I know,' Emily murmured. 'I know.'

'I thought I could never again feel as sad as I did last February,' I coughed with tears. 'But I doo-hoo. It's sadder than the hungry babies in *Angela's Ashes*.'

'Sadder than Mary going blind in *Little House on the Prairie*?'

'Yeah. Sadder.'

But the damage was done. She'd made me smile. After she'd mopped me up a bit and got me to blow my nose, she tempted, 'Will you have a protein shake? It's a local delicacy.'

'Go on then.'

Emily whipped me up a (frankly, delicious) shake and we sat outside in the tiny, sun-drenched back garden, and I was feeling a little bit calmer until she decided to have another go at making sense of me and Garv.

'The thing is, it all feels a bit premature. Too sudden.'

I sat in silence while my arm got hotter and itchier.

'Nothing ends this cleanly,' she insisted.

'It's not clean.'

She tried to jolly me into engaging. 'You've missed out vital parts of the breaking-up process. What normally happens is you go for counselling, you have to have at least two attempts at a reunion. They've got to fail really horribly, and if you think you're bitter now, it's nothing compared to how you'll be then. *Then* it's allowed to be over.'

'It couldn't be more over now because he's . . . with . . .' – I couldn't bring myself to say 'sleeping with' – 'someone else. I could never trust him again. Or forgive him.'

'I understand,' she started. 'But it's because of the –'

'Please, Emily!' I started out sounding snappy but quickly moved to desperation. 'It's over and I need you to believe me because I can't keep going through this.'

'OK. Sorry.' She seemed glad to stop. She looked exhausted. 'So what would you like to do today?'

'Dunno.'

'I've to see my accountant about my IRS returns this morning,' she said. 'You're welcome to come with me, or I could drop you to the beach.'

I didn't want to be on my own. But how stupid would it be to sit in an accountant's office while Emily went through her tax returns? The sun was splitting the stones and I was a big girl now.

'I'll go to the beach,' I swallowed.

'How are you fixed for money?' Emily asked. 'Not that I'm looking for any,' she added quickly.

'Well, Garv said he'd cover the mortgage for a month and I've my credit card. No way of paying it off, though, until I get a new job.' For some reason this worry wasn't as potent as it usually was. 'And I've a bit in my current account.'

In fact, my Ladies' Nice Things account was quite healthy. Though I'd been spending too much lately, I'd been doing it from our joint account and it struck me that maybe I'd been stockpiling money in my own account, somehow anticipating the split with Garv. It wasn't a comfortable thought.

'Why are you asking me about money?'

'I was thinking you might like to hire a car while you're here.'

'Can't I get the bus?'

A funny noise made me look up. It was Emily, laughing.

'What did I say?'

'"Can't I get the bus." Next you'll be offering to walk places. You're a tonic!'

'I can't get the bus?'

'Not really, no one gets the bus. The service is beyond shite. Or so I'm told, I've never actually experienced it first-hand. You need a car in this town. There are some great pick-up trucks for rent,' Emily said dreamily.

'Pick-up trucks? Do you mean jeeps?'

'No, I mean pick-up trucks.'

'You mean . . . like hill-billies drive?'

'Well, yeah, but new and shiny and without hogs sitting up front.'

But I didn't want a pick-up truck. I'd been entertaining a pleasant vision of zipping around in a foxy little silver convertible, my hair flying out behind me, lowering my heart-shaped sunglasses and making eye contact with men at traffic lights. (Not that I ever would, of course.)

'Only tourists and out-of-towners drive convertibles,' Emily scorned. 'Angelenos never do. Because of the smog.'

I remembered that Emily had picked me up from the airport in a huge, jeep-style, four-wheel-drive type of yoke. She'd looked as if she was driving a block of flats, and I'd almost needed a rope and crampons to get up to the passenger seat. 'Pick-up trucks are very now,' she advised. 'And if not a pick-up truck, then get a jeep like mine.'

'But I just need something to get me from A to B.' And it was all right for her, living in year-round sunshine, but when would I get another chance to take the roof off my car and not get soaked to the skin?

'You see, your car is how you're judged in this town. Your car and your body. It doesn't matter if you live in a cardboard box, so long as your car is cool and you're in the terminal stages of anorexia.'

'Well, I think convertibles are cool. That's the car I'd like.'

'But –'

'My marriage has broken up,' I said, playing dirty. 'I want a convertible.'

'OK.' Emily knew when she was beat. 'We'll get you a convertible.'

*

86

Just before we went out, my mother rang. 'That entire seaboard could fall into the Pacific at any moment.'

'Is that right?'

'I'm only saying it for your good.'

'Thank you.'

'Is it sunny there?'

'Very. I have to go now.'

The beach was no distance, I could easily have walked it. If I'd been allowed. I abseiled down out of the car and away Emily drove, perched high and tiny in her mobile block of flats.

The scene ahead of me looked like a postcard. Bathed in citrus light, lines of high, spindly palm trees brushed the jaunty blue sky. Stretching far away in both directions was a wide expanse of powdery white sand, and beyond that was the glinting rush of the ocean.

We've all heard that Californians are gorgeous. That through a combination of good-living, health-consciousness, sunshine, plastic surgery and eating disorders they're skinny, muscled and glowing. As I arranged my towel on the sand I suspiciously watched other people on the beach. There weren't that many – possibly because it was a weekday – but there were enough to confirm my worst fears. I was the fattest, saggiest person on that stretch of sand. Possibly in the entire state of California. God, they were thin. And I was filled with resolve – tinged with despair – that I was going to start exercising again.

Two Scandinavian-looking girls took up a position far too near for my liking. Immediately I wondered if either of them were divorced; I was driving myself mad speculating about the marital status of everyone I met . . .

They whipped off their shorts and tops to reveal tiny bikinis, flat stomachs and golden thighs, shaped and curved with muscle. You never saw two people more comfortable with their bodies; I dearly wanted to shoo them away.

Their arrival meant that I couldn't remove my sarong. Time passed, and when I had managed to convince myself that no one had any interest in me, I slid it off. I held my breath, wondering if the lifeguard would jerk with sudden shock and break into a slo-mo, red-rescue-pack-under-his-arm, pounding-rock-soundtrack run towards me and order, 'I'm sorry, Ma'am, we're going to have to ask you to leave. This is a family beach, you're upsetting folks.'

But no drama erupted and I slathered myself in factor eight and prepared to bake; skin cancer seemed the least of my worries. God, I was white! I should have lashed on some fake tan before I came. Immediately this made me think of Garv – I always snapped on surgical gloves before applying fake tan and he used to say, 'Oooh, matron, a surgical-glove moment!'

Oh, God. I closed my eyes, lulled by the rhythmic rush and suck of the waves, the yellow heat of the sun, the short-lived, skippy breezes.

It was actually quite pleasant until I turned over on to my stomach and found that there was no one to put sun-tan lotion on my back. Garv would have done it. I suddenly felt very lonely and the feeling hit anew, *My life is over.*

As I'd packed, the night before I left Ireland, I'd told Anna and Helen the very same thing. 'My life is over.'

'It's not.' Anna had been visibly distressed.

'Don't patronize her,' Helen had urged.

'You'll meet someone else – you're young,' Anna said doubtfully.

'Ah, she's not really,' Helen interjected. 'Not at thirty-three.'

'And you're good-looking,' Anna struggled on.

'You know, she's not bad,' Helen admitted grudgingly. 'You have nice hair. And your skin isn't bad. For your age.'

'All that clean-living,' Anna said.

'All that clean-living,' Helen echoed solemnly.

I sighed. My living wasn't that clean, it just wasn't as *un*clean as theirs, and my good-for-my-age skin was thanks to slathering on so much expensive night-cream that I used to slide off my pillows, but I let it go.

'And . . .' Helen said thoughtfully. I leant forward on the bed, all the better to be praised. '. . . You have a lovely handbag.'

I sat back, disappointed.

'Funny that,' she mused. 'I'd never have put you down as an expensive-handbag kind of a girl.'

I tried to protest; I *am* an expensive-handbag kind of a girl, I'm almost sure of it. But I wasn't getting into another row with Helen, where I tried to convince her I was irresponsible with money.

Besides, as it happens, it had been Garv who had given me the lovely handbag in question.

'In your granny!' Helen had chuckled. 'You expect me to believe Mr Peel-an-orange-in-his-pocket would shell out over a ton for a *sac à main*. That's French, you know. Anyway, you know the way your life is over? You won't be needing your handbag any more, will you?'

But I wouldn't surrender it, which led her to remark suspiciously, 'Your life can't be *that* over then, can it?'

'Shut up, you're getting my car,' I said.

'But it's only for the month. And I have to share it with *her*.' She jerked her head at Anna.

Then I heard something which catapulted me right back to the present. 'Ice-cream sandwich!'

I sat up on my towel. A young man was passing by, staggering under the weight of ice-cream that he hadn't a hope of selling; not to this crowd of anorexics.

'Popsicles?' he called desolately. 'Blue Gelatos, Cherry Iceys?'

I felt sorry for him. And hungry. 'Go on,' I said. 'Give me an ice-cream sandwich.'

We conducted our business briskly, then he was once more on his profitless way. I wondered if anyone ever shouted abuse or threw stones at him as he plied his high-fat, high-sugar goods along the beach. 'Garn! Clear orf.' The way people do to drug-pushers in other communities.

And then I was alone again. Suddenly I was very glad I was in California, because I could blame the horrible feeling of being out of step with the rest of the human race on my jet lag. It made it not my responsibility, and I could always try fooling myself that I'd feel perfectly normal in a few days.

Watched hungrily by the two Scandinavian-looking girls, I ate my ice-cream. Their expressions were so avid I felt quite uncomfortable. In fact I nearly offered them a bite. I couldn't help feeling that if this was a book, *someone* would have invited me to join in a game of volleyball or at least struck up a conversation with me – the lifeguard or another sunbather. But the only person who spoke to me all day was the ice-cream seller. And I suspected I was the only person who spoke to him.

8

Late afternoon, Emily picked me up from the beach. When we got home there was still no phone call from David Crowe. Her desperation filled the house.

'No news is good news,' I tried.

'Wrong,' Emily said. 'No news is bad news. They keep the bad news from you and cover themselves in glory with any good news.'

'Well, you ring him then.'

A bitter laugh from Emily. 'It's easier to get an on-set pass to a Tom Cruise movie than to talk to an agent who doesn't want to talk to you.'

But she rang him anyway. And he was 'not at his desk right now'.

'I bet he wouldn't be "not at his desk right now" if it was Ron Bass on the line,' she said gloomily.

I took it that Ron Bass was some hot-shot screenwriter.

'I feel a strange but compelling urge to get bollocksed-drunk,' she said. 'Could your jet lag handle going out this evening?'

'What have you in mind?' Would I be forced to go out with a gang of girls and dance to 'I Will Survive', as always seemed to happen to women who'd just split from their men?

'How about dinner somewhere nice?'

'Lovely!' Relief that there would be no Gloria Gaynor made me sound more enthusiastic than I felt.

'That's the spirit. You know what?' she said thoughtfully. 'What you need to do is let your hair down a little.' Even though Emily was very fond of Garv, she'd always thought that I'd missed out on the necessary rites-of-passage high-jinks by getting married so young. 'Go a bit mad for yourself while you're here.'

'I'll see,' I said noncommittally. Jesus, little did I know . . .

'We'll call Lara. Lara likes a drink. And Connie. And Troy. And Justin.'

A quick round of phone calls, and then she just went and got that really pulled-together look. Just bang-bang-bang, like it's easy or something. The dress, the heels, the bag, the hair, all smooth and shiny, shiny, shiny.

Then she opened her wondrous make-up bag and shared with me some of her knowledge. Lotion was smeared on my lips, 'to get that bee-stung look'. My eyelashes were curled with a little machine (I believe it may have been called an eyelash curler). Then she produced a little tube and said, 'This'll get rid of your jet-lag bags.'

'No need,' I countered smugly. 'I have my Radiant-whatchamacallit.'

'Radiant, schmadiant. Wait till you try this.' She dotted some cream under my eyes and – dramatically – I actually felt my skin contract.

'What is it?! Who is it by?' I was all set to run out to a cosmetic counter and hand over the small fortune this magic gear would undoubtedly cost.

'It's Anusol.'

'Huh?'

'Piles ointment. Five dollars a tube, works a dream, all the models use it.'

Do you see what I mean about her always being ahead of the game?

Then a few seconds on my hair with the straightening tongs, and some aloe vera on my ring finger – I'd burnt the tender skin where my wedding ring used to be (which sounded like the title of a particularly maudlin country and western song).

Emily marched to the door, all snappy little sounds. The *tap-tap* of her heels, the *crack* of her handbag clasp, the *click* of her lighter, the *clack-clack* of her nails. I loved it.

We were going to some place on Sunset, she said. The Troy person couldn't come, nor could Connie, who was up to her tonsils in wedding arrangements, but apparently Lara the jarhead and Justin could.

'Are either of them married?' I asked casually.

Emily laughed, 'God, no. Both single.'

'Single single?'

'Is there any other kind?'

'Divorced single.'

With a sympathetic look she said, 'No. They're single single.'

As we drove along, palm trees were silhouetted against the skyline. The sun was setting and the sky was layered with colours: pale blue low down, rising and darkening overhead to a deep luminous blue, in which the first stars twinkled like pinholes in fabric.

We passed the neon lights of gas stations, motels offering waterbeds, billboards in Spanish, used-car lots, signs for Mexican food, chiropractors and houses with really high numbers. There couldn't possibly be 22,000 houses on this road. Could there?

'Maybe,' Emily said. 'Sunset is about twenty miles long.'

Sunset. She means Sunset Boulevard. *I'm driving along Sunset Boulevard*, I thought, feeling like I was in a film.

At some traffic intersection a man stood holding a ragged piece of cardboard, which said in big, crooked letters WIFE WANTED. There was even a phone number. He looked presentable enough, that was the weird thing.

'There we are, Maggie,' Emily indicated him. 'May the best woman win.'

'I'm already married,' I said automatically.

Funny how you forget.

We pulled up in front of a big, white hotel, then some young men were upon us. For a mad moment I thought it might be because of my bee-stung lips and curly eyelashes, but they turned out to be valet parkers.

'So you give them your car key and they park the car and bring it back when you want it!' I'd heard of such a thing, but never before seen it in action. I find parking immensely stressful so I raved with praise for this most civilized of notions.

'But you pay, they're not doing it out of the goodness of their hearts,' Emily said hastily. '*And* you've to give the driver a tip. In we go.'

It was a packed, vibey place. Everyone looked tanned and buffed and gorgeous. However, I wasn't asked to leave. I liked them for that.

As soon as we were seated, Emily said, 'Here's Lara.'

There was a tall, blonde woman swinging herself past tables, and all I could think when I looked at her was: rolling fields of wheat. She had a gilded quality, as if she'd been dipped in golden syrup. There were a lot of beautiful people in that restaurant and she was possibly the best looking of them all.

'Heeeyyy,' she exclaimed at me, when Emily introduced us.

'Hey,' I replied. Normally I'd say 'Hello' or 'Nice to meet you', but I was keen to fit in.

The waiter arrived. Or should I say, the curtain went up. I'd been told that all waiting staff in Los Angeles were resting actors, and this Adonis was so beautiful and so 'on' that he just had to be a thesp.

'Hey ladies,' he dazzled. 'My name is Deyan, I'm your server this evening and I'm going to give until it hurts.'

'Who *is* that?' Lara's face, as she gazed at him, was puzzled. 'Kevin Kline in *In and Out*? Or that guy from *Will and Grace*?'

Not you again, went Deyan's alarmed look. 'It's my interpretation of Jack from *Will and Grace*,' he admitted reluctantly.

'I knew it!' Lara was radiant. 'You know what, Deyan? I'm not really in the mood for Jack tonight. Serve us in the style of . . .' She swept a blue light over me and Emily. 'Who do we want? Choose an actor. Arnie? Ralph Fiennes?'

'I like Nicolas Cage,' I confessed.

'How about it?' Lara questioned Deyan.

'Which movie?' he asked sulkily.

'*Wild at Heart*?' I suggested tentatively. '*City of Angels*?'

He became still and faraway, and I thought he was disgusted at my suggestions. Then his entire body assumed a lanky, boneless quality. 'Rockin' good news,' he drawled. He had Nic's heavy-lidded charm right down!

It was only when I heard myself laugh that I realized it was a long time since I'd found anything funny.

'C'n I git you beautiful ladies a drink?' Deyan husked slowly.

'Vodkatini with Gray Goose, no ice and four olives,' said Lara.

'Apple Martini with Tanqueray and cracked ice,' Emily decreed.

'The same,' I mumbled. 'The apple one.'

'Peanut, you got it!'

I had to admit to being absolutely astounded by this Lara. When I'd first clapped eyes on her swingy, honey-streaked hair and her taut, gold-leaf body, I'd immediately decided that if you looked up 'Airhead' in the dictionary, you'd see a picture of her. But she was intelligent as well as beautiful. I wasn't entirely convinced this was fair.

Across by the bar, Deyan stopped abruptly, dropped as if he was about to kneel on one knee, but stopped about a foot from the floor, swivelled his body back to us, pointed a finger and winked. He mouthed some words, one of which was definitely 'peanut'. I had to hand it to him, he was really working hard.

Then he was back with the drinks. Still in character he began, 'And today's specials are . . .'

Right away my brain went into screensaver mode. I couldn't help it. I wanted to know what the specials were, but something to do with maintaining eye contact for such a long time seemed to interfere with my hearing. It always happened.

'. . . blah blah blah done in a blueberry blah . . .'

'Ooh,' I murmured appreciatively, nodding my head, still locked in that hideous eye-meet.

'. . . blah blah blah served with blah blah and blah.'

'Did anyone listen to that?' Lara asked when he was gone. 'I always get ADD when they start.'

Overjoyed that it wasn't just me, I exclaimed, 'It's like when someone gives me directions. All my energy goes into nodding my head and looking attentive.'

Lara declared. 'You go!' (Big US of A compliment.) 'Me too. I always get the start – "Make a right." Then it's like they scrambled the words and I only get, like, one in twenty –'

'– "Second set of lights,"' I chipped in.

'– "Left on Doheny." Where d'ya find her?' She looked at Emily and pointed at me. 'She's great!'

Her effusive friendliness was over the top, but it still burnt off some of the sense of my own defectiveness. Who was this Lara? Apparently, she worked in a production company.

'A movie-production company?'

She gave me a surprised look that said, *Are there any other kinds?* before nodding. 'Sure, a movie one. An independent.'

'That means,' Emily said, 'they make intelligent movies.'

'But not much money,' Lara laughed.

'Busy week?' Emily asked.

'No. Next coupla weeks I'll be pulling together the launch party for *Doves* but right now I'm taking some down time.'

'I've had way too much down time,' Emily sighed.

I listened attentively. 'Down time' – it seemed to mean 'quietish patch'. One of the things I love about coming to the States is getting the new slang before it comes out in Ireland. To my knowledge, I was the first native of the Blackrock hinterland to use the phrase 'no-brainer', acquired on a trip to New York to see Rachel. It's a bit like seeing all the big films six months before they come out at home.

'I'll probably have nothing but down time for the rest of my life.' Emily was becoming maudlin. 'Bastard agent.'

'It's three days!' Lara admonished. 'Give the guy a chance.'

'Five days. He's had it since last Friday.'

'Three working days. It's nothing. And how's the new script going?'

'Badly. Very badly.'

''Cos your confidence is so low. Hey, here's Justin.'

Justin wasn't what you might call a looker. He had glasses, short, tight black curls, and he was sort of plump. Although to be fair, all he was was probably a pound or two over his optimum weight, but because everyone else in LA was so slender he looked tubby by comparison.

'Sorry I'm late, guys.' His voice was quite high-pitched for a man. 'Desiree's real depressed and I didn't want to leave her.'

I thought Desiree must be his girlfriend, but it turned out to be his dog.

Emily told me that Justin was an actor.

'Would I have seen you in anything?' I asked him.

'Maybe.' But he didn't seem to be taking the question too seriously. 'I play expendable fat guys. You know when they beam down to a planet and one of the crew gets zapped by an unfriendly native? That's me. Or a cop who gets killed in a shoot-out.'

'Don't knock it,' Emily said. 'You've got more work than you can cope with.'

''Sright! In Planet Movie fat guys needed to be expended a lot.

'So!' he said to Emily. 'What happened with your blind-date dinner party on Saturday?'

'Oh God,' Emily groaned. 'Well, I get there and Al, the guy they'd lined up for me, looked OK.'

'Always a bad sign,' said Lara drily.

'He tells me he works in the organ-donor business, and I decided I *had* to fall in love with him. This man saves lives, I thought. So I said, "Tell me about your work."'

'Big mistake in this town,' Lara said to me. 'You ask someone to pass the water jug and you get a ten-minute monologue about how great they are.'

Emily nodded. 'He has to go to car wrecks to check out the dead people's organs, so he starts going on about an accident site. The man had been – this is *awful* – decapitated. "His head was thirty yards away," Al says. "They didn't find it until the next day. It was off the highway, in someone's front yard. The dog found it."'

'Ew,' Lara and Justin shuddered.

'He enjoyed telling me just that bit too much,' Emily agreed. 'I had to go to the bathroom. And when I came back in I heard him telling the entire room, "THE DOG FOUND IT IN THE FRONT YARD". Mind you, I got on really well with this other guy, Lou. He took my number. But he hasn't called me.' Suddenly sobered, she observed tightly, 'I can't have a relationship. No one wants my work. I'm the biggest failure I ever met.'

'No, you're not,' I consoled desperately. I swallowed hard and made myself say it. 'I'm about to get divorced. I can't think of a worse failure.'

'At least you've been married,' Emily said gloomily. 'Although right now I'd settle for sex. Thanks to Brett's botch-job penis enlargement I haven't slept with a man for nearly four months. How about you, Maggie?'

'Not quite that long.' I was much too embarrassed to discuss it in front of Lara and Justin. It had been hard enough admitting I was getting divorced.

'Well,' Lara beamed, 'I haven't slept with a man for *eight years*.'

She had to be joking. All was still as I waited for the punchline. I mean, this woman was off the scale. And if she couldn't get a fella, what hope was there for anyone, anywhere?

'Are you serious?'

'Sure.'

I'd heard about women like her. Emily had said Los Angeles

was full of them – stunningly beautiful, intelligent, nothing too neurotic going on, but they'd been hurt by so many men, who could just take their pick of beautiful women in this town, that they'd decided to throw in the towel and totally shut down emotionally.

'But why?'

'I'm gay.'

Gay. Lara was a *lesbian*. I'd never met a real-life lesbian before. Not knowingly, anyway. Plenty of gay men, of course, but this was a new one on me and I had no clue what to say. Congratulations? Get lost, you're too good-looking?

'I'm sorry.' Lara roared with laughter. 'I shouldn't have done that.'

'So you're not gay?' Suddenly I was comfortable again.

'No, I am.'

9

The following morning dawned bright and sunny. I was beginning to spot a pattern here.

'How are you today?' asked Emily, handing me my breakfast smoothie.

How was I? Goofed, knackered, fearful, disoriented . . . 'Jet-lagged,' I settled on.

'Give it a couple of days, then you'll be fine.'

I could only hope so.

After breakfast, Emily took me to hire a car, but to my disappointment it wasn't as foxy as the one in my imagination, because the foxy one transpired to be about ten times as expensive as the non-foxy model.

'Get it anyway,' Emily urged.

'I shouldn't,' I said. 'I'm not earning.'

'Tell me about it.'

Then the pair of us went to the beach and whiled away several hours, dissecting all sorts of inconsequential stuff, like what a total gobshite Donna's Robbie was – we got great mileage out of that one – and how Sinead looked much better since she'd gone blonde the previous year.

'I'd never have thought it would suit her.'

'No, me neither. Not with her colouring.'

'No, not with her colouring.'

'But she looks great.'

'She really does.'

'And if she'd told me what she was planning to do, I'd have tried to talk her out of it.'

'Me too. I would never have thought it would suit her.'

'No, me neither. I have to say I really didn't think it would.'

'But it's fantastic. Really natural looking.'

'*Very* natural looking . . .' And so on. Lovely, no-brainer stuff, where I didn't have to be clever, or even coherent. Extremely comforting.

But when we got back from the beach, our sleepy, lazy mood changed and we were suddenly encapsulated in a ball of anxiety. The first thing Emily did after she'd opened the door was to skid towards the answering machine, hoping for a message from David Crowe.

'Well?' I asked.

'Nada.'

'Oh, poor Emily.'

'It's too late,' she said the following morning, as she made us our smoothies. 'If it was going to happen it would have happened by now.'

'But your script is brilliant.'

'It makes no difference.'

Despite having perfectly valid problems of my own, I couldn't help but be affected by Emily's hopelessness.

'Isn't life very unfair?'

'Too right. I'm so sorry that all this stuff is going on with me,' Emily said. 'I'm sure you could do without it.'

'Ah, you're OK,' I shrugged.

The thing was – though I'd never have admitted it – that it was almost a relief to be around a big drama that wasn't mine.

Now and again Emily made another half-hearted effort to quiz me up and down about Garv, but I was resistant and she hadn't the energy to persist.

'So what would you like to do today?' Emily asked.

'Duh!' I gestured at the window and the dazzling day beyond it. 'Go to the beach, of course.'

'I'll get my bikini,' she offered, gallantly.

I shook my head. 'There's no need. Stay and do some work, you'll feel better.'

Emily had always been a grafter, and though she claimed she wasn't making any progress on her new script, I knew how guilty she felt if she didn't put in the hours. She'd even done some work the previous evening.

Mind you, as well as writing, Emily spent half her life on the phone, hopping from call waiting to call waiting, like a juggler keeping several balls in the air. There was no such thing as a short conversation.

Connie – whom I still hadn't met – seemed to take up a lot of her time, on account of having drama after drama with flowers, caterers, hairdressers, bridesmaid dresses . . . It made me queasy to overhear. I didn't want anyone ever to get married, I wanted the whole world to get divorced – even single people – so that my life wouldn't feel like such a rare and conspicuous fiasco.

Connie's most recent wedding disaster related to her honeymoon. In a strange version of life imitating art, the resort she'd picked for her honeymoon had been invaded by disgruntled local militiamen, who'd kidnapped seven of the guests. Connie's travel agent was refusing to return her deposit, and though Emily hadn't an ounce of legal knowledge, she was urging Connie to sue. 'You've got rights. Who cares if it wasn't in the contract? Oh hang on, there's my call waiting . . .'

'I'll be back later,' I said, flinging a book into my beach bag.

'Are you sure you're OK?' Emily asked.

'Yes.'

Well, I wasn't too bad – I'd been in Los Angeles for three days and not once had I rung Garv. I'd had two really compulsive urges, but luckily they'd both happened when it was the middle of the night in Ireland, so I'd convinced myself not to act on them.

'You're getting a great tan,' Emily said, sitting cross-legged on the couch and switching on her laptop. 'Drive safely.'

On the way to my car I saw the New-Agey next-door neighbours, obviously on their way out to work. An incongruous pair: she was African-American, haughty and graceful, with a swan-like neck and elbow-length extensions, whereas he looked like Bill Bryson – bearded, balding, bespectacled and kind of jolly. I gave them a nod. Smiling, they approached and introduced themselves: Charmaine and Mike. They seemed very pleasant and didn't mention my aura.

As I said goodbye and turned away, I saw one of the neighbours from the other side, returning from buying coffee for himself and his house-mates, if the Starbucks tray he was carrying was any clue.

'Yo,' he yelled at me, as he marched along in knee-length cut-offs and a torn vest. Even if Emily hadn't already told me the lads were all students, I think I could have figured out that this one wasn't exactly an insurance salesman, judging from his shaved head, many facial piercings and elaborate facial hair. In my few short days in Los Angeles I'd decided that next door could well be a halfway house for Goatees Anonymous. There appeared to be dozens of blokes – although Emily said there were only three – and they all seemed to be afflicted. Some just had wispy, bum-fluff efforts; others, obviously the more hardcore cases like this guy, wore cultivated Fu Manchu mini-beards.

Outside their house sat a long, low, orange car. It looked so clapped out I thought it had been abandoned, but Emily told me it belonged to the boys. It had only cost them two hundred dollars on account of none of the doors opening, so entry and exit was by means of the windows. They called it their Dukes of Hazzardmobile.

'Hey,' I replied, climbing into my car.

I drove the shamefully short distance to the beach and parked. The vista ahead of me was as picture-perfect as it always was. The sand, the sun, the waves, the clear, golden light. Pity I was so wretchedly lonely. Worse still – and I was ashamed to admit this – I was unsettled without the routine and structure of a job and, really, I can't tell you how annoying this was, because I felt like I'd spent most of my working life fantasizing about winning the lotto, jacking in the job and having endless free time to loll around in the sun. Now that I had it, I was afraid of it. Of course, over the years, I'd taken holidays, but this strange, uncharted hiatus wasn't a holiday. I wasn't sure what it *was*, but I knew what it wasn't.

I noticed that my left ring finger no longer looked so weird – the raw-dough colour was becoming more normal, the sunburn had gone down and the outline was plumping out to fit with the rest of the finger. It was like writing in the sand being washed away by the waves.

I spread out my towel and sat in the invisible plastic bubble that kept me cut off from the rest of the world – apart from Rudy, the ice-cream man. He hadn't shown up the previous day. His day off? I asked.

No, he said. He'd been at an audition.

'So what'll it be today?' he asked.

'What do you recommend?' I was keen to prolong the contact.

'How about a Klondike bar?'

A Klondike bar it was, and away he went.

I watched him slog along the beach, getting smaller and smaller the further he went. Where did he put the ice-creams at night, I wondered. Was there a big place they all lived? Like a bus depot, but for ice-creams? Or did he have to bring them home with him? And if so, was he worried about members of his family eating them? It wouldn't matter so much if they paid for them, it'd save him trudging along the beach while people threw stones at him. But they probably wouldn't cough up . . . I drifted off to sleep.

As far as I was concerned, there was no such thing as too many zeds. I was still sleeping that same dead-person's sleep as I had been at home – at least I did once the loudest telly in the Western hemisphere was switched off. Being asleep was a blessed release, and waking up was like being delivered into hell. Each morning when reality hit my first thought was one of terror. 'I can't believe this has happened. I can't actually believe I'm here.' But not long after waking, the horror usually dispersed, just leaving a wispy residue of dread.

When I got back around six-thirty, Emily had fallen asleep on the couch, her laptop on her stomach, and there was a flashing light on the answering machine. One message. Not for me.

A man's voice, speaking in that laid-back, Californian, sing-song way, like this call wasn't a matter of life and death. 'Yeah, hey Emily. This is David. Crowe. Your hardworking agent.' He got particularly sing-song at that bit. 'I just got a call from Mort Russell at Hothouse. He's read your script and he's veeeeery excited.' Another little tune. 'Call me.'

'Emily! Wake up!' I tugged her by the arm and tried to pull her up. 'Wake up, you have to listen to this!'

Her face blank and dazed, I played the message again. Then she was off that couch and on that phone so fast . . .

'Who's Hothouse?' I asked. 'Are they good?'

'I think they're part of Tower,' she mumbled, punching numbers. 'Don't have left for the day, oh still be there, *please*. Emily O'Keeffe calling for David Crowe.'

She was put straight through.

'Yeah,' she said and nodded. 'Yes . . . Right.' Another nod. 'OK . . . When? . . . OK. Bye.'

Slowly she put down the phone. Even more slowly she let her body slide down the wall until she was on the floor. Everything in her actions screamed catastrophe. She turned a strained face to me. 'You know what?'

'What?'

'They want me to pitch it to them.'

It took me a moment. 'But that's good!'

'I know. *I know*. I KNOW.'

Then she wept as I've never seen another human being weep. Torrents. Buckets. Convulsions. 'Thank God,' she bawled into her hands. 'ThankGodthankGodthankGodthankGod . . .'

'You artistic types,' I said, indulgently.

'I have to talk to Troy.' She was suddenly urgent.

A quick phone call – at least it was quick by her standards, a mere twenty minutes or so – then it was all hands on deck. Hair and make-up and dresses and heels; we were meeting Troy at Bar Marmont at eight-thirty. Apparently Troy was a director

107

and he would advise Emily on Mort Russell, Hothouse, pitching and self-esteem, among other things.

'Is he married?' I asked, as I asked about everyone.

This sent Emily into fits of laughter. 'Troy? Yeah, Troy is married all right. To his work. But other than that he's single. Single, single. Single, single, single. The most single person you've ever met.'

'What films has he made?' I asked, as we sped along the 405.

'None that you'd have heard of.'

'Is he no good then?'

'He's brilliant. But he works in the independent sector. He's too uncompromising to survive in the studio system – at least at the moment. He's waiting for his reputation to be good enough so he gets total artistic control on a big-budget block-buster.'

'God, would you look at them!' We'd passed a gym with floor-to-ceiling glass windows, so that everyone on the tread-mills was visible to the whole world. Not only would I hate to have passing motorists witness my red, sweaty shame, but it was eight-thirty on a Friday night! Had they no bars to go to?

'Loads of gyms do that window thing,' Emily said. 'There's always the chance that Steven Spielberg might be passing.'

Bar Marmont was dark and gothic and very un-LA. Plaster serpents snaked up the walls and even the mirrors reflected back gloom.

'There he is.' Emily marched over to a man sitting on his own. After they had greeted each other very excitedly, she introduced me to him.

'Hi,' he said shyly.

'Hi.' I was staring at him. I knew I was, and all I could do was wonder, *What makes a man beautiful?*

I knew there were certain conventions. Big jawlines, prominent cheekbones, long, thick eyelashes. Everyone likes a good set of gleaming white choppers, while soulful puppydog eyes do it for some people (although I'm not one of them). And noses? No. Noses are meant to take a back seat. Everyone thinks it's just better if they keep out of the way.

However, sometimes a person breaks all the rules, and they still end up being devastating. Troy's long face was dominated by his nose. His mouth was a straight, underscored line which gave nothing away. But the light bounced from his olive skin and his dark hair was shorn GI short. His eyes were, perhaps, hazel-coloured. A sidelong glance across the room, as he looked across at the bar, and a greenishness blazed.

'You girls like a drink?' he asked softly.

'Sure,' Emily said. 'White wine.'

'Maggie?' And the eyes were on me. More khaki than hazel.

'Something.'

'You want to narrow it down for me some?' A little upward curve of his mouth.

'Aaah. Something frosty. With alcohol.'

'Something frosty with alcohol. You got it.' He smiled. Oh, and there we are. Gleaming white choppers, all present and correct.

I watched him crossing the room. He wasn't very tall, but there was a careless grace to his movements, as if he wasn't terribly interested in himself.

'Y'OK?' Emily asked.

'Er, yes.'

She rummaged in her handbag, smiling a private smile.

Then he was back. 'Frozen margarita, Maggie. The best in town. So what brings you to LA?'

'Just . . .' I hated this question, just hated it. Then I knew what to say! 'Just taking some down time.'

No one looked at me funny. No one burst out laughing. Looked like I'd managed to use the new slang successfully.

Then it was debriefing time. According to Troy, Mort Russell was 'Insane, but not in a bad way . . . Not *always* in a bad way,' he amended.

'And he's really EXCITED about my script,' Emily twinkled.

'I love your work,' Troy crooned at her. 'I troooly love your work. I want to have sex with your work I love it so much.'

'I love *your* work,' Emily said. 'I'm getting all hot just thinking about it . . . That's the way they go on,' she explained to me. 'Mort Russell probably hasn't even read my script.'

'They just drop a love bomb on you,' Troy said. 'Two days later they won't even take your calls.' Not that that was going to happen to Emily, he insisted.

'So what do you know about Hothouse?' Emily asked.

'They've good people and a lot of energy. You know they made *The American Way*?'

'Was that them?' Emily looked alarmed. 'That wasn't so great.'

'Yeah, but only because they kept firing the directors.'

'You know *Glass Flowers*?' Emily went off on a tangent. 'I heard they had *sixteen* writers on it.'

'True. And it shows. Whatja think of *Sand in Your Eyes*?'

'Not as bad as *Obeying Orders*. Like, I managed not to walk out!'

While I sipped my frozen margarita, Emily and Troy batted high-speed banter about movies they'd seen recently. Mostly they dissed them, but now and again they poured praise.

'*Great* cinematography.'

'Really tight script.'

After a while, I got the rules. If I'd heard of the movie, they didn't tend to like it, but if it sounded obscure, preferably foreign, then it got praised.

'So pitch me your movie, Emily,' Troy said.

'OK. I'm thinking *Thelma and Louise* meets *Steel Magnolias* meets *The Thomas Crown Affair* meets *Lock, Stock and Two Smoking Barrels*,' she said in a rush. 'Only joking. I haven't had time to work on it yet.'

'We have until Wednesday,' Troy said. 'But you know? You'll be great. You,' he pointed at her, 'are Good in a Room.'

'Good in a Room?' I asked.

'It's what they say,' Troy said, 'about someone who's got the art of the pitch. Emily tells a great story, she's Good in a Room. Another frosty drink with alcohol?'

'It's my turn.'

Three drinks later, Troy looked at his watch. 'I gotta take off. Early start.'

'Breakfast roller-blading date?' Emily asked.

'Seven a.m. spinning class,' he replied, and they both laughed.

'They all do that as well,' Troy said to me. 'It's kind of a macho thing, having your personal trainer come by before sun-up.'

Out we went to the valet station and handed over our tickets. I must have been a little bit tipsy, because I couldn't stop going on about how great the whole notion of valet parking was. I told everyone – Emily, Troy, the valet man, the couple waiting next to us – and they all seemed slightly amused. I saw nothing amusing about being a crap parker and scraping cars against pillars in multi-storey car parks. Although I didn't do that in every car, just in . . .

'Here's mine.' Troy's eyes were trained on a valet guiding a jeep towards us. He swung an arm around Emily. 'Baby girl, we'll talk.'

Then an arm around me and a touch on my cheek from the steep-trap mouth. 'And you, Maggie, enjoy your down time.'

He slipped the driver a dollar, swung himself up into his jeep and was gone.

It was midnight. As we drove down Sunset we passed one of the gyms with floor-to-ceiling glass windows. There were still people on the treadmill running to nowhere.

10

The next day was a Saturday and the tight wires of my work ethic unwound and gave me a little relief. Today I really *could* go to the beach and sunbathe legitimately without feeling like a skiver just about to be caught.

David Crowe's call had utterly transformed Emily. Her hopeless lethargy had completely disappeared and activity was the name of the game. After breakfast, we climbed up into her car and drove the two blocks to the aircraft-hangar-sized supermarket. From my years in Chicago, I knew how fabulous American supermarkets were, but even so, I was sure they didn't carry the magnificent array of fat-free products they had here. Everywhere, packaging screaming '0 per cent fat' jumped up and accosted me. I'd found it impossible not to be affected by the pervasive body-beautiful ethic, and virtuously bypassed the occasional cluster of full-fat doughnuts or ice-cream, and instead bought blueberries and salad and sushi. And wine, of course. Emily insisted. 'I must take good care of myself at this important time,' she said, flinging a few bottles into our trolley.

As we wheeled our purchases back to the car, I was startled by someone yelling, 'Hey you!' I turned to see a dirty, bearded man, dressed in rags. 'Hey, you girls, are you listening?' he called angrily. 'A body lies under a fire escape. Male, Caucasian, mid-thirties.'

'What's up with him?' I asked nervously.

'He's always here.' Emily wasn't even interested. 'Roaring and shouting about mad stuff. He's bonkers, God love him, but quite harmless.'

We were barely home and unpacking our groceries when Lara burst through the front door and flung herself so hard at Emily that the pair of them scooted halfway across the room. 'You the maaaaaan!' she cried. 'I'm so happy about the pitch!'

Apparently she was in the neighbourhood because she'd been to her yogilates (whatever that was) class. She offloaded flowers and an affirmation card and a Native American something on to Emily to celebrate the good news.

Then she turned, saw me and exclaimed, 'Go girl! You look so *tan*. Hanging out at the beach?'

'Yeah,' I said shyly, flattered by her admiration. It was good, coming from her, a walking ray of light.

Lara stepped closer and said thoughtfully, 'You know what? Your hair is *so* great.'

Already I'd started to pick up on LA intonation. Telling someone that something is '*so* great' is actually a criticism. 'Your script is *so* great,' – but we're not buying it. 'Your friend that I went on the blind date with is *so* great,' – but she bored me to death and I hope I never see her again.

So when Lara told me that my hair was *so* great, I was pleased for a second, then I wasn't. '*So* great,' she repeated. 'But your bangs' (she meant my fringe) 'are too long. Hello,' she laughed softly, parting my fringe with her long nails, moving hair out of my eyes. 'Are you in there? Hey, there she is!'

'Hi.' I was close enough to see her contact lenses.

'You know what?' Consideringly, she weighed the end of my hair, curling it under with her palm. 'We've gotta get you to my hairdresser. Dino, he is like, the *best*. I'll call him now.'

Already she was halfway across the room, fishing in her handbag, and I breathed out. She'd been standing too close but I'd been afraid to move, what with her being a lezzer. If it had been anyone else I could have stepped back, no bother, but I didn't want her to think that I was uncomfortable around her and her lezzerness. Political correctness is a *minefield*. The palm pilot was out, she was tapping on her little cellphone, then talking. No waiting around. They do everything so *fast* here.

'Dino? Kiss, kiss, baby. I want to schedule in my girlfriend with you. She has the *best* face and she needs a great cut. Tuesday?' She looked up at me with her aquamarine eyes. 'Maggie, Tuesday, six-thirty?'

I felt overrun, taken over. I quite liked it. 'Sure.' Why the hell not? 'Tuesday is good.'

'I got reason to celebrate too,' Lara said, clenching a fist in the air. '*Two Dead Men* has finally dropped out of the top ten!'

'Rock on!' Emily exclaimed, and a general air of celebration prevailed.

Two Dead Men was a spoof gangster comedy film. What had it ever done to Lara?

'Tell Maggie the story,' Emily urged.

'You want to hear it?'

'Course!'

'OK! As you know, I work in a production company, and one of my many, *many* duties is to do script reports. Like, read them, say what the chances of making a good movie are. Anyhoo, two years ago I get this script on my desk, it sucked and I totally trashed it. And the name of this piece of crap? *Two Dead Men*. Only one of the biggest comedy movies of the year!' Her high spirits were infectious. 'The day I read in *Variety* that Fox were going into production on it was one of the worst days of my life. I have prayed so HARD for it to bomb. I have SWEATED when I've seen the weekend grosses. And I came this close –' she held up her thumb and first finger, leaving a tiny space between them, '– to losing my job.'

'But you're entitled to your opinion,' I said.

'Nuh-uh.' She shook her head. 'Not in Lala land. One strike and you're out.'

'I saw the original script too,' Emily said. 'And Lara was right, it was crap. I don't think the writer meant it to be a comedy, but because it was so bad everyone assumed he *had* to be joking.'

'But it's all OK now,' Lara beamed.

All of a sudden a low, rumbling vibration began. I felt it before I heard it and it built with alarming intensity. For a minute I thought it was an earthquake and that my mother had been right. How very annoying.

'Gaaaagghh,' Emily groaned. 'They're at it again. Drumming to the Rhythm of Life. Gobshites!'

'Who?'

'Next door. Mike and Charmaine and a load of professional adults who should know better. Banging Native American drums and hoping to find happiness. They do it on purpose to annoy me.'

'You should never have stolen their "Armed Response" sign,' Lara said.

'Don't I know it! Well, I'm left with no choice but to go shopping and buy something to wear to The Pitch. Any takers?'

Shopping! Apart from a sun-product splurgette in the duty-free, I hadn't bought anything for ages – not since my life had gone belly-up. I experienced a little rush, feeling alert and almost normal, which intensified when it transpired that they both wanted to go to Rodeo Drive. Going to Rodeo Drive was what I *should* be doing, what anyone who came to LA would do, instead of sitting like a lost soul on a lonely beach. OK, so maybe it was a little out of my price range, but a girl could always dream. And use her credit card.

As we left the house, the Goatee Boys were also going out.

'Hey, Lara!' The one with the shaved head exploded in admiration. 'You are the bomb, man, toadally the bomb!'

'Thank you, Curtis.'

'No, I'm Ethan. That's Curtis.'

'Hey.' Curtis shyly raised a plumpish hand.

'And I'm Luis.' A pretty, Latino boy, with Bambi eyelashes and a neat little beard, also waved. 'And you *are* the bomb.'

'I was really hoping,' Emily said wistfully, 'that when term ended they'd pack up and leave and we'd get some proper neighbours in. But it looks like we're stuck with them for the summer.'

The Goatee Boys were going out in their orange wreck. Luis placed his hand on the car roof, vaulted daintily through the open car window and arrived neatly in the driving side. Then Ethan placed his meaty hand on the roof on the other side and also swung in, feet first. But things weren't so easy for plump Curtis, who got stuck Winnie-the-Pooh-like in the window space.

After we'd helped shove him in, we got into Lara's car (a shiny silver pick-up truck about a mile long). The sky was blue, the silvery palm trees were swaying in the gentle breeze and I had a bit of a tan – all in all, things weren't so bad.

I'd half imagined Rodeo Drive to be a type of celebrity compound. Almost a theme park that you'd pay an entrance fee into. Instead, like Sloane Street or Fifth Avenue, it was just a road of famous, expensive shops, staffed by those skinny, snotty cows from central casting. I was well out of my league – I'd worn my very best 'city-girl' get-up and was ostentatiously carrying my expensive handbag like an Access All Areas badge of accreditation, but I was fooling no one. After the first two or three places I confided gloomily to Lara, 'I hate the people who work in these shops, they always make me feel like shit.'

'There's a trick to it,' she sympathized. 'You gotta march in like you own the place, look evil and bored and never, *ever* ask the price of anything.'

So in the next sparse, high-ceilinged emporium, I picked up a handbag – because handbags are the new shoes – and tried to look evil and bored, as instructed. But I can't have been too convincing, because the starved, glam-haired assistant dismissed me with a contemptuous eye-sweep. Then her radar picked up Emily, the label babe, and everything changed. 'Hi there! How are *you* today?'

'Good!' Emily said. 'How are YOU?'

Do you know, for a minute, I thought they actually knew each other, until your woman continued, 'I'm Bryony. How may I help you today?'

On the rare occasions when those girls do speak to me, I'm far too intimidated to answer. In fact I usually leave immediately. (And what's with the 'today' thing? When else was she planning on helping? Next Tuesday?)

I replaced the beautiful bag on its plinth. But clearly I hadn't done it right, because Bryony shot over and, with brisk, angry swivels, moved it half an inch back to its correct position. Then she took a little cloth and polished off my handprints. I felt so humiliated that for a minute I thought I might cry.

'Just remember,' Lara murmured into my hair, 'her clothes

are borrowed. She couldn't buy that sweater she's wearing if she worked here for a year.'

Meanwhile, Bryony had descended on Emily, who was flicking through the hangers with a trained eye. Then Emily was being led to the changing-room, where she started trying things on, flinging them off again and firing them back in crumpled balls at the snotty cow.

'You look GREAT,' Bryony insisted over and over, but Lara kept up a constant stream of 'Hmmm. Let's see it in a different colour. What about the longer skirt? Does that come in a cross-over style?'

Bryony was run ragged carrying out her suggestions.

Eventually I tentatively suggested, 'How about a smaller size?'

'Yeah,' Lara praised, when that sent Bryony racing back to the rails. 'Now you're getting the hang of it.'

We made Bryony bring different styles and different sizes – even shoes and handbags – until it seemed that Emily had tried on every item in the shop several times. Painstakingly, she narrowed her selection down to a shirt-dress and jacket, then beckoned us both into the huge changing-room and shut the heavy wooden door. 'I'm skint,' she hissed. 'Is it very wrong to spend a month's rent on a suit?'

I was all for telling her that of course it was and that she could get a perfectly fine get-up in Banana Republic for a tenth of the price – and not just because I didn't want Bryony to get the commission, I'm not that mean, but out of concern for Emily's finances – when Lara said solemnly, 'You've got to spend money to make money. Gotta look the part for the pitch.

'Sorry Maggie,' she said to me. 'I'd love it to be like that bit in *Pretty Woman* –'

'"Big mistake",' I quoted eagerly.

'"Big HUGE mistake." Yeah.'

Then Emily understood. 'Oh God, was Bryony a bitch?'

'Yes,' said Lara. Then to me, 'But Emily's pitch is totally important and she does look great in these clothes . . .'

'Oh-kay.'

'So what's it to be?' Lara asked Emily.

'I'll get the suit, but not the shoes.'

'Your call.'

'Well, maybe the shoes, but not the bag.'

'Whatever.'

'No point spoiling the ship for a ha'p'orth of tar, I suppose.'

'Ex*cuse* me?' Cow-face had returned.

'I'll take the lot.'

Just before we left, Lara picked up 'my' handbag, manhandled it roughly and put it back all askew and covered with handprints. 'Thank you,' she beamed over her shoulder at Bryony.

'Thank *you*,' I said to Lara.

As we wandered along the street, Emily laden with carrier bags, I indicated a man strolling past us. 'Isn't he the image of Pierce Brosnan? He could get a job impersonating him.'

Lara and Emily took a look. 'It *is* Pierce Brosnan,' Lara remarked, and they continued up the street, clearly unimpressed.

'Where next?'

'Chanel?'

But the Chanel shop was closed because some famous person was inside buying the place up. Madonna, according to a small crowd of Japanese tourists clustered outside. Magic Johnson, a rival group insisted. No, no, a third cluster were adamant, it was Michael Douglas.

Perhaps it was for the best that it wasn't open, Emily said. She'd done enough damage.

'It's five o'clock, let's go for a drink,' Lara suggested.

'The Four Seasons?' Emily said. 'It's close by.'

'Sure.'

'Don't!' I exclaimed.

'What?'

'Don't suggest going for a drink at the Four Seasons hotel in Beverly Hills like it's *not a big deal*.'

'Sorry,' Emily said humbly.

'Yeah, sorry,' Lara said.

The Four Seasons had classical art and huge vases, swagged curtains, thick carpets and mucho, mucho gilt. It all seemed very *patternedy*. My mother would have loved it. As we walked into the bar, a man holding court around a table shouted, 'Billy Crystal is the best goddam director in the whole world!'

'Just in case we didn't know you worked in the movie business,' Emily muttered.

We found a squashy couch and ordered Complicated Martinis and they brought us a little dish of Japanese crackers. As the drink took hold we got a bit carried away.

'It's all starting for you,' Lara promised Emily. 'Look at Candy Devereaux. One minute she's waitressing and thinking about getting the bus back to Wisconsin. Then she writes a dream script and now she's charging a hundred thousand dollars a week, doing script surgeon.'

'Prada will send a truck of stuff over and whatever I want will be mine to KEEP,' Emily said gleefully, stretching out on the couch.

Fantasy stuff and yet . . . In other jobs you're supposed to toil away patiently and incrementally better your lot. But I got the feeling that things worked differently in this town: your luck could turn on a sixpence and you could shoot from the gutter to the stratosphere very, very quickly. I was distracted by a girl passing by with a cleavage as deep as the Grand Canyon. Talk about silicon valley – those breasts couldn't *possibly* be real . . .

'Can I have a part in the movie?' Lara asked.

'Sure!'

'When Lara first came to LA, she was an actress,' Emily told me.

'So how come you're not now?'

'I didn't have what it takes.' She tipped her head back and funnelled crackers into her mouth from her fist. 'I wasn't thin enough. Or beautiful enough.'

'But you're *really* beautiful.'

'She's hot for me,' she drawled.

Emily gave her a stern look, which was interrupted by Lara's cellphone ringing. An animated chat ensued, then Lara snapped her phone away. 'It's Kirsty, she's nearby, she's going to join us for a quick drink.'

Emily made a face. 'A quick alcohol-free, dairy-free, sodium-free glass of water served with a slice of organic lemon in a lead-free glass.'

'She's OK,' Lara said.

'Yeah. She's just so virtuous and humour-free. And she thinks she's gorgeous.'

'But she is.'

'That's no reason to go round showing off.' Emily directed this to me. 'We were all talking about who would play us in the story of our lives – yeah, I know, but it's an LA thing – and Lara there, *beautiful* Lara there, says Kathy Bates. I say ET in an afro wig, Justin says John Goodman, and even Troy says Sam the American Eagle from *The Muppet Show*, and who does Kirsty say would play her? Nicole Kidman, that's who. Says people are always mistaking her for Nicole. She wishes. Well, before she gets here, can I show you something?'

She opened her handbag and slowly produced a keyring. I recognized it. It was from the shop where she'd bought the clothes; it even had the logo, picked out in rhinestones.

'I've been a bad girl,' Emily said, but she couldn't hide a grin.

'Oh my God,' Lara groaned. 'You have *got* to stop!'

'You stole it?'

'Liberated it, I prefer to say. Hey, I'm really stressed right now.'

'I know, but could you not just do a relaxation tape or something?' I said.

'You're just jealous,' Emily accused.

'I know,' I admitted humbly.

I'd only shoplifted once in my whole life – a choc-ice from a newsagent's. I hadn't even wanted it, I much preferred Cornettos, but they didn't have any and Adrienne Quigley had dared me to do it. Anyway, wouldn't you know it? – I got caught. The man was very nice about it and said he'd let me off if I promised never to do it again. Which meant I had to spend the rest of my teenage years looking on enviously as everyone else returned from trips into town with their bags crammed with all sorts of stolen booty: earrings, lipsticks, glittery nail polishes, a length of electrical flex and a handful of screws from a hardware shop. It was Emily who'd nicked the screws and the flex, because she just shoplifted for the thrill, whereas Adrienne Quigley shoplifted to order. I was sick with envy at their daring (and the free stuff, apart from the screws and the flex), but I knew for certain that if I tried it again, I was bound to get caught – and bring everyone else down with me too. There's just something about me. Each of my sisters could get away with brazenness because Claire was feisty, Rachel was funny, Anna was away with the fairies and Helen was fearless. But me – all I had was obedience, it was my only survival tool.

The arrival of Kirsty put paid to my sudden introspection, and actually she did look quite like Nicole Kidman, all tendrilly strawberry-blonde hair and alabaster skin. (Also, she was as thin as a rail, but you could have guessed that, I'm sure. *How* do they all manage it? These women are in their thirties, traditionally not the age to be as insubstantial as a sixteen-year-old. It's a mystery to me.) Kirsty was sparkily vivacious and I couldn't understand Emily's antipathy – until the waiter came and she made him list every mineral water they carried.

Then I offered her a Japanese cracker and she all but shuddered.

'They've only four calories each,' Emily said. 'The waiter said.'

Kirsty quirked a know-all eyebrow around the table. 'They've been sitting there for the longest time, with everyone's hands in and out of them. You wanna eat other people's germs? Go right ahead!'

Instantly the mood became subdued, even shamefaced. No one went near them after that, and when the waiter finally took them away, relief loosened us.

A girl with a tiny pink T-shirt stretched to the limit over a HUMUNGOUS pair of boobs strolled through the bar. Out and proud, it was like the breasts were taking *her* for a walk. Everyone knows LA is Plastic Surgery Central, but when you see these human Barbie dolls with your own eyes, it defies belief . . .

Emily grinned meaningfully at Lara, who regretfully shook her head. 'Too phoney. The fake ones don't feel as good.' She looked down at her own golden cleavage. 'And I should know.'

'Too much information!' Kirsty chided. 'We so do NOT want to know.'

There she was wrong, actually. Was Lara saying she'd had a boob job? I was fascinated, but too embarrassed to push it. Was it true that sometimes they burst on planes? That if you shine a light underneath them they turn green? That in a swimming pool they float like armbands and you can't get them beneath the surface for love nor money?

'Tell Kirsty your news,' Lara prompted Emily.

Emily succinctly told the story of the forthcoming pitch, and in all fairness to her, Kirsty seemed delighted.

'Heeeyyy!' she said. ''Bout time. We've been worried about you, stuck in your little house, becoming a total loser.'

'Excuse me?'

'I love your sandals! Where did you buy them?' Lara hastily said to Kirsty.

'You know what? I bought them last summer and, on purpose, I never wore them,' Kirsty said happily. 'Now everyone wants to get a pair and they can't! Anyway, guys, I gotta take off. Troy is coming over tonight to hang out with me.'

Emily looked like she'd got a crack on the skull from a frying pan.

'Like, really?' Lara interjected. 'Are you and Troy . . . ?'

'Like I'm going to tell you!' Kirsty replied, in high good humour.

Lara walked Kirsty to the valet stand and Emily fumed at me, 'Troy is *my* friend. She only met him through Lara. What the hell does Lara see in her? And what does Troy see in her? Stingy bitch, didn't even pay for her drink. And that stuff with the sandals. Hiding them in a drawer for a year – what was *that* all about?'

'Lara's coming back,' I warned.

But instead of that shutting Emily up, she said 'Good!' then laid into Lara, who was very grown-up about it all. Emily didn't own Troy, she said. Troy could hang out with whoever he wanted. Yeah, the thing about the sandals was a bit weird, but Kirsty's job as a gym receptionist didn't pay much . . .

'Let's get another drink,' she suggested.

After another Complicated Martini, Kirsty's traces had been washed away.

'You coming to Dan Gonzalez's party on Monday night?' Emily asked Lara.

'I thought you weren't going to go!'

'Yeah, well, it's different now. I can hold my head up. I'm a player. So, you coming?'

Lara shook her head. 'Nuh-uh. I'm going on a date.'

At this point, Emily got all screechy. 'Tell us!' she ordered. 'You never said! Where did you meet her?'

'At a club.'

To be honest, I was sort of embarrassed. I just didn't know what to say. If it was a girl going out with a man I'd have been all agog for details, but . . .

'She's way cute,' Lara said. 'She used to be a dancer.'

'A dancer, wow! Hot body?' Emily asked.

'Hot.'

Lara went on to describe the girl, the way men usually get described. How good-looking she was, how sweet she'd acted, how she'd really seemed to like Lara . . .

126

I pushed away my embarrassment and matched Emily screechy noise for screechy noise. I am a woman of the world, I thought.

11

Slowly I shifted the sole of my foot along the fluffy bathmat. The squashy clumps of wool were balm to my aching feet. I shifted the other foot and felt the touch of every fibre against my over-sensitized skin . . . *so soft, so kind* . . . Then back to the first foot again.

How long had I been standing here? Too long. Maybe I should finish drying myself. Someone else might want to use the bathroom.

As I stumbled to my bedroom to get dressed, I knew one thing for sure. *I'm never drinking Complicated Martinis again.* Clearly, Emily was a bad influence. I wasn't what you might call a party animal, but I'd been drunk twice in two days. And I'd never before had a shower while wearing sunglasses – what did that tell me about the company I was keeping?

I wouldn't mind, but I was the only one who was in shreds. I'd woken at eight, feeling like I was coming round from a coma, my habitual terror on waking even more pronounced, and I'd found Lara and Emily sitting in the kitchen, drinking smoothies and chattering, just like normal people. Hardy creatures.

'Y'OK?' Emily had sounded concerned.

'Fine,' I said. 'It's just . . . I can't actually open my eyes. The pain is too bad.'

Emily gave me sunglasses and some painkillers, and suggested

I take a shower. Which hadn't really helped, although the bathmat had, at least while I'd been standing on it.

As I got dressed the sunglasses fell off, but when I bent to retrieve them from the floor, black patches scudded before my eyes so I had to leave them. Then I emerged into the living-room, where the sound of my feet slapping on the wooden floor was too much. I was half-looking for a pillow or blanket on the couch, signs that Lara had slept there, but when I peeped into Emily's room, Lara's clothes were flung on the floor. She must've slept with Emily.

Not *slept* slept. Just slept, slept. Oh, you know what I mean . . .

I got the land of my life to see that while I'd been in the shower Troy had arrived on the premises. I squinched a look at him from my aching eyes. Still strangely beautiful, in a slab-of-granite kind of way.

'Hey, Maggie,' he nodded.

'Howya,' I said, too shattered to be bothered with this 'hey' business. I had to lie down. Carefully I lowered myself on to the couch, flattening my back against the cushions, but even when I'd stopped moving, I still felt as though I was sinking, sinking . . .

Emily and Lara and Troy were discussing the pitch. From far away I could hear their murmuring voices. I found that if I softly moved strands of my hair along my cheek, the pain in my face-bones lessened briefly. Again and again I stroked the feathery strands from my nose to my ear and back again.

'Y'OK, Irish?' Troy was standing over me. 'What's the deal with your hair?'

Too out-of-it to be embarrassed, I told him. Then I told him about the rug in the bathroom.

'What you need is a massage,' he concluded. 'Work those pressure points.'

'From you?'

'No,' he laughed softly. 'From the master. You wait.'

Minutes later the front door opened, bringing a great big bright dazzling morning into the room.

'Close it,' I begged.

It was Justin, beaming and wearing a yellow and red Hawaiian shirt. I actually thought I might vomit.

A clicky skiddy noise on the floorboards alerted me to a second presence. A little white Scotty dog chasing dust motes and generally being cute. Desiree, I supposed.

'Right on time, buddy,' Troy said to Justin. 'Lady here needs help.'

'Oh yeah?' Justin asked in his highish voice. 'What appears to be the problem?' He knelt by the couch and theatrically took my pulse at the wrist.

'Hangover,' I said, flinching at his shirt.

'My fault,' Emily apologized.

Justin laced his fingers together and flexed his hands back and forth, like he meant business.

'OK, where does it hurt?'

'Everywhere.'

'Everywhere. OK, let's fix everywhere.'

I was afraid I might have to take some clothes off, but it turned out it was only my feet he was interested in: reflexology. I'm not proud of my feet. Whenever I'd had reflexology before, shame of my hard skin and my second toe being longer than my big toe had interfered with my enjoyment. But the great thing about feeling like I wanted to die was that the state of my feet didn't seem to matter.

And Troy was right. Truly, Justin was the master.

As he pushed and kneaded with pleasurable firmness, my

pain gradually receded further and further until, to my great surprise, I was restored to myself.

I sat up. The birds were singing, the world was shiny and bright and bearable. The sun was no longer a malign yellow goblin, but once again a dearly loved friend. I could even look at Justin's shirt.

'You,' I said in awe, 'are a miracle worker. You could do that for a living. Is that what you did before you became an actor?'

'Nah, it's just a hobby. I learnt how to do it to try to get a girlfriend.'

'Did it work?'

'No.'

'Not yet, you mean.'

'Nah, I've given up. I'm not just the expendable fat guy at work, I'm the expendable fat guy, period. Now I live just for Desiree. Although,' he added cheerfully, 'I only got her so as I could meet women. I thought I could hang around the dog parks and look for a girlfriend, but that didn't work either.'

'It's IMPOSSIBLE to find love in this town,' Emily interjected. 'Everyone is so into their work. And there's no place to meet anyone.'

'What about bars? Or clubs?' I was sure I'd heard my sisters and friends in Ireland telling millions of stories about going out to a club and waking up the next morning with a strange man in the bed. It seemed to be worthy of comment on the rare occasions that it *didn't* happen and used to make me wistful for the single life.

'Friends of friends is how you usually meet people in LA.' Emily gave Troy a meaningful look. But if she was hoping he'd spill the beans about how he'd got on the night before with Kirsty, she was disappointed.

He loped over to me. 'OK, feeling better now?'

Flat on my back again, I nodded up at him. 'Great. Ready for my ten-mile run.'

'I wouldn't joke about that kind of thing round here,' Emily's disembodied voice said. 'Come on, are we going to work, or what?'

They gathered around the kitchen table like a council of war. Even Desiree was sitting on a chair, paying rapt attention. I later discovered she'd been in a couple of movies.

The doors and windows were all open, bringing the smiley day into the house. At midday Emily rang for brunch from a nearby restaurant and half an hour later enough food to feed an army arrived.

'D'you want any?' she called to me. 'Or would you boke?'

'I suppose I could manage a couple of mouthfuls.' My head pains were gone but I still had the vestiges of hangover nausea.

Troy brought me a plate and when I tried to sit up, he said, 'No need to,' and carefully tried to balance it on my chest. But on account of having breasts and on account of them being, by their nature, wobbly, the plate wouldn't come to rest.

'Maybe you'd better hold it,' he decided, with an embarrassed half-smile. 'Got it?' Then he flashed a direct hit with those greeny eyes and, all at once, he didn't seem a bit embarrassed – and suddenly I was.

When he'd gone, I tried a few cautious mouthfuls and marvelled as they stayed down.

Some time later, Troy reappeared.

'You done?'

I don't know why, but I waited a beat, looking into his face, before saying, 'Yeah.'

Then he lifted the plate from my chest, somehow managing to glance the edge of it off one of my nipples. Instantly both of them contracted and hardened, leaping 3-D-like under my T-shirt towards him.

He looked at them, then looked at me. I knew I should laugh but couldn't. Then I was watching his retreating back, as he returned to the others.

I stayed on the couch, half-flicking through what I thought must be *Daily Variety* but actually turned out to be the *LA Times*. All the news seemed to be about the movie world. Nothing about wars or massacres or natural disasters – only innocuous articles about opening weekends and weekly grosses . . . My eyes closed.

Emily was improvising her pitch, and now and again a remark floated over to me.

'. . . Emily,' went Troy's gentle sing-song, 'you're not convincing me . . .'

'. . . Don't compare it to *Drop Dead Gorgeous* . . .'

At some stage the phone rang, and then Emily was looming over me.

'Are you awake?' she asked. 'Phone call from home.'

Something in the way she said it immediately alerted me and, too quickly, I sat up. It was Garv, right?

Except it wasn't, it was my dad. I'd been about to attempt getting to my feet and walking to another room for privacy, then decided to spare myself the trouble. It was only Dad. But I should have realized something was wrong. Dad hated the phone, he normally behaved as if it gave off noxious gases, so why was he ringing me?

He had something to tell me, he said, halting and mortified. 'Though it mightn't be news to you at all.'

'Go on.' My heart was still pounding from the expectation of talking to Garv.

'Tonight we were coming home in the car . . .'

'Tonight?' Oh yes, Ireland was eight hours ahead. 'Go on.'

'. . . and I saw Paul . . . er . . . Garv. He was with a young woman and the pair of them, they looked . . .' Dad stopped. I was holding my breath and I wished I'd taken the phone into the bedroom. Too late now – dread had paralysed me.

'They looked, um, fond of each other,' Dad went on. 'Your mother said it wouldn't achieve anything by telling you, but I thought you'd prefer to know.'

He was right. In a way. The idea of being made a fool of isn't one that appeals to me. And I'd known anyway, hadn't I? But suspecting very strongly wasn't the same as knowing for sure.

'Are you all right?' he asked awkwardly.

I said I was, but actually I had no idea how I felt.

'Did you recognize the girl?' My heart rate increased dramatically.

'No, no, I didn't.'

I blew out a stream of air. So at least it wasn't one of my friends.

'I'm fierce sorry about this, pet,' he said miserably.

You fucker, Garv, I thought. Doing this not just to me, but to my poor dad.

'Don't worry, Dad, it was probably his cousin.'

'Do you think?' he asked eagerly.

'No,' I sighed. 'But it doesn't matter anyway, it really doesn't.'

Punch-drunk I hung up. What the hell did 'fond' mean? What were they doing? Snogging in the street?

I turned to see a frozen tableau of stares. Even Desiree's head was to one side in compassionate enquiry.

'What's happened?' Emily asked.

I was too shocked to dissemble, and the response from all of them was immediate and steeped in kindness. Lara poured me a drink, Emily lit me a cigarette, Justin rubbed the pressure points on my temples, Troy recommended deep breathing and Desiree gave me a consolatory lick.

'You had already split up?' Lara asked.

'Yeah, but . . .'

'I know. Yeah, but . . .' she repeated, with understanding. 'We've all been there.'

In the middle of the fuss, the phone rang again and Emily answered it. Her face was a picture of reluctance. 'It's your mum.'

I took the phone and made for my bedroom.

'Margaret?'

'Hi, Mum.' I closed the door behind me.

'It's Mum.'

'I know.' And I know why you're ringing.

'How are you getting on? Is it still sunny?'

'Yes. And I still haven't fallen into the San Andreas fault.'

'I've something to tell you and I'm going to give it to you straight. No point beating round the bush. If someone's got something to say, they might as well say it . . .'

'Mum . . .'

'It's that Paul you were married to,' she blurted. 'We passed him tonight in town. He was walking along Dame Street and he was with a . . . a . . . girl. They looked quite enamoured with each other.'

So it's *enamoured* now. *Fond* was bad enough. I swallowed

with effort. The bastard, I thought. The bastarding bastard.

'Your father was all for keeping it from you, but you're like me, you've your pride, you'd rather know.'

True perhaps, yet it still made me angry.

'I'm very sorry.' She sounded suddenly teary. 'And I'm sorry I didn't understand when you said you'd left him. If there's anything I can do . . .'

Abruptly I remembered how, a couple of times, I'd had the urge to phone him; I was transported with insane gladness that I hadn't. Could you imagine if she'd been there? If she'd *answered*? I'd have been so humiliated.

'Did you recognize her?'

'No, no I didn't.'

When I emerged, Troy observed, 'Your mom? Good news travels fast.'

Emily squeezed my trembling hands, trying to stop the tremors, while a flurry of comforting platitudes rained down on top of me. I'd get over it. The pain would pass. It was horrible now, but it would get better . . .

The phone rang again. We all looked at each other. What now?

'Helen,' Emily said, giving me the phone. 'Her sister,' she explained to the others.

Once again I found myself in my bedroom. 'Helen?'

She sounded uncharacteristically halting. 'You're probably wondering why I'm ringing and, in a way, so am I. Something has happened and Mum and Dad said that under no circumstances was I to tell you, but I reckon you should know. It's that prick you were married to. I know I've made things up about him before, but I'm telling the truth this time.'

'Go on.'

'We saw him in town tonight. He was with a girl and he was all over her like a dose of scabies.'

'In what way?' I *was* curious to know what they'd been up to.

'He had his hand on her waist.'

'Is that all?'

'Well, lower down, actually,' she admitted. 'Sort of on her arse. He was squeezing it and she was giggling.'

I closed my eyes. Too much information. Yet I wanted more.

'What was she like?'

'Disfigured.'

'Really?'

'Well no, but I can arrange it.'

'For God's sake, Helen, it's not her fault.'

'OK, him then. I can get someone to hurt him badly. It could be my birthday present to you. Or I'll swap it for your hand-bag.'

'No. Please.'

'We could burn his house down.'

'Don't do that. It's half mine.'

'Oh, yeah.'

'Promise me you won't do anything. I can live with it, I swear.'

'I'm very sorry,' she said, sounding it. I was touched. 'You could at least let me organize to have his legs broken,' she added.

Within seconds of me putting the phone down, it rang again. Anna.

'Another sister,' I heard Emily say to the assembled listeners as, for the third time in ten minutes, I closed the bedroom door behind me.

'Hi Anna,' I said briskly, keen to preempt her pity and

137

awkwardness – I'd had enough of it. 'Thank you for ringing, but I know all about Garv and his new girlfriend.'

'*What?*'

'I know all about Garv and the girl. Mum, Dad and Helen have all rung me separately about it. What took you so long?'

'Garv has a new GIRLFRIEND?' She sounded appalled.

'You didn't know?'

'No.'

'Oh.' I suppose she'd never been the sharpest knife in the drawer. 'So why were you ringing?'

Big long pause, then an audible gulp. 'I crashed your car.'

Another big long pause, then an audible sigh. 'Badly?'

'What does "badly" mean?'

'Did you kill anyone?'

'No. I drove into a wall, no one else was involved. The front is a bit mashed but the back hasn't a scratch on it.'

I took time to digest all this. I should care, but I didn't, it was only a car.

'But, Anna, what were you *doing*?'

'Uh,' she sounded confused, 'driving.'

After a few expensive seconds of cross-continental silence I said, 'Are you hurt?'

'Yes.'

Concern half-heartedly flared in me. 'Is something broken?'

'Yes.'

'What?'

'My heart.'

Right. Shane. But much as I loved Anna, I'd no comfort to give, I was too messed up myself. Time for a platitude. Luckily I had several to hand, as a result of my own circumstances. 'Just hang on in there, it'll get better,' I lied. 'And with the car, I've insurance. Can you sort it out?'

'Yes, yes, I will. Thank you, sorry, I won't do it again. I'm so sorry.'

'It's OK.'

This sort of serious situation called for more of a response than that, but the best I could manage was, 'Anna, you're twenty-*eight*.'

'I know,' she said wretchedly. 'I know.'

12

The news about Garv had devastated me, there was no getting away from it. And the others wouldn't let me ring him.

'Not when you're sore,' Emily said firmly.

A bit wild in myself, I wanted answers. How had this happened? Where had it all gone wrong?

'Had you any idea about this other girl?' Lara asked.

'Yes.'

'But you hoped it would burn out and you two'd get back together?' Troy suggested.

'No.' In all honesty, I hadn't been holding out for a reunion – but there was a big difference between a strong suspicion that something was going on and knowing *for definite*. And knowing for definite meant that I was destroyed, distracted, lost to myself. I began reconstructing my last visit to the house – when I'd been picking up clothes and stuff for Los Angeles. I hadn't noticed any evidence of torrid carry-on. Mind you, I'd told Garv I'd be coming, so he would have had time to clean the Häagen-Dazs stains off the sheets. '*I* left *him*, you know.' My attempt at bravado didn't really convince. Especially when I tagged on, 'Well, it was really a case of constructive dismissal.'

'Let's go out!' Emily suggested, when she saw me looking longingly at the phone again. So we went to a movie. All of us except Desiree, who stayed in the house, wearing a long-

140

suffering, stoical, I'll-watch-it-when-it-comes-out-on-video face.

There seemed to be several hundred cinemas in Santa Monica, a bit like the way pubs are in Ireland. I sat between Justin and Troy, who tried to ply me with foodstuffs. I shook my head when Justin tilted a bucket of popcorn the size of a dustbin towards me and I waved away Troy's bumper pack of twizzlers.

'No?' he whispered in surprise.

'No.'

'Gimme your wrist.'

I extended my arm and carefully he tied a thick, red liquorice lace around it. 'In case of emergency,' and his teeth flashed in the dark of the cinema.

There was never any chance that I'd lose myself and forget my troubles in the film. Especially when it turned out to be a stylish, violent, highly complicated thriller, with bad cops and good villains double-crossing and even triple-crossing each other. I was too dazed to keep up with the myriad changes of allegiance. Unlike Troy, who seemed thoroughly immersed in it: when someone who'd been a baddy turned out to be a goody, he laughed a delighted 'Aha!' and made me jump. On the other side of me, Justin's hand moved from his popcorn bucket to his mouth and back again in a regular rhythm which I found deeply soothing. He only paused from this pattern to whisper, when an innocent – and I must admit, quite plump – 'regular Joe' got caught in crossfire, 'That should've been me!' Or when a goody-turned-baddy's dog's ear got severed by a baddy-turned-goody-turned-baddy, he confided, 'Ew! Boy, am I glad Desiree isn't here to see *this*.'

As we all trooped out at the end, Troy asked, 'Did we enjoy that?'

'I couldn't really follow it,' I admitted.

'Yeah,' he sighed sympathetically. 'Concentration shot to hell?'

'I'm not sure that's the only reason,' I confessed. 'To be honest, I can never really keep up with the twists and turns of that kind of movie.' And I always got Garv to explain it to me at the end, I thought, but didn't say.

It's funny what strikes you, but what seemed terrible and final and wrenching was not that I'd lost my life companion, not that Garv and I would never have a baby, but that I'd have to go through the rest of my life not understanding thrillers. That, and never getting the hang of exchange rates: Garv was like a calculator made human. 'There's three of them to the pound,' he'd explain, giving me a load of foreign currency at the start of a holiday.

'OK, so to find out what things really cost I multiply by three.'

'No, you divide by three,' he'd say patiently.

So as well as not understanding thrillers, all I had to look forward to was an empty future being swizzed by souk traders.

'You've got to talk about it,' Emily insisted, once we were home and everyone had gone. 'I know you don't want to but it'll help, I swear to you.'

You see, now that things were going well for Emily, she had renewed energy to focus on me and my drama.

'You Californians,' I scorned. 'You talk about everything. Like it helps.'

'Better than putting a lid on things and trying to bury them.' Emily knew me too well.

'What good will talking do?' I said helplessly. 'Maybe I should never have married him.'

'Maybe you shouldn't,' she replied evenly.

She'd said it at the time to me. When I'd got engaged, instead of shrieking with excitement and making vulgar jokes about seeing my ring, she'd said soberly, 'I'm afraid you're playing it safe by marrying Garv.'

'I thought you liked him!' I'd said, wounded.

'I love him. Look, I just want you to be sure. Think about it.'

But I didn't think about it because I thought I knew what I wanted. In retrospect, I'd sometimes wondered if maybe she'd been right. Maybe I had settled, maybe I had played it too safe. But it hadn't all been bad . . .

'We had a lovely time together for years.' I could hear my voice shaking.

'So what happened?'

I was silent for too long.

'Go back to the beginning and talk it right through. Go on, it'll help to make sense of it all. Start with the rabbits,' she prompted. 'Come on, you've never told me fully.'

But I didn't want to talk about any of it. Especially not the rabbits. Because you can't really tell the rabbit story without people laughing, and I was in no state to start making fun of the reasons why my marriage had broken down.

It had begun, innocently enough, with a pair of slippers. What happened was, one Christmas someone gave me a pair of slippers which looked like black furry rabbits. I was extremely fond of them. Not only did they keep my feet warm, but they were cute and cuddly without the shame of them actually being cuddly toys. In the event of any confusion, I could point out that they had a function and that I wasn't one of those women who crammed her bedroom window-sill with an army of fluffy dolphins, pastel donkeys and squashy chickens, who looked down with their button eyes on people calling to the house and freaked the life out of them. Oh no. I had a pair of slippers, that's all. They were made of fake astrakhan, and when Garv gave them personalities, he was obviously influenced by the astrakhan because they were both Russian. Valya and Vladimir. I could never tell them apart, but Garv said that Vladimir had a funny ear and Valya's nose was shaped like a cross-section of a bit of Toblerone. (Why he just couldn't have said triangular, I'll never know.) Valya was a bit of a femme fatale and often said stuff like, 'I hef hed menny, menny luffers.' Sometimes she gave me advice on what to wear. Vladimir – who sounded almost identical to Valya – was a Party apparatchik who'd been stripped of his privileges. He was very gloomy, but then so was Valya.

Garv began to conduct the occasional conversation through the medium of the astrakhan slippers. He'd stick his hand inside and wiggle it about and say, 'I em goink to the Vestern-style supermarket. I em queueink for menny, menny days. Vot vill I get for you?'

'Who'm I talking to? Valya or Vladimir?'

'Valya. Vladimir's the one with the funny ear and –'

'– Valya's nose looks like a cross-section of a Toblerone, I know. We need pizzas, toothpaste, cheese . . .'

'Woadka?' Valya suggested hopefully. Valya had a bit of a problem. So, coincidentally, did Vladimir.

'No woadka, but you might as well get a couple of bottles of wine.'

'Bleck-Sea caviar?'

'No.'

'Bleck bread?'

'Actually, we *could* do with a loaf of bread.'

'I em helpink you.' Valya was pleased with herself.

I didn't mind. To be honest, I thought it was cute. Up to a point. But perhaps I should never have indulged him, because after that it was only a short step to the real rabbits.

As briefly as I could, I told Emily about the slippers. Then, ignoring her complaints that the story was only hotting up, I begged to be allowed to go to bed, on the grounds that I'd scratched my arm so much it was bleeding.

13

The phone woke me. I was out of bed and into the living-room before I realized it. In the wake of the previous day's phone calls my nerves were like taut elastic – I was waiting for someone like my first primary-school teacher or the president of Ireland to ring, to tell me about Garv and The Girl.

'Hello,' I said suspiciously.

A sweet, squeaky voice rattled off, 'Mort Russell's office calling for Emily O'Keeffe.'

'One moment please.' I matched the girl's efficient tone.

But Emily was in the bathroom, and when I knocked on the door she wailed, 'Oh no. I'll have to call them back. I'm dehairing my legs and I'm at a vital point.'

When I returned to the phone, some instinct stopped me from sharing this with Mort Russell's office. 'I'm afraid she's away from her desk right now. Can I help?'

'Could Emily call Mort?' the sweet, squeaky girl requested.

I wrote down the number and said, 'Thank you.'

'Thank *you*,' she replied, sunny as you please.

Unlike me. I'd woken at twenty past three, my heart pounding with an irresistible need to ring Garv. I'd tiptoed into the living-room and, in the dark, dialled our home number. I just wanted to TALK to him. About what, I wasn't really sure. But there had been a time when he'd behaved as though he loved me more than anyone had ever loved anyone. I think I needed to know that even if he loved this new woman, it wasn't as much as he'd once loved me.

With a click and a rush of static, the phone began to ring on another continent, and agitatedly I gnawed at the twizzler around my wrist. But there was no one at home: I'd done my sums wrong. Ireland was eight hours ahead, so Garv was at work. My desperation had already begun to cool by the time I was put through to his desk, so when it transpired that he wasn't there and that all I could do was leave a message on his voicemail, it threw me. *Leave a message after the tone.*

I decided not to. I crept back to bed, finished the twizzler and wished I had several hundred more. I'd had some black times in my past, but I wasn't sure I had ever before felt so wretched. Would I ever get over it, would I ever feel normal again?

I seriously doubted it, even though I'd seen other people recover from terrible things. Look at Claire: her husband leaving her the same day, *the same day*, that she'd given birth to their child. And she'd recovered. Other people got married and got divorced and got over it and got married again, and talked about 'My first husband' in calm, easy-going tones, as if not one twinge of pain had ever been felt getting from then – when he was actually someone who mattered – to now, when he was just a walk-on part from your past. People adapted and moved on. But as I curled into a tight ball in the dark, I had a profound fear that I wouldn't. That I'd stay stuck, just becoming older and weirder. I'd stop getting my hair dyed and I'd end up moving back home to look after my aged parents until I was old myself. No one on our road would talk to us, and when children called to the house on Hallowe'en we'd pretend we weren't in. Or else pour buckets of cold water from an upstairs

147

window on to their masked and sheeted finery. Our car would be twenty years old and in perfect condition and the three of us would wear hats when we went out for a drive – when Dad would insist on taking the wheel, even though he'd have shrunk so much that all the other drivers would be able to see of him would be the top of his hat peeping over the dash. People would talk about me: 'She was married once. Used to be quite normal, they say. Hard to believe now, of course.'

The phone rang again, jolting me back to the present. Emily's agent, this time. Well, not actually David Crowe in person, of course, but some lackey who worked for him, setting up a lunch-time appointment.

Eventually, Emily emerged from the bathroom. 'Not a single hair remaining. Now where's his number?'

I handed her the piece of paper, which she kissed. 'How many people would KILL to have Mort Russell's direct line?'

She made the call, got put straight through, laughed and said, 'Thank you, and I totally love your work *too*,' a whole lot.

Then she hung up and declared, 'Guess what?'

'He trooooly, trooooooly loves your script?'

'Yip.' Then she seemed to notice me. 'Oh, sweetheart,' she said, sadly.

'There was another call,' I said. 'David Crowe's office. Will you have lunch with him at the Club House at one o'clock?'

'The Club House?' She clutched me, as though something terrible had happened. 'He said the Club House?'

'It was a "she" actually, but yes. What's the problem?'

'I'll tell you what the problem is,' she called, disappearing and fast reappearing with a book. She flicked through the pages, then read, '"The Club House. Power-brokers' lunch-time haunt where Hollywood's main men break bread and cut deals. Good steaks and salads . . ." Never mind that – but you heard what it said. "*Power-brokers' lunch-time haunt*". And I'm going there!'

With that, she burst into tears, the way she had when she'd first found out Hothouse wanted her to pitch. When the storm of tears passed, she surprised me by asking, 'Would you like to come?'

'But I couldn't. It's a working lunch.'

'So what? Would you like to come?'

Might as well, what else would I be doing? Sitting on the beach on my own, trying not to think about my failed marriage? 'Yeah, OK. But will he let you bring me?'

'Sure! This is the honeymoon period, when they can refuse me nothing. Might as well make the most of it. I was too clueless to capitalize on it the last time. We'll pretend you're my assistant.'

'Won't he think it's weird that I know almost nothing about Hollywood?'

'Well then, don't ask any questions. Just laugh and nod a lot. Please come.'

'OK, go on then.'

A quick phone call later and the deal was done.

The weather had changed. Instead of blue skies, the sun shone through thick cloud cover, glaring at the world with a dirty mustard light. My first five days in LA seemed like a charmed time, by contrast. Not only had the weather been benign, but so had my state of mind. At the time I'd thought I was unhappy, but I was far messier now. And to make matters worse, I could no longer get away with blaming any of my feelings of fear or alienation on jet lag. These were *mine*.

Emily and I drove along Santa Monica Boulevard towards Beverly Hills, and the filthy sky got worse the more we drove inland. Smog, I understood, with a sudden leap of near-excitement. *So* LA. As iconic as palm trees and plastic surgery.

'Is he married?' I asked. 'David Crowe?'

Emily fell silent, then said, 'Please stop doing this to yourself. Lots of people get divorced, you're not so unusual.'

The Club House was noisy and full. Almost entirely with quartets of men who were, incongruously, eating salads and drinking Evian. Emily and I were ushered through the throngs of men to our table. David Crowe hadn't arrived yet.

I suddenly, urgently wanted a glass of wine, but when I asked Emily if that was OK, she regretfully shook her head. 'Sorry, Maggie, but you're supposed to be my assistant. Though, God knows, I could do with several myself. And twenty untipped super-strengths.' Nervously, she clacked her nails on the table until, in a frenzy of frayed nerves, I grabbed her hands. She looked at me in surprise.

'It'll be fine,' I said, pretending that I was holding her hands in reassurance.

'Thanks,' she said, extricating herself and giving the tabletop another good hammering. 'Oh, thank God, here's David.'

Thank God indeed.

She pointed out a clean-cut young man, who looked affable and sure of himself. This meant he was probably a neurotic mess who'd never had a meaningful relationship and who spent five hours a week in therapy. Such, I am told, is the Hollywood way. He gave us a wave and a big, BIG smile. He was no distance from us, yet it took him ten minutes to cross the room, so busy was he stopping at tables, shaking hands, exclaiming with pleasure and generally bonhomieing.

Finally he arrived, held my hand between his two and stared into my eyes. 'So happy to meet you, Maggie.'

He turned to Emily. 'And how's my main girl?!'

All smiles, down he sat, and displayed what a regular at the Club House he was by not even looking at the menu. 'Cobb salad, hold the avocado, dressing on the side,' he efficiently told the waiter. Then he launched into gossipy and entertaining conversation about our fellow lunchers. He was almost like a tour guide.

'As you know, the hierarchy of power in this town shakes down every Monday morning,' he told me.

'Depending on the opening weekend grosses,' Emily said.

'Right! So see that guy over there, in the suspenders. Elmore Shinto. As of this morning, his career is over. Executive producer of *Moonstone*, a ninety-million-dollar project. Word on the street said it sucked. They reshot the ending four times. Opened this weekend and TANKED. Studio's going to take a huge hit on it.'

I was keen to get a look at him, mostly because I was interested in getting a gawk at a man who showed up in public wearing suspenders. As if the Club House was the Rocky Horror Show. Then to my disappointment I remembered that 'suspenders' was American for 'braces'. From the way Elmore was chatting and laughing, he didn't *look* like a man whose career was over.

'That's the way they do things round here,' Emily remarked. 'Always dress it up with a brave face . . . Until you're found rocking in a corner, crazed with cocaine psychosis, and you're carted off to the farm,' she added, with a laugh. '*Then* there's no hiding anything.'

'Er, yeah,' David said, a little uncertainly, then launched into

151

movie gossip. '. . . saved the studio from takeover . . . brought in the original producer . . . three-picture deal . . . script picked off the slush pile . . . ten years to get a green light . . .'

The commentary continued through our unbelievably speedy meal: no starter, and *certainly* no dessert. Since I'd arrived in LA, I hadn't ever once been offered anything other than coffee after my meal. I suspected that if I got a longing for a slice of banoffi, they'd have to ring the dessert chef and get him out of bed.

Over the lunch, David and Emily had discussed pitch tactics a little, but as we left the restaurant the real work began: David stopped at several tables and introduced Emily to meaty-handed moguls.

'Emily O'Keeffe. Hugely talented writer. Pitching her new movie, *Plastic Money*, to Hothouse on Wednesday. You wanna piece you gotta get in there fast!'

I hovered in the background, smiling nervously. The response to Emily varied. Some of the men were patently disgruntled at having their cobb salads and Evian water disturbed, but others seemed genuinely interested. But even with the ruder ones, David – and indeed Emily – smilingly stood their ground, as if they were the hottest stars in town. There was something very exciting about the buzz that David was whipping up before our very eyes. When we finally neared the door, David said quietly, 'That last guy, Larry Savage, has already passed on the script, but betcha he calls.'

'They hate the feeling they're missing out.' I tried to sound knowledgeable.

'They also hate their asses getting fired when Hothouse makes the movie into a big hit and their studio finds out they passed on it.'

Then I heard myself exclaim, 'Oh, holy Christ!'

'What?' Emily asked.

'It's Shay Delaney.'

'Where?'

'There.' I indicated the man with the dark-blond hair, at a table with three other men.

'That's not Shay Delaney.'

'Yes it is! Oh no, you're right, it isn't.' The man had just turned to the room and for the first time I saw his profile. 'But it looked really like him,' I said defensively. 'The back of his head was identical to Shay's.'

14

That afternoon there were two further phone calls from the sweet, squeaky girl at Mort Russell's office. First to know if Emily had any special requests for Wednesday's pitch.

'Like what?' I asked curiously.

'Audio-visual equipment. Herbal tea. A special chair.'

'Well, I'm afraid Emily is in a meeting right now.' She'd gone to her gyrotonic – whatever that was – trainer. Everyone in LA seemed to have a constant parade of appointments with accountants, nutritionists, hairdressers, trainers of strange disciplines and, top of the list, therapists. 'I'll have her call you back.'

Then the girl rang again to give very complicated instructions for parking on Wednesday afternoon. Among other things, she needed the reg. number and make of Emily's car.

'She made a right song and dance about it,' I told Emily on her return.

'That's because in movie studios, parking places are like sincerity,' she remarked.

'Huh?'

'Very, very rare. Anyone else call?'

'Just my parents. They say they're worried about me.'

'They're not the only ones.'

'I'm OK,' I sighed. At least my middle-of-the-night panic had abated. 'And I rang Donna and Sinead.' Once I'd known for sure that neither of them were Garv's girl, I'd felt OK about talking to them. Both of them sounded delighted to hear from me finally, and neither knew a thing about Garv's affair. That was a relief – so at least all of Dublin wasn't discussing it.

'What are you going to wear tonight to Dan Gonzalez's party?' Emily asked.

'Dunno.' I was glad we were going out. Constant activity was what I wanted, to keep ahead of myself and my thoughts. But there was something I had to ask. 'Will Shay Delaney be there?'

A pause. 'He might be. If he's in town.' Another pause. 'Would you mind if he was?'

'Ah, no.'

'OK.'

'Have you ever met his wife?'

'No, she doesn't come with him, I don't think. I suppose with the three children she wouldn't be able.'

'Does he . . . you know . . . play around? Or is he faithful to her?'

'I don't know,' Emily said earnestly. 'I don't see him that often or know him that well. Which would you prefer? That he's faithful or unfaithful?'

'Don't know. Neither.'

Emily nodded thoughtfully at this piece of illogical nonsense. 'Look,' she said slowly, 'you've let him live rent-free in your head for a long time.' Then she stopped. 'I'm sorry, forget I opened my mouth. I don't know . . . I suppose I *can't* know what you went through. Sorry,' she repeated.

'It's OK.'

Then she went to get ready and that was the end of that.

*

Half an hour later she reappeared in pink and black leopard-skin jeans, dominatrix stilettos and some sort of jerkin top. But it wasn't just the clothes: there were bracelets and hair slides and shiny make-up . . .

'How do you do it?' My brow furrowed as I studied her. 'You're like Wonderwoman, the way you transform yourself.'

'You look great too.'

I'd done my best, but I hadn't brought many glitzy clothes to LA (mostly because I didn't have them), and in my black 'party' dress I felt like a mourner next to Emily's exotic plumage.

'Oh why,' I berated myself, 'do I have brick-shithouse tendencies, else I could borrow your clothes. Curl my eyelashes, would you, with your magic eyelash curler?'

Emily could do better than that: she did my make-up so that I was nearly as shiny as her, then gave me some spare hair slides and bracelets.

And then off we went.

The party, in a Spanish-style mansion in Bel Air, was one of those highly organized glamorous ones. Electronic gates with burly types checking your identity, ten Mexican men to park your car and fairy lights winking and twinkling through the trees. In the house, good-looking, talkative people circulated in the high-ceilinged, airy rooms, and enormous vases overflowed with abundant arrangements of lilies. The light glinted off trays of champagne *and* – rather disappointingly, I thought – trays of mineral water. As it was a Hollywood party I'd come expecting drugs, hookers and general high-jinks, and I wasn't prepared to relinquish that vision. Surely that ebony princess looking for the ladies' room was *really* off to snort a gram of cocaine? That alarmingly young-looking Hispanic girl *had* to be a prostitute.

Emily went to pay a fealty visit to Dan Gonzalez, the host, and I stood sipping champagne and watching, hawk-eyed, for signs of debauchery.

'Hi!' A burlyish, youngish man wearing a wing-tipped collar walked up to me. 'Gary Fresher, executive producer.'

'Maggie Gar – Walsh.' They were certainly friendly here!

'And what do you do, Maggie?'

'I'm just taking some down time right now.'

Then, so quickly that I could hardly take it in, he said curtly, 'Nice meeting you,' turned his back and walked away.

Whaaat?

I should have had a job. He wasn't interested in talking to me because I couldn't help him. The realization shocked and depressed me. Party, my granny. More like a dreadful network-ing convention. Next, people would be exchanging business cards. Oh, hold on, they already were, and Emily O'Keeffe was one of them. There she was, in the thick of things, glossy, confident, talking the talk, walking the walk . . .

No sign anywhere of Shay Delaney. He mustn't be in town.

'Hi! I'm Leon Franchetti.'

A startlingly handsome man had materialized in front of me, his hand extended.

'Maggie Walsh.'

'And what do *you* do, Maggie?'

'I'm a pet groomer.' I just couldn't run the risk of being snubbed again and that was the first job to come into my head. 'How about you?'

'I'm an actor.'

I admit it, I was quite impressed. Not as much as I once would have been when my feelings were normal, but . . . 'Cool.'

'Yeah, things have been going pretty good.' I was spellbound by his matinée-idol smile. I was about to ask what he'd been in, but he beat me to it. 'I've just finished a pilot for ABC, should be screening in the fall – I've got a totally great character, with lots of room for growth, I could really stretch myself with it –'

'Excell –'

'Before that I was in *Kaleidoscope*.' Another hypnotizing smile.

'Were you?' I'd seen it, but I didn't remember him from it.

'Not a huge role, but it got me noticed. Oh yeah, it got me noticed.' He flashed me another handsome-devil smile. Oddly, this one didn't affect me like the others had. 'I've also played Benjamin in the House of Pies commercial. "*Where do I get my pie?*"' He stuck out his bottom lip, suddenly looked woebegone, then delivered, with a beam, '"*In the House of Pies, stoopid!*"' It appeared to be the catchphrase from a very crap ad. 'It didn't screen in California, but it was totally HUGE in the midwest. Even politicians were saying it. "Where do you see yourself in ten years time?" "In the House of Pies, stoopid!"'

It was around then that I realized how superfluous I was to the conversation. Emily rescued me, but within minutes I was boxed in by another walking résumé, who gave me chapter and verse on his entire acting career. He asked me one question and one question only: did I work in 'the business'?

When he'd finished with me, I stood alone and watched the room. All the glitter had rubbed off and the people moving and smiling and talking looked like sharks in a shark pool. It was true what Emily had said: it would be impossible to find love in this town. They were all too into their work. Within me a space opened up; there was nothing to distract from my thoughts of Garv. Depression began to circle and settle . . .

Then my heart thrilled at the sight of an old friend across the room: Troy, with his long face and implacable mouth. OK, so I'd only known him since Friday, but compared to this awful crowd of humourless egomaniacs he was one of the closest friends I'd ever had. I hurtled through the throng.

'Hey,' he exclaimed, looking as happy to see me as I was to see him. 'Having a good time?'

'No.'

He turned my wrist to him. 'Uh-oh. The emergency happen?'

I nodded. 'I rang him, he wasn't there. Thank you for the liquorice lace.'

'Twizzler,' he corrected. 'It help?'

'It sure did. I could have done with twenty more.'

'Buddhists say that everything is impermanent – that's a comfort. But not as much as refined sugar. So you're not having a good time?'

'No,' I said hotly. 'I've been monologued at by countless thesps. Such egomaniacs!'

'Acting is a savage profession,' Troy explained softly. 'Every day you get told that your voice is wrong, that your look is over. You get so many blows to your ego that the only way to survive is to overdevelop it.'

'I see.' I was momentarily humbled, then I remembered another wound. 'Wait till you hear what happened when I first arrived!' I related the story of the man walking away when he heard I didn't have a job. 'Where I come from,' I scorned, 'people aren't interested in you because of what you do.'

'No, they're interested because of what you look like,' he said drily.

I paused. 'Fair enough,' I conceded. 'And I haven't seen one person snorting cocaine. Call this a Hollywood party. Although do you think she might be a hooker?' I indicated the very young Hispanic girl.

'That's Dan Gonzalez's daughter.'

I could feel the disappointment on my face and Troy laughed a low, gentle laugh. 'You're not going to find drugs and sketchy stuff at this kind of party. They're here to work. But,' he said, 'if you want I'll take you out some night and show you a different side to LA.'

'Thanks,' I said, coolly. Irritated by the flood-tide of heat that roared up my neck and exploded in bright colour in my face.

As Emily and I drove home, I was oddly mesmerized by the freeway traffic. Five lanes of cars streaming forward, everyone proceeding at the same speed, with the same distance between every car.

Sliproads fed newcomers into the main body. They settled into their place with balletic grace, without missing a beat. At the same time, cars were leaving, extricating themselves smoothly and zipping up sliproads until they disappeared from view. Constant motion, constant grace – I found it beautiful.

What was wrong with me? Finding traffic beautiful. Finding big-nosed, slab-of-granitey men beautiful.

I was covered in confusion. It was a long, long time since I'd found someone other than Garv attractive and I couldn't help but worry about my unconventional choice.

15

A mild crisis had arisen. David Crowe wasn't able to make Emily's pitch.

'Something's come up,' Emily said bitterly. 'Some*one*, he means. More important than me.'

But Mort Russell's 'people' still wanted the meeting to go ahead as arranged.

'So David said I'm to bring my assistant with me.'

'What assistant?'

'You!'

'Me?'

'You get nothing for nothing in this town,' Emily mourned. 'You'll be paying for that caesar salad at the Club House for the rest of your days.'

'But Emily, I'll be no help. I know nothing about pitches.'

'You don't need to. You just have to flank me and laugh at the funny bits. Maybe carry a clipboard.'

'But . . . But what'll I wear? I didn't bring any suits, I'll have to buy something.'

'Third Street Boulevard is only five minutes' drive from here – go now!'

Obediently I obliged – like shopping was a hardship – and spent a couple of hours going round the normal shops where the assistants acted pleased to see me, unlike the snotty cows in Rodeo Drive. But, as we all know, the first law of shopping says

161

that when you're urgently looking for something specific, you've no hope of finding it. The few suits they had had the peculiar effect of making me look like a prison warder. Half-heartedly I picked up some stowaways: an embroidered denim skirt and a white vest top.

Then I stumbled upon Bloomingdales. I know it's naff, but I love department stores – so much better than those funky little boutiques where you've to ring a bell to get in. The type where they only have eleven items of stock, which you can survey and dismiss in 2.7 seconds but have to spend fifteen minutes going 'Mmmm, lovely,' in order not to seem rude in front of the assistant, who is never less than ten inches from you, explaining how the silk was handspun in Nepal, cold-dyed in natural plant colours, etc. It's excruciating and I often end up buying something just to extricate myself.

So what I love about department stores is that it's operation free-flow. Apart from an occasional woman jumping out and trying to spray you with perfume, no one bothers you. And there must be a moral in that somewhere, because within seconds I'd pulled out my wallet and welcomed aboard another stowaway: a face gel that promised to make me look radiant. Then followed a brief moment of madness when I almost bought Garv some Clinique for Men stuff – my head turned by the free gift that was on offer – then luckily I remembered I hated him.

But the bottom line is that I wasn't any better off in the suit department. My other purchases made me feel good only for about forty seconds, and by the time I got home I was needled by guilt – I shouldn't be buying stuff while I had no job – and also by fear – Emily was a little volatile at the moment. Tentatively I broke the no-suit news to her, and she responded by snuffling like a warm-up act for full-blown hyperventilation, so I said very quickly, 'Couldn't I borrow something?'

'Who fucking from? Charles Manson? The Easter bunny?' Wildly, she appraised me, then visibly calmed. 'Let's see, you're about the same size as Lara. Except maybe in the chest area.'

'Did she really have a boob job?'

'She was an actress.' Emily sounded as if that explained everything. 'Anyway, could you call her and borrow a suit?'

'Well, I'm seeing her later, anyway. She's taking me to get my hair cut, remember?'

'Is she?' Emily looked a little startled. 'When was that decided?'

I thought back. It had been a morning. Sunny. But that was no help, they were all sunny. But hold on, Lara had been off work . . .

'Saturday, remember?'

'Oh, yeah, of course, sorry.'

At six o'clock, Lara swept me off in her silver pick-up truck to Dino's salon. 'OK sweetheart, let's make you even more pretty than you already are!'

Whizzing up Santa Monica Boulevard, I said – daringly, I thought – to Lara, 'So how did your date go last night?'

'Good,' she said cheerfully. 'It's totally too soon to call it, but she's a funny girl and we had a good time. She said she'd call me. Like, she'd better!'

Lara parked the pick-up truck in a space that would have held three normal cars and ushered me into a white, Grecian-style salon. Lots of urns and ivy and columns.

'Dino!' she called.

Dino was huge, with enormous sideburns and tight, flamboyant clothes. Ropes of muscle rippled beneath his skin. Gay? Not necessarily.

'The beautiful Miss Lara!'

Lara pushed me towards him and said, 'This is Maggie. Hasn't she got the BEST face?'

'Yeeaaah,' Dino drawled with interest, and ran a hand parallel to my cheek, conveying that he found huge potential in me. Hope stirred. I was going to be changed for the better. 'Hey, I gotta tell you my news,' he said to Lara with such anticipatory drama that I thought at the very least he'd won the state lottery. It transpired that he'd bought a tongue-scraper. 'I do not know how I lived without it up until now. My breath is the FRESHEST.' He breathed a big 'Haaah!' into Lara's face to demonstrate.

'Fresh,' she agreed solemnly.

'You gotta get one, it'll change your life,' he predicted.

Now that he mentioned it, I had seen ads for them. But I'd dismissed them as silly nonsense, in the same category as vaginal deodorants. Could I have been wrong?

'Sit here, in my special chair. The light is better,' Dino guided me. Then with frowning concentration he was mussing my hair, lifting the ends to chin level, changing my parting to the middle, pulling my fringe back from my face . . .

By my side, Lara watched the variations in the mirror.

'She's totally got a great jawline,' Dino remarked, with professional-sounding dispassion. 'The best!'

But I haven't. I've got a very mediocre jawline, and I know it.

'Look at those eyes,' Dino ordered.

I looked. They were just my eyes, nothing to write home about. But they were an awesome colour. Leastways, that was what Lara said. From the way the pair of them were love-bombing me, you'd swear I was gorgeous.

'I think we're gonna go pretty short here,' Dino said. 'Your head shape is good enough to take it.'

I opened my mouth to object, then realized that I didn't have to.

It was Garv, you see.

Despite popular opinion, he'd actually been very easy-going. At least, about most things. But there was some stuff that he simply was not open to negotiation on.

1. He would have no truck with electric blankets – dying of cold was preferable. He insisted that if you stayed in an electric-blanket-warmed bed for too long you'd – and I quote – 'pop up like a slice of toast'.

2. He hated me getting my hair cut. Visits to the hairdresser were fraught, because even when I only got a blow-dry, Garv used to examine me on my return and insist that they'd lopped off four inches. And getting a trim was a total nightmare – no matter how often I explained to him about split ends and what Bad Things they were. While his insistence on long hair used to irritate me, I indulged him, because when I could never find time to go to the gym and so lost most of my muscle tone, he didn't once complain.

But as Dino's hands sketched shapes around my face, I suddenly saw that I was free to do whatever I liked with my hair. I could shave my head if I wanted.

'I don't want it too short.'

'Your face can take it.'

'But my hair can't. It goes into awful curls if it's shorter than three inches. I look like a cauliflower.'

There have been many hairstyles over the years: the Shingle; the Bob; the Purdey; the Rachel. Well, I lived in terror of the grim halo of curls they called the Irish Mammy.

'I hear you,' Dino said, clicking open and closed a huge pair of steel scissors, practically pawing the ground.

'You've got to wash it, first,' Lara murmured.

'I *know*.'

As dark clots of wet hair fell to the white tiles, the weight on my head noticeably lightened. It felt strange: it was ten years since I'd had anything other than a trim. Now and then anxiety leapt, as I forgot how much my life had changed. Garv would *kill* me. Then I remembered he wouldn't. He couldn't.

'How'd your date with the dancer go?' Dino asked Lara. 'Gimme the 411 on her.'

As the old me fell away, the pair of them chatted easily. Then I was being blow-dried with my head upside-down, then finally I was being turned to the mirror, face to face with a sleeker, sparklier version of myself. By comparison, the earlier me seemed pathetically crude and lumpish – and very long ago.

Words finally found me. 'I look different. Younger.'

'The right cut is as good as a facelift,' Dino said.

And almost as expensive. It cost a staggering one hundred and twenty dollars! With a twenty-dollar tip! I could have got four haircuts at home for the same amount and had enough change for a bag of Maltesers for the drive home. But if that's how they do it here . . .

As we left, Dino said, 'You know what? You have great

eyebrows, but they could use a shape . . . You know what I'm thinking?' he questioned Lara.

'Anoushka!' they declared together.

'Who?'

'Eyebrow shaper to the stars,' Dino explained.

In a by-now-familiar scenario, Lara already had the palm pilot and the cellphone out. 'Madame Anoushka? My girlfriend is having a brow crisis.' She looked at my eyebrows. 'It *is* an emergency, Madame Anoushka.'

For some reason I couldn't be bothered being offended.

Lara paced anxiously, then, 'Saturday, five-thirty?' She turned to me. 'OK?'

I nodded. Why not?

Next stop, Lara's Venice apartment to pick up clothes for the pitch. I liked Venice. There was something bleak and charming about the clapboard houses with their peeling paint, the secret, hidden little streets which darted away from the road, the dusty trees weighted low over front yards, casting a mysterious, sub-aquaish light.

Lara's apartment took up the entire top floor of a big, wooden house. From her windows you could hear the swish and roar of the ocean.

'My closet is through here.' She marched into her bedroom, me in her wake. Then I took one look at her bed and all I could think of were porn film titles. *Hot Lesbian Love Action. Ladies Who Munch. City Lickers.*

I couldn't help it. This was the first lesbian bedroom I'd ever been in – I defy anyone not to have the same reaction.

Blithely unaware, Lara was pulling clothes from the closet – not a pair of dungarees in sight.

'There's this pant suit. Or how about this skirt and jacket? Lemme show you the shirt that goes with it . . . Try this on,' she kept urging. 'Try that on.' And when I finally got round to doing so, she stepped out of the room while I got changed.

Then, my arms full of business-like clothes, Lara gave me a lift – or ride, if you prefer – home to Santa Monica. Night was falling and the light draining away. As we drove down an avenue lined with palm trees, their silhouettes black against the fading sky, I noticed again how lanky and skinny they were. They say some people get to look like their dogs. Well, Angelenos get to look like their flora.

As I ran in home, I glanced through the window into Mike and Charmaine's front room. To my great surprise there were loads of people there, sitting amongst flickering candles. They all had their eyes closed. In fact, they were so still I wasn't even sure they were breathing. With a strange thrill, I wondered if I'd stumbled on a Jim Jones grape-flavoured-Kool-Aid mass-suicide-pact-type thing.

While I'd been out, Emily had gone into a pre-pitch frenzy and tried on every item of clothing she owned. They were scattered on the bed, the floor, the chairs, flung over her television, and she was on her hands and knees pawing hysterically through them.

'I have nothing to wear tomorrow!' She didn't even look up.

'But what about the lovely things you bought on Saturday?'

She shook her head. 'I hate them. They're all wrong.'

Only then did she notice my hair. 'Holy Christ, I'd hardly recognize you! You're BEAUTIFUL.'

'Listen to me. There's something funny going on next door –'

'Police raid?'

'No, the other next door. Loads of them, not moving. They look dead! Should I call 911?'

'They're meditating,' she said. 'They do it every Tuesday night. Listen, Mammy Walsh rang.'

'She's worried about me and I'm to come home?'

'She's worried about you and if it doesn't stop raining soon she's going to wind up in the mental hospital.'

'Nothing about me coming home?'

'Nothing.'

'Good.'

'So did Lara give you a suit for tomorrow?'

'Yes.' I picked a shirt off the floor. 'Come on, I'll help you hang up some of this stuff.'

'All right,' she sighed, grabbing a bundle of hangers. 'Lara has a great apartment, hasn't she?'

'Yeah.' Then I thought of those porn film titles again. 'You know, Lara's the first lesbian I've ever met,' I admitted. 'At least, knowingly.'

'Me too.'

'I wonder . . .' I trailed off.

'What they get up to in bed?'

'No!' Well, yes.

'Dildos, I imagine. Oral sex. Christ, I wouldn't be into it myself,' Emily said with distaste. 'It'd be like licking a mackerel.'

I hung up a few more items, then I said, 'But everyone is a little bit bi, aren't they? That's what scientists say.'

Emily paused in her hanging-up and she gave me a forbidding look. 'No,' she said firmly. 'Don't even go there.'

16

When the real rabbits had finally showed up, at least Garv hadn't pretended they were a present for me. I'd heard stories of other men doing that – buying a kitten or a puppy which they'd really wanted for themselves and presenting it to their girl. Thus adding insult to injury, because the girl not only has to share her home with an unwanted animal, but has to feed and clear up after the little shagger also.

Garv arrived home from work one evening carrying a cardboard box lined with straw, which he placed on the table.

'Maggie, look,' he whispered, clearly about to burst with excitement.

Torn between dread and curiosity, I looked in, to see two pairs of pink eyes looking up at me, two little noses twitching.

'Funny-looking pizzas,' I said. He was supposed to have brought home our dinner.

'Sorry,' he said, full of good nature. 'I forgot. I'll go back out.'

'They're rabbits,' I accused.

'Baby ones,' he grinned. A girl at work had had some going spare, he said. 'We don't have to keep them if you don't want, but I'll do all the taking care of them,' he promised.

'But what about when we –'

'– Go on holiday? Dermot will mind them.'

Dermot was his younger brother. Like most younger brothers, he'd do anything for a couple of bob.

'You've thought it all through.'

Instantly, his glow began to fade. 'I'm sorry, baby. I shouldn't have just landed them on you like that. I'll give them back tomorrow.'

Then I felt *awful*. Garv loved animals. He was affectionate and indulgent and he wasn't just saying he'd return them so that I'd relent. His contrition was genuine.

'Wait,' I said. 'Let's not be hasty.'

And so began the Year of the Rabbit.

The black and white one was a boy and the pure white one was a girl.

'What'll we call them?' Garv asked, holding them both on his lap.

'I don't know.' *Bloody nuisance?* 'Hoppy? What else do rabbits do?'

'Eat carrots? Ride rings around each other?'

Eventually we decided that the girl would be Hoppy and the boy would be Rider.

I would have preferred not to have had two (well, I would also have preferred not to have had one), but Garv said it would be cruel to keep just one, that he'd be lonely. And because I didn't want them breeding like . . . well, *rabbits*, I insisted that they got done. The first of many visits to the vet.

Before we did anything else, though, we had to buy them a hutch.

'Can't we just keep them in the garden?' I asked. But apparently not. They'd burrow under the garden wall and into the next-door neighbours', then off out into the wide, blue yonder. So we bought a hutch, the biggest in the pet shop.

Most days, after work, Garv let them out for a run around the garden, to give them a taste of the wild. Although trying to catch them to put them back in the hutch was like trying to put toothpaste back in the tube. They were *impossible*. I remember standing at the kitchen window watching Garv belting around outside in his sober charcoal suit. Each time he'd almost caught up with one, it would spring away from his outstretched arms and the chase would begin again. All we needed was the Benny Hill theme music and for someone to fling a sack of ball bearings at them. It was hilarious. Sort of.

Don't get me wrong, they were very cute in their way. And when they hopped over to see me when I got home from work, it was sweet. And Garv had a way of carrying them, with their head over his shoulder, the way you'd burp a baby, that used to have me in convulsions. Especially, for some reason, when it was Hoppy: she did a great wide-eyed expression of surprise that was very funny. We ascribed them personalities, the way we had with the slippers. Hoppy was a mischievous flirt, Rider a smooth ladies' man with an arsenal of cheesy chat-up lines.

But on one of their turns around the garden the little bastards ate my lupins, the lupins that I'd planted myself, with my bare hands (nearly), and I'm afraid I slightly took agin them. I also resented having to shop for them – if we hadn't managed to get to the supermarket for ourselves we could just get an Indian delivered. But we couldn't get away with ordering a couple of extra onion bhajis for them. Instead, we were obliged to make regular trips to the Bad Place for their bags of carrots, bunches of parsley and funny pellet yokes.

Then came the day when Garv marched in, waved something at me and declared, 'Present!'

I whipped it from his hand, tore off the paper bag . . . and stared. 'It's a bit of wood,' I said.

'To gnaw on,' he said, like he thought he was making sense.

'To gnaw on,' I repeated.

He understood before I did, and couldn't stop laughing. 'Not for you. For Hoppy!'

More presents followed: a ball, a mirror for the hutch, a baby-blue clutch bag (for me, so I wouldn't feel left out). And one day, I got home from work to find half the garden dug up.

'What's going on? Have you murdered someone?'

But the truth wasn't much more palatable – Garv was making something called a run, because he felt it was cruel to confine the boyos to a hutch.

In a way, it was a relief that Garv had dug up the garden to make the run: at least we'd never have to worry about cutting the grass again. But in another way, it wasn't a relief at all. I thought he was getting too fond of Hoppy and Rider. But when I mentioned it to Donna, she told me to cop on to myself. Who ever heard of anyone being jealous of a pair of rabbits?

Not long after, Hoppy got sick and Garv was clearly worried. He took a morning off work to take her to the vet, who diagnosed an infection due to – of all the weird things – misaligned teeth. It was no big deal: the vet clipped her teeth and prescribed a course of antibiotics. But a few days later, we went out for dinner with Donna and Robbie, and Garv began telling them about Hoppy's bout. About how he'd known something was wrong, because she was normally alert and reactive, but she wouldn't even gnaw on her new bit of wood. Donna and Robbie made sympathetic noises, and Garv went on about Hoppy's high temperature and how Rider had tried to tempt her to eat a bite or two of onion bhaji. (One very busy week, when we hadn't had time to go to the supermarket, we'd discovered that they actually quite liked them.)

As Garv went on, Donna and Robbie's indulgent expressions

faded and hardened, and I had a tight place in my stomach that no amount of wine-swallowing would dissolve.

'How's work?' Donna eventually cut across Garv.

'Work?' He sounded confused. '*My* work? But you never let me talk about my work, it's too boring.' As enlightenment dawned, he began to laugh. 'Oh right, I see. I'll shut up about them, so.'

Donna rang me early the next day and said, 'Maggie, I think you might be right, he *is* a bit too devoted. Stick him on to me there, I'll tell him myself.'

The crunch came not long after, when my sister Claire came to visit and remarked on the amount of rabbit paraphernalia lying around. Garv was putting them into their travelling baskets to bring them to the vet for their jabs.

'Jabs?' Claire exclaimed. 'It's almost as bad as having a child!'

17

*SCENE: Sunny day. White clapboard house,
with small front yard. Front door opens.
Two women emerge. One, tall, carrying an
empty folder and wearing a jacket that
bags slightly in the chest area. The
other, short, skinny, well-dressed,
smoking manically.*

SHORT GIRL. I need to go to the bathroom
again.
TALL GIRL. No, Emily, you don't!

*They cross the lawn, just as the
sprinklers spurt high jets of water from
the ground, catching the short girl and
extinguishing her cigarette. She shrieks.
Like a reaction in a scientific
experiment, her glossy, shiny hair
immediately begins to fuzz and bulk.*

Cue laughter.

Oh, stop!

I couldn't stop thinking in screenplay speech. Emily had
practised on me long and hard into the night, and, between

appointments at the hairdresser's and reiki practitioner, through the morning also.

We were both in shreds.

I was *literally* having a bad-hair day. As usual, I'd woken up feeling like it was the end of the world. And that was even before I went to the bathroom and saw my hair – what remained of it. When I thought of all the hair I'd lost, the eight or nine inches which had dropped to the floor and been peremptorily swept away, I cried. Interestingly enough, I wasn't crying because my haircut was symbolic of the end of my marriage. I'm fairly sure I was crying because in all my excitement at Dino's I'd only gone and signed up for a high-maintenance cut, and now it was too late.

Fecking hairdressers. It always looks great when you leave the salon. (Well, it doesn't, but let's not get into the times when we've been fighting back tears even while we've been shoving them a tip. I'm talking about the rare occasions when we're actually happy with what they've done.) Everything is dandy until the first time we wash it, and then for love nor money we cannot re-create that just-out-of-the-salon look. Despite all the hype, there is one way and one way only to achieve that just-out-of-a-salon look and that's when you're just out of a salon. Even now, all I'd done with my hair was sleep on it funny and already I'd lost control of it. It took water, styling wax and a hairdryer at its highest setting before I could bring it to heel.

Emily had taken the precaution of bringing her own hair to the hairdresser's. She returned briefly and walked around the house saying, '. . . camera pans over a pair of breasts in a T-shirt . . .' Then she went out again.

While she was gone, the sweet, squeaky girl from Mort Russell's office rang for her.

'I'm afraid she's away from her desk right now.' She'd gone to her reiki – now I knew what *that* was – practitioner. 'Can I help?'

This time she wanted to know, for identification purposes, what our DNA make-up was. Well, almost. She needed me to fax over copies of our driving licences, because she needed to see our photos.

'I'm sorry to bother you like this,' she said. 'But we've got to be security conscious.'

I could well believe it. There was every chance that crazed scriptwriters, desperate for an appointment, could try to break in, hold studio chiefs hostage and force them to listen to their pitch.

'See you at three-thirty,' she said.

She'd been so lovely every time we'd spoken that, on impulse, I asked her her name.

'Flea,' she replied.

Instantly I realized my mistake. I'd been far too friendly. Crossed professional boundaries. Stung, I mumbled a goodbye and hung up. Flea, indeed! Oh, make fun of the poor Irish eejit just off the plane. And what's your surname, lovey? Pit? Bite? Bag?

'. . . Camera pans over a pair of breasts,' I heard. Emily was back.

'My chakras were in a terrible state,' she announced. 'Good job I went.'

Then she started muttering to herself in the mirror. 'The universe is benign, they will option my script, the universe is benign, they will option my script . . .' She varied this affirmation with, 'The perfect pitch is twenty-five words or less, the perfect pitch is . . .'

'I thought you didn't believe in chakras,' I said. 'And don't you hate all that New Age stuff?'

Her answer humbled me. 'When you're desperate, you'll try anything.'

In the end, I talked Emily into wearing her new outfit. She brushed her hair for the millionth time, put on the umpteenth layer of lip-gloss, then we squared our shoulders and sallied forth. Just in time for the sprinklers to spring into sudden life and launch their jets directly at Emily. As her hair expanded like bubble bath, she almost had hysterics.

'It's a disaster,' she shrieked. 'I'm going to have to cancel!'

'Quick, back to the hairdryer,' I suggested.

'We don't got time,' she wailed. 'The only thing I can do is to keep combing it. But I've got to drive!'

'We'll take my car.'

'We can't bring your crappy hire-car – what'll they think of us?'

'Actually, we can't bring my crappy hire-car because our parking space is allocated for your reg. number,' I remembered.

'I'll drive, you comb.'

We sped across LA, Emily talking to herself, her face like flint, me combing energetically and doing my best to ignore the startled looks we were getting at stop lights.

The studio, like most of the studios, was in a place called 'The Valley'. From what I could gather, most people would rather live in a cardboard box in Santa Monica than in a five-bathroomed mansion in The Valley. Apparently it was naffer than Liebfraumilch, Andrew Lloyd Webber and mullet hairdos put together, and one of the worst insults you could level at anyone was 'Valley Girl'.

After we'd been driving about forty-five minutes, Emily interrupted her affirmations. 'This is The Valley.'

For all the talk, it didn't look that remarkable, to be honest. People weren't lining the streets guzzling Blue Nun, dancing to *Phantom of the Opera* and teasing their neckcurls, as I'd almost expected.

'Nearly there now,' Emily said, heaving a breath from her diaphragm.

Just then we ran into heavy traffic.

'Come on, come on, come on! Oh, Jesus!' Agitatedly, Emily pounded her steering wheel, then handed me her cellphone. 'Give Flea a buzz and tell her we'll be five minutes late.'

'Flea? You mean that's really her name?'

'Yeah, Flea.' Emily sounded impatient.

'Like the insect?' I couldn't let it go.

'No. F-L-I. It's short for something. Felicity, maybe.'

'Right!' Short for something. Felicity, maybe. *Not* making fun of the poor Irish eejit just off the plane!

Then we were driving through the gates, then the man was checking our name was on the list, then we were parking in the special space that had been allocated for us. It was like an out-of-body experience and, despite my anxiety, a long-forgotten feeling stirred – excitement. For months – though it felt more like for ever – my positive feelings seemed to have been running on half-power; I hadn't been able to spark up any genuine unbridled joy or excitement.

But I couldn't get too carried away, because I knew how important this was to Emily's life. She was nearly out of money and chances, and she'd be going back to rainy Ireland and working as a checkout girl if she didn't pull this one off.

Then we were walking through the glass doors — for a moment, I thought Emily was going to faint. Then we were looking at posters on the wall of box-office-breaking movies the studio had produced — which was my cue to think that *I* might faint. Then we were introducing ourselves to the nauseatingly thin, beautiful, unfriendly receptionist hidden behind the enormous flower arrangement on the curved wooden desk. As soon as she heard Emily's name, her implacable expression lit up.

'Hiiiiii. I'm Tiffany. I love your script,' she said warmly.

'You've read it?' I was impressed. Even the receptionist had read it.

A startled, caught-in-the-headlights look skipped across Tiffany's gorgeous face, and when she spoke she sounded as though she'd been inhaling helium. 'Sure,' she squeaked nervously. 'Sure. I'll tell Mr Russell you're here.'

As Tiffany clicked down the marble-floored hall, Emily said, between angry lips, 'She hasn't read it.'

'But she —'

'*No one* has read it. Except the person whose job it is to reduce 190 pages of screenplay to three lines.'

'Shush, she's coming back.'

'Mr Russell will see you now,' Tiffany said.

Emily and I rose slowly and followed her back down the hall, passing more framed posters of famous movies as we went. My ears pounded and there was a loose-hinged wobbliness about my knees. I couldn't even begin to imagine how Emily must feel. So much depended on this.

Tiffany opened a door into a tastefully understated room, where three men and a dinky blonde girl — Fli? — were grouped around a table. They stood up and one of them, all teeth and tan, extended his hand and announced himself to be Mort Russell. He was a lot younger than I had expected, but he had that fear-generating charisma that very powerful people have.

'Emily O'Keeffe,' he proclaimed, making it sound like an accolade.

'Guilty as charged.' Emily stepped forward with a confident smile, and I relaxed just a tiny bit. She seemed to have a handle on things.

After Mort had loved-up Emily a little, he introduced her to the other people there. The girl was indeed Fli and the two other men were vice-presidents of some ilk. Which wasn't necessarily as impressive as it sounds. In the States, you could be a tea lady and be called Vice-President of Beverage Providing. (Indeed, I'd once been a vice-president myself.)

Then Emily shoved me and my empty folder at them and they professed themselves to be 'So, *so* happy' to meet me. You'd swear it was one of the nicest things that had ever happened to them.

'Nice to meet you,' I replied. I was under strict instructions to say nothing else.

Coffee was offered and accepted – no Hobnobs, or bikkies of any kind, unfortunately, but other than that the mood around the table was friendly and informal, and the four of them couldn't have been nicer. Loudly, enthusiastically, they all professed how much they loved *Plastic Money*.

'It's, ah . . .' Mort sketched a shape in the air. 'Gimme a word,' he ordered one of his boys.

'Edgy.'

'Yeah, edgy.'

'But commercial,' the other provided.

'Oh yeah, gotta be commercial.'

'And funny,' the first one supplied.

'Funny is good. We *like* funny. So pitch it to me,' he suddenly ordered Emily.

'Sure.' She smiled around the table, shook back her hair and started. 'I'm thinking *Thelma and Louise* meets *Snatch* meets . . .'

To my horror, you could actually *hear* how dry her mouth was. Every word was accompanied by a type of clicking noise as she unpeeled her tongue from her hard palate.

Fli slid a glass of water towards her.

'Water,' Emily explained, with a goofy grin, before taking a quick gulp from it. Then, to my giddy relief, the velcroey sounds stopped and suddenly she was like a hare let out of a trap.

All the practice had been worth it. She did her 'twenty-five words or less' summary. Then she did a longer description of everything that happens, and even though I'd heard it all before, she was so good that for a moment or two I almost forgot where I was and nearly enjoyed myself.

She finished by saying, 'It's going to make a great movie!'

'All right!'

They all clapped and I wondered if I should join in or whether it would be seen as applauding myself, but they'd finished before I could decide.

Then Mort spoke, and I could hardly believe the words that came out of his mouth. 'I see this as a big, BIG movie.'

A thrill flamed through my entire body and I shot the fastest look at Emily. Her smile was restrained.

Above his head, Mort made a screen shape with his hands and we all obediently looked up at it. 'Big budget, big stars. Seventy million dollars, minimum. I see Julia Roberts and Cameron Diaz. Am I right?'

The others all nodded enthusiastically, so I did too.

'Who're we gonna get to direct our movie?' Mort asked the lads.

They named a couple of Oscar winners. Then came talk of fast-tracking it, green-lighting it, opening on three thousand screens across the country. It was the most exhilarating thing that had ever happened to me. Then we were shaking hands and Mort was promising that he was looking forward to working with me.

As Emily and I walked back down the hall, I literally couldn't feel my feet.

Another flurry of goodbyes in reception, then we were walking away. Aware of their eyes on our backs, neither of us said anything. I was shaking with unexpressed elation. Still in silence, we got into the car, where Emily lit a cigarette and sucked at it, like it was a thick milkshake coming through a narrow straw.

'Well?' I eventually said, and waited for the pair of us to SCREECH and hug with excitement.

'Well,' she said, consideringly.

'But that was fantastic! You heard the man! Julia Roberts! Cameron Diaz! Three thousand screens!'

'Don't forget, Maggie, that I've been here before.'

I thought she was being very negative and told her. 'So now what happens?'

'Now we wait.'

'Now we wait,' I repeated, feeling cheated and resentful.

'Mind you,' she conceded, 'we could get drunk while we're doing it.'

18

An impromptu party was what was called for, Emily decided. She spent the drive home with her phone clamped between her shoulder and ear, inviting people over. 'I don't know if we're celebrating,' she kept saying. 'But we're definitely partying.'

Lara was under instructions to come round at six, to accompany Emily to the Liquor Locker to buy up the place. Every time I saw Emily spending money, I got a pang of anxiety, but this time for once felt no worry. The good times they were a-coming.

We were home by five-thirty. As I hung up Lara's suit, I asked Emily if tonight's do would be a dress and heels affair.

'Christ, no. Shorts and bare feet.'

Shorts and bare feet it was. While she waited for Lara, Emily tapped and fidgeted distractedly. Then her face fixed on a thought.

'Look,' she said defensively. 'There's something I want to do. Don't laugh, but will you run in to Mike and tell him to come with his smudge stick?'

'I won't laugh,' I assured her earnestly, 'because I haven't a clue what you're talking about.'

'Mike, next door – beardy New Ager?'

'Oh, Bill Bryson? Go on.'

'He's always offering to banish the negative energy in here. It's called smudging. I just feel that maybe I'd have a better chance of getting good news if the house was full of positive vibes.'

I didn't laugh. Instead I felt the full force of her terror. She must be out of her mind with worry to contemplate doing something she had such contempt for.

'Will you go?'

I was happy to. Constant activity was keeping me one step ahead of myself. Sooner or later, I knew the bubble would burst and I'd be flung down hard against the ground. But not just yet. So out I went and rang next-door's bell, but no one came. I rang again, and still the door remained unanswered. Then I gave the large wind-chime which hung in the porch a smack, setting off a mad tinny jingling, but that got no response either. At this stage any sensible person would have given up, but the thing was I knew he was there. I knew he was there because I could *see* him. There was a big pane of glass in the front door, through which he was clearly visible, sitting on a floor cushion, making 'O' shapes with his thumbs and middle fingers. I'd just decided to leave and promise Emily I'd get him for her another time when I saw him get to his feet and amble to the door.

'Hi,' he smiled. 'I was finishing a meditation. Come in.'

To my surprise there was no flurry of 'Sorry to keep you waiting's. Maybe spiritual people don't apologize.

I stepped into the dim room, to be hit by a sweet smell. Rose oil? Or lavender? How would I know? In the background I could hear the plinking of more wind-chimes. From somewhere else came the rush of running water, which in any other house I'd assume was from a burst pipe – but, somehow, not here.

Dreamcatchers dangled from the windows, embroidered throws decorated the chairs, and wooden carvings – mostly of men with bulging eyes and disproportionately large penises –

hung on the walls. Every object looked like it meant something, and from the odd placing of the furniture I was prepared to bet that the place had been Feng Shuied to within an inch of its life.

'Hi, Bill,' I said.

'Mike,' he corrected, with a gentle smile.

Cripes! 'Oh, sorry, Mike. Emily sent me.'

'She'd like to be smudged?' It sounded like he'd been expecting this. 'I'll get my stick.'

The effect of the house – the smells, the sounds, even the men with the big mickeys – was immensely consoling, and as we left I said as much.

'It's a safe place,' Mike agreed, slamming the front door behind him with such force that it sent the porch wind-chime swinging away with a wild jangle. Just as quickly it was penduluming its way back – and heading directly for my face. Before I knew what was happening, it had delivered a smart belt to my right eye: pain shot through my socket, red exploded behind my eyelids and all I could hear was a riot of discordant notes – like a broken piano.

'Whoops. Shouldn'ta slammed the door,' Mike laughed softly. 'Y'OK?'

'Great!' I exclaimed, wondering if I'd been blinded, acting the way you have to act when you get injured in front of someone you don't know very well. Even if your head falls off you have to say things like, 'Just a scratch! Besides, I never use it much anyway!'

As it happened, I *was* fine. My eye watered a bit, then stopped. But I felt very close to tears and maybe Mike was aware of it, because he held my arm as we walked the short distance between the two houses.

Emily let us in and, clearly torn between embarrassment and vulnerability, she explained her situation.

'Sure,' Mike said cheerfully. 'Is now a good time?'

'How long will it take?'

He sucked his teeth and shook his head regretfully, just like a swizz-merchant builder would. All that was missing was a cigarette tucked behind his ear.

'Let me guess, you haven't got the parts,' I heard Emily mutter.

'Sure I have!' He waggled his stick and Emily had the good grace to pinken. 'But the energy in here is so bad one session won't clear it. But, hey! Twenty minutes now and we're ahead of the game, right?'

Intrigued, we watched him carry out his juju. Smudging appeared to involve lighting tapers, waving the stick into corners of rooms, muttering incantations and doing a type of hopping Red-Indian-on-the-Warpath dance.

'You know, you don't need me, you could do this yourself,' Mike panted at Emily, his belly rising and falling with each hop.

'Ah, I'd never get the dancing right.'

'But the dancing is optional!'

After Mike finished, he assured Emily with great kindness, 'This'll give you a fighting chance, but if they don't buy your movie, it's not the end of the world.'

'It IS the end of the world.' Emily was very firm on this.

Mike laughed gently, much the same way he had after I'd been savaged by his wind-chime. 'Be careful what you wish for – you might get it,' he said, then left, promising to drop in later with Charmaine.

Not long after, Lara arrived and Emily went out with her to buy the drink.

'Can't I come?' I asked, discovering how very reluctant I was to be left on my own.

'But you don't have a connoisseur's interest in alcohol, the way Lara and I do,' Emily said. 'And we need someone here to let people in.'

'Woman sits alone in room,' I said, resentfully. 'Unhappy. Clearly abandoned by friends.'

Lara laughed but Emily replied, 'Camera tracks her as she gets up, opens a couple of bags of peanuts and fires them into bowls in order to be helpful.'

I was sure that no one would arrive while they were out, but they'd only been gone five minutes when Troy walked in.

'Hey, Irish!'

'Young man, casually dressed,' I said.

Troy stood by the door, his poker face confused.

'Stands by door, looking confused,' I said.

'Crosses room,' Troy replied, quick as a flash. 'Notices girl has had her hair done. "Cute," he says.'

I laughed, delighted at how fast he'd got it.

His straight-line mouth quirked in acknowledgement. 'Coming right back atcha!' He threw himself into a chair, and flung his leg over the arm with loose-limbed ease. 'So how'd it go today?'

I sat on the day bed, my legs stretched out in front of me, and related everything that had happened in Mort Russell's office. All the time, Troy watched me, nodding intently when I mentioned anything good.

'Were they all lying when they said they'd read her script?' I asked.

'No. If they've seen a twelve-line résumé, they honestly think they've read it. For real.'

'So what do you think?' I finished with, keen to hear something other than Emily's negativity.

'Could be good.' But he sounded more thoughtful than hopeful. 'Could be good.'

He lapsed into faraway silence, and into the quiet I asked, 'Where do you live?'

'Hollywood.' He pronounced it 'Hoh-hollywooooood,' and spread his fingers to demonstrate sarcastically the name in lights. 'Only the name is glamorous. Sketchy neighbourhood, which means rents are low.'

'And is that far from here? I've no idea where anywhere is in relation to anywhere else in LA.'

'I'll show you.' He unfolded himself from his chair and came to balance on the bottom of the day bed.

'OK, this is the ocean.' He pointed to a cushion. 'This is Third Street Promenade, and you live here.' He jabbed at a spot on the day bed. 'Make a left on to Lincoln and drive for, oh, 'bout a mile.' He dragged his finger in a line along the fabric. 'Excuse me,' he said, as his finger bumped up on to my bare shin. 'Until you get to the freeway entrance. Take the 10, going east.' His finger did an abrupt left turn and was no longer crossing my shin, but was whizzing up to my knee. I was a little surprised, but he didn't seem to think it was a big deal, so I took my cue from him.

He paused, with his finger on my knee. 'Then when you get to downtown, you change on to the 101, going north.' Now his finger was speeding up the bare skin of my thigh. 'To Cahuenga Pass, which is about here.' He paused, his finger resting unnervingly near the top of my thigh. 'Actually, no, more like here.' He moved his finger marginally higher. 'Then,' he took a breath, his expression determinedly innocent, 'you make a right.' His finger curved on to the soft, hidden skin of my inner thigh. We both looked down at his hand, then quickly looked up at each other again. 'Just for a coupla blocks.' His matter-of-fact tone was confusing. He was giving me directions, right? But his hand was between my legs.

'And I live right here.' He demonstrated his whereabouts by gently circling the tip of his finger on my tender white flesh. 'Just here,' he repeated, continuing to stroke the inside of my thigh.

'Thank you.' I was sure he could feel the heat coming at him from down there.

'You know what?' His smile was suddenly wicked. 'I live pretty near to the Hollywood Bowl, but if I showed you where it was, I bet you'd slap my face.'

It took a moment to understand what he was talking about.

'Prob'ly,' I managed, while a small, sweet spasm jumped from my Hollywood Bowl.

One final touch from his feather-light fingertip, a regretful look at my denim crotch, then he was getting to his feet. 'Do you want a beer?' he asked as he headed to the kitchen.

Tons of people came. There wasn't even time for the obligatory standing around in the empty house, looking at the acres of drink, feeling fearful and friendless, the way people usually do when they have a party.

One of the first to arrive was Nadia, Lara's new girlfriend. She was a lollipop girl, her head big with dark, swingy hair, her limbs shrunken sticks. I wasn't surprised by her sexy glamour – after all, meeting Lara had dissolved my subconscious preconception that all lesbians look like Elton John – but I was surprised by the instant dislike I took to her. Two seconds after being introduced, she snapped gum in my face and confided loudly, 'Right this afternoon, I got me a Playboy wax. There is totally not one pube left on me!'

'Lovely!' I said, mildly mortified. 'Will you have a peanut?'

She shook her enormous head, barely drawing breath before launching into an account of how she'd had to get on her hands and knees and stick her butt high in the air so that the beautician could properly get at her. Then she'd had to lie on her back and put her ankles behind her head. They'd tell you *anything*, these Angelenos. Compulsive Disclosure Disorder, that's what they had.

Then came Justin and Desiree, who brought two jockish men and three dogs with them. They'd all become friends when they'd gone to the dog park, trying to meet girls. Next at the door was Emily's friend Connie, a short, strident, bandy-legged Korean-American: sexy the way very sure-of-themselves people are sexy. She was accompanied by her sister Debbie, her friends Philip and Tremain, and her fiancé Lewis, who barely spoke – I suppose she was such a great talker that his ability had simply atrophied. This was the first time I'd actually met Connie, and I hadn't wanted to; something to do with her imminent wedding. Emily had been my bridesmaid and she was going to be Connie's too, and I felt on the wrong side of the being-married divide. Connie had a happy future ahead of her, while my happy future was far behind me.

Tendrilly Kirsty showed up and unsettled me by making a beeline for Troy. Mike and Charmaine showed up too, as well as a load more people whom I didn't know from a plate of chips. Even David Crowe dropped in briefly, charmed his way past everyone, then left again.

'He didn't stay long,' I remarked.

'Are you kidding me?' Emily grabbed Troy away from Kirsty and ordered him, 'Tell her the joke. The agent joke.'

Deadpan, Troy began. 'Man gets a visit from the cops. "We've bad news, sir," they say. "Someone broke into your house and killed your wife and child." The man is distraught and says, "Who could do such a terrible thing?" And the cop goes, "I'm sorry to have to tell you, sir, that it was your agent." And the man says, "My agent? My agent came by my house?! Oh boy!"'

'See?' Emily said.

'I see.'

The house was full and the party had spilled out into the backyard. Somehow, in the warm, twinkly-blue night, I ended up in conversation with Troy and Kirsty. Kirsty had just been to a two-hour power yoga class and was extolling the benefits of exercise, when I said vaguely that I really should go to a gym while I was in LA. To my astonishment, Kirsty said, 'That's a neat idea.' She looked me up and down and concluded, 'You could drop, say, five, six pounds.' She swept a critical gaze from my feet to my upper arms. 'And you could use some toning. It's worth doing,' she said with utmost seriousness. 'I mean, look at me. I work out and I –' she did a little wiggle of her little hips, 'am in purr-itty good shape.'

OK, so most of it was for Troy's benefit and it was probably all true. Of course I'd be delighted if I woke up one morning and found I'd miraculously lost half a stone during the night – who wouldn't? But nevertheless, I was speechless. I'd never before come across a woman who claimed, by her own admission, to be in good shape – I thought it was simply Not Allowed. That you say it about everyone else, whether it's true or not, while berating yourself for being a hippo/heifer/Jabba the Hutt, even if you've been on the grapefruit diet for the past month.

All right, maybe it's dishonest, but it somehow seems less offensive.

In that moment, I hated Kirsty so much I wanted to hit her, and for the first time in ages I got a stab of pain up into my back tooth. Even though I'd only spoken to her to prevent her having a one-on-one with Troy, I had to get away. Muttering some excuse, I promptly got buttonholed by Charmaine.

She was nice, if a little intense. Yes, she stood just a teensy, weensy bit too close to me, and whenever I moved back a little, she moved forward a little more, until my head was almost fully immersed in a lilac bush, with only my nose peeping out, but no one's perfect. She wasn't exactly a laugh a minute, but I got the feeling she was broadly sympathetic to me, so I ended up telling her about me and Garv.

'Do you still love him?' she asked kindly.

'I don't know,' I said despairingly. 'How would I know?'

'How did you know when you were sure?'

'Dunno. It just sneaks up on you, doesn't it?'

'No one event?'

'No.' But then I remembered something. 'The snail!' I exclaimed.

'Huh?'

I explained. Garv, being a man, had been the one in charge of all insect removal: spiders in the bath, moths around lights, wasps on window-sills were all his department. I never used to lift a finger, just used to yell, 'Gaaarv, there's a wasp!' and he'd come with his rolled-up newspaper and do battle. But he had a thing about snails, a bad thing; he was so grossed out about them, he was almost phobic. And when we'd been going out about six months, a snail crawled up his car's windscreen, then settled in for what looked like a long stay. (On the driver's side, too, at eye-level just to make it worse for Garv.) A high-speed burn along the dual carriageway didn't budge it, so in the end I put on some rubber gloves, lifted it off and threw it at a passing Nissan Micra, packed with nuns. I wasn't wild about snails either, but I did it because I loved Garv, and ever since then I'd been head of snail extermination.

'So right now, would you remove a snail from his wind-screen?'

'Probably not.'

'There's your answer.'

'Right.' That made me improbably sad.

Then – emboldened by drink – I made some reference to Charmaine reading auras.

'Yes,' she said.

'Do you?'

'Yes,' she repeated.

'So what's mine like?'

'Are you really sure you want to know?'

Well, after that I *really* wanted to know.

'It's a little toxic,' she said.

All of a sudden I was upset, despite the fact that I didn't actually believe that I – or anyone else, for that matter – even *had* an aura.

'Toxic – that's bad, isn't it?'

'Good and bad are just labels.'

That old cop-out.

'You should learn not to be so judgement-based,' she instructed, in a manner which sounded very judgemental.

I disentangled my head from the lilac bush and went back inside, to discover that the Goatee Boys had got wind of the knees-up. They had commandeered the stereo – replacing

Madonna with some Death Metal racket – and had formed an impromptu mosh-pit in a corner of the front room. Luis, the small, dark, pretty one, showed a great aptitude for moshing. While the others just ran straight at each other and violently bounced stomachs, Luis invested his moves with delicate steps and socket-defying hip-swervage.

To my surprise, beardy Mike was in the thick of it, having what looked like the time of his life. I suppose he had the belly for it. Every time he gave someone a good mosh, he sent them flying halfway across the room. A particularly enthusiastic bump scooted little Luis several feet and he only stopped when he crashed into a chair.

Once they'd picked him up and established that he wasn't badly hurt, they tried body surfing, passing one of them over the heads of the others, but it all fell apart when they tried to hoist Mike up and found they couldn't.

They dispersed, to reveal the shaven-headed one, Ethan, in a corner, gloomily bent over the coffee table. Because he had the most hardcore goatee – a pointy, satanic beard and a long, Zapata-style moustache that extended to his chin – I'd always thought of him as the leader of the other lads. Closer inspection revealed that he was playing with a penknife. He had his hand splayed, palm down, on the table and he was flinging the penknife at the table, aiming between his fingers. Sometimes he missed his hand but, as evidenced by the cuts between his fingers, sometimes he didn't.

'Stop it!' I exclaimed.

'It's my hand, man.'

'But it's Emily's table!'

'I'm bummed out, man.' Mournfully, he looked up at me. 'This is what I do when I'm bummed out.'

'But –' I said helplessly, worried about the table. Then I had a solution. 'If you want to self-harm, could you not try burning yourself with cigarettes?'

'Smoking, ew! Totally gross.' He sounded mortally offended.

It transpired that he was hurting because he'd tried to get off with Nadia and she'd spurned him. But as soon as I told him she was gay, he brightened. 'Yeah? For real? With Lara? Oh, wow, man. What do they do?'

Something I'd been wondering myself, actually.

'I don't know,' I said sternly. 'And leave the table alone!'

Back out to the garden to check on Troy and Kirsty. They were still talking to each other. Before I could decide how I felt, Lara and Nadia, arm in arm, skipped over to me.

'Having a good time?' Lara beamed.

'Yes . . .' I trailed off, as Nadia snaked her hand under Lara's arm and began caressing her breast.

'Hey!' Lara laughed. 'Cut that out.'

Nadia withdrew her hand but only to lick her finger and recommence stroking. Lara's erect nipple appeared through the damp cotton and I felt acutely uncomfortable. If a man did that at a party everyone would loudly condemn him as a lech and a gobshite, but because Nadia was a lesbian I had to behave as if I was totally down with it.

All night, I was aware of Kirsty talking to Troy. Even when I couldn't see them, I could sense their closeness and it didn't make me happy. So the high point of my evening was that they didn't leave together. She effed off around midnight and I was hard put not to stand in the middle of the road, roaring after her car, 'You can't be in *that* good a shape, now can you?'

Troy stayed quite a bit longer and when he finally left I

half-expected a special goodbye. But he kissed Emily and said, 'Baby girl, we'll talk,' then he kissed me in exactly the same friendly way and said, 'Night, Irish.'

Bit by bit, the crowds drained away until it was nearly just Emily and me left. While we were arranging all the bottles to be recycled, sweeping the splinters off the coffee table, wrapping broken glasses in newspaper, I blurted – the drink talking, 'I've a confession to make. I have a . . . crush.' Yes, that was the right word. 'Troy. I find him attractive.'

'Take a number and get in line.'

'Oh. It's like that?'

She pointed her finger, winked and said in an Elvis-type voice, 'Don't fall in love with me baby, 'cos I'll only break your heart.'

'Don't tell me he said that!'

'Not as such.' She seemed amused. 'It's just the way he acts. You'd swear everyone's mad about him . . . Although,' said with less certainty, 'maybe they are.'

'But he has a big nose,' I protested.

'Don't seem to bother the ladies none.'

'What ladies?'

'With Troy there are always ladies.'

'Are you talking about Kirsty?'

'Sure.'

'But do you know for a fact that there's something going on with them?'

'*Intuitively*, I know for a fact.'

Then I got it. 'Has anything ever happened with *you* and Troy?'

'Me and Troy?' She began to laugh. It started as a quite normal chuckle, then progressed to where she was leaning on the kitchen counter. 'Sorry,' she said, her face contorted with hysterics. 'It's just . . . the idea of me. Me and Troy!'

She was off again. I picked up a bin liner and started flinging cans into it.

Later, in bed, I thought about Troy. I'd been surprised, indeed almost put out, when he'd touched my leg. But now I thought about it differently. I savoured the memory, replaying it again and again. The heat of his hand running up my bare skin, the leap of desire at the moment his finger had reached the top of my thigh and turned inwards. Again. His finger reaching the top of my thigh and turning inwards, his finger reaching the top of my thigh and turning inwards . . .

A dreamy weakness began to steal through me. I'll take my chances, I thought. I've played it safe for too long. I *will* fall in love with him and he's *welcome* to break my heart.

In that halfway state between waking and sleeping, my defences slipped for a moment and in rushed thoughts of Garv and Truffle Woman and their public displays of affection.

Immediately I thought of Troy.

'Ha!' I said to myself, with sleepy defiance.

19

It must have been all that talk of falling in love, because that night I had The Dream. I'd had it on and off since I'd been eighteen: maybe once a year, perhaps not even that often, and it was nearly always the same. I'd spot Shay Delaney in a crowded street and I'd start running and pushing, trying to catch up with him. Above the January-sales throng I'd see the back of his head, moving further and faster away from me, and I'd try to go quicker, but more and more people would get in the way, tangling themselves in my legs, tripping me up, blocking my path, until he was gone.

I used to wake up swollen with longing, dreamy with re-membered love, irritable and snappy with Garv. For the entire day following the dream, these feelings would wrap themselves around me like a hangover, and it was only once they'd worn off that I worried about them. I hardly thought about Shay from one end of the year to the next, but did these dreams mean that I still loved him? That I didn't love Garv?

Consolation came via an unexpected route: a science pro-gramme I watched one bored Sunday evening, maybe eight or nine years ago. It was about the earth's relationship with the sun. The commentary said that even in the depths of winter, when our side of the earth is facing away from the sun, its draw is so powerful that we're still pulled to it. Once in a while the cold side of the earth gets its way, which is why we sometimes get days of bizarre warmth and sunniness in the middle of February.

Maybe I'd misheard it, because when I thought about it properly it didn't really make much sense, but it still operated as a consolation: a weight lifted from me and I understood that of course I loved Garv, but that there were times when I'd still be drawn back to Shay. It didn't mean anything.

But this night the dream was different, because when it started it was Shay I was running after, but at some stage he became Garv. I ran as hard after Garv as I ever had done after Shay. It was so important to catch up with him, I was tender, *sore* with love for him – that giddy, lifting wonder of when we'd first fallen in love. I *remembered*, I felt it with such clarity. But he slipped through the crowds and my legs wouldn't go fast enough, then he was gone. And I awoke with tears on my lashes, carrying years' worth of loss.

In the sunny kitchen, Emily was already up and hyper with it. 'I've been awake since six,' she announced. 'Waiting for that phone to ring!'

Oh, right, news of her pitch. The dream was still with me, so I was finding it hard to be present in the here and now. I was like a badly tuned radio which was picking up two frequencies. One in the foreground, another more ghostly one fading in and out in the background.

'But it's only nine now,' seemed to be the right thing to say. 'They're hardly likely to be at work.'

'Lazy, LAZY bastards! Anyway, Mort has David's home number – he could have called him last night or early this morning, if he was very keen. Every second that passes without news is another nail in the coffin.'

'You're being overdramatic. Is there any coffee?'

Two mugs of muscular coffee managed to shake away some of the wraiths that were wrapped around my mood, and life came into clearer focus.

'This place doesn't look bad, considering we had thirty people here last night, drinking their heads off. You'd hardly know.'

'Yeah,' said Emily. 'Apart from the souvenir on our couch.'

Oh cripes! A cigarette burn? Or had someone puked? Had anyone been that drunk? Could have been a bulimic, mind you.

'Worse,' Emily said. 'It's Ethan. I don't know how we missed him last night. I've already tried waking him up and he growled at me like a dog. Little prick.'

Sure enough, Ethan was curled up on the couch, clutching his penknife between his paw-like hands, five o'clock shadow bristling on his skull. In slumber his goateed, bemetalled face was sweet.

'That boy needs to get home to shave his head. Give him a kick,' Emily urged.

'Couldn't we just shake him?'

'More fun to kick him.'

'OK.' I tried a tentative jab on his shin, but he shifted and muttered something about nailing my motherfucking head to the table.

I looked enquiringly at Emily. 'Best leave him for a while,' we agreed over-enthusiastically. 'A young man needs his sleep. More coffee.' We headed back to the kitchen.

On top of the fridge was an open bottle of white wine that we'd missed in last night's clear-up. I noticed that a cork was still wound around the corkscrew. That could be used to seal the bottle for later.

'Pass me the sesame,' I said to Emily.

A long stare from Emily, and a bottle of sesame oil arrived in front of me. I looked at it, realized what I'd done, and saw that she was already subjecting me to an are-you-quite-sane examination.

'What d'you want sesame oil for? To stir-fry your raisin bran?'

'Ah no, I meant can you pass me the corkscrew.'

'That's not what you said. You said "sesame". Unless I'm going mad, and I'm really not in the mood for that.'

I contemplated lying – it'd be easy enough to convince her she was halfway around the bend – but saw how unkind that would be. 'It's just a word. That Garv and I used to say,' I explained, awkwardly. 'When we opened a bottle of wine, we'd say "Open Sesame". So the corkscrew got called "sesame". I'm sorry, I forgot.'

'Is that why you keep putting my toothpaste on my toothbrush for me every night? It's something you and Garv did?'

'Wh-at?' I stuttered.

'Every night since you've got here,' she said patiently, 'after you've gone to bed, I've gone to the bathroom and my toothbrush is waiting, with toothpaste on it. If you're not doing it, then who is?'

I had to admit it. 'It is me. I hadn't realized I was doing it. I can't believe it.'

'And it's something you and Garv did?'

'Yeah. Whichever one of us went to bed first would get the toothbrush ready for the other person.'

'That's the sweetest thing I ever heard,' Emily glowed, then quickly quenched it when she saw my face.

The grief I'd felt when I'd woken up was back. I was carrying the full weight of a lost language and all the rituals that would mean nothing to anyone else, but were part of whatever had bound Garv and me together. And there were loads of them: when he made my dinner and put it on the table, I had to rush into the room and declare, 'I came as soon as I heard!' And if I forgot, he'd withhold the nosh and prompt me, 'Say it. Go on – I came as soon as I heard!'

Trying to explain why that was funny or comforting would be like trying to describe colour to a blind person. Not that I'd ever have to, because now it was all gone. An entire way of life.

Clearly, I was pumping out waves of regret, because Emily urged, 'It's OK to say it.'

'Say what?'

'That you miss him. Even *I* miss him.'

'OK,' I sighed. 'I miss him.'

But I missed more than him. I missed me. I missed the way it used to be, when I didn't have to pretend to be anything other than me. Now there were all these people around, and I was tired of having to act. Even with Emily I wasn't as fully me as I once was with Garv. And it showed up in the smallest of things, like the telly being on too loud. With Garv I'd just roar at him and he'd turn it down, but with Emily I had to keep my mouth shut and burn holes in the lining of my stomach instead.

'I had a dream,' I announced. I sounded like Martin Luther King.

'Tell me,' Emily said, then thought to add, 'Marty.'

'Well, you know the plot already.'

'Is this the Shay Delaney dream?'

'Yes, and it started with me running after Shay, but he turned into Garv.' I described the frantic running, the desperate need to catch up with him, the terror as he slipped further and further away, the bereft grief when I understood that he was gone. 'So, go on,' I ended. 'Make me feel better.'

Emily's very good at that sort of thing.

'We process things in our dreams that we're not able to in our waking hours,' she said. 'You were married for nine years, of course you feel shite. The end of any relationship is a wrench. I mean, even after I've been going with someone for three months, I feel suicidal when it's over. Unless I ditch them. Then I'm over the moon.'

I was beginning to feel a good deal more normal, then Emily ruined it all by asking, 'Is there any chance, though, that maybe you and Garv could try again?'

The room seemed to darken.

'I know he's had an affair,' Emily said.

'Having,' I corrected. 'He's *having* an affair.'

'It could be over, for all you know.'

'I don't care. The damage is done. I'd never be able to trust him again.'

'But it could be worked out – other people have done it.'

'I don't want to. Since February . . . I can't describe it, Emily. It was like . . . like being locked in a car boot with him.'

'Jesus!' she said, startled at my imagery. I was quite startled myself, to be honest. I'm not normally good at that sort of thing.

'A car boot that was shrinking,' I added, just to outdo myself.

Emily gasped, her hands to her throat. 'I can't breathe!'

'That's exactly how I felt,' I said thoughtfully. 'Anyway, I'm just having a bad day . . . Another one,' I added.

'Let it go, man,' a dopey voice interrupted. It was Ethan, leaning against the door frame, clearly enthralled. 'If it don't come back, it was never yours. If it comes back, it's yours to keep.'

'Out!' Emily ordered, her arm straight, her finger pointing. 'We've enough armchair philosophers around here.'

As he loped to the door, Emily checked the time again. 'David has *got* to be at his desk by now!'

And he was – but he couldn't really tell her anything. As was his way, he made positive noises. 'They really loved you!' But she wanted hard news. A yes or no. Are they in or are they out? And he couldn't tell her.

'He's scared,' she surmised, hanging up the phone.

'Why would he be scared?' I forced joviality.

''Cos this town runs on fear. If Hothouse pass, it'll reflect badly on him and his lousy judgement in backing a loser. Makes him a loser by association.'

Food for thought. I'd always thought of agents as kind of impartial catalysts. Middlemen who brought people together but who remained unaffected by the process. I'd been wrong.

'And Mort Russell is probably scared that if he buys it, the head of the studio mightn't like it,' she continued gloomily. 'And scared that if he *doesn't* buy it, someone else might and make a hit of it. Meanwhile, I'm fucking terrified that *no one* will buy it. How do you feel, Maggie?'

I checked my anxiety levels. Same as they always were. 'Scared stiff.'

'Welcome to Hollywood.'

A ring on the doorbell had us making enquiring faces at each other. Emily nearly broke her neck skidding across the floor, spurred on by visions of Mort Russell standing on her doorstep holding a your-worries-are-over cheque.

But it wasn't Mort Russell, it was Luis, one of the Goatee Boys. Up until now, they'd only existed for me as a blur of interchangeable facial hair, but at last night's party they'd come into separate focus. There were indeed only three of them. Ethan: big, meaty and shaven-headed. Curtis: blondy, balding, plumpish, with the least impressive goatee of the lot. It was wispy and flyaway, as though he'd been crawling under a bed and had got a load of fluff stuck to his chin. I found something slightly odd about him, but that might just have been because Ethan had told me that in high school Curtis had been voted pupil 'Most likely to go postal in a public place with an automatic weapon.'

And, standing in front of me, Luis. Neat, pretty – and polite! He'd come to thank us for the party and to invite us over for dinner some time. He claimed to be an excellent cook – a result, apparently, of his Columbian heritage. 'Call by whenever,' he invited.

'Sure.' Emily brusquely closed the door.

'Don't you want to?' I asked.

She rolled her eyes at me. 'Oh, come on!'

Muttering something about being thirty-three and not fifteen, she grabbed the phone and spent several unbroken hours on it, hopping from call waiting to call waiting, discussing the pitch, having the same conversation again and again, speculating and, in effect, saying nothing.

I could have gone to the beach or reverse-shopping – I'd decided to return the embroidered denim skirt, because when I tried it on at home it made my knees look funny – but instead I listlessly watched a telly evangelist, weighed down by the return of my earlier, regret-filled mood. I thought about Garv. He'd had a lot of good points. But then again, plenty of bad points. They ping-ponged around so much in my head that in the end I grabbed one of Emily's yellow pads and wrote them all down.

List of Good things about Garv

1. Understanding exchange rates and the plots of thrillers.
2. Having a lovely, tiny bottom. (It was really gorgeous, especially in combats.)
3. Thinking I am the most beautiful woman on the planet. (Though he probably doesn't any more.)
4. Seeing the good in everyone. (Except for my family.)
5. Doing his own ironing.
6. Bringing me to jazz concerts and such like, to further my cultural education.

List of Bad things about Garv

1. Bringing me to jazz concerts and such like, to further my cultural education.
2. Loving football and being proud of me because he thinks I understand the offside rule. (I don't.)
3. The electric blanket business, obviously.
4. And the way he was about my hair.
5. Not talking to me about Things. (I know all men refuse to talk about Things and shrug, 'Ah sure, we're grand,' when a nine-year marriage is falling apart, but it still distressed me.)
6. Sleeping with other women.

But my childish list of facts made no impact on my gloom. I still felt spooked – heavy with sorrow and a hope-flattening sense that I was a failure. That I was a mess and my life was a mess. And my future was a mess. And my past was *definitely* a mess.

Realizing that the day was shaping up to be a write-off, I

took a towel out to the backyard for a spot of sunbathing, and within seconds I was mercifully asleep.

I awoke choking on a jet of water – the sprinklers had started – and came back inside to find Emily still on the phone. She was getting directions from someone. 'Oh, I know it. The block where all the plastic surgeons are? Right.' She hung up. 'Coming out for dinner tonight?'

'Who'll be there?' I tried to sound casual.

'Lara, Nadia, Justin, Desiree, you and me.'

No Troy?

'Troy's got to work,' she said kindly, sensing my unasked question. 'He's meeting some producer guy. And you know what he's like about his work.'

I didn't, but anyway. I was disappointed – and still no word from Mort Russell. Although, while I'd been asleep, Helen had phoned. I was touched by her concern. Until I discovered there wasn't any. All she'd done was try to discuss sexy surfers with Emily. 'And she wouldn't believe me when I said I didn't know any!'

As we drove through the dazzling evening to Beverly Hills, we came upon a little commotion outside a mini-mall. Two boys were being arrested. They had their hands on the roof of the black and white and one officer was frisking them, while another swung handcuffs, ready for use. I'd never before seen someone being arrested. It gave me a little living-on-the-edge thrill, of which I was immediately ashamed.

The restaurant was mostly outdoors, the tables beneath a pretty green and white striped awning, separated from the street by a white trellis. Nadia and Lara were already waiting at our street-side table. As Emily and I wove through the tables to get to them, I felt there was something slightly odd about the place, but I couldn't put my finger on it until Justin arrived, Desiree trotting by his side.

'Thanks a lot, guys.' Thin-lipped and high-pitched, Justin chided Lara and Nadia. 'You invite me to a dyke restaurant. I could get lynched.'

And then I realized what was so strange: the clientele were all women. Justin was literally the only man. Suddenly the open staring, the two winks and the one wide smile I'd received all made sense. And I was beset with anxiety; had I been wrong to wink back? Giddily, Nadia 'fessed up that coming here had been her idea. 'I love this place. Isn't it the greatest?'

'The greatest,' Justin muttered, mortified. 'Let's eat.' As he perused the menu, every now and again he flashed an 'I'm just an expendable fat guy, you have nothing to fear from me' look about the place, but he couldn't relax.

We ordered, everyone except me asking for things that either weren't on the menu or for the menu description to be customized. It seemed to be the LA way to be as awkward as possible in restaurants. Then, just as I was about to tuck into my dinner, my fork froze in my hand as I saw something that didn't fit with the rest of the world. A woman, her entire head and face swaddled in bandages, was being led along the sidewalk by a young, great-haired babe. As they got closer, we could hear the girl murmuring tenderly, 'OK, Mom, there's a step coming up. Two more steps, then down again. OK, here's the car.'

They stopped at a four-wheel drive parked only a few yards from our table. In silence, we watched the woman stand blind and passive, waiting for the car door to be opened.

'What happened to her?' I muttered queasily. 'She looks like a burns victim.'

Instantly I was fixed with indulgent smiles all round. Even Desiree's liquid eyes looked kindly and amused.

'Plastic surgery,' Lara said, *sotto voce*. 'Looks like she got her whole head lifted.'

'Really?'

'Sure.'

But why not? LA was a shrine to beauty and every paper I opened urged me to GET those saddlebags sucked conveniently away, HAVE every hair on my body burnt off with a laser, DEFINE those blurry cheekbones with no-fuss collagen injections. (And who CARES if after six months the collagen slips down to your chin and you look like the ELEPHANT man and you have to have LIPOSUCTION on your COLLAGEN?)

'Take it easy, Mom.' Gently the woman was being guided into the passenger seat, but she didn't lower her head enough and managed to bump her face on the door surround. A little squawk escaped the mouth slit and a spontaneous flinch rippled through the entire restaurant. Everyone had stopped eating.

Then the woman was in. As her daughter scooted round to the driver's side, she sat in her four-wheel drive, looking like *Return of the Mummy*. I had to be careful about slagging off plastic surgery, what with Lara's fake jugs, but what *must* that face be like under those bandages? A raw steak? I couldn't help wincing, 'It looks barbaric.'

'Hey!' Lara playfully shook my arm. 'Don't faint on us. She's happy. She'll spend a couple of days in bed, then she'll have a launch party for her new face.'

'What about her daughter?' I don't really know what I meant by that. I just thought it must be terrible for her to see her mother in such a state.

'Don't worry about her!' Emily comforted. 'She'll be OK

soon. At Beverly Hills High they get nose jobs for their sixteenth birthday present!'

'I got a nose job,' Nadia announced proudly. 'Not just for me, but so my kid will be born with, like, a totally great nose.'

A paralysed silence descended. Desiree actually got down off her seat and trotted away. Lara smiled at me but she looked a little sick.

'What? WHAT?' Nadia had picked up on the atmosphere and was looking from one of us to the next. 'What'd I say?'

Then, 'Oh, I get it. It's because I'm gay. You think gay women can't have children. Well, get over yourselves.'

'Sperm donors!' Emily declared and conversation erupted, a bit too enthusiastically.

20

There was something I'd forgotten to put on my list of bad things about Garv. Now, what was it? Putting empty orange-juice cartons back in the fridge? Pronouncing 'certainly' as 'certintly'?

No, it wasn't either of those, it was:

7. Wanting to have children when I was afraid of it.

Claire had been bang on the money when she'd remarked that the rabbits were almost as much trouble as children. Of *course* Garv's fondness for Hoppy and Rider was something to do with wanting children. Even an amateur psychologist who'd failed all his amateur psychologist's exams could have figured that one out. And I sort of knew it myself, even if I did my very best *not* to know.

Before Garv and I got married, we'd discussed the subject and decided that, while we both wanted children, we also wanted a few years on our own first. That suited me fine, because at twenty-four I felt too young to be a mother. (Even though I knew other twenty-four-year-olds had lots of kids; the only explanation I could come up with was that I was immature.)

The thing was – and I'd have been the first to admit it – I was terrified by the thought of having a baby. And I wasn't the only one. Most of my friends were of the same mind, and we spent many happy hours perplexed by the notion of natural childbirth. Occasionally a horror story was produced about some girl – a distant cousin, someone one of us worked with, no one too like *us*, if you know what I mean – who'd recently had a baby without pain relief. Or stories of nice, normal women who'd had epidurals lined up for months, but who got to the hospital too late and had to have an eight and a half pound baby without so much as a junior aspirin to take the edge off the agony. Such conversations usually came to an abrupt conclusion by someone begging, 'Stop! I'm going to black out!'

But the ink was barely dry on my marriage certificate before both Garv's and my parents mounted a round-the-clock Pregnancy Watch. Soft cheeses were whipped away from in front of me. If I so much as belched (not that I ever dared to in front of his mum and dad), it generated a Mexican wave of pleased, knowing eyebrow raises. When I ate a dodgy mussel and spent two wretched days lying on the bathroom floor, they were practically knitting bootees. Their expectations made me feel panicky – and resentful. Just because I'd never stepped out of line before didn't mean that, just to please them, I was going to start dropping sprogs like I was shelling peas.

'They can't help it,' Garv said. 'It's just because we're the first one in each family to get spliced. Humour them.'

'Will it all be OK?' I asked anxiously, bothered by visions of my in-laws holding me down and forcibly impregnating me with a turkey baster.

'It'll all be OK,' he reassured.

'Everything?'

'Everything.'

'*Everything* everything?' (You know the way you can get, sometimes.)

'Everything everything.'

And I believed him. Broodiness, I was sure, was one of those things that belonged Sometime in My Future. A change that automatically occurred with the passage of time; like all of a sudden wanting to sit down in pubs, when standing up, being goodnaturedly pushed and shoved, had been fine – indeed *enjoyable* – for years. I'd watched it happen to other people – I saw no reason why it wouldn't happen to me.

We hadn't been married long when we moved to Chicago, and suddenly I was studying at night and we were both working very long hours, trying to get a toehold on our respective career ladders. Having children would have been out of the question; we'd barely have had the time or energy to conceive the poor creature, never mind take care of it.

Then, astonishing news came from London: Claire was pregnant. On the one hand, it was a blessing because my mother would have her longed-for grandchild and the pressure would be off me. But on the other hand, I felt peculiarly usurped. It was Claire's job to reduce my parents to hand-wringing despair; it was my job to please them. All of a sudden, she's puking day and night and cutting my most-well-behaved-daughter's legs out from under me.

And Claire had been one of the greatest party animals of our time, so what had prompted the decision to have a baby? I asked her, hoping she'd confide that James, her husband, had said it was a good tax break. (That's the kind of man James was. It was a godsend when he had the affair and left her.) But the hardest fact she could come up with was that it 'felt right'. This I liked the sound of: if it 'felt right' for a wild woman like Claire, the time would definitely come when it would 'feel right' for me.

A few days before Claire's due date, I happened to be in London for one day's work. It was months since I'd seen her, what with me living in Chicago, and when she collected me from the tube station I barely recognized her. She was enormous, easily the most pregnant person I'd ever seen – and she was proud, excited and mad keen to involve me in the whole process. The minute we got back to the flat, she ordered gleefully, 'Look at me, I'm HUGE!' Then she whipped up her sweatshirt and gave me a full frontal.

I was delighted for her happiness, but as I looked at her gigantic, blue-veined belly, I felt a little squeamish at the thought that there was a human being in there. But what made me even more squeamish was that it had to get out, through an orifice which it was clearly far, far too big for.

I found myself wondering just what *had* Mother Nature been thinking of? The process of gestation and giving birth was definitely one of her poorer ideas – the biological equivalent of being painted into a corner.

However, one of the plus sides of being around a heavily pregnant woman was that her flat was full of food. Cravings food – an old biscuit tin was an Aladdin's cave of different chocolate bars, and there was a freezer crammed with ice-cream.

We parked ourselves before the biscuit tin and ate our fill (this took some time), then we were ready to lie on her bed and watch telly. But before we did so, Claire pulled off her sweatshirt. And why not? It was her home. And why should she have a problem undressing in front of me? I mean, I'm her *sister*. But as I stretched my neck to see over her bump to the screen (put it this way, if it had been a subtitled programme we'd been watching, I wouldn't have had a clue what was going on), I tried to blank out the colossal belly which rose, like Ayers Rock, from her body. I began to wish we lived in Victorian times. Modesty, there's a lot to be said for it.

'I shouldn't have eaten that second-last Bounty. The baba's got the hiccups,' she said tenderly. And indeed, before my aghast eyes, her bump convulsed with rhythmic twitches. 'Do you want to feel?' she said. If she had asked me if I'd like to stick my hand in a blender I'd have been as enthusiastic – *more*, probably – but I couldn't think of any way to refuse without giving offence.

I produced my hand and let it be guided, and when she placed it on her stomach a shudder shot up my arm to my scalp. I couldn't help it. I'd have preferred to take the giblets out of a turkey.

She passed my palm over something bumpy. 'Feel that? That's her head,' Claire said, and it was all I could do to suppress a whimper.

Then, as if I wasn't finding things hard enough, Claire remarked idly, 'She could come at any minute.'

Sweat popped on to my forehead. *Not tonight, God*, I prayed. *Please God, don't let her come tonight.*

Claire had always sworn that if she was ever 'unlucky enough' (her words) to have to give birth, she'd start mainlining heroin the minute her waters broke. But when I tentatively enquired how many lines of defence she'd prepared for her fight against labour pains – Pethidine? Epidurals? Heroin? – she shook her head and said, 'Nada.' My horror must have been stamped on my face, because she roared laughing and explained, 'Having this baba is the most exciting thing that's ever happened to me! I want to be fully present for it.'

Clearly she'd gone over to the Dark Side – which I found strangely consoling. If someone like Claire could be contemplating a natural birth, then there was great hope for a scaredy cat like me.

All the same, the following morning I was awake and dressed a full hour before I needed to leave, and not even the charms of the biscuit tin could persuade me to linger. Claire wandered around the flat yawning and muttering to herself, 'I'm ready to pop.' Eventually, she lumbered to the car to drive me to the Tube, and when I saw the underground station, relief made me light-headed. Long before the car had come to a halt, I had the passenger door open and my foot on the road, sparks flying from my heel.

As I leapt out, I blurted, 'Thanks for all the chocolate and good luck with the excruciating agony of childbirth.'

I hadn't meant to say that. I tried again. 'Er, good luck with the labour.'

She had the baby two days later, and no matter how hard I tried, she wouldn't admit that it had hurt that much. It was around then that I realized there was some sort of conspiracy afoot. Whenever I tried pumping any woman who'd had a baby for specifics on agony, pain relief etc., they wouldn't play ball. Instead they just said dreamily, 'Ah yeah, I suppose it stung a bit, but afterwards you've got a baby. I mean, a BABY. You've created a new life, it's miraculous!'

I expected that the passage of time would take care of my fear, that I'd grow out of it. So what I did was I told myself I'd have a child when I was thirty. Partly, I suspect, because I thought thirty was so far away it would never come.

21

'As the crisis in Santa Monica moves into its second day . . .' I woke with my usual horrible jolt to the sound of Emily talking to herself, '. . . conditions inside the house are bad. Morale is low among the hostages . . .'

So I could take it that Mort Russell hadn't arrived in the middle of the night, with a contract under his oxter.

But shortly after I got up, someone rang. Someone who caused Emily to giggle a lot and wind her finger in her hair while talking to him. It was Lou, the guy she'd met at the dinner party where the organ-collecting bloke had been her date.

'I'm going on a date with him tonight,' she said, when she finally hung up. 'He's taken nearly two weeks to call, he's given me no notice, but I don't care. I'm going to go out with him, have sex with him, then never hear from him again. That,' she said with satisfaction, 'will take my mind off Mort Russell not calling!'

I was staring out the window.

'What are you looking at?' she asked.

'Curtis. He's after getting stuck again.' I stared a while longer. 'They're calling us to help.'

'Oh, for God's sake!'

After we'd helped dislodge Curtis – this time he'd been trying to get out of the car, not in – we returned home. I'd half-planned to spend the morning taking a turn around the Santa Monica mall – my knees still looked funny in the denim skirt – until I saw Emily producing an armload of cleaning products from under the sink and pulling on rubber gloves. Housework! What with staying with her rent-free and all that, I felt obliged to help. Or at least to offer and hope she said no. But to my disappointment she said, 'If you wouldn't mind, the floor could do with a wash.'

Ah well, it'd be good exercise for me. As I filled a bucket with floor cleaner and water, Emily sighed, 'Thanks. Conchita is coming on Monday. I like to have things nice for her.'

'Who's Conchita?'

'My cleaning lady. Comes every fortnight. Goes mad if the place isn't clean.'

There was no need to challenge this piece of seeming illogicality. I don't know anyone who doesn't clean up before their cleaning person comes. I started mopping my way across the wooden floor and was working up a good satisfying sweat when the front door opened and in came Troy.

'Right across my nice clean floor,' I scolded.

'Whoops! Sorry.' He laughed softly but there was an urgency about him. 'Guess what?!'

'What?' Emily had appeared.

'Cameron Myers!'

Cameron Myers was a box-office heart-throb. Young and pretty.

'What about him?'

'You know I met with Ricky the producer last night? Well, I'm in his house, and Cameron Myers pays him a visit! Turns out Ricky's an old buddy of Cameron's. But this is the best bit. I tell Cameron my name and he says, "Didn't you direct

Free-Falling?"' A quick aside to me – 'That was my first movie, Irish. Then he says that it rocked!'

Emily went hysterical and I did my best to match her, but Troy silenced us. 'It gets better. Today's his birthday and he's taken the penthouse in the Freeman to hang with his homies tonight. And this is where it gets *real* good – he told me to drop by! And bring a date!'

Anticipation began to stack up inside me. I felt my shoulders tense and my whole body move forward . . .

'So how about it, Emily? You might get to meet some people. Sorry, Irish,' he lifted his arms helplessly, 'I only get to bring one person.'

The sensation of defeat was acute, but in an unexpected reversal of fortune Emily was shaking her head. 'I can't come. Got me a date.'

'A date?' Troy stared at her, then revealed his perfect teeth in an amazed laugh. 'Who *is* this guy, that you're turning down Cameron Myers' birthday party for?'

'No one special, but I'm burnt out from all this movie stuff.'

Troy gave her an enquiring look and Emily turned her mouth down apologetically. 'Maybe I'm just not tough enough for this town.'

A few seconds of silence, then Troy concluded, 'Or maybe you just need a day off.'

'Thanks,' she said, with weary relief. 'Why don't you bring Maggie tonight?'

'Would you come with me?' He sounded surprised, even humble – which in turn surprised, then touched me.

'Yes.'

'You mean you'd come out with me alone?'

If you'll do that thing on my leg again. Except, of course, I didn't say it.

'Emily hasn't warned you about me?' Now he was joking. And flirting. 'I am baaaaaad news.'

'I'll risk it,' I said, wishing I didn't sound so prim.

'Great.'

'What's Cameron Myers like?' I asked.

'Mmmm,' Troy said thoughtfully. His eyes roamed across the ceiling while he contemplated. 'Let's see. What's Cameron like?' The searching silence endured a good time longer, then finally Troy decided. 'Short! I'll pick you up at eight.'

As soon as the door had closed behind him, all my hope and fear was distilled to one sentence. 'I've got to get my hair blow-dried.'

But I didn't know Dino's address. Besides, I couldn't afford him.

'Go down to the corner to Reza,' Emily said. 'She's as mad as a brick, but she'll do in an emergency.'

I hurried to the end of the street, where a small hairdresser's was sandwiched between the Starbucks and the surveillance-equipment shop. The salon was empty save for a magnificent, exotic-looking woman of indeterminate age. Brick-mad Reza? Very dyed black hair bouffed to her shoulderblades and many gold chains nestled in her wrinkled but full décolletage. She glared, as if mortally insulted, when I asked if she had a free appointment, then surprised me by saying, 'Now!'

'No?' Had I misheard?

'No! Now!'

'Um . . . great.'

'I am Reza,' she declared.

'Maggie.'

I explained that I wanted my hair to be smooth, full and shiny. Reza bunched her blackberry lips and said, in an interesting accent, 'You have this bad hair. Fat . . . ?' With expanding hand gestures she sought the right word.

'Thick?' I offered.

'Coarse!' she concluded triumphantly. 'Very bad. The worst kind. Is very hard work to get this bad hair shiny. But I am strong!'

Excellent.

The wash she gave me was so thorough I'm surprised that she didn't draw blood with her nails. 'Strong hands,' she grinned grimly, then proceeded to give me whiplash as she vigorously towel-dried.

As she revved up the dryer – for some reason making me think of a logger about to cut down a tree with a chainsaw – she asked from which godforsaken place did I hail, to end up with such dreadful hair.

'Ireland.'

'Iowa?'

'No, Ireland. A country in Europe.'

'Europe,' she said dismissively. She might as well have said, 'Pah!'

'And where are you from?'

'Persia, but we are not bullsheet Persian. We are Bahai. We don't mess with the bullsheet politics, we love everyone. NO!' She turned to yell at a girl who had appeared at the door. 'No appointment today! We are FULL UP!'

Crushed, the girl disappeared, and without missing a beat, Reza turned back to me. 'We give all peoples their respect. Rich, poor, black, white. Hold your stupid head! You have this BAD hair!'

More than once in the next half-hour my ear lay flat against my shoulder, as she tugged and pulled the coarseness from my hair. Finally, my neck feeling as though it had been pummelled by a baseball bat, Reza switched off the dryer and turned me to the mirror. 'You see.' She couldn't hide her pride. 'Is good. I am strong!'

And my hair *was* nice. Except for my fringe. However she'd managed it, it was almost circular, as if it had been wrapped around a sausage roll. But I saw no point in mentioning it, she would have just laid the blame at the feet of my bad, fat hair.

Then came the delicate matter of payment and she was surprisingly expensive. Perhaps it was extra for hair as terrible as mine.

'OK,' I sighed, proffering my Visa card – which she energetically spurned. 'Bullsheet credit cards,' she muttered. 'Only cash.'

Then came more muttering about 'Bullsheet IRS,' and I passed her some notes and left.

I made my way home pressing my fringe against my forehead, and had the bad luck to be spotted by Ethan, who opened a window and yelled, 'Hey, Maggie! Your bangs look kinda weird.'

Within seconds all three of the boys were on the street, examining me.

'You look like Joan Crawford,' Curtis concluded.

'And your goatee looks like candy floss, only I'm too polite to say it,' I replied. Before I even had time to be appalled at my crassness, they all ROARED laughing, and already Luis had a plan to help me.

'You gotta flatten the hair and keep it flat. Come inside.'

One of the features of this strange post-Garv time was that I seemed to have no power to resist doing things I didn't want to do. I found myself accompanying them into their dim, smelly house and letting Luis ease a pair of tights on to my head, the waistband snug around my fringe. The only saving grace was that they were new tights, straight out of the packet. Ethan told me they kept such stuff on the premises in case any of them got lucky with a girl.

'Keep them on until you have to go out tonight,' Luis advised.

I thanked the three of them – I mean, what else could I do? – and carried on home, the legs of the tights dangling down my back. When I let myself in, Emily looked up from her laptop and remarked, 'Jesus, Reza has lost it altogether.'

And still no word from Mort Russell. Emily abandoned her writing and, humming calmly to herself, pottered around the house, polishing the mirrors, doing her nails. Now and then she rounded on the phone and shrieked, 'Ring, you fucker! Ring, RING, RING!!!!!' Then it was back to the humming.

Meanwhile, I was fretting about what to wear to the party and wondering if I should race down to Santa Monica to try and find something, but I was all too aware of the first law of shopping and knew I hadn't a hope.

'How about that new embroidered denim skirt?' Emily suggested.

'I can't, it makes my knees look funny.'

'No, it doesn't.'

'Yes, it does.'

'Try it on and show me.'

'Come into my room.'

Twenty-nine seconds later, a perplexed Emily was forced to admit, 'Christ, it does. I don't know how. Normally your knees look fine.'

She began rootling through the suitcase on the floor, looking at my clothes and commenting, 'That's a lovely skirt . . . I've that T-shirt in pink.' Then she paused and groaned, 'God, these are gorgeous.' I looked. She'd found my turquoise sandals and was pulling them out from under a pile of socks. 'Gorgeous. And they're new. Look, the price-sticker is still on them. How come you've never worn them?'

'Just waiting for the right occasion.'

'Which I believe might be this evening.'

'Ah, no,' I swallowed. 'Not tonight.' At her sharp look, I explained, 'They're high and uncomfortable. I want to be relaxed this evening.'

I wasn't sure she really believed me, but she let it go.

In a mutation of the laws of physics, the day was interminable, but it also went far too fast. Each individual second endured for quite some time, yet all of a sudden it was five-thirty – too late to get news. Emily spoke to David, who said that Hothouse were obviously taking the script seriously, that the time-lag indicated that Mort was discussing it with his bosses. But Emily wasn't reassured.

'He didn't get enough of a buzz going,' she said sadly. 'I've seen what happens when the hype works. The agent rings the executive in the morning and fires him up so much that he's shelled out two million dollars by lunch-time. Often without having even seen the script.'

'I don't believe you.'

'Honest to God. I can give you four separate instances where a studio paid shedloads without having read a single word. The agent offered them a one-hour window to make a pre-emptive bid. They all came through – too terrified of someone else getting the chance.'

'But what if it's a bad script?'

'It often is, but by the time the studio discover they've paid two million dollars for a dog, it's too late. The writer's sunning himself in the Caribbean and is already on his next project.'

'That's insane.'

'It's an insane kind of town. Anyway, might as well try and enjoy my weekend,' she said sensibly. Then she put her face in her hands and screeched, 'I can't fucking BEAR this.' She emerged with a shaky smile. 'Just taking a moment. Right, where's my make-up bag? C'm'ere till I do your face.'

'But you've to get ready for your date.'

'Ah, it's as easy to do two people as it is to do one. And it's not every night you go to a movie star's birthday party in the penthouse of LA's most fabulous hotel.'

When she put it like that . . . 'Look, are you *sure* you don't want to go?'

'Quite. There's a good chance I'll get laid tonight. A bird in the hand and all that. Are you sure *you* want to go? You don't seem very thrilled.'

She was right. Going to Cameron Myers' birthday party was dream-come-true stuff and I wasn't as fizzy as I should be. As I once would have been. I felt ashamed of myself. The only time I'd come close to feeling any real excitement lately had been at Emily's pitch – and I was starting to wonder if I'd been mistaken about it.

'I just don't seem to be great at enjoying myself at the moment. Everything, even the brilliant stuff, is a bit flat.'

'You're depressed. This whole thing has really taken its toll on you. Naturally enough.'

'The part I'm most looking forward to is going out with Troy,' I admitted.

'It's great you're his date,' she agreed. 'He might have asked Kirsty otherwise.'

'That bitch!' I exclaimed. 'I never told you what she said to me at the party . . .'

I related the story, while Emily did her usual stunt with the make-up and hair slides and stuff. I ended up wearing the same black dress I'd worn to Dan Gonzalez's bash – I'd nothing else – but Emily did something to me with a chiffon neck-scarf and said my look was 'very Halston'. Then came the moment of truth: we finally removed the tights from my head – and my fringe was as flat as Holland. I owed those boys.

At half-seven, as Emily clacked out the door, a fragrant, glittery vision, she paused and turned back to me. 'Just in case you were thinking . . . about Troy. A word of advice. Human Teflon.'

'That's two words.'

'Wonderful to have around, but . . . he's non-stick. Enjoy yourself, but don't expect anything. Promise?'

I promised, then promptly forgot about it. I had to take my enjoyment where I could find it.

22

The Freeman was new, the most glamorous hotel in a town crammed with glamorous hotels. We could hardly get into the noisy lobby, so jammers was it with people meeting for drinks, waiting for dinner and tripping over sculptures. Everyone was astonishingly good-looking – and most of them were staff. It took a long time to get anyone's attention – like Troy muttered, they hadn't been hired for their ability – but eventually we were directed to a special elevator, which was policed by two bouncers who frisked us for cameras and tape-recorders.

The elevator shot us straight to the top floor, playing havoc with my already swoopy stomach. And when the lift doors opened, straight into the penthouse, I nearly got snowblindness. It was all white. White walls, white carpet, white tables and huge, white-leather sofas. I got a fright to see a disembodied blonde head floating in mid-air above one of the couches – then I realized it was just a girl whose white-leather catsuit had merged in with the white leather of the couch.

Troy and I stepped reticently from the lift and exchanged a nervous smile. 'Where's Cameron?' he murmured.

I looked around: there were only about a dozen people there, but never had I seen such a condensed distillation of gorgeousness. It was like walking into an episode of *Beverly Hills 90210* – girls displaying lots of bare, tanned, toned flesh and boys with square teeth and noticeably well-cut hair, all laughing and holding Martini glasses. *What on earth am I doing here?*

This impression intensified when my sweep across the room landed on Cameron Myers. And I have to say that, despite my excitement-facility not operating at full capacity, I did go a bit dizzy and starstruck, as though a plane had flown just two inches over my head. He was on his knees in front of a plain white hole in the wall, a very modern fireplace.

'Hey!' He scrambled to his feet when he saw Troy – and I must admit he did look much shorter and dinkier than he does on screen. 'You came!'

'Happy birthday, man. Thanks for inviting us. This is Maggie.'

'Hello.'

I was almost on a level with Cameron Myers' perfect symmetrical face, with the white-blond hair, the blue, blue eyes, and the tight, evenly tanned skin. He was nearly as familiar to me as one of my family, and yet . . .

Wait till I tell them back home. They'll never believe me.

I realized I was staring, so I shoved four orange orchids at him. 'These are for you.'

He seemed genuinely touched. 'You brought me flowers!'

'But it's your birthday.' I gestured at the room. 'I'm sorry they're not white.'

He laughed a sweet laugh and I had the urge to pick him up under my arm, start sprinting and not stop until I had him safely locked in a cage. He was so cute, like a puppy.

'There's frosty drinks in the kitchen. Help yourselves.'

'I'll get them,' Troy said, and headed off across the room, leaving me alone with Cameron Myers.

'Hey, do you know how to do this?' He gestured helplessly at the instant-fire packets at his feet.

'Er . . . yes, it's easy.'

'I love a real fire. It's kinda homey. Will you help me?'

What could I say? It was July. It was Los Angeles. It was eighty degrees out there. But he was Cameron Myers and he wanted a fire.

'OK.'

Once the fire was crackling brightly and Cameron had rung down for marshmallows, Troy handed me a Martini, murmured, 'How about this place,' and took me on a walkabout. It was huge. The 'reception room' (as they say) must have been sixty foot long, and there were three enormous bedrooms, so full of dazzling white cotton it hurt to look at them. There was a kitchen, an office, countless bathrooms – even, would you believe, a screening room. All around were dotted soft, white, cashmere throws, white suede cushions, white porcelain vases. Maybe it was good Emily hadn't come. She might have been tempted to start nicking stuff.

'Who are all the other people here?' I whispered. 'Any of them famous?'

'Don't think so. Wannabes, Maws –'

'Maws?'

'Model-actress-whatevers. Another word is "mattresses" – models-actors-waitresses. Now, get a load of *this*!' He opened a door on to a roof garden. 'Wow.'

We stepped out into the sultry night – far hotter than in the air-conditioned rooms – the air dense and musky with the smell of flowers. There was a hot-tub, steaming into the night. But most impressive was the astonishing view.

'No smog tonight,' Troy observed, as we leaned over the balcony, staring, awestruck. Far below us were pristine Spanish-style homes, neatly parked cars, the springy tops of palm trees and the jewel-bright turquoise of underlit swimming pools. The pools were like stars – at first I only noticed one, then another, then suddenly, popping up out of nowhere, there were too many to count. They dotted away randomly into the distance, until they became too small to see. Beyond the nearby streets, the megalopolis of Los Angeles was laid out like a grid of Christmas lights, a city of the future which stretched for miles until it blurred into a horizon of electric colour.

The odd thing was that I couldn't see a single human being. But they were out there – countless hopefuls caught on the grid, like so many flies in an endless spiderweb. Infinitesimally, I felt the collective weight of all the dreams on that net of light: the beautiful girls waiting tables, while waiting for their one big break; the would-be actors, writers and directors who'd poured into this reclaimed desert from the four corners of the globe; hundreds of thousands of individuals hoping that they'd be one of the pitifully few who made it. Such longing, such dogged determination: I imagined I could nearly see it, rising into the night sky like steam.

'Awesome?' Troy quirked his straight mouth.

'Scary.'

'Yeah. Want to sit down?'

There was a wide choice of wicker chairs and top-of-the-range sunbeds (with about twenty different inclines), but '*This* is the one for us.' Troy seemed amused by a squashy, swinging sofa suspended by ropes from an overhead beam.

After a twinge of fear that the ropes wouldn't hold our weight (*my* weight, really. Could you imagine the shame if I clambered aboard, only to yank the hooks out of the beam and send the whole thing crashing to the floor?), I got totally into it. We took an end each, and curled on the cushions, our feet almost touching.

Look at me, I thought, amazed by myself – swinging in the warm night, high above the city, sipping a Martini with a sexy, sexy man.

Yes, now about the 'sexy, sexy man'. They say that you don't know how sad you've been until you feel happy once more. Similarly, you don't realize how much you haven't fancied anyone until it happens again. Troy's easy grace, his greenish eyes, his very nearness, generated something in me – what I could only describe as readiness.

'I could get to like this,' he said softly. From his tone and the accompanying sidelong glance, he wasn't just talking about the view/frosty-drinks/swinging-sofa set-up. I might have lived a fairly sheltered life, but I'm not a complete ditz.

'Me too.' I kept my inflections neutral.

'You're sure? You really do feel OK? You know, after those phone calls about your husband?'

'Fine.' Well, I felt fine at that precise moment.

He nodded. 'Cool.'

'Tell me about your meeting last night.' Emily had implied that his work was important to Troy, so I wanted to know.

He told me a little about the three projects he was trying to get off the ground, the various setbacks, how hard it was to get finance, and I encouraged and commiserated where appropriate, but it was like we were speaking in code.

If only he'd touch me. The skin on my leg almost tingled with the need for his hand . . .

'Is there a Maggie here?' Someone had stuck their head around the door. 'Cameron needs ya. His fire has gone out.'

The mood broken, Troy made a regretful face and said, 'Better go in.'

Back inside, more people had arrived, but there were still

only about thirty of them. Cameron beckoned me across the chilly tundra and yelled raucously, 'Come on baby, light my fire!'

'Lord,' I murmured, 'what have we missed?' It looked like the high-jinks factor had gone up several gears while we'd been outside. But as soon as I'd fixed the fire and Troy and I had commandeered one of the white-leather sofas, I discovered how mistaken I was. Cameron's boisterousness was about as rowdy as things got: as parties go, this one was very well-behaved. And as movie stars' parties go, it was a bitter disappointment.

'No one's had their face slapped, there's been no jiggery-pokery in the hot-tub, not one television has been thrown in the swimming pool,' I said sadly. And apart from a couple of slender joints doing the rounds, there wasn't even any obvious drug-taking.

'Irish, you're obsessed!'

I shrugged. 'Just trying to make up for lost time.'

Around the fireplace, weaving in and out in a tight knot, all of the 90210 crew seemed to know each other. And while they were perfectly cordial to Troy and me, they weren't overly friendly. For once I didn't care, because Troy was the only person I wanted to talk to. He resumed telling me about his work while I widened my eyes and licked my lips and looked up from under my lashes – and then realized I was sipping from an empty glass. Had possibly been at it for quite some time.

Troy indicated it. 'Another?'

'I'll get them.'

I crossed the vast expanse of whiteness to the kitchen, but as I got there, the door was shut in my face. Behind the door a girl gasped, 'Do you want *everyone* to see? And where did you get it?'

I paused, my hand frozen on the door knob, as a male voice tempted, 'Want some?'

'I can't! You shouldn't!'

'A little isn't going to hurt.'

'Jeez, listen to yourself!'

I was afraid to go in. What manner of illegal mood-alterer were they indulging in? Cocaine? Angel dust? *Heroin?* But my curiosity got too much, so I opened the door – and found the pair of them bent guiltily over a tub of Ben & Jerry's Chunky Monkey. They looked up, a picture of shock, and the girl actually said, 'This isn't how it looks.'

Full of glee, I skittered back to Troy and, with my mouth intimately close to his ear, confided what had happened. 'Not exactly rock and roll, is it?' I couldn't stop grinning.

'No,' he laughed. 'This isn't such a great party, is it? Come on, suck down that drink, I'll take you home.'

The words were out of my mouth before I'd even known I was going to say them. 'Whose home?'

Instantly, I dropped my eyes, afraid to look at him. I was shaking with hope, with my own audacity, with dread . . .

'Maaaggie,' he whispered, and cautiously I peeped up again.

His expression was quizzical. He was wondering if he'd misunderstood, then saw that he hadn't. He laughed – a funny, regretful laugh. 'Oh, boy.' He sounded almost weary. With a heart banging with nerves, I watched him stand up and sling an arm towards me.

'Let's go.'

23

In his jeep I faced away and stared out of my window, because I couldn't bear looking at him and not touching him. In silence, he drove too fast. But when we got caught at a red light, I made the mistake of turning and glancing at him, and then his mouth was on mine. I hadn't known what kind of kiss to expect, because his mouth was hard but he was gentle – but when it happened I was actually shocked by the quality. It wasn't just my being out of practice that made me think he was an expert kisser. He was teasing, tantalizing and more than a little dirty.

We kissed through three changes of the lights. At the time, I didn't know that was what was happening, but afterwards I made sense of the noises I'd been faintly aware of – the mad beeping must have been when the lights changed to green and we didn't move. The sound of acceleration was us being overtaken, then a fresh burst of mad beeping must have been when the next lot pulled up behind us on the red and the lights went to green again.

Somehow we were driving again, even faster, then we were parked on a trash-strewn street, he was opening a graffitied metal front door and we were going up some concrete stairs. His apartment was tiny and untidy, full of books and piles of manuscripts. Then we were lying on his bed, facing each other.

'Are you sure you want to do this?' he murmured, stroking

along my hairline with his thumb, sending little shivers through me.

All my life I've been cautious and held off on things until I'm sure they're right. But this could not happen fast enough.

'I'm sure.'

'You've just broken up with your husband . . .'

I had no interest in playing games, holding on, hoping to drive him mad. I wanted this and I wanted it now.

'It's been six weeks. And it's been over for much longer than that.' I was breathless. Not just with longing, but with fear that he was going to turn me down.

'Because I am bad news,' he said gently.

'So you've already told me. D'you want me to sign a disclaimer clause?'

He laughed, and I took his hand and placed it on my shin. 'Show me again how to get to your apartment from Santa Monica.'

'I can do better than that.'

He pulled off his T-shirt and his chest was shiny-smooth and hairless. Then went the rest of his clothes, to reveal a body that was narrow-hipped and sinewy, and blessed with that perfect, olive skin. If I tell you that he was the most beautiful man I'd ever seen, I'm probably exaggerating, but you get the picture.

Then he was helping me out of my dress and telling me how much he wanted me.

Claire had told me about the first time she'd had sex after she'd split up with James, how nervous she'd been with the new person. And after I'd left Garv, I'd found it impossible to imagine ever sleeping with another man – literally impossible. But this was a lot easier than I'd expected.

'You're beautiful,' he whispered, gently unknotting my 'Halston' scarf from around my neck, then just as gently tying it around my wrist – then tying the other end to his bedpost. Oh my God! 'Stay there,' he ordered, disappearing and – oh, Jesus! – returning with slender ropes. 'This OK?' he asked, tying my other wrist to the other side of the bed.

'Don't know. I've never done it before.'

''Bout time you did,' he laughed, then he was holding my foot in his hand and attaching a rope to my ankle. Soon all four limbs were tied and I was spread-eagled on the bed.

And now I was afraid. What if he was a serial killer? What if he was going to torture and kill me?

Then he was inching his way up my leg with his tongue, taking his own sweet time, lingering on my kneecap, and by the time he'd got to my thigh, I'd decided that if he was a serial killer, I didn't care. Up, up, he moved, still not high enough, up a little more, then back a bit – I nearly choked – then finally he'd arrived where I wanted him to be.

I'd forgotten how fabulous sex could be. Put it this way, it had been a long time since Garv and I had had sex on the kitchen table. (The fact that we were still waiting for it to be delivered didn't help, of course.) This was pure, selfish pleasure, all for me. The circles began to build, pleasure stacking and intensifying, reaching for the almost unbearable sweetness until it got to the top. I quivered on it, helpless, until the burst dispersed and I returned to myself, striving for breath.

'You're very good at this,' I half-laughed.

He grinned and drawled, 'I practise a lot.'

Then he was kneeling between my legs with an impressive, angry-looking hard-on and swinging the tip against me, then removing it, then it was in half an inch, then out again, then in a bit more, then out again, and all I wanted him to do was thrust right up into me and fill the need. But in the midst of it all was the worry about contraception – the last thing I needed was to get pregnant by Troy.

Then he was pulling a foil square from a drawer, rolling a condom on in one fast, unbroken motion, then he was plunging into me, and it was wild. Though my arms and legs were tied, I flipped with desire beneath him. Then he was whimpering, 'Oh Jesus, oh Jesus.' His eyes shut, his head arched back. At the moment of climax his body spasmed into paralysis and nothing moved except his spurts pumping inside me.

Limbs suddenly floppy and weak, he collapsed on to me, our chests heaving. Then he pulled himself up on to his elbows and looked at me with amusement. 'Jeez,' he said, softly. 'You love this, doancha?'

He untied me, and the second time we took it slower – a lot slower. Side by side, barely moving, locked at the groin, we ground further into each other with the smallest of actions and I stared into his eyes and forgot who I was.

The sun was already starting to come up when we got to sleep, then suddenly I was awake and the yellow light of full-on morning was filling the room. Panicked, I turned my head on the pillow and there he was. Awake and watching me. He rolled closer, fixed me with sleepy green eyes and said, 'Our first morning together.'

His lazy drawl made everything sound like a joke so I laughed, then moved my hands under the sheet until I found what I wanted – velvety skin over iron – and slithered down the bed to it. 'Your turn.'

Afterwards he insisted on returning the favour, then said

with a regretful sigh, 'I'd love to do this all day, but I got work to do. C'mon, I'll drive you home.'

Coming out of his apartment, we stumbled across a cluster of tourists, laden with maps and Leicas, wandering around the manky streets looking bewildered. Wasn't Hollywood supposed to be glamorous? As we climbed into Troy's jeep they studied us over-hopefully, desperate for us to be famous, and we pulled away with them still staring hard.

On the drive to Santa Monica, neither of us spoke. I had my eyes closed as I basked in a great sense of well-being. Then Troy's voice was saying, 'Wake up, Irish, we're home.'

I opened my eyes. We were outside Emily's and all the Drummers to the Rhythm of Life were streaming out of Mike and Charmaine's and into waiting Mercs and Lexuses.

I roused myself. 'Thanks for the lift, and the party and, you know . . . everything.'

'My pleasure.' He slid a hand under my hair to the nape of my neck, and touched a brief kiss to my mouth.

'Call me,' I yelped, hopping down out of the jeep.

'Sure,' he grinned. 'I'll write you every day.'

24

The sunlit house was unexpectedly silent; Emily wasn't home yet. She'd obviously got lucky also. For once, I didn't mind being on my own, I didn't mind *at all*. I was aglow – with my sore wrists and ankles and my stiff inner thighs, I'd never felt more alive. After a shower, where I looked in awe at the bite mark on my stomach, I drove to the beach to catch some rays. I liked this picture of myself. A convertible-driving independent woman, happy with my own company.

I'd only been stretched out for a few minutes when along came Rudy, laden down with ice-creams.

'Where'd ya go? Been worried about ya,' he said.

'Busy week,' I said. 'Any tri-colour Klondikes?'

As I arranged myself and my ice-cream beneath the dazzling sun, a vision of a fresh start wound around me seductively. This place had everything: great weather; fantastic location; lovely people. I could put my disastrous life in Ireland behind me, begin again and, this time, get it right. After my time in Chicago, surely someone would employ me and sort out a green card for me – there must be thousands of jobs in the studios for people with legal experience.

Then I let the door open on a secret, exciting hope: maybe Troy would be part of my new life. I revelled in a happy idyll of me and him, laughing happily together. Strolling through a fruit and veg market – in films, people who've just got off with each other spend a lot of time wandering amongst fresh produce, and it's always OK to stroke aubergines suggestively without a stallholder shouting, 'Oi, no 'andling the goods!' Or for the man to pluck a juicy, red strawberry from a stand and feed it to the woman without getting arrested for theft.

I entertained myself thus for most of the afternoon, and it only came to an end when I had to go home because I was dying to go to the loo.

Back at the house, I raced to the bathroom and was surprised at the stinging sensation. Then I remembered what had caused it and suddenly it became pleasant. Oh yeah, of course . . .

Still no sign of Emily, but there was a message on the machine from her. She'd spent the day with Lou, they were going out again tonight, I wasn't to expect her home. 'Call me on the cellphone if you've any problems.' As if it had just occurred to her, she added, 'But maybe you're not back either. I'll try you at Troy's.'

That was the only message. At least it was the only message for *me*. There were about ten thousand for Emily. Justin and Connie, someone called Lamorna, another person going by the name of Dirk.

It was then that the implications of Emily's message began to filter through: I'd be spending the evening alone. That was OK, I could ring Claire – then I remembered I couldn't because of the time difference. Fine, I could ring Rachel in New York, and afterwards I could compound my happy, independent-woman status by going to the movies on my own. Doubtfully I thought, yeeess, I could do that. Then I let myself think the thought that had been begging to be formed – unless Troy rang. There might be a possibility of repeating the fantastic sex of the previous night and this morning . . . Suddenly, I was in a state of raging arousal.

There was a noise at the door and I looked up in wild hope. Could I have conjured up Troy? With a pistol in his pocket?

Not quite. It was Lara. 'Ready?' she beamed. 'For Madame Anoushka?'

I froze. 'Oh Lord, I'd completely forgotten!' Madame Anoushka, who would save me from my terrible eyebrows. I had an appointment with her for five-thirty. 'Give me ten minutes,' I begged, and bolted to the shower to wash off the day's sand.

Three minutes later I was dragging a towel over myself, and while I foraged for clothes Lara came in to talk to me. As I located a bra, I had a panicky moment of wondering how I'd put it on without her seeing my chest, then was too rushed to bother. Let her see it. Nothing she hadn't seen before! Hadn't I always been annoyed by homophobic men who acted as if every gay man they met was going to come on to them? And wasn't I behaving in exactly the same way?

Anyway, I didn't for one second think she was going to make a move on me. I suppose I just wondered how I measured up, if she thought my jugs were nice.

I was dressed in under nine minutes – 'I'm impressed!' Lara said – then into the silver pick-up truck, once more heading for Beverly Hills. Sure, I was hardly ever out of the place! As we drove, she asked about Cameron Myers' birthday party and I told her about the apartment, the view and Cameron's fire, but she didn't ask if anything had happened with Troy, and I didn't quite know how to bring it up.

Madame Anoushka was an icy white Russian who was shocked by the poorly plucked state of my eyebrows. 'Bed,' she pronounced. 'Werry bed.'

So bed that she had to sit down for a moment and heave a deep, heartfelt sigh. Then she rose to her feet and the challenge. 'Ve fill do fot ve ken,' she said, painting some molten wax on my eye socket. Her accent was reminding me of someone, generating a maelstrom of hard-to-place nostalgia. Then I remembered: Valya and Vladimir. Garv and his shopping lists. It was as though a door to a draughty place had opened inside me. Then, mercifully, Anoushka ripped off a strip of wax and the agony wiped out the memories.

The process was preposterously unpleasant. As Anoushka plucked, it was like being assailed with a thousand little darts, my eyes dribbled water and I hovered uncomfortably on the edge of a sneeze. All the while, she gave orders in her Valya accent.

'Tveezers,' she barked, like a surgeon in *ER*. 'More wex.'

I pushed down an impulse to ask if she'd had menny, menny luffers. Anyway, I'd say she would have had, she was a fine-looking woman.

After what felt like ages, the plucking frenzy started on my other eye and it was, if anything, worse than the first. I prayed for it to be over.

Eventually everything went still – like the calm after all the popcorn has popped – so I opened my eyes and began to struggle to my feet. Only to be stopped by Anoushka insisting, 'No!'

Obediently I lay back and shut my eyes again. But nothing happened, and I cautiously squinched open one eye to find Anoushka studying me with great concentration.

'The hardest part is knowing when you're finished,' Lara said admiringly. 'All the great artists say that.'

Over the next ten minutes, a single hair was plucked from

my right eye and none from my left, then Anoushka saw fit to declare, 'Finish!'

Sitting up, I looked into the mirror: my nose was red and my eyes were rheumy, as though I'd been crying for a week. I reminded myself of someone. Who? Oh, *myself*. Last February. But my eyebrows were lovely, no doubt about it.

'Better than a facelift,' Anoushka said. Now where had I heard that before? And once again, it was almost as expensive.

When we got back into Lara's pick-up truck, a change occurred. All of a sudden, she was uncomfortable, and the feeling filled the small space. 'There's something I've got to say to you,' she said, then picked up my hand. Alert, I stared into her blue eyes. Oh God, here it comes. Lezzer snog! Senses instantly heightened, I noticed that she smelt of strawberries, that her legs were so long her car seat was as far back as it could go . . . She pulled my hand to her face. Was she going to kiss it? And then me?

'I feel bad saying this,' she sighed, 'but you have the worst nails. You have *got* to get to a nail bar.'

It took me a perplexed moment to realize she'd returned my hand to me. No lezzer snog. Just another instalment in Lara's mission to groom me to LA standards.

'Have you, like, *ever* had a manicure?'

'Of course I have.' I'd had one when I'd got married, hadn't I? And other times too, I'd say.

'But not in a while, right? OK, there's a place in Santa Monica, on the corner of Arizona and Third. Nail Heaven, Taiwanese girls, they're the best! Tell them I sent you.' I waited for her to grab her palm pilot and book me in, but she didn't.

'You're not . . .' I tried to sound normal, 'getting me an appointment?'

'You don't need one, not for nails. This is a civilized country! Hey, you don't hate me, do you?'

'No.'

'Phew! So what'll we do now? Go for a drink, or get some dinner, or . . .'

Before we could decide, her cellphone rang. 'Yes –' Her eyes slid to me, 'I've got her.'

It was Troy! Tracking me down! Mad for sex with me!

But it wasn't. It was Justin. Emily had called him and he was under instructions to take care of me that evening.

'Can I come too?' Lara asked.

'No Nadia tonight?'

'No.' Suddenly subdued, she switched on the ignition, and we drove over to Justin's house – a red-roofed mini-hacienda, with lots of Spanish archways and wrought-iron window shutters. He wore a blue and green Hawaiian shirt that I hadn't seen before. He must have hundreds.

'Hi, how are you?' I asked.

'Pretty sore,' he answered, his voice even higher than usual.

'Why, sweetie?' Lara asked with concern.

'Some other guy keeps getting the parts I'm up for. Look at him!' He hit a copy of *Daily Variety* with the back of his hand, then showed us a little photo of the other guy. It was uncanny – he was so similar to Justin, they could have been brothers, but this guy was just that little bit plumper and cuter and his face was even more open and uncomplicated than Justin's.

'All I can do is be fat and expendable,' Justin said, slumped in depression. 'If I can't do that, I've no job. I'm a total loser.'

Lara and I pitched in, reminding him he could give great foot massages and was an excellent cook (according to Lara), until eventually he perked up. 'Aw, I'm sorry, guys. So what'll we do? We could catch a movie?'

'Suits me.' Going to a film was always a great opportunity to eat loads of confectionery under cover of darkness.

'How about *Flying Pigs*?' Lara said.

'Nah, I hated his last one,' Justin said.

'Which? *Introspection*?'

'No, *Washday Blues*.'

'Did he do that?'

I tuned out as the pedigrees of the many, many films currently showing in greater Los Angeles were discussed – this is the one complaint I'd have about hanging around with people who work in the film industry, they know too much – and tuned back in only when they'd finally nominated a candidate. Something called *Seven Feet Under*.

'A black comedy,' Justin explained. 'Directed by the guy who made –'

'Grand, whatever.' I was more interested in the bag of M&M's I'd be eating while I watched it.

On our way out of the house, I noticed the name on Justin's mailbox: Thyme.

'Justin Thyme? That's a great name. Is it –?'

'No.' He beat me to it. 'Not my real surname. I made it up to try and stand out from the thousands of other expendable fat guys out there.'

By Sunday morning, I was itching for Emily to come home.

And for Troy to ring me.

When was he likely to? What were the rules? Perhaps it was way too soon – it had been less than a day. Then I checked my watch – OK, just over a day. Nothing, no length of time. I could ring him, of course. That's what people did, normal people that I had to start behaving like. But I didn't have his number.

Aimlessly, I opened a couple of cupboards, found nothing of interest, then sat staring at the floor, wishing Emily would come home from her sexathon with Lou. Sundayitis – the same wherever you are.

When the phone rang, the adrenalin rush felt like a heart attack. Nerves a-jangle, I picked up on the second ring. But it wasn't Troy, it was my mother.

'Are you all right?' she asked.

I nodded assent, too disappointed to speak.

'Is it nice there?'

Quickly, I got it together. 'Lovely, *lovely*!' I so didn't want any pressure to go home. 'Nice people, gorgeous weather –'

'Is it sunny?' she cut in.

'Sunny? Splitting the stones!'

'I'd love a bit of sun,' she said wistfully.

I got a strange little inkling and began backtracking. 'Mind you, it can be smoggy too. Very overcast. And there's always the chance of an earthquake.'

'It hasn't stopped raining here since the day you left. I'd prefer an earthquake.'

'Ahaha,' I laughed nervously, changed the subject, then said goodbye and resumed staring at the floor.

Emily got home around two o'clock. Lou had love-bombed her all weekend: taken her out for fabulous meals, practised his shiatsu on her, then last night they'd driven up to Mulholland Drive to watch the lights of the city and he'd said that this was something they'd tell their grandchildren.

'Classic commitmentphobic,' she said gaily.

'What are they?'

'They do instant intimacy – just add water and stir. Then you never hear from them again.'

'You almost sound happy about it.'

'It's nice to know there are some things you can depend on . . . Unless he actually *meant* all that stuff about telling our grandchildren,' she added scornfully. 'That'd be even worse!'

No need to tell her that Mort Russell hadn't called: she'd checked her messages several times.

'So how are you?' she asked.

How was I? Troy still hadn't rung, which had whipped up a ball of anxiety in my stomach. But hadn't I always been one for deferred gratification? When he finally came through, the wait would have been worth it.

'You look . . . different.'

Oh my God, was it that obvious?

She studied me thoughtfully. 'Your eyebrows!'

'Oh, ah, right. Lara took me to Madame Anoushka.'

'Tell me about Cameron Myers' birthday party.'

'Weeelll,' I said, unable to keep my delight from spreading right across my face. 'It was great.'

'How? Tell me everything.' Then her expression altered. 'Oh, shit.' She looked surprisingly shocked. 'You slept with Troy.'

'What's wrong with that?'

'Nothing,' she insisted. 'Nothing . . . OK,' she admitted, 'it's just a bit weird for me. Like, for nine years you've been Garv's wife, you've been here – how long? – less than two weeks and you're sleeping with other men. And you were never a goer – not really – and, you know, it's a bit hard to get used to, that's all.'

'I've got used to it.'

'Great.' She made a very obvious attempt at being fine, and with a big smile asked, 'Was it fun?'

'Fun isn't the word.'

'Fair play to you.' For a second, it looked like she was about to say something else, then she stopped.

25

About three years ago, two things that I never thought would happen, happened. My thirtieth birthday arrived and, after five years in Chicago, Garv was offered a promotion in the Dublin office and we decided to move back to Ireland. Garv settled into his new managerial position, I got a six-month contract at McDonnell Swindel and suddenly it was baba time!

But, to my distress, I still didn't feel 'ready'. It was great being back in Ireland, but I missed Chicago. In addition, adjusting to my new job was stressy; I hated the insecurity of a short-term contract, but that's all that anyone offered me. *And* we had nowhere to live: we'd expected our return to the Emerald Isle to be the traditional one of an Irish person who goes to Ameri-kay: they make good, then come back and dispense largesse like it's going out of fashion. So it came as a big shock to discover that while we'd been away, Ireland had had the temerity to go and get an economy for itself.

Dublin was boomtown and the price of property had gone through the roof. We arrived back at the very zenith, when shoeboxes were changing hands for several million quid and if someone stood still long enough, someone else would apply for planning permission to build sixteen apartments on them. The upshot of all this was that instead of snapping up a city-centre mansion with the proceeds of our Chicago apartment, it took us five months before we managed to buy a house in the suburb of Dean's Grange, several miles from the city.

Before us, it had been owned by an old lady – the kitchen and bathroom were museum pieces and small, gloomy rooms were the order of the day. So we fashioned plans to modernize: new kitchen, new bathroom, knocking through walls, adding skylights and all that. Lord Lucan Construction duly arrived, knocked down most of the house, then promptly disappeared. And every day that the pile of cement in the front 'garden' stood unattended was another day that I didn't have to commence babymaking.

But all the time the net was tightening. Just before we'd left Chicago, nearly every couple we knew were having children, and we'd barely touched down in Ireland when I noticed they were at the same lark there. Only a week after our return, Garv's sister Shelley had a baby boy, Ronan. Garv and I went to visit her in hospital, a bunch of grapes under our oxter, where we found that Shelley's partner Peter had conjoined with a bottle of Power's to celebrate the birth of his first child. 'GARV!' he shouted, when he saw us coming down the corridor. 'Garv, Garv! C'mere till you see the fruit of my loins!' He thrust his pelvis at us with such vigour that he almost fell over, then, bouncing between the shiny green walls, he got Garv in a headlock, dragged him to the infant's cot and berated him, 'De murkil 'f new life. 'Sa MURKIL!' I was mortified for him, especially when he was asked to leave as he was upsetting the other fathers. But Garv seemed quite moved by it all.

I hadn't been able to avoid noticing that Garv was keen on sprogs. He liked them and they liked him back. They were particularly fond of messing up his hair and pulling off his glasses and poking him in the eye. When they cried, he held them and spoke sweetly and they stopped crying and looked at him with a kind of wonder and everyone said (except my family), 'He'll make a great dad.'

Sure enough, Garv started making noises about us reproducing, and I cursed my bad luck. In other relationships, it seemed to be the women who wanted to have children while the men would do anything to get out of it. In fact, according to popular folklore (and women's magazines), these child-shy men riddled the landscape like landmines. Every time Garv brought up the subject, I always managed a legitimate reason why now wasn't the right time. But it dawned on him that my reluctance wasn't simply temporary, one weekend when we were babysitting Ronan. (Well, I say weekend, but it was only Saturday night, all that Peter and Shelley dared leave him for. And they rang about eighty times in that twenty-four-hour period.)

It was the first time that we'd minded Ronan for more than a couple of hours, and we weren't at all bad at feeding, burping, changing and cajoling him. It was good fun because, you see, I had nothing against babies *per se*. Just the idea of having them myself. When Ronan cried a couple of times in the night, Garv got up without complaint. Then in the morning he brought him into bed with us and sat him on his lap facing us. Already Ronan was chortling, and when Garv held on to his chubby wrists and blew raspberries at him, Ronan nearly shrieked his head off. Garv was laughing almost as much, and with his bare chest and off-duty hair, he looked like the hunky man in that Man and Baby portrait. I got such a pang of confused yearning, it almost hurt physically.

A great day was had by some and when Peter and Shelley came to collect Ronan, they asked, 'Was he good for you?'

'Good?' Garv said. 'He was brilliant! We don't want to give him back.'

'You'll have to get working on a little cousin for him, so,' Shelley said.

Quick as a flash, I indicated the raw walls and said, 'How could we bring a baby into this building site?' They laughed and I laughed and Garv laughed – but his laugh wasn't as loud as ours. Even then, I knew that it had been one excuse too many and not long afterwards the rabbits showed up.

Time passed and I still didn't feel 'ready'. Some of my fears had lessened, specifically the one about the pain of childbirth; I knew enough women who'd had children to know that it was definitely survivable. But whenever I heard stories about people having their first baby at thirty-nine, it brightened my day. Then there was something in the paper about a woman of sixty having a baby using some artificial process and that, too, was good news. But, a lot sooner than I expected, my thirty-first birthday arrived and tipped me into panic: I'd said I'd have a baby when I was thirty and I was now a year older than that. When would my full-blown maternal instinct arrive? I was running out of time. If it didn't get a move on, it would show up just in time for my menopause.

Like I say, Garv is no fool. And finally, he sat me down gently – but firmly, mind. He can be firm when he wants to be – and made me talk about it. *Really* talk about it, instead of fobbing him off as I had been doing for the previous twelve months.

'I'm just not ready,' I admitted. 'And it's not really the pain any more, I'm a bit better about that.'

'Good woman, we'll get you the finest epidural that money can buy. So what is it, then?'

'Well, my job.'

Once I said it out loud, I realized what a problem this was. For over five years, both in Chicago and Ireland, I'd been working very, very hard, pushing against the current, and I was still waiting for my job to plateau, to get to a position where I felt 'safe'. Where I was established enough to be able to take maternity leave, sure that I'd be re-employed, and free from the worry of my colleagues undermining me in my absence and poaching my work. But I was on my third temporary contract.

'You'll get maternity leave and . . .'

'But how easy will it be to get back in? And what will it do to my promotion prospects? If I take four months off, how will I ever get to be Frances?'

'So you can sleep under one of the desks and wash in the staff toilets like a bag lady? Anyway, they can't discriminate against you, it's against the law.'

Easy for him to say. He hadn't heard a partner at my firm (a man, of course) complain about someone on maternity leave, 'If I took four months off to sail around the Med, and expected to be paid for it, they'd laugh in my face!'

This was what I was up against. Compared to his, mine wasn't much of a career, but it was important to me. Even though it drained and stressed me, to a certain extent I defined myself by it.

'OK. Anything else?'

'Yes. What if it turns out to be like one of my sisters? Like Rachel and the drugs, say? Or Anna and the insanity. Or Claire and the rebelliousness. I'd never be able to control them, they'd have my heart scalded.' I stopped. 'Listen to me, I'm already sounding like my mother. Anyway, I'm too irresponsible to have a child.'

That made him laugh. 'You're not irresponsible!'

'I am! You and me,' I urged, 'we have a lovely time. We can go away for weekends at the drop of a hat. Think of Hunter and Cindy!' Friends of ours in Chicago, who'd had a baby and, overnight, had their life up-ended. Once upon a time the four of us had gone on trips together, but post-baba they'd seemed perpetually ensnared by their screaming child, while Garv and I had swanned off to the lakes for the weekend, feeling guilty and relieved. 'We couldn't leave a baby with Dermot, the way we can with Hoppy and Rider. And parenthood never stops,' I pointed out. 'Not until the babies are grown up. And maybe not even then.'

'OK, a baby will cause you agony, have your heart scalded, finish your career and destroy your social life for the next twenty years. Other than that, have you any objections?'

'Yes.'

'Tell me.'

'It sounds stupid.'

'Tell me anyway.'

I made myself voice it. 'What if . . . like . . . anything happened to it? What if it got bullied at school? Or if it died? What if it got meningitis? Or was knocked down? We'd love it so much, how could we bear it? Sorry for being so mad,' I added quickly. I'd never met anyone else who felt like this. Friends who'd got pregnant had admitted to mild regrets, but they'd all been along the lines of 'Well, that's our last romantic weekend away for the next three years,' or 'I'm reading as much as I can now, because you can't concentrate on a book for the first two years. Your brain just goes.' No one had expressed the kind of morbid misgivings that I had. The closest anyone had got was when they said, 'I don't care if it's a boy or a girl, so long as it's healthy.'

But Garv said, 'I do understand how you feel.' And I knew he did. 'But if we thought that way all the time, we'd never love anyone.'

For a moment, I was afraid he might suggest that I had therapy. But of course he didn't – he was an Irish man.

Unlike most of my friends, I'd never had therapy. Emily said it was because I was too afraid of what I'd find out. I agreed – I said I was afraid of finding out that I'd paid forty pounds a week every week for two years to entertain a stranger with the story of my life.

'Can you see anything positive at all about getting pregnant?' Garv asked.

I thought long and hard. 'Yes.'

'Yes?' The hope in his voice shamed me.

'Chocolate.'

'Chocolate?'

'Food generally. I could eat as much as I liked and never feel guilty.'

'Well,' he said, with a heavy sigh. 'It's a start, I suppose.'

Another year passed, I turned thirty-two and I still didn't feel 'ready'. More than I had, admittedly, but not quite enough. Until one day, feeling like I was giving up after years on the run, I just crumbled. I knew I had to. The silent struggle was exhausting and I suspected that things with Garv and me had gone a bit weird since Hoppy and Rider had arrived. I loved Garv and I didn't want things getting any worse.

When I turned myself in, Garv almost burst with happiness. 'What changed your mind?!'

'I don't want you becoming one of those women who steal babies from outside a supermarket,' I said.

'You won't regret this, I promise,' he enthused.

And while I suspected that I probably would, my resentment was defused by the knowledge that he didn't understand how great my qualms were. That he genuinely thought that once he'd knocked me up, all my trepidation would be washed clean away in a great tide of oestrogen.

'So will I buy a thing that tells me my temperature and all that?' I asked.

Garv looked startled. 'No! Can't we just . . . ?'

So we just . . .

The first time we had sex without contraception, I felt as if I'd jumped out of a plane without a parachute, and even though we'd been told it could take between six months and a year, I was still watchful of my body.

But despite the risks we'd taken, my period arrived, and not even the squeezing cramps could dampen my relief. I relaxed a little – I'd bought myself another month. Maybe I'd be one of the women who could take up to a year.

Not a hope. I conceived in the second month; and I knew about it within minutes. I didn't immediately start demanding peanut butter and wasabi sandwiches, but something in me didn't feel settled, and when I abruptly took agin Tesco Metro BLTs, I *knew*.

Mind you, I'd been fairly sure the previous month too, when I *hadn't* been. But within days it was clear that this was no neurotic imagining. I really was up the pole. How was I so sure? It might have had something to do with the fact that until after eight in the evening I couldn't even keep down water. Or if anyone passed within three feet of my boobs I wanted to kill them. Or that I was chalk white. Except for when I was mint green. It was all wrong. When Shelley had been five weeks pregnant, she'd gone on a walking holiday in the Pyrenees (Why, indeed? Your guess is as good as mine), covered ten gruelling miles a day and never once felt lightheaded. Claire hadn't even known she was pregnant for the first month and was out partying day and night, without recourse to a single bucket.

But I was the sickest person I'd ever met, which was especially hard for me because I didn't usually get sick often. Even my brain was affected – I couldn't *think* straight. Just to make it official, we did a pregnancy test and when the second blue line rose to the surface, Garv cried, in a manly, I've-an-eyelash-caught-in-my-eye sort of way. I cried too, but for different reasons.

Sick though I was, I just about managed to keep working – though God only knows how much use I was to them, and the only thing that kept me going was the vision of my bed at the end of the day. By the time I reached home, almost whimpering with relief, I'd make straight for the bedroom. If Garv had got home before me, he'd have already flung back the covers and all I had to do was crawl in between the cool, forgiving sheets. Then Garv would lie beside me and I'd grasp his hand and tell him how much I hated him.

'I know,' he crooned, 'I don't blame you, but I promise that in a few short weeks you'll feel better.'

'Yes,' I whispered, gratefully. 'Thank you, yes. And then I'll kill you.'

Sooner or later, I struggled to sit up and Garv knew the drill. 'Puke bowl?' he'd ask solicitously, as we prepared for yet another round of dry retches.

'Watching the game, having a Bud,' Garv murmured, as I

Whassup'd into the pretty fuchsia basin he'd bought specially for the occasion.

It was after the first month that something began to ripple through me, a sensation so unfamiliar that I couldn't categorize it.

'Indigestion?' Garv suggested. 'Wind?'

'No . . .' I said, in a daze. 'I think it might be . . . excitement.' Garv cried again.

Call it hormones, call it Mother Nature, call it whatever you want, but to my great surprise I suddenly really wanted the baby. Then, at seven weeks, when we went for the first scan, my love just exploded. The grainy, grey picture showed something tiny, a little blob that was slightly darker than the other blobbiness around it, and it was our baby. Another human being, new and unique. We'd made it and I was carrying it.

'It's a miracle,' I whispered to Garv as we studied it.

'De murkil 'f new life,' he agreed solemnly.

In wild, celebratory mode, we took the rest of the day off work and went for lunch at a restaurant that I sometimes went to with clients and consequently had never been able to enjoy before. I even managed half a chicken breast without barfing. Then we wandered around town and he persuaded me to let him buy me a JP Tod's handbag (the one that Helen now covets). It was so expensive I'd never have been able to buy it for myself, not even out of my Ladies' Nice Things account. 'Last time we'll have the money for this kind of thing,' he declared skittishly. Then I bought him a CD of some saxophonist whom I knew nothing about but whom he loved. 'Last time you'll get the chance to listen to music,' I declared, also skittishly. It was one of the nicest days of my entire life.

That was when we decided to give Hoppy and Rider to

Dermot. He'd become very fond of them, and though we were sad to lose them, we'd decided they'd have to go anyway when the baby arrived. We'd heard enough horror stories about jealous animals attacking babas, and even though Hoppy and Rider had never shown signs of narkiness, we felt we couldn't take any chances. So, tearfully, we waved them off to Dermot's, promising to visit them regularly.

Around then, other things changed too. I'd never been mad about my body. I mean, I didn't hate it enough to starve or cut it, but it had never been something to celebrate. But with my pregnancy came a profound shift; I felt ripe and gorgeous and powerful and – I know this sounds funny – *useful*. Up until then, I'd regarded my womb in the same way as the keyring on my Texier handbag: it was neither decorative nor useful, but it came with the rest of the package, so I was stuck with it.

Another by-product of my pregnancy was that I felt blessedly normal; for so long, my lack of maternal instincts had had me thinking I was almost a freak. For the first time in a long time, I felt in step with the rest of the world.

You're supposed to wait until after the twelfth week to tell people, and I'm normally very good at keeping secrets, but not in this instance. So on week eight we broke the news to our families, who expressed delight – most of them, anyway. 'I reckoned you for a Jaffa,' Helen coldly told Garv.

'What's a Jaffa?'

'An orange which doesn't have any seeds.'

He still looked confused, so she elaborated. 'I thought you were firing blanks.' Then she added, 'When I could bear to think about it at all.'

Next I rang Emily, one of the few people who'd known the full extent of my reluctance to get pregnant – and only because she'd been of the same mind. She was one of those people who, if you asked if they liked children, would reply, 'Love them! But I couldn't manage a whole one.'

I broke the news that I was eight weeks pregnant and when she asked me, 'Are you happy?' I heard myself reply, 'I've never been so happy in all my life. I was a fool to have waited so long.'

There was silence, then a sniff. 'Are you crying?' I asked suspiciously.

'I'm so happy for you,' she wobbled. 'This is wonderful news.'

It was on a routine visit to the bathroom one Saturday afternoon when I saw it. This wasn't the spotting they'd talked about. This was crimson and *everywhere*.

'Garv,' I called, surprised at how normal I sounded. 'Garv! I think we'd better go to the hospital.'

Out by the car, I decided I wanted to drive myself. I was quite insistent, something to do with control, probably. And Garv, who rarely loses his temper, stood in the street and yelled, 'I'LL FUCKING DRIVE.'

I remember every part of the journey to the hospital in almost hyper-reality. Everything was acutely sharp and clear. We had to go through town, which was so thronged with Saturday-afternoon shoppers we could hardly get the car through the streets. The sheer number of people made me feel entirely alone in the world.

At the hospital, we parked in an ambulance bay and to this day I could still tell you what the woman on admissions looked like. She promised that I'd be seen as soon as possible, then Garv and I sat and waited on orange plastic chairs that had been nailed to the floor. We didn't speak.

When a nurse came for me, Garv promised, 'It'll be OK.'

But it wasn't.

It was a nine-week foetus, but I felt as if someone had died. It was too early to tell the sex and that made me feel worse.

A shared loss is harder, I think. I could handle my own pain, but I couldn't handle Garv's. And there was something I had to say to him before the guilt devoured me whole. 'It's my fault, it's because I didn't want it. He or she knew where it wasn't wanted.'

'But you did want it.'

'Not in the beginning.'

And he had nothing to say to me. He knew it was true.

26

On Sunday evening, Lara came over.

'Not out with Nadia?' Emily asked.

'Nah, she got her butthole bleached and can't sit down.'

'Excuse me?' I spluttered. 'Her butthole? Bleached?'

'It's the latest thing in plastic surgery,' Lara explained. 'Lots of girls do it. To make it look pretty.'

'Like getting your teeth whitened,' Emily chipped in. 'Except it's your butthole instead.'

'You're making this up!'

'We're not!'

'But who'd see . . . when . . . ?' I stopped. I was better off not knowing.

'I got me a present.' Lara thrust a box at us.

'Lovely,' Emily enthused. 'What is it?'

'It's my new state-of-the-art caller display. So sophisticated it can almost tell me what my caller is thinking. Listen to the functions!'

As she listed out all the things it could do, she reminded me of Garv – boys and their toys – and I wondered whether there was a link between loving gadgets and wanting to have sex with girls.

We took ourselves and a bottle of wine out to the sunloungers in the fragrant back garden, where Lara tried to quiz Emily on her thirty-six-hour date with Lou. But Emily tetchily dismissed

263

him: 'I had a good time but he's not going to call.' She was far more interested in analysing her work situation.

'The new script just isn't coming together, so if Mort Russell passes on *Plastic Money*, that's it. Game over.' She blew into her hands and her face was pale. 'I've got no other choice, I really am going to have to go back to Ireland.'

Lara shook her head. 'I've been thinking about this. There must be other work you can do.'

'Yeah, I hear they're hiring at Starbucks.'

'No, other *writing* work. Script polish.'

'What's that?' I asked Emily.

'I take a poxy script that's about to go into production, make it coherent, add jokes and make the main characters three-dimensional and likeable. For that I get a pittance and someone else gets the credit.' Emily sighed. 'Obviously I'd love it, but there are so many writers in this town and we're all chasing the same pieces of work. David says he's tried for me.'

'Agent, schmagent. The time has come to get out there and hustle yourself,' Lara encouraged.

'I do!'

'You need to do more than look pretty and give out your cards at parties. You've got to *bother* people. That's if you really don't want to go home to Ireland.'

'I really don't.'

'OK. I'll see if I can swing something and so will Troy. And what about that Irish guy? You know the one from Dark Star Productions. Shay something? Shay Mahoney?'

'Shay Delaney.' Beside me I could feel Emily's sudden awkwardness.

'Yeah, him. Wonder if he's got any shit Irish films that could use a polish.'

'I'm sure he's got plenty of shit Irish films that could use a polish,' Emily said. 'But no money to pay for it.'

'You never know,' Lara mused. 'Call him. Convince him.'

Emily made noncommittal noises and I was relieved. I didn't want her to ring him.

'Oh, enough doom and gloom already!' Emily declared. 'We need cheering up. Lara, will you tell us your "I'm OK, you're OK" story?' She snuggled into her lounger, like a child preparing for their bedtime story. 'Off you go,' she encouraged, with the air of someone who'd heard this many, many times. '"I'd been nineteen for seven years and it was starting to show . . ."'

Lara took a deep breath, and began. 'OK, I'd been nineteen for seven years and it was starting to show. I'd been the prettiest girl at my high school, and seven years earlier I'd come to LA hoping to be the next Julia Roberts.'

Emily was happily mouthing the words along with her.

'But LA was full of chicks who'd been the prettiest girls at high school and I was nothing special.'

I began to object that Lara was *very* special, but she stopped me.

'Tell it to the hand. Look around you, this town is full of babes. They are everywhere and a thousand new ones arrive every week, can you *imagine*? But at the time I didn't know this. So I start looking for work, hit a brick wall and end up having to do pay theatre.'

'What's that?'

'Productions you pay for a part in.'

'*You* pay *them*?'

'Yeah, but there's always the chance that some hotshot director will spot you and you get to put something on your résumé. Anyhoo, after that, I got a few walk-on parts where *they* paid *me* and I thought I was on my way. In between acting jobs, I waited tables and got my boobs and lips done.'

'Biggened,' Emily explained. 'And some casting director told her to drop ten pounds –'

'Was her name Kirsty?' I asked sarcastically.

At that point, the story of Lara's life stalled while Emily had a little rant about Kirsty telling me I needed to drop ten pounds. (I had exaggerated to make her seem worse.) Lara soothed and smoothed, then Emily resumed. 'Right! Some casting director told her to drop ten pounds, though she was already x-ray skinny – so she upped her exercise to four hours daily. Then she began starving herself and only ate twelve grapes and five rice-cakes a day.'

I didn't believe her. No one could survive on that.

'It's true,' Lara confirmed. 'I was constantly hungry.'

'Even though you were on pills,' Emily reminded her.

'That's right. I knew every doctor who gave fake pre-scriptions. I took so much speed – that's what diet pills are – my mouth was always dry, my heart was racing . . .'

'. . . I was permanently homicidal,' Emily chimed in with the last bit.

'I was so poor and so unhappy. Six days out of seven I managed to stick to my diet. But – and it was like Russian roulette, I never knew which chamber was loaded – on one of the days I broke my diet. And how! Three pints of ice-cream, a pound of chocolate, four bags of cookies . . . then I made myself puke it all up.'

'Bulimia,' Emily intoned gravely at me. 'For all the good it did her.'

'You got it. Instead of graduating to speaking parts, even the walk-on parts stopped happening. They said my look was over. Big, blonde Aryan types were out and wide-eyed waifs who looked like they'd been abused as children were in.'

She paused and Emily prompted her, '"I'd been to twenty-three auditions in a row without a single call-back."'

'I'd been to twenty-three auditions in a row without a single call-back and I hadn't had a paying acting job in over two years. I'm stony broke and all the time I'm getting older, my ass is slipping, my face is getting lines, and every week a thousand *real* nineteen-year-olds are getting off the bus and hawking their fresh teenage bodies round town. I can't, just can't go back to waiting tables, so I slept with a director – a *man* – who promised me a part. It never happened. Then I got so desperate I slept with a *writer.*'

'Why's it worse to sleep with a writer than a director?'

Emily and Lara both chuckled. 'Because writers in Hollywood have no power,' Emily explained. 'They're the amoebas of the Hollywood food chain, even further down the scale than the caterers on a movie set.'

'Then,' Lara bit her lip, 'just when I think it can't get any worse, my girlfriend threw me out. She'd found out about me sleeping with the director. I had no job, no money, no girl, no self-respect – no rice-cakes, even. The long, dark cocktail hour of the soul.' She laughed, but saw fit to add, 'It was horrible – I can't tell you. The dream was over, I knew I was beat and it just about broke my heart. I saw myself going back home to Portland on the bus and I felt like the biggest failure in the history of the world. So there you go – my sordid life as an actress!'

'At least you never did a porn film,' I comforted.

'Oh, I did.' She sounded surprised. 'I even put it on my résumé. For a while.'

'But the moral of the story,' Emily prompted. 'Let's not get sidetracked.'

'The moral of the story is I thought I would never be happy again,' Lara said. 'I was twenty-six years of age and all washed up. I'd had plastic surgery, I'd given years of my life, I'd used up every bit of my hope and I had nothing to show for it. I hated myself and I wished I was dead.'

'She tried slitting her wrists,' Emily said.

'But I couldn't even do that right. Did you know you're supposed to do it longways instead of crossways?'

'Yes.'

'Smarter than me. But here's a thing – my life did get better. I made the decision to let go of my dreams, because they were killing me, and I stopped asking the impossible from myself. I changed my attitude and decided to focus on what I had rather than what I didn't have. And most of all, I decided I wasn't going to be bitter.'

'So you went back to school,' Emily said.

'So I went back to school and two days – *two days* – after I got those little letters after my name, I got hired by a production company. So I still got to work in the movies, right? I hadn't wanted to work behind the scenes, I'd wanted to be in front of a camera, but I sucked it up and got with the programme. And yeah, there are times when I see a girl's face on the silver screen and I wish it was me,' she said. 'But most times I'm down with it. I love my job – except for when I nearly got canned for missing *Two Dead Men*. I love the movies I work with and I got over the girl. So there you go.'

'I love that story,' Emily sighed. 'Makes me think that whatever happens, I'll be OK. And so will you, Maggie.'

We lapsed into a silent glow of hope and, for the first time, heard a conversation floating over the hedge from next door. The Goatee Boys were also taking the evening air in their backyard.

One of them said, '. . . crusty and kinda green . . .'

This gave rise to groans and 'Oh man!'s.

'Like peeing razor blades,' the first voice said, and more groans ensued.

'Venereal disease,' Emily whispered, her face alight with disgust. 'Ssshhh, listen. One of them has VD.'

Sure enough, we listened and there was more talk of peeing fire and a visit to the quack.

'Which one of them is it?' Lara asked. 'Ethan? Curtis?'

'Betcha it's Ethan.'

'It doesn't sound like him.'

'And Curtis is too weird, who'd sleep with him?'

'You'd be surprised.'

We earwigged a bit more. Whoever it was, their winkie was like a war zone and the doctor had only added to the grief because he'd put a type of furled umbrella down into the afflicted willy – then opened it! Behind the fence, cries of horror rose up into the night and I myself felt the first signs of queasiness.

'It's not Luis,' I insisted. 'He's too sweet.'

'So who is it, then?'

'I've got to know.' Emily pulled her lounger across, stood on it and poked her head over the fence. 'Which one of you is it? *Luis?* I'm surprised.'

Still standing on the lounger, she turned back to us. 'It's Luis, and they want to know if we want to come over. They're doing tequila shots. Dude, that's most excellent!'

Despite her sarcasm, she seemed happy enough to go round. So did Lara, and I had no problem at all with it: nearly everything I did in Los Angeles was strange and new, this was no different. But as we passed through their darkened house, I got the fright of my life when I saw a seven-foot-tall figure looming blackly out of a corner. It transpired to be a cardboard Darth Vader – Curtis's most prized possession. 'I got a C-3PO too, and a Chewbacca suit,' he boasted. 'And three of the original posters.'

God, he was peculiar. To humour him I said brightly, 'So you're a Trekkie.'

'*Star Wars*.' He sounded appalled. 'Not *Star Trek*.' Under his breath I heard him mutter with contempt, '*Girls*.'

Indeed.

They'd dragged their flowery old sofa out into the back, where Luis was installed, with a slight air of the invalid about him. His hands seemed to hover and flutter protectively over his groin. Or maybe it was just to fend off prying eyes: Emily, Lara and I all stared long and hard at the diseased area.

'You girls look like you got x-ray vision,' he said nervously.

'You'd better believe it.' Lara gave a menacing wink.

Ethan doled out shot glasses of tequila, then stopped in front of me. 'You look different,' he said thoughtfully.

'No pantyhose on her head.' This from Luis.

'No-o, not just that.' He paused to give Curtis a sharp poke and hissed like a mammy, 'Get off the sofa and let the ladies sit down,' then resumed his scrutiny of me. 'You haven't . . . had your moustache shaved off?'

'She's had her eyebrows done,' Lara contributed.

'Ahhh, gotta be that!'

And so began a pleasant, mellow night which only ended when an argument broke out over who should have the worm at the bottom of the bottle. ('Stop!' I berated Lara and Emily, who were both flushed from the tussle. 'It's Ethan's bottle. He should be allowed to have it.')

Then we all went home and slept soundly.

27

I awoke to find a woman, approximately four foot high, banging a swiffer around my room. Conchita, I could only imagine.

'Sorry I wake you,' she beamed.

'I was awake anyway,' I lied back, grabbing some clothes.

In the kitchen, Emily was hurriedly putting on her sandals. 'Didn't I forget to get Conchita's bun, so I've to run up to Starbucks. She refuses to touch the bathroom unless we give her a sugar hit.'

'I'll go,' I offered, still on my keeping-busy kick.

'Are you sure? Well, thanks. But listen, she won't eat anything with bananas or blueberries,' she yelled after me.

Outside, yet another beautiful day was presenting itself for inspection. Considering it was a Monday morning, the world was suffused with triumphant yellow light, and everything looked picture perfect – the pretty little houses, the even-skin-toned lawns, the velvet petals of the blazing pink flowers.

In Starbucks I got us a chocolate muffin each, even though all Emily would do with hers was to crumble it into bits, then announce she was stuffed. Then I set off for home again, passing Reza's salon as I went. She was within, grimly tugging the hair off someone. I waved at her and she glared at me. Just as it should be! God was in his heaven and all was well with the world.

But the second I walked back into the house, I knew something bad had happened. Emily was shaking on the edge of the couch and Conchita was ministering to her.

'They passed,' Emily declared.

For a confused moment, I thought she was talking about exams or a driving test. Where I come from, 'passed' is a *good* word – the opposite of 'failed'.

'Who passed what?'

'Mort Russell. Hothouse passed on my script. David just rang.'

Shock rooted me to the spot. They couldn't have passed. What about Julia and Cameron? What about the three thousand screens? It took a moment for my hope to dwindle away, to understand that none of it would be happening. The lying bastards!

Emily was hyperventilating with squeaky gasps and she was shuddering as if she was crying, but her eyes were dry. 'What am I going to do? I'm fucked, I'm so totally fucked. I've no money, not a red cent. Oh my God, oh my God!'

From her apron pocket, Conchita produced a little bottle and said, 'Xanax. To calm her down.' I made sweeping, go-for-it, no-time-like-the-present motions with both my hands.

'Can I've two?' Emily asked.

'Ob course.'

But when Conchita shook some pills into the palm of her hand, there was a little ruck and before I knew what had happened Emily had roughly grabbed not two, but four xanax and crammed them into her mouth.

'Sorry,' she mumbled – but only once they were good and swallowed.

Conchita and I exchanged a look. Who were we to deny her?

Another wave of disbelief hit. 'But they were so enthusiastic,' I voiced. 'It sounded like a done deal.'

'That's the way they all carry on.'

'Did they say why they passed?'

'They *said* it's not what they're looking for right now,' Emily gasped. 'But I don't know what the truth is. Probably they just hated it.'

'Sssssh,' Conchita urged, pulling Emily to her bosom and stroking her hair.

'But –' I started up again, a thousand indignant questions forming, but Conchita nitched them with a firm shake of the head.

The three of us sat in silence while the hopeless day ticked by. I was at a complete loss. Everything had been geared around this coming through, and though I'd had my worries, I'd never really considered that it wouldn't. What was Emily going to do now? Come home to Ireland with me? But I didn't want to go home. Especially not now. Now that Troy – It was then that I realized he still hadn't called me. Unless he'd called while I'd been out getting the muffins, and it so wasn't the right time to ask . . .

'Maybe you go to bed?' Conchita suggested and Emily nodded obediently.

'Four xanax, she sleep until Websday,' Conchita told me.

I was on the verge of asking for a couple of pills for myself when the phone rang. My immediate thought was of Troy, but when I answered, a woman's voice said, 'Hold for David Crowe calling for Emily O'Keeffe.'

'She's busy right now.' Having a nervous breakdown. 'I'm her assistant. Can I help?'

But the woman was gone and after a few clicks the next voice I heard was David. 'Hey, Emily!' he chuckled.

'It's Maggie. Emily's a little upset.'

'Sure. But I got good news. Larry Savage over at Empire took a look. He wants to meet with her.'

'Well, that's great! When?'

'Right now.'

'Oh, that's a shame,' I said regretfully. 'She can't go right now. She's just taken four xanax.'

A pause. Not a cordial one.

'Now you listen to me,' he said, all traces of affability gone. 'She needs to get it together *now* and get over to Empire. We can't push this meeting back. She's got to get in today before Larry finds out that Hothouse passed, xanax or no fucking xanax. Coffee, cocaine, I don't care how, but she'd better get it together. And if she can't do it, *you* do it. I've put my ass on the line here.'

All the moisture had retreated from my mouth. It was as dry as carpet. What had happened to David Crowe, charm monster? I was frightened of him, genuinely frightened. He sounded so dangerous, so vengeful.

And I had got the gist of what was happening. Some machiavellian machinations meant David had managed to con Larry Savage into thinking that Mort Russell was still interested. There was a tiny window of opportunity before Larry discovered that Mort had passed. If Larry found out, then David was in the shit. And Emily's last chance was gone. So the pitch had to be today.

I glanced into Emily's bedroom. She was lying down, her eyes closed, Conchita stroking her forehead. There was no point asking her what we should do. And *I* hadn't a notion. I thought of Lara – she could help, even though she was up to her eyes organizing the launch for some movie called *Doves*. Or how about Troy?

274

'Could you give us a couple of hours?' I glanced at my watch, it was ten-twenty. 'Say until midday?' That should be enough time for either Troy or Lara to get here, and then they could take over, they'd know what to do.

'No. I can't give you five fucking minutes,' he snapped. 'The clock is ticking and news gets round this town way fast. It's this morning, or never. By lunch-time it'll be all over.'

Desperately, I tried to focus, to think intelligently. *Oh, Jesus Christ!* 'Oh, OK . . . what can you tell me about Larry Savage?'

'Larry, Larry, Larry . . . what's to say?' There was a clicking sound like David was banging his pen off his teeth. 'Weeell, he's rumoured to have sex with animals. But, hey, it's only a rumour!'

I pushed down my frustration and asked, 'Any career information?'

'A coupla years back he made *Fred*. Remember it? Old English Sheepdog who saves the circus from closure?'

I remembered it.

'Seen it?'

'No. I was more than five years of age at the time.'

'Cute,' David said unpleasantly. 'Well, lie. Tell him you loved it.'

'OK. Now, can you tell me how to get to Empire?'

Irritably, David gave sketchy directions, and just in case there was any chance that I might calm down, he ended the conversation by saying, 'This is Emily's last chance. Make sure she doesn't fuck it up.'

'Right.' With a pounding heart, I hung up the phone and hurried in to Emily. Who, floating away on a pink xanax cloud, was having none of it. 'Al go ch'morr', she said sleepily.

'Tomorrow's too late.' Hysteria skimmed my voice as I explained the situation.

Luckily, Conchita displayed an astute grasp of the workings of Hollywood. 'The man find out the other man have passed, he not berry happy!' She hoiked a startled Emily from the bed.

'Emily, you'll have to make yourself sick,' I said urgently.

'Huh?'

'Stick your fingers down your throat and make yourself throw up. To get rid of the tablets.'

Dazed though she was, she looked disgusted.

'I'm sorry. But desperate circumstances call for desperate measures.'

Conchita and I marched her to the bathroom, where despite issuing some impressively inhuman gawking noises from her gullet, she couldn't recall the xanax.

'I'j nevr make ablimic,' she said, slumping against the bowl, her forehead beaded in sweat from her efforts.

'One more time,' I encouraged. 'Just try once more.'

'K.'

But though she strained until her face was bright red and running with tears, there was still no joy. What was I to do with her?

Conchita was on top of things, though. 'Emily, you get in the shower! And you –' she pointed at me, 'make coffee. Strong!'

After her shower, we dressed Emily and tried to get a comb through her hair.

'You look good,' Conchita encouraged.

Emily shook her head and said sadly, 'Everything is wrong.'

'Like what?'

'My 'spensive suit's in jrycleaner's, I haven't been reiki'd, my hair's a Jackson Five special.'

'Nebber mind,' Conchita said, forcing a cup of treacly coffee on her. 'You got a pitch, lady!'

When we were ready to leave, Conchita whipped out a little plastic bottle of holy water and flung generous handfuls of it at us. As a drop splattered on to Emily's face, she turned to me in confusion.

'Maggie, is this actually happening? Or mi jreaming it?'

'It's happening,' I said grimly, marching her to my car and wondering how the hell you got to The Valley.

The drive was horrible. My heart was banging against my ribs and my breath didn't want to be drawn – there is nothing more terrifying than the LA freeways when you don't know where you're going. Lanes and lanes of aggressive cars on all sides of you. My right arm was begging to be scratched. To make matters worse, I was trying to make Emily practise her pitch.

'Camera pans over a breast of pairs . . .'

'Good,' I tried to encourage. 'Good.' I saw a sliproad approaching and peered around, looking for signs. 'Is this where we turn off?' And how did I cut across three lanes of traffic to do so?

By the time I'd discovered it wasn't our turn, Emily had meandered off into silence. I managed to take my eyes off the road just long enough to see her chin nodding on her chest and a delicate trail of dribble heading south to her second-best suit. Christ! That was all we needed. Her falling asleep mid-pitch.

I shook her and begged, 'Drink some Jolt, try and stay awake. Please!'

'Oh my God, Maggie,' she mumbled. 'This is a nightmare.'

I felt for her, because she genuinely understood how serious the situation was, but simply couldn't control herself.

'I can't do it,' she said.

'You can.'

'I can't.' There was a pause and I knew what was coming next. 'Will you do it?'

'What? The pitch?'

'Yes.'

What could I say? With dreadful resignation I said, 'You'd better remind me how it goes.'

So then I was trying to remember the pitch as well as concentrate on directions. My palms were so wet they were sliding all over the steering wheel and I still couldn't seem to get enough air.

Some time, today will be over, I told myself. Some time in the future this horrible day will have ended. Then I changed it to, Some day I'll be dead and at peace and none of this will matter.

More by luck than judgement, we finally arrived at Empire Studios. You couldn't miss it. On top of each of the two gateposts they had twelve-foot-high Freds.

I rolled down the window and gave our names to the man with the clipboard, who confirmed we were on the list. 'Welcome to Empire Studios.'

'Nice dogs,' I nodded at the Freds.

'Oh yeah?' The man laughed. 'Thing is, guy who made them had a grudge against the studio. When it rains, it looks like the dogs are peeing.' Then he cheerfully waved us through.

Empire Studios looked very different to Hothouse. Hothouse had been high-rise glass and steel, but this studio looked like it had been built in the thirties: rows of unassuming-looking, white, two-storey buildings. It reminded me of a holiday camp.

Not that it meant that Empire was any less successful or powerful than Hothouse, it just meant it had been around for longer. And the reception area was covered with posters from mega-successful movies, just like it had been at Hothouse. The only difference was that this time it didn't thrill me. It all felt like a nasty sham and though my knees were wobbling the way they had done there, this time it was from fear, not excitement.

'Take a seat,' the text-book-beautiful receptionist said.

'Are you OK?' I whispered to Emily, as we sat down.

'Yeah, I just feel like I'm dreaming.'

'Try and stay awake,' I encouraged desperately.

'I'll try.'

A few minutes later, we were met by Larry Savage's assistant, a pleasant-looking woman called Michelle.

'I loved your script,' she told us warmly. 'I truly loved it.'

It was all I could do to stop myself from curling my lip at her.

'This way, please,' she said, walking us through the heat to Larry Savage's chalet.

I'd seen Larry Savage – briefly – once before at the Club House, and he looked just like I remembered: an identikit Hollywood executive. He had the tan, good teeth, well-cut lightweight suit and – no doubt – a convincing line in bullshit. I'd become very cynical very quickly.

He was on the phone as we were ushered in. 'I don't freakin' care,' he was shouting. 'We test-screen the ass off it. If no one salutes, then it's straight to video.' An angry pause, then he yelled, 'No, you kiss MINE!' Then he clattered the phone back into its cradle and turned to Emily and me. 'Actors,' he said, with a rueful smile.

'Yeah,' I rolled my eyes sycophantically, then effected introductions.

'All righty. I read your script,' he began.

I almost put my arm up to shield us from the avalanche of fake compliments. Funny, edgy, great dialogue – hadn't we been here before?

'I hated it!' Larry Savage declared.

Now I hadn't been expecting *that*. Then I wondered if it was going to be one of those 'I hated it so much I want to pay you three million dollars for it' riffs?

Unfortunately, it wasn't.

'I hated it,' Larry repeated. 'Me, I like animals!'

'So we've heard,' Emily slurred beside me.

I gave her arm a sharp little pinch.

'Fred, Babe, Beethoven, now *that* was a movie . . .' Larry sighed wistfully. 'But the studio is looking for smart.' He bitch-slapped the script in front of him. 'This is real smart.' He managed to sound glum about it. 'It's sassy, snappy, pacy. But I got an idea, hear me out here!'

We nodded. Not that it made any difference, he fully intended to have his say. 'These girls in your movie go on the run. How about their pet dog goes with them, stows himself away in the trunk of the car, they discover him when it's too late to bring him back, but they're real happy. Then he tips them off when the rangers are coming. Y'know, he wakes 'em by pulling the bed clothes off with his teeth.' Suddenly Larry started speaking in falsetto. '"What's up, Chip? Had a bad dream, boy? Go back to sleep, boy. Oh, you won't? You think the rangers are coming. Wake up, Jessie, wake up!!!"' He returned to his normal voice. 'The pet doggie saves the day. Got a problem with that?' he barked (appropriately enough) at Emily.

Mutely, she shook her head.

'Terrific.' Suddenly he was all smiles. 'I look forward to working with you. Your people will be hearing from my people.'

Then, an arm around each of our shoulders, he was walking us back out into the too-bright sunshine.

As Emily lurched to the car, she mumbled, 'Did I dream that bit?'

'The bit about the dog saving them from the rangers?'

'No, the bit where he said my people would be hearing from his people.'

'He said it all right.'

'But nobody *ever* says that in real life.'

'This isn't real life.'

It was only when we were clambering into the car that we noticed that neither of us had had to pitch to him.

'After all our practice,' I laughed. 'But it's probably for the best.'

'So how d'you think it all went?' Emily asked, dazedly. 'Any chance he might buy it and save my life?'

I considered it – there had been no talk of fast-tracking, green-lighting, three thousand screens or major stars. But Mort Russell had done all that and it had amounted to nothing, so who knew? And did Emily really want to rewrite her witty, sexy script as *Chip, the Wonder Dog*? But before I got to say any of that, Emily had fallen asleep on me. She slept for the entire hellish journey home, so she never knew that I took a wrong turning on the 405 and ended up halfway to Tijuana, passing turn-offs to all sorts of dodgy neighbourhoods before I managed to turn around.

Once back in Santa Monica, there was still no rousing her, so I had to call in on the Goatee Boys and get Ethan to help carry her from the car. Which was almost more trouble than it was worth, because he made me take her arms and insisted that he'd carry her legs, and I knew, just *knew* it was so he could look up her skirt. Then, when we'd flung her on the bed, he suggested hopefully, 'We better undress her. Like, in case she can't breathe and stuff.'

'No! Thank you, Ethan! Goodbye!'

I wanted to get rid of him fast, because as we'd stumbled into the house I'd noticed there was a message on the machine. It had to be from Troy. And sure enough, when I hit 'play' a man's voice said warmly, 'Hey, baby . . .' I exhaled with relief. But another second in, my reprieve curdled into bitter disappointment. This wasn't Troy. It was Lou, Emily's commitmentphobe. But what the hell was he doing ringing her? According to her prediction, she was never going to hear from him again. And here he was, calling her 'dollface' and suggesting that they catch a movie tomorrow night.

Abruptly all hope departed, like air from a burst beachball. For the past two days I'd been pumping myself with faith, warding off doubt – and suddenly I had no defence. Why hadn't Troy called me? It was Monday afternoon, almost evening – I'd last seen him on Saturday morning and he'd said he'd call me. Well, I'd asked him to call me and he hadn't said no. But I hadn't heard a word. Why?

At that, my worst suspicions began to multiply like bacteria in a Petri dish. Had I a horrible body? Was I boring? Had I not been good in bed? After all, I'd been out of practice for so long that I could have been atrocious and not known. But he'd *seemed* to enjoy himself. Then again, Mort Russell had *seemed* to love Emily's script and hadn't. Was this city just one big hall of mirrors, where nothing was what it seemed?

Immobilized by despair, all I could see ahead of me was an empty, burnt-out future. Then I remembered the vile day I'd had: anyone would feel discouraged after it. I tried hard to generate a tiny amount of positivity. Troy was probably just busy. Emily had said he was fanatical about his work. And the night we'd spent together, he'd really seemed to like me. We'd had fun. He *would* ring me.

Just about convinced, I turned my attention to the telly, and spent several catatonic hours in front of it, too tired even to eat. At around eleven, I heard noises from Emily's room. She must have finally woken up. When I went in, she was sitting up in bed like a princess.

'You know what, Maggie?' And her smile was anxious. 'I had the strangest dream.'

28

The night's sleep wrought an astonishing change in me and I came to full of benign thoughts. Troy was going to ring me today, I just *knew*.

For once, my mood matched the weather. Most mornings since I'd come to Los Angeles I'd woken up with foreboding, shocked on a daily basis at finding my life so altered. But today my expectations were as sunny as the elements.

Emily was in the kitchen cradling a huge, crackly cellophaned bouquet. 'Look,' she said. 'Lou sent them. What's he up to?' She was genuinely perplexed. 'This must be some new mutation of the commitmentphobe syndrome. They knew we were getting resistant to the One Fantastic Night thing, they *knew* we expected never to hear from them again, so they've had to raise their game. He wants us to go out again tonight. Well,' she laughed, 'he must think I'm a bigger fool than I look!'

'You don't think for a second that he could be sincere?'

A firm shake of the head. 'I do not. Because if he did mean all that stuff about telling our grandchildren, that would be the worst. To have grandchildren, you first have to have children and you know my views on – Oh, Maggie, I'm sorry!'

'It's OK.'

'I just wasn't thinking –'

Just then the phone rang and I jumped to answer it, knowing, with the same certainty that one and one equals two, that it would be Troy.

It turned out to be David. Well, I'd never had great psychic powers, that gift had gone to Anna.

David was once again sweetness and light. Not a mention of yesterday's rage – and certainly no apology. 'Hey, Larry loved you two!'

'That's funny,' I said stiffly. 'We barely opened our mouths. Has he found out about Mort Russell passing?'

'Don't know, but who cares now? You girls hooked him.'

'Did he tell you he wants to make it as an animal movie?'

'Details, details,' he dismissed airily. 'I gotta great feeling about this. Stand by for good news.'

When the phone rang again, I let Emily get it. Then I was sorry, because this time it really *was* Troy!

My heart gave one big, almost painful thump and my anticipation built and built as Emily went on for ages, filling Troy in on the dramatic events of the previous day. 'It's *déjà vu*,' she exclaimed at him. 'I'm *still* waiting for the phone to ring. Same shit, different studio!'

I pottered around in her vicinity, waiting for Troy to finish being polite to her and get to the real business of the call. But on and on they went, and I stopped pottering, I was wearing myself out. So I plonked myself in a nearby chair until *finally* she got round to making winding-up noises. I half got up, my arm stretching for the phone, which is when Emily did something unfathomable. She hung up. It seemed to happen in slow motion, her finger hovering over the red disconnect button, then moving in for the kill. Completely at a loss, I goggled at her and at the phone, which should still be connected but for some incomprehensible reason wasn't.

'What?' Emily looked confused.

'Didn't he ask . . . didn't he want to talk to me?'

'No.' Then, still staring at me, 'Oh shit.'

'Oh shit' was right. Troy's message to me could not have been clearer.

'Maggie, I didn't . . .' Emily squirmed and her manifest anguish belittled me. She pitied me and even though she'd commiserated on the end of my marriage, for a reason that I couldn't articulate, this stung a lot more.

'Maggie, I didn't realize you were expecting . . . something from him.'

'I wasn't.' My voice was barely there.

She was wrestling with some dilemma. With mortifying gentleness, she said, 'There's something you're probably better off knowing. When I called him on Saturday, Kirsty answered the phone.'

'You don't know for sure that something's going on with them.' My defiance was pathetic. 'And even if there is, he might decide he preferred me.'

'You're right.'

That did it. 'I think I want to lie down for a while.'

'No, Maggie, please . . .'

But I closed my bedroom door and redrew the curtains that I'd flung open with such anticipation less than an hour before, and climbed, fully clothed, between the sheets. This is what it's like, I understood. This is what it's like to be single and out there. I mean, I hadn't really thought that Troy and I would end up together and that I'd stay in Los Angeles and live happily ever after. Not for more than five seconds, anyway. But I hadn't expected it to be a for-one-night-only extravaganza either.

So much for living dangerously; it wasn't half as nice as

people made out. Unless the fault was in me. Maybe it was an acquired taste, like olives. I should probably just keep at it until I'd learnt to enjoy it.

Some time later, Emily tiptoed in. 'I'm really sorry,' she whispered. 'How do you feel?'

'I don't know.'

'Humiliated?'

'Yip.'

'Rejected?'

'Yip.'

'Betrayed?'

'Yip.'

'Not good enough?'

'Yip.'

'Lonely?'

'Yip.'

'Ashamed that you lay down and gave it up so easily?'

I closed my eyes. Lord, did she have to be so graphic.

'*Not* ashamed that you lay down and gave it up so easily?' She sounded puzzled.

'Yes, ashamed.'

'That's what I thought. Didn't think you'd changed that much. Have I forgotten anything?'

How about missing my husband? I thought, but didn't say. Both losses had merged into one and I was grounded by their combined weight. For a while, when I'd been with Troy, I'd danced on stardust. Now the glitter had fallen from the sky and all was drab and grey again. While I'd been caught up in Troy, I'd flirted with another life, with being someone else.

Now I was back to being me and I longed to scuttle back to the safe haven of marriage, where this humiliation would disappear. But I couldn't even ring Garv – until I'd found out for definite about Truffle Woman, I'd felt that option was always available to me if missing him got too bad. Now that door was closed. Anyway, wanting to go back to Garv because another man had humiliated me was hardly a healthy reason.

'Have you any idea . . . ?' I asked Emily. 'Why . . . Troy . . . might do this to me?'

'That's just the way he is,' she explained earnestly. 'He likes the ladies but he's too into his work, not interested in a relationship.'

She didn't say that she'd told me so. She's nice that way. Anyway, he'd as good as warned me himself when he'd said, 'I am baaaad news.' But he'd been laughing when he'd said it and, like an eejit, I thought the laugh meant that he was joking.

'He should have left you alone,' she said. 'You're too vulnerable.'

'Too stupid, you mean,' I muttered, hating myself for being so naïve, inexperienced, out of practice. I'd fallen for the oldest trick in the book – a man had been nice to me and I'd thought it meant something.

'Don't be hard on yourself – this is normal, you're on the rebound! You're on your own for the first time in years, you're more than a bit lost, who could blame you for going looking?'

All of a sudden, I was furious with Troy. Him and his concern and his twizzlers and compliments about my hair and calling me 'Irish'. To think I'd once thought he was ugly, with his long features and his hair-grip mouth. Someone with a nose that size had no right to go round breaking hearts!

And small wonder the sex had been so fluid and unclumsy: he was an expert, the guy had a black belt in riding. Christ, he even had special bondage ropes! What did that tell me about his dedication?

Then I cringed as I remembered the most embarrassing bit of all – to think I'd asked him to . . . to *call* me. All those years listening to my single friends and had I learnt *nothing*? You never let on you want to be called. If *he* says he'll ring *you*, you've to murmur, 'Whatever,' like you so couldn't give a damn. What you don't do is throw your hat in the air and burst into 'Happy Days Are Here Again'. Isn't it funny how we all know the rules, but we never think they apply to us?

I was going about this break-up lark all wrong. The usual procedure is you feel awful, then a little bit better, then another little bit. And then a big bit. But the more time had gone on since Garv and I had split, the worse I felt. How much further did I have to proceed into this heart of darkness before I came out the other side?

How was Garv getting on with the single life? Was he faring better than me? Or was he as miserable too? Probably not: he was a man, they always seem to find this sort of thing easier. And who exactly was his girlfriend? How serious was it? Those tormenting thoughts which had been dormant for a while were now back in force.

'I'm giving up on men,' I said bitterly. 'Do you know what I'm going to become?'

'Oh no,' Emily moaned softly. 'Don't say it, because someone round here might take you up on it. Anyway, you have it all wrong. Lesbians are just as bad as men, as far as I can see. They say they'll call then they don't. They sleep with you, then ditch you –'

'I wasn't going to say lesbian,' I interrupted. 'Although it's a thought.'

'Noooo,' she covered her eyes.

'What I was about to say was I'm going to become one of those fabulous single women who go on about choices a lot.' Bitterly, I pretended to be airy and launched into, '"It's just *great* being single because I can *choose* which side of the bed to sleep on. I can *choose* who I want to spend time with, and who I don't. I don't have to waste time on my partner's *boring* family or workmates. No negotiations, no compromises." It'll be fantastic. I'll have tons of friends, a huge mother-ship hand bag from Coach, linen drawstring pants and beautifully cut but practical hair.' Somehow I'd mutated into Sharon Stone.

'Or maybe I won't,' I finished with a sigh. Maybe I'd just end up moving back in with my parents so we could become our street's version of the Addams Family. I would grow a moustache. Eventually I would bow to the inevitable at the hairdresser's and ask for an Irish Mammy.

I wanted to go home. I was so hurt and embarrassed by the way Troy had rejected me that I wanted to put as many miles as possible between me and him. For a while, the dazzling Californian sunshine had bleached out the sharp contours of my pain, but my eyes had adjusted until my anguish was just as severe here as it had been in Ireland. Like a painkiller that becomes less and less effective the more it's used, Los Angeles had stopped working for me. I'd always suspected this would happen, but I didn't expect it to be so soon. I'd only been here two weeks and my initial plan had been to stay for about a month. Ah, well . . .

I was acutely aware of how much I didn't belong here. Mind you, where did I belong? 'Home' didn't really exist any longer. But there was so much music to be faced in Ireland that sooner or later I was going to have to bite the bullet and return – and in the wake of my humiliation at the hands of Troy, I wanted to leave for the airport immediately. I looked for my suitcase; I still hadn't fully unpacked, mostly because I had no closet-space – it wouldn't take me ten minutes to gather up my stuff and ship out of here. The image of me getting on a plane was as comforting as a padded plaster on a blister.

But what about Emily? How selfish would it be to leave her at this nerve-wracking time? Reluctantly, I concluded that I should wait until we heard from Larry Savage. Either he'd buy her script and she'd be fine, or he'd pass and her adventures in Lala land would also come to an end. Whichever happened, we'd know very soon.

That decision made, I rang my parents to tell them I was homeward bound: the mere act made me feel like I was already on my way.

Dad answered, with his customary terror. 'Which one of you is that? Oh, Margaret.' I waited for him to be overcome with the noxious gas given off by the phone, but to my surprise he stayed talking. 'Have you been to Disneyland yet?'

I hadn't.

'You should go, it's marvellous! And they've other ones too. Some Six Flags place. They say it has the world's highest rollercoaster.'

'Think of your neck,' I said firmly. 'Anyway, how do you know about the Six Flags place?'

'Read about it on the Net.'

'*What* net?'

'The Internet Net.'

'What are you doing on the Internet Net?' I couldn't hide my surprise. Surprise which bordered on indignation.

'Helen set it up.'

'He's never off it,' Mum's voice cut in, on the extension. 'Cruising on the Net, looking at pornography.'

'I do not look at pornography!'

'There's no need to shout. And I know all about what goes on on that Net.'

'I'm not shouting, I only sound loud because you're just upstairs from me. And there's other things go on on the Net besides pornography.'

'Like what?'

'Holidays.'

A pause, then a suspicious, 'Flights?'

'Yes, flights.'

'To sunny places?'

I had a clear and unpleasant insight into where all this was heading, and decided to nip it in the bud. 'I'm coming home soon. In the next few days.'

'*Are you?*' High-pitched and irritated and perfectly in unison.

Just as I'd suspected. Well, hopefully that had knocked that on the head.

But later I spoke to Emily about it. 'I've a bad feeling Mum and Dad might be planning a visit here.'

'Don't be silly,' Emily said.

'No, I'm serious.'

'So'm I. They couldn't come here because they haven't had it booked since last November. They're not exactly spontaneous, are they? I mean, their idea of being mad-cap and spur-of-the-moment would be to plan a weekend break for next spring.'

Thus comforted, I put my fears from my mind.

*

But I hadn't reckoned on Helen and her surfermania and it all came to a dreadful head three short hours later.

'. . . booked the flights on the Internet Net,' Mum was saying. 'No need to bother with travel agents, you just type in your details and they give you all these choices. This Net is a great invention!'

'But I want to go home.'

'Well you can't,' she said pleasantly. 'We'll need you to show us the sights. Sure, what difference can a few more days make, anyway?'

For God's sake. I had to bite my knuckle to stifle a scream of frustration.

'Where will you stay?' Then I added very quickly, 'There's no room here.'

'We wouldn't dream of imposing,' Mum said graciously. 'I spoke to Mrs Emily and she gave me the name of the hotel that she stayed in when she came over. Only down the road from Emily's and very friendly, she says, and the breakfast is nice and you get little yokes . . .'

'What little yokes?' I asked wearily.

'Shower caps, sewing kits, the lend of an umbrella. Not that I'd be needing an umbrella,' she sounded suddenly fearful, 'because I'm coming to get away from the rain. If it starts raining in Los Angeles, I'm just booking myself into the mental hospital and let that be an end to it.'

'Well, you know what they say?'

A mistrustful pause. 'That you shouldn't put butter on a burn?'

'They say, it never rains in California.'

'Good,' she said firmly.

'It pours!'

But even that wasn't enough to deter her.

'They arrive on Tuesday,' I reported to an appalled Emily.

'Oh, good Christ.'

29

I clung grimly to sleep as though to the side of a cliff. Reluctantly I rose towards consciousness until I was covered only by a thin veil of sleep, but still I refused to surface. It was the sound of the ringing phone that finally made me give in and face the day.

God, was I sorry that I had. My first thought was of Troy and his horrible, humiliating rejection of me. The second was that, with my family coming to visit, I was trapped in Los Angeles.

Unless . . . unless they'd messed up their Internet reservations. The more I thought about it, the more I saw that the chances of them either a) getting seats on a flight that actually existed or b) booking themselves on a flight to Los Angeles instead of say, Phnom Penh or Tierra Del Fuego were very slim indeed.

I began to cheer up, and when Emily tapped quietly on my door I was able to smile at her. Until she handed me the phone and whispered, 'Mammy Walsh.'

Within seconds, my worst fears were confirmed. It was a perfectly straightforward American Airways flight from Dublin to LAX – and they were definitely booked on it. 'I rang this morning and got confirmation,' Mum said cheerily. She even had a flight number. In fact, she'd even reserved their seats and a vegetarian meal for Anna! Which was the first I'd heard of Anna coming.

'How long will you be staying?'

'Helen's got to be back to do Marie Fitzsimon's wedding – seven bridesmaids, three flower girls, the bride, the mother of the bride and the mother of the groom – so we won't get the full two weeks –'

'*Two* weeks!' I'd have to stay here and face Troy for another two weeks! For the love of Christ!

'– so twelve days is how long we're coming for. Now have a word with your father, he wants to know should he bring his shorts.'

As soon as I was off the phone, things got worse; Emily wanted to have a little 'chat' with me. 'As you know,' she began awkwardly, 'I still haven't heard from Larry Savage and I'm not holding out much hope. Lara made a suggestion the other evening –'

I already knew what was coming.

'– about me looking for other work doing script polishes.'

I couldn't bear it any longer. 'Ring him,' I said.

'She suggested several people, one of them being . . . Oh! Do you mean it? Shay Delaney – you wouldn't mind if I rang him?'

'Why would I mind?' Like, what grounds did I have?

'Maggie, please be honest with me. Just say the word and I won't go near him.'

'Go for it.'

Anxiously she asked, 'Are you sure?'

'Completely.'

'Thanks, thank you. I'm just so desperate for work and I know it was a long time ago, you and him, but first cut is the deepest, as they say. So I was afraid you might be cross with me, and –'

'It's fine,' I interrupted, a little too brusquely. 'Just fine.'

Quickly, she said, 'I won't ring him. I'm sorry I even asked you, it was wrong of me.'

'Ring him, I don't MIND!' The yell hung in the air, shocking us both, then I took a breath and forced a more reasonable tone. 'I don't mind, I promise. Just don't make me keep saying it.'

Bu–'

'Nnnneh!'

'Are you sure?'

'Yes.'

'OK.'

I was hoping that she'd take days to get round to it, but she rang him immediately – so I went to my room, where I could listen avidly without being observed. She didn't get to talk to him, but when she said, 'So he *is* in town right now?' I watched my fingers begin to tremble, although nothing like as badly as the day I'd met him and I hadn't been able to undo the zip on Dad's anorak afterwards. Emily spelt out her name for whoever she was talking to, 'O'Keeffe. O-K-E-E-F-F-E, yeah, O'Keeffe. It's Irish. No, *Irish*. So if you could have him call me, that would be great. Bye.'

Then she came looking for me. 'Maggie? He wasn't there.'

'Wasn't he?' I said neutrally, like I hadn't been standing behind the door, holding my breath in order to overhear and slowly turning purple.

'No. No, he wasn't. So what would you like to do today?' she asked solicitously. 'We could go to the beach or for a drive – or how about we go out for lunch?'

'You've work to do.'

'I can skip it.'

I couldn't help laughing. 'I'm O-K!'

'Bu–'

'Nnnneh!'

She was clearly reluctant to let it go, but at least she didn't start disagreeing with me again.

'Do some work,' I urged.

'All right.' She switched on her laptop and disappeared into her writing. I switched on the telly, hoping for a similar type of escape, and so began another day without someone buying Emily's script: I had a sudden surreal flash that I was in some sort of Beckettian play, and that the rest of my life was going to be spent stuck in this house with Emily, waiting for good news that never came.

After thirty minutes of unproductive channel-hopping, my nerves couldn't take any more so I decided we needed food, and set off for the supermarket.

The raggedy shouting man was there, like he always was, this time roaring about police shoot-outs and heroes taking a bullet. I must have been giving off kick-me-when-I'm-down signals, because as soon as I got out of the car he lit up, sprinted straight across the parking lot at me and yelled 'Zoom!' right into my face.

My heart pounded with shock. Though Emily had said he meant no harm, he seemed out-of-control crazy. Skirting around him and his manic eyes and his bad smell, I hurried across the tarmac, trying to avoid the indignity of full-blown running. I was close to tears by the time I reached the air-conditioned haven of the supermarket.

Then there was the worry of how to get back to the car without being accosted by him, so when I had finished shopping, half-ashamed of my wussiness, I asked one of the bag-packing boys to escort me. Just as well I did, because as soon as we appeared through the sliding doors, the raggedy man yelled angrily at me, 'You're supposed to be ALONE!'

'He's kinda harmless really,' the boy tried to reassure me, as we put our heads down and rattled the trolley at high speed across the parking lot.

'Mmmm.' But I was no longer that concerned for my physical safety. It was what the nutter had said: 'You're supposed to be alone.' It sounded almost prophetic and I was indescribably depressed by it.

'We've a visitor,' Emily said as I staggered into the house with the shopping bags. I assumed it was Ethan. Since the night he'd slept on the couch, he was a regular guest, under some illusion that he was welcome. He kept showing up to hang out and watch television.

But it wasn't Ethan, it was Mike, armed with his smudge stick and lepping about good-oh.

'Hey, Maggie,' he grinned. 'Just clearing a little more of the toxic energy in here.'

'Good man,' Emily urged. 'Get rid of it all, so I'll get good news from the studio.'

'That's not how it works.' Mike gasped a little from his exertions. 'What it means is the right thing will happen.'

'And the right thing is that they'll buy it for a million dollars.'

'I keep telling you, be careful what you wish for,' Mike grinned.

When he was taking a breather from the dancing, he turned his attention to me. 'And how about you, Maggie?'

'I'm OK,' I said unenthusiastically.

'Yeah?'

'Mmmm.'

He beamed at me, a full-on, beardy beam and said, 'When you're in a dark place, you know what you gotta do?'

I shrugged. 'What?'

'Hold your face up to the light.'

I hadn't a clue what he meant, I don't really get that woolly, mystical talk, but for the second time that day I was a little tearful.

'Be kind to yourself,' he said.

'How?'

'Nurture yourself. Take time out to smell the flowers or listen to the ocean.'

'Um –'

'You'll know what's right for you. Maybe do a little meditation and listen to your own stillness?'

'Ah, OK.'

'Hey, if you girls aren't doing anything tonight, why don't you come by ours? We're having one of our fable-telling evenings.'

Both Emily and I froze as we frantically sought some sort of excuse.

'Er, what goes on at this fable-telling evening?' I asked. It was the best I could do.

'Some beautiful people come by and we tell stories from our different cultures.'

'When you say beautiful people,' Emily said, 'you're not talking about Gucci-sunglasses-streaked-hair-and-speedboat beautiful people?'

Mike laughed. 'I mean beautiful on the inside.'

'I was afraid of that. Anyway, asking me to come to a fable-telling evening would be like inviting a dentist over for dinner, then getting him to do a couple of root canals between courses. I'm telling stories all day long, it's my job.'

Mike shrugged equably. 'I hear you.'

I shoved my feet into my mules. 'OK, I'm off.'

'Where?'

'I'm holding my face up to the light and I'm going shopping. I don't know how I didn't think of it before now.'

'Excellent!' Emily said. 'Good for you.'

I took myself down to Santa Monica, where I spent an unexpectedly happy afternoon wandering along Third Street Promenade in the sunshine, popping in and out of Aladdin's Caves of fabulousness.

So much was happening that I was once again glad to be in LA: a man with a clipboard gave me two tickets for a test-screening of a new movie; I saw someone who might have been Sean Penn buying a packet of Lifesavers; a man painted from head to toe in silver, juggling silver balls, was being filmed by a small crew. All the time the sun shone and the funny-knees-denim-skirt shop gave me a sympathetic hearing. 'Why are you returning this garment?' the girl asked, her pen poised over the form (oh yes, you've to fill out a form when you return things).

'It makes my knees look funny.'

'Makes . . . knees . . . look . . . funny,' she said as she wrote.

Then she went to her manager to see if making knees look funny was worthy of an actual refund or just a credit note. It was close, she told me, it had gone to the wire, but in the end the manager felt that as the garment couldn't actually be regarded as defective, I was only due a credit note.

For the rest of the afternoon, I didn't even do my usual stunt of buying too much of the wrong things. Money changed hands only once – when I bought two little T-shirts with stuff written on them. Emily's said 'I want, I want, I want' and mine said 'Boys are Mean'.

Feeling miles better, I arrived home, where Emily professed herself to be in love with her new T-shirt. 'I'll wear it tonight. Will you come out for a drink later?'

'And play gooseberry with you and Lou?'

'Lou?' she said scornfully. 'He can get lost with his flowers and his phone calls – does he take me for a total idiot?'

'So who's going out tonight?'

'Me. Troy.'

I managed a short, bitter, 'Hah!'

'Oh please, please don't be like that. Troy sleeps with everyone and he stays friends with them.'

'I'm obviously very old-fashioned, then,' I said stiffly.

'Please come out with us.' She was a knot of anxiety.

'Who's inviting me? You? Or him? And be honest!'

'Both of us.'

'Did he say anything about me?'

'Um . . .'

'Don't lie!'

'No, I suppose he didn't.'

Hurt though I was, I could see some good in this; if he was planning to avoid me for the rest of my visit, it would cut down on opportunities for me to feel humiliated.

'You go out,' I urged. 'Enjoy yourself, you've been working all day. And before you ask again, I'm FINE.'

Off she went, and though I had numerous invitations – the fable-telling evening on one side of me or watching a digitally remastered *Rosemary's Baby* on the other – I parked myself in front of the telly, defiantly wearing my 'Boys are Mean' T-shirt. To pass the time, I planned scathing put-downs for Troy, unable to decide between maintaining a dignified silence or shrilly berating him for his alley-cat morals. It was extremely enjoyable.

At some stage the news came on, with a piece about the Irish peace process, and I got the fright of my life: for a moment I thought the colour on the telly was broken. Everything was grey, and the Irish politicians were so pallid, as if their skin had never seen sunlight. And as for their teeth . . .

Oh dear. I'd crossed the invisible line: now I thought glowing skin and expensive dentistry were normal. With a sigh, I resumed my imaginary conversations with Troy.

Some time later, a car screeched to a jarring halt outside, a door was slammed, then came the clatter of heels on the path. I listened to them, wondering where they were going, and located them just as they burst into the room, bearing a mussed and distraught Lara.

'Where's Emily?'

'Out with Troy. What's wrong?'

'Oh my God!'

'A glass of wine?' I suggested.

She nodded and followed me into the kitchen.

'What's wrong?' I asked again. Had she been mugged? Or in a car crash?

'It's Nadia. She called me tonight, and on my new caller display panel her number came up as "Mr and Mrs Hindel". Can you believe it – Mr and Mrs Hindel! She's married. The bitch is married!'

I poured the wine faster and said, 'It could be a mistake. She might have been married once but they could be separated now.'

'Oh no, she admitted it all.' Lara caught sight of herself in the mirror and groaned. 'God, I look like twelve miles of rough road.' In fairness, I'd seen her looking better: her lovely tan was mushroom-coloured. 'She was totally up front about it – she was just a sexual tourist having an adventure.'

After a painful gap, Lara squeezed out, 'She was just using me.' And she began to cry in a contained, dignified way that brought a lump to my own throat. 'I really liked her,' she wept, the way women usually weep about men. 'It hurts just as bad when it's a girl.'

'I know, I know.' Well, I knew now, didn't I?

'I thought she was someone special.'

'You'll meet someone else.' I stroked her hair.

'I won't!'

'Shush, you will. Of course you will. You're beautiful.'

'I feel so bad.'

'You do now, but you'll get over it. She wasn't the one for you.'

'Yeah, you're right.' With a watery smile, she said, 'I'll give myself a week to obsess about her, then I'll get over her.'

'That's the spirit,' I encouraged.

'Thanks.'

Foreheads almost touching, we shared a rueful, can't-live-with-them-can't-shoot-them look and, all of a sudden, she was taking my face in her hands and kissing me softly on the lips. I was startled, but even so I noticed that it wasn't unpleasant.

That was the moment, of course, that Emily chose to come home. I saw her shock before I saw her face; white and appalled, it loomed through the night-time window at me. In more of a hurry than usual, she burst into the house and looked, in confusion, from Lara to me.

'What's going on?' she asked.

'You're not going to *believe* this.' Lara began her tale of woe.

Both Emily and I listened intently to Lara, but we weren't meeting each other's eye much. Not at all, in fact. We didn't even exchange words until eventually I said, 'I'd better go to sleep. I need my full fourteen hours.'

Then Emily called after me, 'Troy says hey.'

'Does he? 'Night.'

I went to bed and shut my eyes and for once I wasn't thinking about Garv. I wasn't even thinking about Troy. I was thinking about Lara.

30

The next morning, in the time between chopping the bananas for my first-thing smoothie and putting them in the blender, we were informed of Emily's salvation – Larry Savage had bought her screenplay!

Naturally enough, she nearly screeched the house down with relief. And nothing, not even the proviso that she had to rewrite the script to include Chip the dog, could dent her joy.

'I'll change my entire cast to orang-utans if he wants!' Emily declared. 'So long as he gives me the money.'

'How much will you get?' I asked, feeling pretty uplifted myself.

'Writers' Guild minimum, the stingy bastard,' she said airily. 'It's nearly an insult!'

But an insult that ran to almost six figures. With the promise of half a million dollars if they actually made the movie.

The thing was, though – *would* they make it? I knew from my own small experience that this was impossible to gauge; no matter how enthusiastic a producer was, they still had to convince the studio executives and the Green-Light Guy that it was a movie worth making. And that was easier said than done. But still, we wouldn't worry about that today . . .

Emily surgically attached herself to the phone and began a ringathon: that night we were having another party, a *proper* party, and this time we really had something to celebrate.

Meanwhile, the good news was criss-crossing amongst her friends, and those that hadn't already spoken to her were ringing in, so call waiting was doing overtime. 'Hold on a minute, the other line is going,' I kept hearing.

And one of those call waitings was Shay Delaney. I knew immediately: the air molecules around Emily seemed to re-arrange themselves into a guilt-filled configuration. What a terrible pity he hadn't rung the previous night and left a message, because I could have wiped it and Emily would never have known. And what an even worse pity that I'd never have the guts to do something like that.

When the telephone frenzy had played itself out, Emily approached me as I sought out a clean T-shirt in my suitcase.

'I invited Shay Delaney to come tonight,' she said apologetically. 'In the heat of the moment, it just slipped out. Do you mind?'

'Bit late if I do,' I said briskly, continuing to rummage in my suitcase.

'I could uninvite him.'

As if.

'I'll do it right now.'

'No, it's OK.' Tonight was Emily's long-awaited celebration, I had no right to spoil it. And Shay Delaney was ancient history.

Emily decided the party should be catered. I was doubtful – my only experience of caterers was of acquiring dozens of sample menus, taking six weeks to deliberate over them, then finally deciding it would be cheaper to pay my mother to make ham sandwiches and apple tarts. But in Los Angeles, you just pick up the phone and say, 'I want Vietnamese finger food, miniature pastries and pink champagne for forty.' And four hours later, three buffed out-of-work actors are efficiently transforming your house into a white-clothed, crystal-glinting venue, bursting at the seams with Vietnamese finger food, miniature pastries and pink champagne. As smooth and speedy as Formula One engineers changing a tyre, they were, and the moment the last champagne glass was placed in the triangular configuration and the last sprig of coriander placed on the pile of glass noodle spring rolls, they were on their way again.

'Off to save someone else's party?' Emily asked.

'You got it.'

'Well, thank you Super Caterers, how can we ever repay you?'

'Just doin' our job, ma'am.'

'And the invoice is in the mail.'

'And we know where you live.'

'We'll be back for the glasses and stuff in the morning. Enjoy!'

Once they'd gone, Emily decided we'd try the pink champagne. 'Just to make sure it isn't poisonous.'

We clinked glasses and Emily said, 'I couldn't have done it without you. To my lovely assistant, Maggie.'

'To a brilliant script!' I said gallantly.

'To Larry Savage!'

'To Chip the dog!'

'To a cast of orang-utans!'

In the dreamy, happy silence that followed, I heard myself ask, 'Does he know I'm staying with you?'

'Who?'

'Shay Delaney.'

'No. Well, I never mentioned it.'

Just like that, my bubble burst and I was at the mercy of all the stupid feelings you get when someone was once your sole preserve but now you're out in the cold, excluded and irrelevant.

And speaking of excluded and irrelevant, 'Is Troy coming tonight?'

'Yeah.' Emily looked uncomfortable. 'I know you don't want to see him, but he's been my friend for a long time and he's helped me so much with the script. I couldn't not invite him.'

I saw her point, but this put paid to my hope that Troy would have the decency to steer clear of me for the rest of my stay and thereby spare me any further mortification. It stung that I wasn't even worthy of being avoided!

'Well, if Troy's coming,' I said, whipping off my 'Boys are Mean' T-shirt, 'I'd better find something else to wear.'

'Why?'

'In the words of the song: He's so vain, I bet he'll think this T-shirt's about him.'

Shortly after seven, people started arriving. Justin and Desiree were the first to show up. Next, bearing a bottle of champagne, came Lou the commitmentphobe, who was swarthy, sexy and extremely pleasant. When I whispered to Emily how nice he seemed, she replied, 'Oh, these guys are clever, I'm not saying they're not.'

Then I saw Troy's jeep parking across the road, and to my shame I immediately began wishing for the best: that he might take me to one side and whisper an apology about how he'd been too busy to ring me – even though I knew for a fact *it wouldn't happen*.

And how right I was! As he alighted from his car, I got a pain in my stomach when I saw that he was accessorized by Kirsty. Then they were crossing the road and coming through the door. Before I had time to wonder how he'd behave, he was walking straight over to me. My heart constricted with hope . . . then he was planting a brotherly kiss on my cheek and saying, real goofy and friendly like, with none of the innuendo I'd come to expect, 'So Irish, you were the one driving the getaway car!'

'What?' I asked shrewishly. Funny that, I'd *meant* to sound calm and cool.

'You saved the day on Monday, right? Driving Emily across town to Empire. Even offered to do the pitch, yeah? If it hadn't been for you, well, who knows . . . Oh, thanks,' he took a drink from Justin. 'Hey guys, how about we raise our glasses to Irish?'

Justin and Lou obediently raised their glasses with Troy and chorused, 'To Irish!'

Interestingly enough, mind, Kirsty's glass of low-fat water didn't budge and her lips remained zipped.

'Hey, we haven't met – I'm Troy, Emily's friend.' Troy thrust his hand at Lou by way of introduction.

'Lou,' Lou replied evenly. 'Emily's boyfriend.'

'Oh,' Troy said. 'Yeah, right.' He was looking at Lou and Lou was looking at him – what I recognized as an Alpha-male moment. If they'd been lions they'd have been circling each other, sizing up their respective strengths.

'So where is she?' Troy looked around for Emily.

'Here!' she called, emerging from her bedroom.

Both Lou and Troy stepped forward, but Troy got there first and spread his arms in homage. 'The success story! Need a director?'

'Eat my shorts,' Emily laughed.

'So what's the catch?' Troy asked.

'Why should there be a catch?'

'C'mon Emily, you know these guys, there's always a catch. How bad is it?'

'Chip the dog gets a part.'

'You happy to do that?'

'If the man is happy to give me the money.'

'Whatever happened to art?' Troy teased. 'Whatever happened to principles?'

'Amazing how easy it is to compromise when you're broke and scared,' she grinned.

'Yeah, I know,' Troy smiled. 'Congratulations, baby girl, I'm way happy for you.'

At this point, Kirsty decided that there was too much grinning and camaraderie going on with Emily and Troy, so she stepped between them and started whining to Troy about her mineral water having the wrong size bubbles, or something.

They arrived in their dozens: Lara, David Crowe, Mike and Charmaine, Connie and her entourage, Justin's two friends from the dog park, a gang of scriptwriters from Emily's Learning Annex class, another bunch from gyrotonics. It was so much like a rerun of last week's premature shindig that when I found the Goatee Boys moshing in the front room, I groaned, 'Groundhog day.'

Everyone brought presents: the studio had sent half a garden of flowers earlier; David Crowe had arrived with an arrangement only marginally smaller. It was a happy night, a night of celebration. Most of the people present were connected in some way with the world of movies, so Emily selling a script gave everyone a lift – a victory for one was a victory for all.

But I didn't feel happy or celebratory, not even close: I was burning up from Troy's treatment of me. Bad enough to use me for a one-night stand, but I wasn't even important enough for him to hide his carry-on with Kirsty from. At least he respected *her* enough to lie to her. And I was complicit in my own humiliation – by keeping my mouth shut, I was going along with it and making it easy for Troy.

It was all wrong, but I could see no way to make it right. What would be achieved by telling Kirsty I'd slept with Troy, then bitch-slapping her like we were on the *Jerry Springer Show*? Apart from the fact that I'd enjoy it?

So not only did I hate Troy – and Kirsty – but I hated myself. And, though I didn't like facing it, I was angry with Emily for inviting Shay Delaney. Small wonder that I felt I hated the whole world. My sole consolation was that I didn't hate Kirsty just because Troy was dancing attendance on her; luckily I'd already hated her.

I wandered around ungraciously shoving trays of food at people who seemed indignant at the implication that they occasionally ate. If it hadn't been for Justin I'd have had no takers at all.

'Gotta take care of this,' he said, wobbling his belly and popping a jumbo prawn into his mouth. 'I got my job to think of. Now, what about you, Princess?'

'Sure, another three or four more can't hurt,' I said, reaching for a prawn.

But he was talking to Desiree, tempting her with a spring roll, which she disdainfully turned her nose up at.

'See that?' he asked anxiously. 'She usta love Pacific Rim.'

'Maybe she's sick. Why don't you bring her to the vet?'

'She's not sick. It's worse than that.'

'What do you mean?'

'I'm scared she has anorexia.'

'Anorexia? But . . . but she's a *dog*.'

'Dogs can get anorexia,' he said sadly. 'There was a thing in the *LA Times* about it.'

'Please tell me that you're joking.'

'Maggie,' he said sadly, 'I wish I was.'

I picked up my tray and set off on another thankless circuit and wondered: What kind of place was this where even the dogs got eating disorders?

'See you at the pastries in five,' Justin called after me.

Justin and I kept bumping into each other in the garden at the tray of pastries. They'd lured me back so often I was actually beginning to get embarrassed and, sure enough, a short time later, Justin and I both showed up beside them.

'We've got to stop meeting like this,' I said, and in the hope that if I couldn't see them, I wouldn't be as tempted to eat them, I turned my back – and came face to face with Troy and Kirsty. *Shite.*

'Having fun?' Troy asked.

'Um, yeah.' I turned around, located a thumb-sized chocolate eclair and threw it at my mouth. I just couldn't help myself.

'Great news for Emily, huh?'

'Yeah, um . . .'

Then, like I was possessed by a sugar demon, I was picking up a dime-sized doughnut. (When you ask for 'miniature' in LA, that's exactly what you get.) Kirsty watched it carefully, following its journey from the tray to my mouth, then asked with fake sympathy, 'That's, like, number *at least* seven. Are you pre-menstrual?'

The taste of rough sugar vanished from my mouth, to be replaced with the taste of hatred.

'You know what you gotta do?' she carolled. 'You gotta try zinc. Zap those sugar cravings! But forget glucose, forget candy! I got something even better!' A statement like that was bound to attract a lot of attention in Los Angeles. Several heads turned to her and when she was satisfied that her audience were hanging on her every word, she continued. 'Better'n all of them is – a frozen grape! Just buy grapes at the market, put them in the ice compartment, and any time those old sugar cravings come calling, scare 'em away by eating a frozen grape. Totally sweet and zero, read my lips, *zero* calories.'

All I could say was, 'Grapes have more than zero calories.' A poor attempt, but better than nothing.

'She's right,' Justin said, making mischievous eye contact with me. 'Grapes are very high in fructose. You're looking at fifteen to twenty calories a grape.'

'More,' I lied. I hadn't a clue. 'Depending on the size of the grape. If it's a big one and has a particularly high sugar content, you could be looking at as many as –' I paused for effect, '– FIFTY calories.'

'Seems to me you should stick with pastries,' Justin concluded, reaching for a tiny custard pie. 'Better for you!'

With that, Justin and I exchanged a high five with our eyes, then peeled away, leaving Kirsty with her reputation as a food guru in tatters.

Just when I thought I was in the clear, Shay Delaney arrived.

All evening I'd been as tense as an exam hall, wondering if he'd show, but the more time had passed the less likely it had been that he'd appear. Naturally enough, the minute I decided he wasn't coming was when I spotted a tall, dark-blond head across the garden. It couldn't be . . .

It was.

Every one of my muscles tensed as I waited for him to notice me. And waited. And waited . . .

He seemed to know almost everyone. Heads were thrown

back and laughter floated at me as he worked the garden and chewed the fat with David Crowe, Connie, and Emily's friend Dirk. Well, they say the movie world is very small.

Finally, unable to bear the suspense, I placed myself in his path.

Just like the last time, he looked gratifyingly shocked. 'Maggie Garvan!'

'Walsh,' I corrected, defiantly – the last time we'd met I'd have died if he'd found out about the breakdown of my marriage, and now I was determined that he should know about it.

'Walsh?'

'Yeah, Walsh.'

'Oh. So, what are you doing here?'

'Taking some down time.'

'Staying with Emily?'

'Yes.'

And then – just like the last time – 'Well, *great* to see you,' and he stuck out his hand for me to shake, then off he went, leaving me in a huge pool of anti-climax. I wanted to call after him, *Don't you want to know what happened? Why I'm Walsh now instead of Garvan?*

My mood darkened further. It was no fun being at a party where I'd been rejected by two of the men present. Why didn't they just fly Garv in to complete the set? Even though I'd had a laugh at Kirsty's expense, she was the one with Troy by her side. And there was Shay Delaney, hail-fellow-well-met-ing his way around the party, but he wasn't coming within a mile of me.

Well, I thought with a sigh, maybe he feels guilty. And maybe he should.

Without warning, Curtis bumped into me, jogging my drink and squeezing his weight down on to my toes. As sticky champagne slopped over my hands, rage leapt in me and at that moment I'd have had the strength to throttle him with my bare hands.

Maybe Kirsty was right, maybe I *was* pre-menstrual.

Tetchily, I sucked the champagne off my fingers and, all of a sudden, I got that tingly, hair-lifting feeling you get when someone is staring at you. I looked up and around the garden and my gaze landed on Lara. She was watching me. When she saw I'd noticed her, her face changed and she playfully rolled her eyes after Curtis, then flashed me her radiant smile, which seemed more radiant than usual. I smiled back, feeling a little head-spinny, a little off-balance, and a funny anticipation began to flicker in the pit of my stomach.

Most people left around midnight. Most people except for those I really wanted to see the back of: Troy, Kirsty and Shay arranged themselves in the kitchen around Emily, talking excitedly and roaring laughing. While, glowering with resentment, I trudged back and forth from the garden, carrying glasses, bottles and leftover food. Lara and Ethan flitted around me, loading the dishwasher in Lara's case and finishing any half-drunk glasses in Ethan's. Both, in their way, were helping.

'Excuse me,' I said, pushing past Troy to get to the bin and accidentally-on-purpose sticking a fork into the back of his leg.

'Ow!'

'Sorry,' I said, trying my very best not to sound it.

As I crumpled a paper plate into the bin, plans were being made for the following night: Troy, Shay and Emily felt that they could help each other out in their respective careers, and they were going out for dinner to discuss it.

'You'll come too, won't you, Maggie?' Emily invited.

'You might find it kinda boring, Irish,' Troy said, a little too quickly for my liking.

'Probably.' I straightened up from the bin, looked at him hard and tried to invest my tone with unpleasant meaning.

But before it got any nastier, Lara interjected cheerily, 'Hey, Maggie, come out with me tomorrow night. Those guys are going to be talking work, but you and me – we can have fun!' She winked flirtatiously at me and confusion dulled my reactions. I wasn't imagining this. Was I?

No, I wasn't, because next thing she was sliding her arm around my waist. 'Don't worry, guys, I'll take care of Maggie. Real good care. Right, Maggie?' She tickled my waist with her fingers and I twisted around to look into her aquamarine eyes. As so often with her, I felt railroaded – and I liked it.

'Right, Lara,' I said, with a huge, happy smile, then brazenly moved to kiss her. It was quite chaste – i.e. no tongues – but had a sweet, lingering quality, so that when we opened our eyes and turned back to the others, we were slap bang in the middle of what could only be described as an 'atmosphere': Troy, Kirsty, Emily and Shay were pictures of disbelief and confusion.

'Oh man,' Ethan groaned, rearranging his crotch.

As soon as they'd all gone home, Emily pounced. 'What's going on with you and Lara?'

'I don't know. Nothing.' But honesty compelled me to add, 'Yet.'

'Yet? Maggie! You mean you're planning . . . ?'

I nodded. 'Yeah, maybe. Probably.'

'But you're straight!'

After a stretch of silence, I made myself say it. 'I'm not sure I am, you know.'

317

'What the HELL are you talking about?'

'Well . . .' It was difficult for me to voice this. Very difficult. 'You know –' I swallowed hard. 'You know if you're watching a porn film?'

Emily's face was a picture. Though we'd discussed almost everything else that had ever happened to us, pornography was a neglected area.

'Please don't look at me like that!' I implored. 'It's not like it sounds. I don't have any, but if I'm away in a hotel with Garv and they have it on the in-house movies, then sometimes . . .'

'Mmm.'

'I've never admitted this before, but I wasn't interested in the men in the films.' I looked at her, hoping for some sort of encouragement, but she was expressionless. 'They were just plastic-looking, over-developed bodies. To be honest, I actually found them quite repulsive.'

'That's because they *are* repulsive, with their mullet hair-dos and their bushy moustaches.'

'How did you know that's what they looked like?'

'They're all like that.'

'Are they really? Right. Well, apart from Garv I've never told anyone this ever before, but . . .' I stopped, not sure if I could continue. Then I almost choked as I blurted out, 'Emily, it was the girls that I wanted to look at. I fancy them.'

'You don't fancy them,' Emily said in despair. 'You just want to *be* them! Everyone feels like that. It's normal.'

I shook my head. 'I don't think so. I might be a lesbian. At the very least I'm bi.'

Emily's exasperation drained away and she assumed an expression of concern. 'Maggie, I'm worried about you. I mean it. Think for a moment about all you've lost in the last while.

It's no wonder you're looking for love, or affection or whatever. Especially after the way Troy rejected you.'

'Troy didn't reject me.'

'Sorry, wrong choice of words. When he didn't . . . When he decided not to . . .'

'He didn't reject me, because you can only be rejected if you *let* yourself be rejected.' I'd heard something similar to that recently and I'd liked it. Trouble was, I didn't think I had it quite right. Troy had definitely rejected me.

'Right, but what I'm saying, Maggie, is that after all you've been through it's no wonder you don't know what you want. Last week it was Troy –'

'Now there was a mistake.'

'– and now you think you want Lara. But you don't.'

'That's where you're wrong.'

'I'm not! You're all confused.'

'I'm not confused. Listen to me, Emily – Lara smiled at me tonight and something good happened in me and for the first time in ages I felt . . .' I sought the right word. '. . . OK. It felt right. I'm sorry you're finding this so hard, but I can see why. You've always known me as heterosexual and you've got slightly homophobic tendencies . . .'

'Now just a minute!'

'But you do! You said you'd hate to lick someone's mackerel.'

'Lara is one of my best friends, I love her to death. Just because I don't want to do what she does in bed doesn't mean I disapprove. I mean, I'm not that keen on anal sex either, but I don't care if anyone else does it.'

Emily put her face in her hands. 'This is all my fault. I told you to let your hair down.'

'And I'm glad you did. I've played it safe for far too long.'

'Put it back up,' she implored. 'Before you do yourself any more damage, put it back up.'

'No.'

'Today is Thursday,' Emily whispered to herself. 'They're coming on Tuesday.' She bit her knuckle and whimpered, 'She'll kill me. Mammy Walsh will kill me.'

31

Larry Savage proceeded to extract his pound of flesh – with immediate effect. No sooner had her celebratory hangover kicked in than Emily was summoned to his chalet to 'bounce around' some script changes.

'This morning's not so great,' I heard her say, then she put her hand over the speaker and mouthed desperately at me, 'Alka Seltzer, please!' Then, after a little pause, she said, 'Yes, sir, I understand sir. Eleven o'clock. I'll be there.'

Hanging up, she rushed to me. 'Maggie, how good is your shorthand?'

I handed her a fizzing glass. 'Non-existent.'

'Oh. How good are you at writing fast?'

'Not bad.'

'Get dressed. We're going to The Valley. We've got us some face time with Mr Savage.'

But first it was my unpleasant duty to call to the Goatee Boys' darkened house and rouse one of them to wait in for the catering guys to collect their stuff. I was afraid of seeing any of them naked, but especially Curtis.

Luckily, the only one who showed any sign of life was a half-dressed Ethan, who pulled on a singlet and announced that he was considering a career change.

'But don't you first need a career,' I suggested gently, 'before you can consider changing it?'

Entirely unfazed, he told me his great idea: he was going to start up a new religion.

'Come on,' I beckoned him to the door. 'Hurry.'

'My mom says she doesn't care, so long as I pick something and stick to it. She says I've got to stop changing courses and I think starting a new religion is a pretty cool career move.'

I wasn't so sure. Don't you end up being crucified, that sort of thing? But far be it from me to rain on his parade.

'And what kind of things would you believe in?' I asked, opening our front door and ushering him in. 'Or haven't you got that far?'

'Sure I have!' Then Ethan outlined the cornerstone of his new faith, which was that the disciples have to have lots of sex with Ethan.

'Oh, Christ,' Emily muttered, putting on her lipstick in the mirror.

'"Oh, Ethan" is what you'll be saying soon,' Ethan cheerfully corrected her.

'I don't think so,' she said stonily. 'The catering guys will be here inside an hour, then you can go home. And just to let you know, I have my underwear drawer arranged in a special way. I'll know if someone's been through it. Capisce?'

'Capisce. Hey, Maggie, are you really going to go out with Lara tonight?'

'Yes.'

'Woooh! Lesbianism rocks!'

Emily sighed, but said nothing.

Out at Empire, we were given a warm welcome by Michelle, Larry's assistant.

'Congratulations,' she said, hugging first Emily, then me. 'It's a great script, we're all really excited about it.'

The door to Larry's office was closed, but he could be heard, clear as a bell, shouting at someone, 'Sue me! So freaking sue me!'

'Larry's just on to his mom,' Michelle smiled. 'He won't be long.'

Sure enough, one final valedictory bellow, then the office door was wrenched open and Larry emerged, full of beans.

'Have we got a deal or have we got a deal!' he beamed at Emily. 'Congratulations, kiddo.'

'Thank you for buying it,' Emily beamed back. 'And thank you for the flowers.'

Larry waved away her thanks. 'Don't mention it. Studio always does it. Standard procedure.'

'OK.' With an arm around each of us, Larry guided Emily and me out into the sunshine. 'This morning we're meeting with two studio executives. We gotta get these guys on side if we want this movie to be made. Got it?'

We nodded energetically. Oh, we got it all right.

At the boardroom chalet, the two executives – a stick-thin blonde called Maxine and a clean-cut, square-jawed man called Chandler – both gushed at Emily about how much they loved *Plastic Money* and how it was going to make a great movie. For a trillionth of a second I was excited, then I copped on to myself.

As we gathered around the table, Larry produced a copy of the script, and when some of the pages fell open there were thick, red lines scored through paragraph after paragraph and in some cases dragged across entire pages. I can't describe the feeling. I hadn't written the script, so I wasn't attached in the same way that Emily was, but I still felt sick. For some reason, it made me think of visiting someone in prison and seeing them bearing obvious signs of beatings.

Michelle distributed photocopies of *Plastic Money* to the rest of us and Larry called the meeting to order. 'OK. Let's try and knock this into shape! First off, that whole plastic surgery stuff has to go. Too weird, too edgy.'

'But that's the whole point,' Emily explained calmly. 'It's an exploration of society's fixation with the body beautiful, it makes important points about our value system –'

'Well, I don't like it. Get rid of it. All of it!'

Shock had my jaw swinging like a sign in the wind. I'd heard about studios buying scripts then proceeding to eviscerate them. But I'd always thought such accounts were wildly exaggerated to generate sympathy or laughs: clearly they weren't.

Emily swallowed hard, then she asked, 'So what's their motivation for holding up the bank, then?'

Larry leaned across the table and sing-songed at her, 'Well, I don't know. I'm not the writer!'

Emily went white.

'How about a blind girl needs an operation to restore her sight,' Chandler suggested.

Larry clicked his fingers. 'I *like* it!'

'Or a bunch of underprivileged kids have a ball park,' Maxine said, 'but a big corporation wants to turn it into duplexes, so they need the money to buy it?'

'Yeah,' Larry said thoughtfully. 'Could work.'

'If there's no plastic surgery, the name will have to be changed,' Emily said, slightly shrilly. '*Plastic Money* makes no sense now.'

'Yeah, you're right. We'll change the name to *Chip*.'

Emily looked even more upset and I was dismayed; I'd hoped

that he'd intended Chip only to have a bit-part, not the starring role.

'If the name is *Chip*, you don't think people might think it's a movie about *a* chip?' Maxine wondered.

'Would they?'

'Maybe – after *Chocolat*.'

'So we call it *Chip the Dog*,' Larry said.

'That's great!' Chandler said. 'That's so great. But what about those animal-rights guys? They see a movie called *Chip the Dog*, they're going to tell us that people might see it as an order. Like, you *gotta* chip the dog!'

'Unless we change the dog's name,' said Michelle.

'I like Chip.'

'Yeah, I like it too.'

'How about Chuck?'

'*Chuck the Dog*? Bad as *Chip the Dog*.'

'How about calling him Charlie?'

'So now it's a drug movie!'

As the discussion raged, Emily maintained a flinty silence. I was forbidden to speak, but even if I'd been allowed I wouldn't have wanted to, muzzled by a potent mixture of depression and boredom.

Larry announced that we were 'working through' lunch, so at twelve-thirty enough food to feed a multitude was delivered to the chalet and laid out prettily – and very quickly – on a table in the corner.

I was starving, but everyone else put tiny amounts of food on to their plates: one strand of noodle; half a baby tomato; four pasta shells; one rocket leaf. So we were taking a little and often approach – OK, I could do that too . . .

We all sat back down with our food and Larry continued to

demand suggestions from us, so it took me a while to notice that I was the only one who'd cleared my plate and that there were no signs of anyone paying a return visit to the buffet. I forced myself to be patient, perhaps they were just slow eaters ... but then the plates were being absently pushed aside as ideas were scribbled in the margins of our scripts. Lunch was over. Over before it had begun, and I was still so hungry.

I wondered if I could just get up and help myself. But we were all sitting down and fully immersed in work. Could I just get up and walk over and put more food on my plate, then put that food in my mouth? What would they think of me?

Wistfully, I looked at the table. Its legs were almost buckling from the weight of uneaten food on it. An entire quiche – *untouched*. A deep-pan pizza, its perfectly circularity unbroken. It was the pizza that did it. All at once, I was pushing back my chair and straightening my knees.

Larry Savage looked at me in surprise. 'Where ya going?'

My resolve departed abruptly. 'Nowhere,' I said, sitting right back down again and studying my script.

My regret was immense. If only I'd known I only got one chance, I'd have made the most of it.

Suddenly that sounded very profound.

We worked through until two-thirty, then Larry wrapped things up. 'Time out, guys. My acupuncturist just got here.'

Her head bowed, Emily straightened the papers in front of her. 'I'll get writing.'

'You do that. We need these rewrites fast.'

'By when?'

'Say, Friday.'

'*Next* Friday? Or the Friday six weeks from now?'

'Haha. Next Friday.'

'No, Friday's not so good for me.'

'Thursday, then. Or Wednesday?'

'Oh. Oh, OK then, Friday's fine.'

Exhausted, we got into the car. Emily was grey.

'Are you OK?' I whispered.

Her face was wretched. 'Why did he buy it if all he wants to do is butcher it?'

'I don't know.'

'What was it that eejit next door said?'

'Follow me and I will get jiggy with thee?'

'No, the other eejit from the other next door. Mike. "Be careful what you wish for," he said. Well, he was right – I wished for someone to buy my script and now I wish they hadn't.'

'It might be a great film. You never know.'

'No, it's going to be a piece of shit,' she said, and tears began to spill down her face. 'My lovely script that I worked so hard on until it was perfect, perfect, perfect. I was so proud of it and now it'll never see the light of day. No one will ever see it. Seven months I slaved on it, to make it wonderful, and now he wants it totally rewritten in a week. It can't be done! And he's taken out all my one-liners, all the funny stuff is gone, and any of the touching moments now involve a fucking DOG!'

I rummaged for a tissue while she howled like a child. 'I'll be ashamed, Maggie, I'll be so ashamed to have my name on a cheesy, schmaltzy, moralizing movie about a dog.' She tried to catch her breath. 'About a dog called *Chip*.'

'Could you pull out?' I suggested. 'Just tell him to stick his money and you'll find someone else to make your movie, thanks very much!'

'No. Because no one else does want to buy it. I know all that and I need the money to live on. But there's no doubt that everything comes with a price tag.'

'Just refuse to make the changes,' I urged. 'Tell him this is the movie he bought and this is the movie he should make!'

'Then he'll fire me and I'll get paid almost nothing, but they'll still own my script. They'll just get some other writer in to make the changes.'

'They can't do that!' But I knew they could; in my time I'd worked on enough contracts to know how much power the big studios retained. I'd just never seen it in action before.

'They don't just buy your script, they buy your soul. Troy is right to try and get all his work produced independently.' Emily's sobbing began to quieten down and she smiled regretfully. 'You make a deal with the devil, no point complaining if you get a pitchfork in the arse.' Then tears began to spill again. 'But that script was like my baby. I loved it, I wanted the best for it, and it kills me to see it torn apart like that, my poor baby.' Aghast, she stopped. 'Oh, Maggie, I've done it again. I'm so sorry.'

32

When you have a miscarriage, you get given a huge amount of information, but you actually discover very little. People bombarded me with well-meant advice, which varied too much for comfort: some said we should try again immediately; others insisted it was vital that we grieve the loss before moving on.

But nobody could tell me the one thing I wanted to know, and that was: Why had it happened? The best that Doctor Collins, my gynaecologist, could come up with was that fifteen to twenty per cent of pregnancies routinely end in miscarriage.

'But why?' I persisted.

'It's nature's way,' he said. 'Something must have been wrong with the foetus, so that it wouldn't have been able to survive on its own.'

I'm sure that was meant to be comforting, but instead it enraged me. In my mind's eye, my child, wherever it was, was perfect.

'But it won't happen again?' Garv asked.

'It could. It probably won't, but I'd be lying to you if I said it couldn't.'

'But it's already happened to us.' Meaning we'd had our quota of bad luck.

'Just because it's happened once is no guarantee that it can't happen again.'

'Thanks a bunch,' I said bitterly.

'Another thing,' he said warily.

'What?' I snapped.

'Yeah, what?' Garv echoed.

'Mood swings.'

'What about them?'

'Expect them.'

I went over the past nine weeks with a fine-toothed comb, searching for the thing I'd done wrong. Had I lifted heavy objects? Accidently gone on a loop-the-loop rollercoaster? Booked myself into a German measles hospital? Or was it just down to the fact – now unimaginable to me – that I simply hadn't wanted it and he or she had known?

They provided a nurse-counsellor-type person, who told me that there was no way that the baby would have known that it hadn't been entirely welcome. 'They're thick-skinned little creatures,' she said. 'But it's natural to blame yourself. Guilt is one of the emotions everyone feels when this happens.'

'And what else?'

'Ooh, anger, grief, loss, frustration, fear, relief –'

'Relief?' I glared at her.

'Not for everyone. And did I mention irrational rage?'

Because we'd told so few people that I was pregnant, there weren't many who knew I'd miscarried. So almost no one made allowances for us as we tried to fill the hole in our lives.

And it was a hole. We'd already thought up names – Patrick if it was a boy, Aoife if it was a girl.

The due date had been April 29th and already we'd started looking at baby clothes and planning the decoration for the bedroom. Then overnight we no longer had any need of teddy-bear wallpaper or revolving lamps that throw patterns of stars on the walls, and that was hard to get used to.

Even more painful was that I'd been excited about getting to know my child. I'd been looking forward to a lifetime with this new person, who was part of me and part of Garv – and abruptly it had all been whipped away.

You know how it is when your boyfriend ditches you – out of nowhere the world is full of loving couples, holding hands, kissing, clinking champagne glasses, feeding each other oysters. In the same way, as soon as I'd lost my baby, out of the woodwork suddenly emerged busloads of heavily pregnant women, ripe and gorgeous, carrying their swollen bellies with pride. And worse still, there were babies everywhere I turned: in the supermarket, on the street, by the sea, at the optician's. Perfect little creatures with their dolphin-smiley mouths and lustrous skin bursting with freshness, flapping their pudgy arms, clapping their sticky hands, kicking their socks off and making high-pitched, swooping, singing noises, like bald mini-Bjorks.

Sometimes it was too painful to look at them, but at other times it was too painful not to, and Garv and I used to eyeball them with hungry gazes, thinking *We nearly had one of them*. Then Garv usually whispered, 'We'd better stop, we're being weird, the mother will call the peelers on us.'

My instinct was to get pregnant again immediately, so that we could almost pretend that the first loss had never happened, and Garv said he wanted to do whatever made me happy. So I went straight out and bought a temperature thing, because I wanted to leave nothing to chance. My life was pared down to just one all-consuming need, and terrible fear tormented me. What if this time it took a year? What if – unthinkably – it never happened? But we were lucky: I'd miscarried at the start of October, and I was pregnant again by the middle of November. It's hard to describe the giddy mix of relief and happiness I felt when the blue line appeared on the stick; we'd been given a second chance. Breathless, we squeezed each other and we both cried, as much for the loss of the other child as the joy of the new one.

But almost straight away the joy was overtaken by anxiety. Blind terror, actually. What if I lost this one too?

'Lightning doesn't strike twice,' Garv said, even though it does, and it wasn't lightning anyway.

I became so very, very careful; I stopped going to pubs, because I was afraid of inhaling cigarette smoke; I drove at about fourteen miles an hour (quite fast for Dublin, actually), so there'd be no danger of any sudden braking; I refused to give cream cheese house-room, and I never permitted myself the luxury of a belch – quite understandable when you consider that I even worried about *breathing* too hard, in case it dislodged the baby.

Horrible dreams dogged me: one night I dreamt that the baby had died and was still inside me, another night I dreamt I gave birth to a chicken. And this time round, there was no skiving off work and buying handbags from JP Tod's; we'd been so badly punished the last time for being happy that we were scared of doing anything that smacked of celebration. Mind you, I wasn't at all as sick the second time – apart from when I found something very funny (almost never), and my laughter segued seamlessly into dry-retching. (I was a model dinner-party guest.)

We cautiously took the reduced nausea as a good sign. Though there was no medical basis for it, I said to Garv that the terrible sickness the first time round had probably been a sign that something was wrong. Then he repeated it back to me and thus we tried to reassure each other and ourselves.

But every twinge in me could indicate the onset of disaster. One night I got a really bad pain in my armpit and I was absolutely *convinced* that this was it. Garv tried to restore calm by pointing out that my armpit was miles from my womb, but I countered defiantly, 'Yeah, but when people have heart attacks they get a pain in their arm,' and then I could see I'd put the fear in him too.

But we survived that night, and in the seventh week we went for our first scan, where anxiety stripped the event of the joy we'd had with the first baby. I kept asking if everything looked OK and the nurse said over and over that it did.

But how could she tell? If I was completely honest, the picture they gave us looked more like a poor black-and-white photocopy of 'Starry, Starry Night' than a baby.

As we approached the ninth week, the tension built and built. During the ninth week itself, time slowed down to the ticking of each individual second. We breathed as though the air was rationed. Then – unbelievably – it had passed without incident and we'd moved into the clear blue waters of the tenth week. The cloud lifted and suddenly we were gulping breaths like the air was chocolate-flavoured – you could actually *see* the change in us. I remember smiling at Garv and watching him smile back at me and being shocked at how unfamiliar it was.

Week ten passed. Week eleven arrived and we went for our second scan, where we were a lot giddier and lighter than at the previous one. Then something happened which upped the ante more than I could ever have imagined – as I was lying on the table, the nurse indicated that we should be quiet, she flicked a switch, and the sound of our baby's heartbeat filled the room. A lightish pitter-patter, so fast it was absolutely belting along. It is impossible for me to convey the depth of my wonder and joy. I was transported with it. As you might expect, we both cried buckets, then we had a little laugh, then shed a few more tears. Our awe just knocked us sideways. And the relief was glorious: it had a heartbeat. Things must be fine.

And just as soon as we were over week twelve, we'd really be in the clear. 'Two days to go,' I said that night, as we squeezed hands before we went to sleep.

The pain woke me. There hadn't been pain the last time, so I wasn't immediately alerted. Then when I understood what was happening I went into a dreamscape: *I can't believe this is happening to us.*

When bad things happen, I'm always taken by surprise. I know some people react to disaster by stomping around shouting, 'I knew it, I just fucking KNEW this would happen!' But I'm not one of them. Bad things are supposed to happen to mythical 'other people', and it comes as a shock when I discover that I am one of the 'other people'.

As we hurried out to the car, I looked up to the night sky, silently begging God not to let this happen. But I noticed something that seemed like an omen. 'There are no stars tonight,' I said. 'It's a sign.'

'No, baby, it's not.' Garv slid his arms around me. 'The stars are always there, even in the daytime. Sometimes we just can't see them.'

The sense of déjà vu as we drove to the hospital turned reality into a nightmare. Then we were sitting on the orange chairs again, then someone was telling me that everything would be OK, and once again it wasn't.

It was still too early to tell the sex, not that I cared. All that mattered was that this was the second time I'd lost a child: a ready-made family, gone before it had arrived.

This time it was far, far worse. Once I could live with, but not twice – because the one thing we'd had the last time, that we didn't have now, was hope. I hated myself and my defective body that was failing us so terribly.

People provided stories that were supposed to be comforting. My mother knew a woman who'd had five miscarriages before carrying to term and now she had four fine children, two boys and two girls. Garv's mother could go one better: 'I know a woman who had *eight* miscarriages and then she had twins. A lovely pair of boys. Mind you,' she added doubtfully, 'one of them ended up in prison. Embezzlement. Something to do with a pension fund and a villa in Spain . . .'

Everyone tried to instil optimism back into Garv and me, but I didn't buy it. Hope was utterly absent and I was in the grip of a burgeoning belief that this was all my fault. I'm not given to fanciful nonsense, talk of hexes and jinxes and the like (that'd be Anna you're thinking of), but I couldn't chase away the conviction that I'd brought all of this on myself.

33

I opened the front door. Emily was on the day bed bent over her laptop, working hard.

'Hi,' I said cautiously.

'Hi,' she replied, equally cautiously. 'Good night?'

'Yes. You?'

'Yes.'

'How were Troy and Shay?'

'Fine. Helpful. They both say hey.'

I nodded at the computer. 'So, ah, how's *Chip the Dog* going?'

'Nightmare. I'm getting cramps in my stomach from writing this stuff. Did you get off with her?'

A pause. 'Yes. Sorry.'

'Not at all, whatever floats your boat. So what was it like?'

'It was . . . different.'

'Like licking a mackerel?'

'It was only the first date,' I said. 'What kind of girl do you think I am?'

'Jesus Christ,' she said faintly. 'And what did you do?' Then she hit her forehead. 'Doh! Not like that!'

'We went to a movie. Look, I'm going to have a shower and get some rest.'

'Sure, you must be exhausted. I mean, I'm not saying . . . Oh Christ,' she clicked, 'see you later.'

I went into my bedroom, closed the door, then sat at Emily's desk and wearily flicked through some of her unsold scripts, looking to be distracted.

I wasn't exhausted; I was terrified. I was way, *way*, WAY out of my depth here. This business with Lara – what had I been *thinking* of?

I wasn't a lesbian. I suspected I wasn't even bisexual.

The whole night had been a disaster, starting with Lara turning up looking radiant; her hair was swingy and shiny and she wore a clingy jersey dress. Nothing wrong there – until I suddenly understood that she'd *made a special effort*. She'd made a special effort *for me*. Momentarily I was flattered and seconds later I was freaked out.

We went to Santa Monica to a movie where neither of us understood the plot, and when we got outside into the sweltering night it transpired that each of us hoped that the other would be able to explain it. That didn't bode at all well, and I had a powerful compulsion to ask Lara what she knew about exchange rates, except I was afraid of discovering that she was as clueless as me.

'What now?' I asked. 'Will we go for a drink?' There were hundreds of very attractive-looking bars and restaurants all around us. But Lara firmly shook her head and said, with a message-laden smile, 'Nuh-uh. My place.'

It was as though a full cage of butterflies had been released into my stomach. *Nerves*, I told myself. *Not terror. Nerves.* On account of my shyness and inexperience, of course. But Lara would be masterful enough to take control and make it easy for me.

So back to her place we went, where she opened a bottle of wine, put some soft jazzy-type music on the stereo and lit scented candles. It was the scented candles that brought home to me the full extent of my mistake. It was so *romantic*. She definitely meant business. A lead ball displaced the butterflies and there was no longer any ambivalence about how I felt. I wanted to go home, I wanted to run away as fast as I could – but instead I had to curl up on the sofa, sip Chardonnay and exchange mischievous glances in the flickering light.

Valiantly, I tried. I managed to dredge up a sickly smile each time Lara warmed her eyes at me, but as she moved closer along the sofa, my panic built.

Desperately, I tried to keep talking but I was so uptight I sounded like I was interviewing her for a job. 'How many screens will *Doves* be opening in? Is it fun organizing the launch party for it? Oh, a nightmare, is it? Oh dear.'

I longed to leave, but couldn't see how I could possibly extricate myself; the words that might release me wanted to be uttered yet remained locked in my throat. What was stopping me was that I'd gone into this with my eyes open. As soon as it had been offered, I could have told Lara to get lost, but instead I'd given every appearance of fancying her – because at the time I had. Now, though, was a different story, but I felt I'd no right to tell her I'd changed my mind.

A glass and a half of Chardonnay in and Lara suddenly leant right over to me, almost on top of me. *Here we go.* Automatically, I shrank away from her and the relief was intense when I realized she was just refilling my glass. With a shaky hand I picked it up and gratefully gulped back most of it.

'Hey, don't get too drunk on me,' Lara chided sweetly.

'Er, no.' And my anxiety started anew.

I actually prayed, offering to do a deal with God: if he'd get me out of this, I'd never do anything risky again. But God must have been on the other line, because next thing Lara had moved closer and was stroking my hair away from my face. Then she'd kissed me, which hadn't been too bad, and put her hands under my top and caressed my breasts, which hadn't been too bad either. At that juncture I felt it was my turn to do something, so I kind of pulled at her shoulder strap to show willing. But I wasn't expecting her to shrug her dress off her shoulders, down to her waist, then whip off her bra and weigh her breasts in her hands. As soon as she touched herself, her nipples sprang at me and it would have been sexy in other circumstances, but I was paralysed by the inappropriateness of it all. 'Don't be chicken,' she said, so I took a deep breath and gingerly started caressing her breasts, partly to return the favour and partly because I was curious about what implants felt like – but as I'd never felt anyone else's breasts except my own, I'd nothing really to compare them to.

A bit more caressing and clothing removal ensued; Lara was beautiful, there was no doubt about it, and she was soft and downy and sweetly fragrant. And yet, when we were pressed crotch to crotch, it felt all wrong – we were both too flat. I realized how much I liked men's bodies.

Whatever bravado or curiosity or neediness had propelled my initial response to Lara had all drained away and I was keenly aware that I'd bitten off more than I could chew. Not that I was chewing anything – God, no! No power on earth could have persuaded me to do any mackerel licking.

They say that only a woman can truly know what another woman wants and Lara certainly did her best. But I couldn't divorce my body from my mind and just let go and give myself to any pleasure that might come from the experience. I felt like an out-and-out fraud and, worse still, I felt silly.

Luckily, Lara had seemed to really enjoy herself and waved

away any of my inhibitions with an airy, 'Hey, it's your first time.'

'Thanks,' I said humbly.

'Soon,' she said, 'we'll have you strapping on a twelve-inch dildo!'

Jesus Christ!

I'd barely slept all night. Then she'd dropped me home this morning on the way to her yogilates class. The Drummers to the Rhythm of Life were just arriving – one or two of them said hello, clearly getting used to seeing me arrive home on a Saturday morning, still in last night's clothes.

'I'll call you tomorrow,' Lara said, driving off. 'We'll go out. Tell Emily I said hey.'

And now here I was, flicking through Emily's old scripts and unable to concentrate on anything. So what was I to do? I couldn't break it off with Lara – not only did she really seem to like me, but I'd have to 'fess up to just being a sexual tourist. And after Nadia had let her down so badly! I simply couldn't do it.

Anyway, I'd no idea how to go about breaking it off with someone, it was so long since I'd done it. What do people say? 'It's not working out'? 'I need some space'? 'Can we still be friends?'

But if I didn't break it off with her . . . ?

I could see my future unrolling itself in front of me. I'd have to stay in Los Angeles for ever and be a lesbian. I couldn't see any way out of it. I'd have to do all sorts of lezzery things that seem enticing in the occasional fantasy, but not that alluring in real life. And I'd be worn out from the regime of personal grooming that Lara would expect from me: my hair and eyebrows would need twice-weekly maintenance, and she'd brought up the question of my raggedy nails again. She'd make me go for the Brazilian wax and God knows what else.

How had I ended up in this mess? Having sex with a *girl*? This wasn't me, this wasn't the way I behaved – someone must have led me astray. But much as I'd love to, I could blame no one but myself. I forced myself to face one of the reasons I'd flirted – yes, flirted – so shamelessly with her: I'd been *showing off* in front of Troy and Shay. I'd been hoping to shock them or hurt them or something, because they had both, albeit in very different ways, hurt me.

What had I become? Before Lara there had been Troy, and even though the sex itself was fantastic, the entire experience left me feeling bad about myself.

At least one thing was pretty clear, I thought wryly: any suspicions I'd ever harboured that I was a bad-girl peg jammed uncomfortably into a good-girl hole had been allayed. I'd often told myself that it was a shame I'd got married at twenty-four, that I'd done myself a disservice by forgoing anonymous sex with mysterious strangers. Deep in my heart I'd felt that if I was presented with the opportunity to showcase my dormant wild-girl side, I'd be able to misbehave with the best of them.

But I'd been wrong. I wasn't cut out for one-night stands. Unlike women like Emily or Donna, casual sex didn't excite me; it depressed me. God, how disappointing that I was what I'd always behaved like: a dyed-in-the-wool serial monogamist. Well, who knew? Emily was right to be worried about me: I was out of control.

In despair, I sat at the desk for an indeterminate amount of time. Then I began to think of Emily, who was desperately trying to cram seven months' work into a week. I got up and went out to her. She was still at her laptop, typing furiously.

'Emily, can I do anything to help?'

She paused, her shoulders hunched and her purple-ringed eyes giving her the look of a raccoon.

'I could make you something to eat. Or I could rub your neck. But not in a lezzery kind of way,' I added, lest there be any confusion.

Slowly, she lowered her shoulders. 'You know what, there is something you could do. I need to get out for a few hours this evening. I don't care what we do so long as we do something. You decide.'

'OK.' I thought about it. And I knew exactly what I wanted to do. 'I'd like to go out with a gang of girls and get drunk and dance around our handbags to "I Will Survive".'

'Fabulous,' Emily breathed. 'Who would you like to come? Lara, obviously –'

'No, she's busy! Um, how about Connie?'

'Connie? I didn't think you liked her.'

'Ah,' I shrugged.

'Is it all the wedding arrangements?'

'It doesn't matter as much now.'

'*And* you've stopped asking me if everyone is married. Maggie, I finally think you're on the mend. Now if you'd only stop getting off with people . . .'

'I will, I promise. There'll be no more.'

Connie was on for it and so was her sister Debbie. We got very glammed up in short skirts, heels and shiny make-up and went to the Bilderberg Room – so naff it had suddenly become very cool – where the men were aggressively forward and fashionably attired in Starsky and Hutch retro. We were barely in the door when one said to me, 'Here I am! What were your other two wishes?' I jostled away from him, and moments later I was running my hands through my hair when I encountered another hand in it. Belonging to a brat called Dexter, who then asked me to go home with him.

But all four of us were there to dance, not to meet men, and we deflected assholes like Wonderwoman deflects bullets – which only made us even more popular. Complicated Martinis kept being bought for us, which we drank but didn't say thank you for. And although our handbags were small enough to swing from our shoulders without injuring bystanders, for the sake of tradition we placed them on the floor beneath the glitterball – Emily's Dior saddlebag, Connie's mother-of-pearl Fendi, Debbie's LV clutch and my JP Tod's special – and danced around them.

When Connie decided she wanted to fix her lips, all four of us steamed haughtily across the floor, ignoring offers of drinks and/or fabulous sex, and went to the ladies' room, which was a landscape of brown-cork tiling – even on the walls. The woven wicker chairs were like a 'Readers' Wives' special and the smoked-glass mirrors were very 'Last Days of Disco'. Highly stylish, of course, but not so great if you were trying to see if you'd got lipstick on your teeth.

There was only one other woman in there, squinting at the smoky glass and trying to reapply her mascara. On the washstand, beside her handbag, lay something slightly odd – a pair of handles like the ones usually found attached to expensive carrier bags, the type of handles that are made of hard plastic and clip together along their length. They weren't odd in themselves, what was odd was that there was no bag attached. But I only noticed all this on the edge of my consciousness, until the woman threw her mascara back in her handbag, tucked it under her arm, then – I thought I was seeing things – picked up the handles and swung them as if there was an invisible carrier attached. The Emperor's New Bag.

In silence, we all turned to watch her leave, and as soon as the door had shut behind her, Emily, Connie and Debbie erupted into excited talk.

'It was, wasn't it?'

'Got to be!'

'Who? What?' I asked, realizing that the woman wasn't, as I'd thought, a poor lost soul and mad as a bike.

'Doctor Hawk's handles!' From their shining eyes it was clear I was meant to know what they were talking about. Slowly I shook my head and Emily explained.

'You know how we all carry baggage from our past?'

I had to admit I did – in fact, I was beginning to realize just how much stuff I was carrying.

'So Doctor Lydia Hawk is a shrink who's got this, like, pioneering approach. She translates emotional baggage into physical baggage. For the first month you see her you've to carry a proper suitcase.'

'And it can't be one of the ones with wheels,' Debbie elaborated. '*And* it's got to be full of stuff – Doctor Hawk packs it so it's way heavy and you've really got to carry it. Ev-err-y-where. To the drugstore, to work, out on dates . . .'

'And as you get better, the bags get smaller. Until you're shrunk enough to get given Doctor Hawk's handles. You've got to carry them for a whole year as a reminder.'

'And they cost a thousand dollars.'

'Ten thousand,' Connie corrected.

'That's insane!' I said. 'They're only plastic handles. You could just tear them off any carrier bag that you get for free.'

They all disagreed, three heads of big hair swishing emphatically from side to side. 'Nuh-uh. Got to be the special Doctor Hawk ones, else they don't work.'

'There are only twenty pairs in the whole world,' Connie marvelled. 'They are totally the coolest things.'

Sometimes I thought I was getting the hang of how they do things in Fantasy Land. Other times, like right then, I felt as clueless as the day I'd arrived.

But never mind – back out for more dancing! The music was unreconstructed seventies disco – 'Mighty Real' and 'Disco Inferno' and other wonderful stuff that I remembered from my childhood – and the high spot was when Emily had a word with the DJ and next thing 'I Will Survive' was bouncing off the mirrored walls. One of the braver blokes tried to break into our circle just when the song got to the 'Go on now, Go!' bit, so we shouted it at him until he withdrew again, then we danced like there was no tomorrow.

34

I found myself certainly wishing there hadn't been one the following day, when Emily announced, 'Lara's on her way over.'

'To see you?' I asked hopefully.

She gave me a funny look. 'No, to see you.' She spelt the words out like I was a moron. 'Her. Girl. Friend.'

Oh Lord.

The day had begun very nicely, starting with Lou taking us both out for breakfast. Lou had arrived last night when Emily – loosened by several free Complicated Martinis – rang him at two a.m. and invited him over. He'd arrived within twenty minutes and claimed that he'd spent the evening watching a ball game on TV and praying she'd ring.

'Sheesh,' Emily had exhaled, making a meal of being disgusted by his insincerity.

Then in the morning he'd taken us to Swingers, a cool, crowded diner where the ambience was vibey and flirty, even at ten o'clock in the morning – long, hot looks being exchanged over blueberry pancakes, and that was just the waiters – where he was fun, entertaining and as nice to me as he was to Emily without in any way coming across as sleazy. He insisted on paying for us both, and on the drive home stopped at a drugstore and bought cigarettes and sweets for Emily, gave her three good suggestions for *Chip the Dog* and told her to call him if she needed anything. 'And I mean *anything*,' he stressed, with unmistakeable meaning.

As he drove away, I had to say to Emily, 'I think he's really nice.'

'Only because you've been out of the game for too long,' she said, booting up her laptop and arranging herself at the kitchen table with an ashtray, coffee cup and packet of Mintos. 'But he's actually evil.'

'Evil! That's a terrible thing to say.'

'And it's not terrible to cold-bloodedly set out to make a woman fall for you, then do a disappearing act?'

'But are you *sure* that's what he's doing?'

''Course I am.' She scrolled down her screen and muttered, 'Now where did I get to? Oh here we go. Chip the dog has just bitten the property developer.' She flung her face into her hands and whimpered, 'I can't believe I'm writing this stuff. I hate myself!'

'Think of the money,' I replied, just like she'd told me to. 'Think of all those lovely things, like being able to eat, and pay rent, and put gas in your car.'

'Thank you, thank you.' She began to type and everything was grand until Lara rang to say she was coming over.

Half an hour later, Lara burst into the room, as golden and gorgeous as always, except instead of filling me with admiration it now terrified me. She stopped at Emily and looked over her shoulder at the screen. 'Hi, sweetheart, how's it going?'

'I've gone beyond shame, Lara. I'm a Hollywood whore.'

'Hey, who isn't? Emily, would you mind if I spent a little time with Maggie in private?'

Emily winced but managed, 'Work away.'

'I know this is a little weird,' Lara said softly.

Emily just shrugged and, feeling wretched, I took Lara into my bedroom, closed the door and braced myself for passionate snogging.

'So whatcha do last night?' she asked, moving around the bed and sitting at Emily's desk chair.

'Went to the Bilderberg Room with Connie and Debbie.'

'Sounds great!'

'Er, yes, it was. Good music.'

'Like what?'

I listed some of the songs and all the time I was wondering, *When is the snogging going to start?*

'I went for dinner at Shakers,' Lara said. 'Up in Clearwater Canyon. Great food. You should go.'

'OK.' The waiting had got too much to bear, so I stood up – I had to because she was quite a way from me – forced her to her feet and pulled her to me. But before I could plant my lips on hers, she'd placed the palm of her hand on my chest and straightened her arm.

'No.'

'No?'

'I'm really sorry, Maggie, but I don't think we should do this.'

' 'Cos of Emily being outside?'

'No. I don't think we should do it, period.'

I mouthed her words, repeating them back to myself until it sank in. 'You want to break up with me?'

'Um, yeah, you got it.'

'But *why*?' What was wrong with me? Why did I keep getting rejected?

She fixed me with her blue laser beams and said candidly, 'I was sore after Nadia and I was curious about you. It seemed like a good idea at the time, you know . . . ? I'm way sorry.'

'So didn't you fancy me at all?'

'Sure!'

'Since when?'

'Since . . . ah, since the night I found out about Nadia and you were real nice to me.'

'Not since I first came to Los Angeles, then?' I didn't know why this was so important, but it was.

'Not straight off, no. See, you're a little confused right now, 'cos of your marriage and Troy, and I'm real sorry but I think I took advantage of you.'

'Um . . .'

'Like, you're great, you're really great.'

'But not great enough.'

'It's not that, it's like . . . I don't know how to say this . . .'

'I'm not your type?'

'Don't be pissed at me,' she said sadly.

Very hurt, I swallowed. 'So what is your type? Girls like Nadia, I suppose.'

'Yeah, I suppose.'

'And why? She had a great body?'

Uncomfortably, Lara assented.

Now, I wasn't expecting that. I thought men made choices based purely on physical attraction, but I expected girls to be less shallow. Doesn't a good personality count for anything any more? I wondered bitterly.

'You've got a great body too,' Lara said, so nicely it took some of my mortification away. 'But because she usta be a dancer, you know . . . And, like, she really took care of herself.'

'It was my nails, wasn't it?'

'It didn't help,' she admitted.

'And . . .' I made myself say it, 'was my . . . you know . . . bum . . . um, bit . . . the wrong colour?'

She shrugged. 'I didn't really see it. But Maggie, it's not about that. I'm pretty sure your natural inclination is not to be with girls . . .'

There, she'd said it.

'. . . and I swear to you that if I didn't break up with you, you'd break up with me real soon.'

I paused, wondering if I should play the pity card or go for pride. Pride won. 'Actually, I wanted to do it today, but I didn't know how.'

'*What?*' she said sharply. 'And here I am feeling totally like the worst person ever!'

'Yes.' All at once the silliness of the situation struck home and I began to laugh. 'Tell me, Lara, tell me honestly, was I terrible?'

She stared at me and a smile creased her face as she filled up with mirth. 'No, but I've gotta say I've had better.'

'Me too.'

And suddenly we exploded into convulsions, huge belly laughs of relief and liberation and the full-on insanity of it all.

When we eventually quieted down I said, 'But we'll still be friends, right?' And that was enough to start us all over again.

'Keep Wednesday night free,' she said, before she left. 'For the première of *Doves*.'

When the door had shut behind her, I cornered Emily. 'I've good news for you. It's all off with me and Lara.'

She stopped her frantic typing. 'What happened?'

'She broke it off with me. Says I'm not her type.'

'So what's the story? You hate her now like you hate Troy and every time she comes over here you'll stick a fork in her leg?'

Aghast, my heart pounded. 'No, we're friends.'

'That's a relief.'

'Emily, I'm sorry.'

'For what?'

'Sleeping with all your friends. I won't do it again.'

'You can sleep with who you like. It's the bad atmosphere when it doesn't work out that I don't like.'

'I won't be sleeping with anyone else. I was off the rails and out of control, but I'm OK now. I'm sorry. It's back to being clean-living Maggie – I'm just not cut out for anything else. I might even join an enclosed order.'

Emily shook her head. 'Some sort of middle ground might be nice.' Then she added, 'But thank Christ you knocked that lezzer lark on the head before the arrival of Mammy Walsh. Else we'd have all been in the soup.'

I heartily agreed.

35

After the second miscarriage, I cried for four solid days. I know people often say things like 'I cried for a week,' when they mean they cried on and off for a few days, but I really did cry non-stop for four days. I even cried in my sleep. I was hazily aware of people coming and going, tiptoeing around my bed and whispering to Garv, 'How is she now?'

By the time I stopped crying, my eyes were so swollen I looked like I'd been beaten up and the surface of my face was white and crusty like those dried-out salt lakes that you see in the desert.

In the past, when I'd heard about women having miscarriages, I couldn't imagine their sadness, because I suppose I wondered how you could miss something you'd never had. I could identify with other losses – if one of my friends got dumped by their boyfriend, I felt lonely, rejected and humiliated for them. Or if someone belonging to a friend died, I could go some way to understanding the shock, the grief and the very weirdness of death, even though my grandparents were the only people I'd loved who'd died.

But I hadn't been able to imagine the grief of losing a baby. Not until it had happened to me. Not until it had happened to me twice.

And the funny thing is that in ways, it's similar to the other losses. I felt as lonely, rejected and humiliated as if I'd been dumped – lonely for the person I'd never get to know, rejected because they didn't want to stay in my body and humiliated by my very defectiveness. And I also felt shock, grief and weirdness, like someone had died. But there was an extra dimension to my sadness, something that went to the very essence of my humanness. I had wanted a child, and the longing was as visceral and inexplicable as hunger.

Throughout it all, it was as though a pane of glass separated me from the rest of the human race, so isolated was I. I felt almost no one could understand the exact nature of my pain. Those who'd miscarried would – although I didn't know anyone – and those who were unsuccessfully 'trying' for a baby, and maybe some people who'd already had children would. But the vast majority wouldn't get it. I intuited that, because for a long time I'd thought the way they did.

The one person who truly shared my loss was the one person I could barely look in the eye – Garv. Having to go through it all with him made it worse and I couldn't figure out why. Until I realized that I couldn't stop thinking about something that had happened when I was about twenty: a child from the neighbourhood had run out from between two parked cars and been knocked down and killed by a motorist who hadn't had a hope of stopping in time. The parents of the dead boy were devastated, of course, but there was also a lot of sympathy for the man who'd been driving. I overheard several people say, 'My heart goes out to the driver – the poor man, what he must be going through.'

Well, I was the same as the driver. I was responsible for Garv's grief – it was my fault, and it was horrible living with it.

But Garv coped a lot better than I did. In the fortnight after the miscarriage he kept the household running, monitoring my visitors, replacing my *Mother and Baby* magazines with *Vanity Fair*, and ensuring I ate. I flailed around, failing to reclaim normality, and refused to talk about what had happened. I couldn't even use the word 'miscarriage' – when anyone started on about it, I interrupted and called it a 'setback'. And when they said, 'OK, setback,' and continued trying to probe me, I'd say, 'I don't want to talk about it.' I was so resistant that even the most dedicated of friends kind of gave up.

Then someone came up with the idea that Garv and I should go on holiday. All of a sudden, everyone was in agreement that a holiday was a great idea, and it felt like everywhere we turned there was another spooky face intoning, 'It'll dooo yoooou the world of gooood.' Or 'A few days lying by a poooool reading a crappy boooook and you won't knoooow yoooourself.' It was like a horror film. 'You yourself were conceived on holiday, Margaret,' Mum said, accompanying this information with a wink and a disconcerting leer. 'Don't tell us, for God's sake, don't tell us,' Helen begged.

In the end, Garv and I felt we'd no choice. I had no energy to resist everyone's urgings and the idea of staving off real life for another week was too tempting to resist.

So off we went to a resort in St Lucia, spurred on by visions of silvery palm trees, powder-white sand, hot yellow sun and goldfish-bowl-sized cocktails. Only to discover that three days before we'd arrived, they'd had a hurricane – even though it wasn't the hurricane season – and their beach had fallen into the sea, along with most of their palm trees. Not only that, but my bag, crammed with gorgeous, newly purchased beachwear, never turned up on the airport carousel. Salt was rubbed vigorously into the wounds by the JCBs which commenced work rebuilding the beach every morning at seven a.m. outside our window. And the icing on the cake was the fact that it pelted rain, and no, it wasn't the rainy season either.

But the cherry right on the very top of the icing on the cake was the attitude the hotel staff took to my missing bag. No matter how hard I tried to convince them that I wanted my stuff urgently, it didn't seem to cut any mustard. Every morning and every evening Garv and I made enquiries as to its where-abouts, but nobody could ever give us any hard information.

'They're so laid back here,' I complained.

'Laid back?' Garv said grimly. 'They make the Irish look as hard-working and efficient as the Japanese.'

On the fifth day, it all came to a head when we showed up, once again, at the front desk. Even though we'd gone through the whole missing-bag thing with Floyd every morning for the previous four days, Garv had to explain it all afresh to him.

Unconvincingly, Floyd pressed a couple of keys on his key-board and looked at his screen. I twisted my head trying to get a look at it, because I harboured a suspicion that the computer wasn't even switched on.

'Be comin' tomorrow,' he drawled.

'But you said that yesterday,' my jaw was clenched, 'and the day before.' I thought of Garv having to wash my T-shirt and shorts in the handbasin again tonight and me having to put them on damp in the morning and be laughed at by the other well-dressed girls there. Then I thought of my bag, filled with jewel-coloured bikinis, flower-splashed sundresses and, worst of all, my new unworn sandals, and I became a little hysterical. Even now, when I think of those sandals my gut twists with pain. Not because I'm a shoe junkie – my first love has always been handbags, really – but because Garv went to so much trouble to get them for me. I'd seen them in a shop in town the week before we'd come away. I'd even tried them on and was all set to buy them when into the shop came a woman with a baby. It was tiny, clearly a newborn, its delicate eyelids fluttering with sleep, its marshmallow hands curled into fists.

I had to leave. I'm not exaggerating, I *had* to leave, or I would have lost it and started crying again – and once I started I found it very hard to stop.

At home, I collapsed on Garv. 'It wasn't just the baby,' I said. 'I know it's stupid, but it was the sandals too. They were perfect, they would have gone with everything. And I left them . . .' I hovered on the brink of a great crying torrent.

'I'll get them for you,' Garv offered, and a muscle leapt rhythmically in his jaw. 'Where were they?'

'No, it's OK.' Anyway, I couldn't remember which shop – all I knew was it was in Grafton Street. Next thing I know, Garv is placing a pad in front of me. 'Draw them,' he says. 'Put down colour, size, everything you know about them.'

I tried to talk him out of it, but he was insistent. Which only made me feel worse. It was a sign of how bad things were, of how close we were to toppling over the edge, if he had to employ such extreme measures to try to make me happy.

Like a private eye, he pounded the pavements in the centre of Dublin, armed only with my diagram. He went into shoe shop after shoe shop with the folded bit of paper, asking people, 'Have you seen these shoes?'

He tried Zerep, who didn't have them, but thought that Fitzpatrick's might. Fitzpatrick's hadn't seen them either and tried to send him to Clarks. But Garv said I wouldn't have been in Clarks, that their shoes were too comfortable, so they suggested he try Jezzie. Who tried to fob him off with a pair that were too low and didn't have a ridged sole. Off his own bat

356

Garv tried Korkys, and though the staff couldn't help, a customer – a shoe aficionado – overheard and insisted that the sandals were in Carl Scarpa. And sure enough, paydirt was hit in Carl Scarpa.

'I just hope they fit,' Garv said, opening the bag when he got home.

'They'll fit.' I was quite prepared to chop my toes off, if necessary. I was so appalled at the trouble he'd gone to, especially in view of my unworthiness, that I wouldn't have been able to admit to anything being wrong.

He held them up. 'Are they the right ones?'

I nodded.

'Your ruby slippers,' he said, handing them over. And though they weren't ruby – more of a turquoise, really – or slippers, I put them on, clicked my heels together three times and said, 'There's no place like home.'

Tightly we held on to each other and for a while there I thought we might make it. Isn't it strange that sometimes the memory of an act of kindness can cause more pain than the cruel stuff?

Meanwhile, Floyd just didn't give a damn whether the bag containing my sandals and everything else ever turned up.

'Where is it?' I begged. 'It's been lost for nearly a week now.'

Floyd fixed me with a dazzling melon-wide grin. 'Relax, mon.'

And maybe in other circumstances I would have. Perhaps if I'd had a proper night's sleep in the previous month, if my nerves hadn't been stretched see-through, if I hadn't hung so much hope on this holiday. Instead I heard myself shout, 'No, I won't fucking relax.'

Garv put his hands on my shoulders and firmly marched me

to a pretty white bench. 'Sit here,' he ordered. Resentfully I sat while Garv leant over the desk at Floyd. 'Now listen to me,' he threatened. 'That's my wife. She hasn't been well. She's come here to feel better. There's no beach, the weather is shite, the least you could do is find her bag.'

But despite his macho intervention, the bag didn't turn up till the final day and our mood didn't turn up at all.

At the airport coming home, the pall of depression that hung over the pair of us could almost have been photographed. We'd thought the holiday would heal us, but it had only highlighted the divisions. Not only was I not pregnant but we were further apart than we'd ever been.

As I thought about all the terrible things that had happened with the weather and the bag and the food poisoning (oh yes, two gippy tummies, one overworked bathroom, let's not go there), I wondered if Garv and I were jinxed. Then an unexpected terror got me as I understood that the disasters had actually been the best thing about the holiday – because they meant Garv and I had had things to talk about. The only times we'd been animated or in agreement had been when we were venting about what a kip it was or when we were planning the various tortures we'd inflict on the JCB drivers or Floyd or the chef who had given us the dodgy swordfish.

For the first time ever, as far as I could remember, Garv and I were running out of things to say to each other.

36

The exity bit of LAX, where the recent arrivals emerge, was choked with people waiting. As well as the Dublin plane, a flight had recently landed from Manila, and another from Bogota, and it looked like thousands of relatives had turned out to greet the passengers. I'd already spent almost forty minutes standing with a stretched neck, being jostled and shunted by the vacuum-packed throng. Every time the glass doors slid back to reveal yet another family group, a happy wail went up from some-where, and a fresh heave had me stumbling all over my neigh-bours as people sought to burrow through to their visitors.

The more time that passed without my lot appearing, the more lighthearted I became – they must have missed the plane. Great, I could go home to Ireland. What a pity I hadn't thought to bring my stuff with me, I could just have left there and then. But at the exact moment I'd decided they definitely weren't coming, my senses pricked up and my hopes slid away. I still couldn't see them, but I knew they were about to show – not thanks to any sixth sense, but because I could *hear* them, their voices raised in disagreement.

And then they appeared. Mum with a mysteriously orange face – the mystery was explained later when I saw the palms of her hands, also a browny-orange colour. She'd been at the fake tan again. No matter how many times we told her she just couldn't handle it, she wouldn't listen.

I caught a quick glimpse of Dad, almost invisible behind an overladen trolley. He was wearing khaki shorts. Fetchingly accessorized with varicose veins, argyle socks and black lace-ups. Behind him came Anna, and I got a surprise – actually, a shock – when I saw her. She'd had her hair cut – *styled*. She looked great. And then came Helen, her long, dark hair glossy, her green eyes sparkling, her mouth curved in a contemptuous smile as she surveyed the waiting multitude. Even from a distance, I could see what she was mouthing: 'Where the fuck is she?' With a sigh, I positioned my elbows outwards, like I was about to do the Birdie Song, and prepared to push.

The reason for the delay? One of Anna's bags hadn't turned up, and only after they'd filled out the forms was it spotted taking a twirl for itself on the Bogota carousel. Also the trolley wasn't helping. Capricious and unpredictable, it had caused skinned ankles and bruised calves all round. Put it this way – if it was a dog, you'd have muzzled it.

But I was happy to see them, happier than I'd expected, and I had a moment of feeling protected – Mum and Dad were here, they'd mind me. But something about Dad's thin, white and blue legs was telling me it wasn't fair to expect to be taken care of. Instead, because I'd been in LA for three weeks already, I'd be responsible for their welfare – even though I hardly felt able to take care of myself, never mind the four of them.

With much barking of knuckles I got their huge amounts of luggage into Emily's block of flats and, under a blue, blue sky, we headed for the freeway to Santa Monica while they discussed my new look.

'Your hair hasn't been that short ever.'

'It must have been short when she was born,' Helen said.

'No, it wasn't.'

'How would you know? You weren't there. I have to say, Maggie,' Helen mused, 'you look great. Your hair really suits you that length and you've a gorgeous tan.'

I waited for the catch. However, the trap wasn't for me, but for Mum.

'A gorgeous tan,' Helen repeated. 'Nearly as gorgeous as Mum's. Hasn't she a great colour?' she asked unkindly.

'Yeah, lovely.'

'I've been sitting out in the garden at home,' Mum said.

'Between showers,' Helen twisted the knife.

'The Irish sun can be very strong,' Mum persisted.

'Must be, if you can get that sort of colour when it's pissing down.'

The sniping continued until – a mere six blocks from Emily's – we got to the Ocean View hotel. To my surprise, it was accurately named: you *could* actually view the ocean from it. All that separated it from the vast, twinkling expanse of the Pacific was a road, a line of palm trees and a cycle path.

'Look,' Anna said, all excited, as two six-foot, toffee-tanned, pony-tailed blondes rollerbladed past. 'Welcome to California.'

Inside, the hotel was nice and bright and had a swimming pool and the advertised umbrellas, but Mum seemed edgy and distracted, moving around her room, opening drawers, touching things. She only relaxed when she discovered that they hadn't hoovered under the bed. She's a bad housekeeper herself and she hates feeling out-cleaned.

'It's quite nice here,' she finally conceded.

Helen was less impressed. 'We came this close,' she held up her thumb and forefinger, 'to staying in the Chateau Marmont.'

'She told me it was a convent,' Mum said indignantly. 'If it wasn't for Nuala Freeman, who told me the kind of place it really was –'

'Glamorous,' Helen interrupted. 'Full of the stars of screen and stage. It would have been great.'

One of the reasons they – at least Mum and Dad – had come to LA was out of concern for me, and they hadn't even unpacked before I was called to provide an account of my emotional health. Somehow, Mum had backed me into a corner, thrust a concerned (and orange) face at me and asked softly, 'How've you been these past few weeks, since . . . you know?' Up close, her neck was streaky, but her eyes were kind and I wondered where I should start – 'I found out for sure that my husband has someone else, then I had mild bondage with a big-nosed man who didn't call me, then I ran into Shay first-cut-is-the-deepest Delaney again, who did his best to ignore me even though we'll always be linked, at least in my head, then I had sex with a woman with breast implants and she rejected me too. I've been to very dark places and behaved so out of character that I've scared myself, and I'm still no wiser about what's going to become of me and my life and my future and my past.' So which bit should I tell her first? I mused. The lesbian sex? Being tied to Troy's bedpost?

'I'm fine, Mum,' I said weakly.

Her loving expression remained on me and I noticed she'd missed a patch just below her ear. For some reason this squeezed me with hopeless tenderness.

'Are you sure?'

'Yeah.'

'Thank God,' she sighed. 'I was afraid you might go . . . a bit mad for yourself.'

'What news from home?' I was keen to change the subject.

'Well, you heard about us being broken into, did you?'

'No! What happened?'

Moving her orange face even closer to mine, Mum told the story. Apparently, one morning as Dad was going downstairs to make Mum's cup of tea, he met an unfamiliar youth climbing the stairs. 'Morning,' Dad said, because an unfamiliar youth climbing the stairs was, in itself, nothing unusual. With five daughters, the chances of this sort of encounter of a morning were high. But then Dad noticed that the youth had two of his golf trophies under his arm. And that the microwave was by the front door. And so was the telly. 'What are you doing with my golf trophies?' Dad had asked uncertainly.

'Ah fuck!' the youth had said moodily, bouncing the trophies on to the ground, bolting down the stairs and out into the wide, blue yonder. It was then that Dad saw the key still in the front door – left there when Helen had come home the previous night. The youth was no swain of one of his daughter's, but an opportunistic, early-morning burglar.

'It was the mercy of God that your father got up,' Mum said. 'Or else the bed would have been stolen out from under us. And another night Anna came home scuttered, put some beans on the ring, then fell asleep.'

'I was still there when that happened.'

'Oh, were you? We could all have been burnt in our beds. Mind you,' she said ruminatively, 'I suppose we could count ourselves lucky to still have beds to be burnt in, the way things were going . . . Now tell me,' abruptly Mum changed the subject and dropped her voice to a hiss. 'Is my face a bit much?'

'No, Mum, you're gorgeous.'

'Only it's fake, you see. I was putting it on and nothing was happening and I put some more on, a good handful, and when

I looked in the mirror this morning this is what I was greeted with.'

'But you know the colour doesn't come up immediately, Mum, we keep telling you, you have to wait.'

'I know, but I'm always afraid that I haven't put on enough. Anyway, I think it's marvellous to have a bit of a colour, but Helen has been at me, making fun.' She paused, swallowed, then made herself continue. 'She's been calling me Outspan Head. Kept telling the air hostesses, "Outspan Head can't work her earphones, Outspan Head wants another blanket." She even told the man at immigration that that was my real name, not the name on my passport, and it wasn't funny, they can't take a joke, those men.'

'Maybe Helen's jealous.'

'Jealous!' Suddenly it all made sense to Mum. 'Sure of course she is! That's what's up with her. But you're OK yourself? And you're coming home soon?'

Then Dad made the same sort of enquiries about my general well-being, though of course, being a man and worse still being an Irish man, he did it more obliquely and without eye contact. 'You're looking . . . healthy.'

'I'm fine, Dad.'

'You've been . . . eating properly and all that?'

'Yes, Dad, I'm fine and you're not to worry about what you told me about seeing Garv.'

'It *was* his cousin?'

'Ah no, it wasn't. But don't worry, it's still OK. Right, I'll go on home. I'm sure you're all knackered, I'll see you to-morrow.'

From the clamour of disagreement that ensued, this was clearly the wrong thing to say.

'But it's gone midnight in Ireland,' I protested. 'What about your jet lag?'

'The best way to deal with jet lag is to try and stay awake, then go to sleep at the normal time,' Mum said knowledgeably. I looked at her in wonder. Since when had she become such an expert traveller? 'That's what Nuala Freeman said.'

'Oh well, if Nuala Freeman said it, it must be true,' Helen said bitterly. And I had to agree with her; Nuala Freeman sounded like a right pain in the bum.

'And we have to have our dinner,' Mum said. 'How can we go to bed before we have our dinner?' They are creatures of routine, my parents.

'Is it too late to go to Disneyland today?' Dad asked.

'It's half-four, you old fool,' Helen said.

'But it stays open till midnight,' Mum supplied. 'Nuala Freeman said.'

Before Helen could round up a lynch mob for Nuala Freeman, I quickly told Dad that it was a two-hour drive to Disneyland and that we'd be better off going another day. I suggested that they unpack and spend some time by the pool, then we'd go out for an early dinner.

'What about you?' I asked Helen and Anna. Surely they'd want to go out, get pissed and look for surf gods? But they decided to come – they had to eat and Dad was paying.

'And what about Emily?' Mum asked. 'I told Mrs Emily I'd look in on her and make sure she's eating properly and looking after herself.'

'Emily's very busy,' I said, but Mum had got that look.

'All right,' I caved in. 'But I'd better bring her car home in case she needs it. I'll tell her to expect us all later.'

'Then you'll be right back?'

'Yes.'

I whizzed home, warned a knackered-looking Emily that they'd be calling in to her for a quick drink before dinner, then returned to the Ocean View, where we whiled away a not-unpleasant couple of hours, unpacking and bickering.

At six o'clock, we walked the six blocks from the hotel to Emily's. Even though this was Santa Monica, where people were occasionally spotted getting from A to B without vehicular assistance, the sight of five people walking on their hind legs caused almost as much of a stir as it must have done when the prehistoric tree-dwellers first came down to terra firma and decided to give it a go. Cars kept slowing down to stare at us, like we had two heads each. 'What's up with them?' Mum tisked, as yet another car beeped us. 'Helen, what have you been doing?'

'Nothing!' She didn't sound innocent, so I relaxed. It's when she sounds innocent that you really have to worry.

When we got to Emily's street, Helen noticed the surveillance-equipment shop at the end of it and made us all go in, where she quizzed the man up and down about what the stuff was for.

'Mostly domestic use,' he said. 'We got hidden cameras and tiny microphones if you suspect that your husband is having an affair and want to tape his . . . like . . . activities.'

The jokey way the man said it meant he thought it was out of the question that a husband of Helen's would ever have an affair and need to be taped, but a pall suddenly settled on our little group and everyone avoided meeting my eyes.

'And I supply quite a few private detectives.'

'Private detectives!' Helen's already glowing face lit up even further. 'I wouldn't mind being a private detective.'

'Right, we'll be off so!' Dad said, fear in his voice. I don't think he could take another career change from Helen just yet.

Back on the street, as we passed Mike and Charmaine's, Mike stood up and had a good, decidedly unspiritual gawk at us through his window. Then, as Helen and Anna filed up Emily's short path, the dirty, torn sheet that passed for a curtain in the Goatee Boys' front window twitched. Convulsively.

Emily, God love her, was still labouring away at *Chip the Dog*, and she was exhausted.

'Hello Mrs Walsh. Gosh, you've a great colour.'

Mum hesitated, then preened. 'I take the sun well.'

We all filed into the front room, where Justin and Desiree were sitting; they'd come by to help Emily with some of the doggier parts of her screenplay.

'How's Desiree's anorexia?' I asked, sucking in my face to indicate great thinness.

'Way better,' Justin said happily, then added, 'since she started on Prozac.'

Right. For a minute there I thought normality had come to pay a visit. Clearly I was wrong.

Wine was uncorked and introductions were effected.

'What do you do?' Dad asked Justin. Dad could only relax with people once he knew what job they did. He was at his happiest in the company of local-government officials.

'I'm an actor, but –'

'That's right!' Mum said appraisingly. 'I've seen you.'

'You have?' Clearly this had never happened to Justin before.

'I have. In *Space Hogs*, wasn't it? They sent you down to that planet and the scaly plant thing ate you.'

'Er, yes. Yes!' Justin's dinner-plate face lit up. 'That was me.'

'You gave an excellent performance, but to be honest I thought it was idiotic beaming you and the other space corporal down like that. Wouldn't anyone with an ounce of sense know 'that you wouldn't last five minutes with that scaly plant thing?'

'Yes! Totally right! But the way it works is . . .'

As Justin explained the whole expendable-fat-guy thing to Mum, I was surprised to see Mike and Charmaine had arrived. They *claimed* they were coming to see how Emily was getting on with her desmudged house, but if I didn't know better I'd think they'd just come in out of nosiness.

Dad was very pleased that Mike worked in health insurance – which I hadn't known. I'd always thought he'd have some airy-fairy, touchy-feely form of employment. Then Emily brought Mike over to meet Mum.

'This,' Emily said dramatically, 'is Mammy Walsh. And this –' She turned to Mike, but Mum interrupted and with her most charming smile said to him, 'Oh, I know who you are.'

'You do?'

'You've so many famous friends,' Mum complimented Emily, then turned back to Mike. 'You write those travel books, don't you? And didn't you have your own TV series for a while? What's that your name is?'

'Mike Harte,' Mike said politely.

'No, no, it isn't. It begins with a "W". Oh, it's on the tip of my tongue – what is it?'

'Mike Harte,' Mike repeated, just as politely.

'No! I have it – it's Bryson, Bill Bryson, isn't it?'

'No, Mammy Walsh, it's not.'

'Are you . . . are you sure?'

'Sure I'm sure.'

An uncertain silence followed, and Mum became a strange purplish colour. I could only assume she was blushing beneath the tan. 'Sorry, you look very like him.'

'Hey, that's OK,' Mike said, extremely nicely.

'I have news!' Emily attempted a very clumsy diversion. 'Lara phoned!' Automatically I winced, certain that the mere mention of Lara's name would bestow Mum with psychic knowledge that I'd slept with her. '*Doves*, the movie Lara's been working on, is having its first screening tomorrow night and you're all invited!'

Naturally enough, this caused considerable excitement and semi-papered over the Bill Bryson faux pas.

'Will there be famous people there?' Helen wanted to know.

'Maybe, but do you know who *will* be there?' Emily screeched, still on her hostess-with-the-mostest kick. 'Shay Delaney! You remember Shay Delaney, Mammy Walsh, don't you?'

'Indeed I do.' Mum was quickly recovering her aplomb. 'And a lovely boy he was, too. I'll be delighted to see him again.'

I swallowed it away, pushed it down. I wasn't going to feel it, whatever it was that wanted to be felt. I'd enough to cope with.

In no time, Mum was back on top, and even though it was Emily's house, she was the one who was filling people's glasses, checking they were OK, acting in every sense the Irish matriarch. The Mickriarch. But when she tried to refill Charmaine's wine glass, Charmaine protested, 'I've already had one.'

'Have another,' Mum pressed her, the way Irish mammies do. 'A bird never flew on one wing.'

Charmaine tilted her head to one side and repeated slowly, 'A bird never flew on one wing. But that's beautiful. Such wisdom.'

Was she being sarcastic? I wondered. But there wasn't one bit of badness in her.

'Excuse me,' she said. 'I gotta tell Mike that.'

'That one's all sweetness and light,' Mum said mistrustfully, watching Charmaine's slender back and swinging braids.

'She's a very spiritual person,' I said.

'Oh, she's a Catholic?' Mum perked up.

'No, she said she was a *spiritual* person,' corrected Helen, who'd been following the entire exchange.

After that, Mum had clearly become of great interest to Mike and Charmaine, because they kept watching her. When Anna began to droop with jet lag and Mum chivvied her, 'Snap out of it, you're like a tree over a blessed well, there,' Mike elbowed Charmaine and, with a look of wonder, they mouthed at each other, 'A tree over a blessed well!'

A short, intense conversation ensued, then Charmaine gave Mike a little push and said, 'You ask her.'

'No, you ask her,' Mike said back.

Their heads were together again and they had another little mutter, then Mike was touching Mum on the shoulder. 'We gotta go, tonight's our meditation night.' He sounded disappointed. 'But it was a great pleasure to meet you, Mammy Walsh, and we were wondering if, while you're here in LA, you'd like to join us for one of our fable-telling evenings.'

Of course, she was thrilled. Just *delighted*. But she had to pretend that she wasn't – that's the way it's done in her world. 'I'll be very busy while I'm here, I'm going to a film premeer tomorrow night and my husband wants me to accompany him on Thursday.' She was doing a good job of sounding important and gracious until she added, 'To Disneyland.'

'We can work around your schedule.'

'How about Thursday night, when you get back from Disneyland?' Charmaine suggested.

'I can't promise,' Mum said solemnly, 'but I'll do my best.'

'We'll look forward to it.'

37

'So what does today hold?' Emily was in her pyjamas, drinking Jolt and smoking the first of that day's sixty cigarettes.

'Chauffeuring them round Beverly Hills with the "map" of the stars' houses, then on to the Chinese Theatre to see the stars' handprints set in concrete.'

Emily cringed at the naffness. 'For the first time, the idea of *Chip the Dog* doesn't seem so bad. It just goes to show, there's always some poor bastard worse off than yourself.' She gave a feeble smile, but she was so exhausted the skin beneath her eyes looked bruised.

'I wish I could help you,' I said fervently.

She shook her head. 'It reminds me of cramming for exams – no one can really do it except me. And I can't complain, I'm getting well paid for it.' But she looked so woebegone, my heart went out to her. 'It's the shame that I can't take. I'm cringing with every word of the schmaltzy crap I'm having to write. That's what's really depressing me. And the conference calls don't help.' She gave the phone a vicious glare – Larry Savage kept ringing, looking for progress reports and making her have conference calls with him and Chandler while they forcibly suggested cuts and additions. 'If they'd just let me get on with it, it mightn't be so bad. But every time I finally manage to sew up a scene, they make me change it, so I feel like I'm getting nowhere.'

'Do you think you'll be able to come tonight?'

'Ah, yeah. I'll need a break.' She suddenly remembered something. 'Look, sorry about telling you about Shay Delaney like that. I sort of panicked with the Bill Bryson thing and couldn't stop talking.'

'It's OK, no biggie,' I said quickly, keen not to dwell on it. 'Who else'll be there?'

'Do you mean Troy?'

I winced. 'S'pose.'

'He'll be there. How do you feel about him now?'

'Oh, you know,' I said airily, 'mortified, embarrassed.'

'Do you still want to sleep with him?'

'Are you insane? Last man on earth and all that.'

'That's great. You're not so messed up that you've become a rejection addict.'

'And what's that, oh pop-psychology one?'

'You know – the more he pushes you away, the more you want him.'

'God, that'd be worse, no doubt about it. As it is, I just feel really stupid.'

'You're not the first woman to have been taken in by a man and you won't be the last, so go easy on yourself. All that's wrong with you is that you're out of practice,' she added with a smile. 'Soon you'll have been duped by tons of men, and Troy will fade into nothing!'

'Speaking of being duped, how's Lou?'

'Clever, I'll give him that. Playing at being Mister Perfect. But I'm several steps ahead of him.' Coolly she blew out a plume of smoke.

Down at the Ocean View, they'd all been awake since four a.m. and were looking for kicks. Spirits were high as we set off beneath a cloudless blue sky for Beverly Hills and purchased a 'map' of the stars' houses. Everyone knew the maps were, at best, inaccurate and out of date, but who was I to ruin anyone's excitement?

First stop was Julia Roberts' house, where we spent a good twenty minutes parked on a well-kempt deserted road, trying to see through solid metal gates.

'She'll have to come out some time,' was Dad's reasoning. 'To buy a paper or get a pint of milk or something.'

'You haven't a clue,' Helen scorned. 'She has people to do that. She probably even has people to read the paper and drink the milk *for* her.'

We resumed our silent vigil.

'This is really boring,' Helen said. 'Although it's good practice for when I set up my private-detective agency. A lot of that will be surveillance work.'

'You're not becoming a private detective,' Mum said tightly. 'You've got Marie Fitzsimon's wedding on Monday week and you'll send her down the aisle looking like a princess, or you'll have me to deal with.'

'Don't you need qualifications to be a private detective?' Anna said.

Helen thought about it. 'Yep. First, I need to develop a drink dependency. Shouldn't be any problem considering the gene pool I come from. Secondly, I need a wacky family.' Helen swept an approving eye over the assembled group, over Mum's patchy face, Dad's argyle socks and Anna's I-get-dressed-in-the-dark chic. 'Once again, ladies and gentlemen, we appear to be in luck!'

'Someone's coming out. Someone's coming out!'

'Calm down, Dad.'

But it was just a Mexican gardener with a leaf-blower.

Dad rolled down the window and shouted at him, 'Is Julia around?'

'Hooleeya?'

'Julia Roberts.'

'Thees ees not Mees Roberts' khouse.'

'Oh,' Dad said in consternation. 'Well, do you know which one is?'

'Yes, but eef I told you, I would have to keel you.'

'Fine help you are,' Dad muttered, rolling the window back up. 'Come on, who's next?'

After visits to the 'houses' of Tom Cruise, Sandra Bullock, Tim Allen and Madonna had yielded nothing but views of electronic gates and Armed Response signs, we gave up on it and went to the Chinese Theatre, which was overrun with tourists seeking their favourite actors' handprints, then putting their own hands in and having their photo taken. Dad paid homage to John Wayne's hands, Mum couldn't get over the tininess of Doris Day's shoes and Anna seemed very touched by Lassie's paw print. Helen, however, wasn't so impressed.

'This is boring,' she said loudly and tagged a passing official. 'Excuse me, sir, where can I find Brad Pitt's arse?'

'Brad Pitt's arse?'

'Yes, I heard it was here.'

'Didja? OK. Hey, Ricky, where can this lady find Brad Pitt's arse?'

'What's an arse?'

'An ass,' Helen translated helpfully. 'A butt, if you prefer.'

'Do we have Brad Pitt's butt? Hey, LaWanda, where's Brad Pitt's butt?'

But LaWanda wasn't as stupid as the rest of them. 'We don't got it,' she snapped.

'Did someone steal it?' Helen asked sympathetically.

LaWanda eyed Helen angrily. 'You weird.'

'Because I want to see a concrete copy of Brad Pitt's arse? It'd be weird *not* to want to see it.'

'Brad Pitt ain't gonna come on down here, drop his pants and sit his ass in wet con-*crete*. He a star!' By now LaWanda was giving the hand and doing that side-to-side, head-popping thing they do on Jerry Springer. I knew what usually followed. Before Helen got the crap beaten out of her, I moved her on.

Later, I dropped them back to the Ocean View, with instructions to get ready for the film screening, then to come round to Emily's.

'And we're to get dressed up?' Dad asked, hoping the answer would be no.

'It's a film premeer,' Mum scolded. 'Of course we are.'

'Are we?' he asked me again.

'You might as well.'

Though *Doves* was only an independent film – which meant no household-name stars and no one in Ireland being impressed because they'd never hear of it – all the same, it was worth looking our best.

And then, I don't know what got into me, but I decided I'd take a trip to Arizona and Third and get my nails done.

I found Nail Heaven easily. Not only was it on the corner of Arizona and Third, just like Lara had said, but it had a pink-neon hand in the window and a blue-neon sign that said 'nails, nails, nails' (only the 'n' wasn't lighting properly so what the sign actually said was 'ails, ails, ails', but what harm?). Down a couple of steps and in I went.

It was run by Taiwanese girls, Lara had said. The best. Behind a desk sat a beautiful, doll-like receptionist, whose name badge said 'Lianne'. As I explained myself to her and apologized for not having an appointment, I was distracted by her nails – they were about two inches long and each one was individually painted with the stars and stripes. All at once, a wealth of nail-related possibilities opened up – maybe I'd get mine done the same!

'You don't need appointment,' Lianne said – just as Lara had promised – then she grasped my hand and bent over it to examine it. 'Ooohhh,' she breathed, sounding quite shocked – and suddenly I saw what she was seeing; the uneven, crooked nails, the scraggy cuticles, the general air of neglect. I'd never thought it had mattered before. How wrong I was!

Just in case I wasn't already feeling ashamed, Lianne began to laugh – childish, sweet hee-hee-hees – before lifting her glossy head and excitedly summoning her colleagues to have a look. In seconds I was surrounded by slender, white-coated girls, high-pitched garrulous chatter and lots more laughter as they examined my hand, as if it wasn't attached to me, but was a strange object found abandoned in the street.

'On vacation?' one asked.

'Yes. From Ireland.'

'Ah,' she nodded, like it all made sense now. 'Iowa.'

Quick-fire questions in Taiwanese began to hop between the girls and the word 'Mona' kept appearing. Finally, when some conclusion had been reached, Lianne said, 'Mona will do you.'

'Which one of you is Mona?' I asked, looking from blossom-like face to blossom-like face, and for some reason this question was enough to start the laughter all over again. I could sort of understand why when Mona emerged from some back room, a heavy-set lady quite a bit older than the other beauticians.

'She very goo',' one of the young girls whispered respectfully to me.

'She rike a charrenge,' whispered another.

Mona examined my fingernails. 'The feet too?' She leant over for a look at my toes poking through my sandals and all but winced.

'I'm not sure I have the time.'

'We do them same time as hands. One girl hands, other girl feet,' she said scornfully.

'OK then.'

She summoned one of the younger girls, and in no time they had my hands and feet soaking in soapy water.

'You need the hot wax. It's goo' for your skin,' Mona said.

'Fine.' If the job's worth doing, it's worth doing properly, right?

Just then a tall, well-kempt woman stalked in, wearing a beautifully cut trouser suit and an air of panic. She had a quick word with Lianne, who shouted a few urgent-sounding imprecations around the salon and within moments people were rising from their work stations and gravitating to the front of house. There was an atmosphere of importance, of professionals falling into well-rehearsed roles, and for some reason it reminded me of the time, years ago, when I'd had to go to Accident and Emergency with a badly sprained ankle. I'd been in agony, my foot had swollen up to the size of a football and I was whimpering in pain, when out of nowhere gurneys were rattling past me, bearing bodies that were losing blood hand over fist. Paramedics were running beside them, holding drips and shouting stuff like, 'He's still breathing.' Apparently there had been a terrible car crash on the Stillorgan dual carriageway and my sprained ankle, painful though it was, was suddenly (and rightfully) bottom of the priority list.

From the minute the well-dressed woman had rushed into Nail Heaven, there was the same attitude that this was a *real* emergency. While she told the terrible story of her 'prize nail' and how she'd got it caught while changing a toner cartridge, Mona rose to her feet, followed by her assistant, and a path opened up for them.

'Oh, Mona, thank God!' The woman thrust the injured nail at her. 'Can it be saved?'

When Mona had taken stock and eventually concluded, 'It's bad. I'll do what I can,' I almost expected them all to start scrubbing up and donning green gowns and masks.

While the worthier woman was being fast-tracked to full nail health, I sat abandoned, my hands and feet in basins of soapy water. Some kind-hearted soul placed a magazine on my thighs, but, on account of my hands soaking, I couldn't turn the pages. Then I moved my foot a fraction and the magazine slid off my knee and down into the basin of water that my feet were in.

'Sorry,' I muttered, as the same kind-hearted soul retrieved it and shook out its swollen, pulpy pages. I wondered if she'd bring me another.

She didn't. I looked at the two other women there who were having their hands and feet done. Neither of them had let their magazines fall into the soapy water. What was it about me that I sometimes felt I'd been born without life's rule book?

Eventually, after she'd saved the prize nail, Mona returned to me bringing her helper and they set to work, filing, buffing, pushing back cuticles, rubbing at callouses, and then it was time for the hot-wax treatment. A basin of molten wax was placed on the floor in front of me and I was told to put my foot in. But the second I came in contact with the wax, I hopped my foot right back out and yelped, 'It's much too hot!'

'But it's goo' for your skin,' Mona cried, clamping a vice-like hand around my knee and trying to force my foot back down into the basin.

'But missus . . . Mona, it's too hot.' We struggled for a few seconds, me pushing my knee up, her pushing it down, then Mona cheated by standing up and giving herself extra leverage. Right away my foot was plunged back into the scalding wax.

'It hurts,' I begged.

'It's goo' for your skin,' Mona repeated, her hand steady on my quivering knee.

All the other girls were in convulsions, shrieking with laughter behind beautiful hands.

After a short but agonizing wait, I was allowed to lift my foot out. But as soon as a layer of wax had cooled and whitened around my foot, she plunged me back in again. The laughter started anew. In, out, in, out went my foot. The pattern was repeated four or five times, each time as painful as the first.

Some years ago, there was a programme on the telly called *Shogun*. In it a man is dunked repeatedly in boiling water until he dies. For some reason I thought of that. And funnily enough, I thought of it again when we did the second foot.

Then they wrapped my be-waxed feet in plastic bags tied at the ankles with pink ribbons, and if I hadn't seen this done before I'd have been looking around for the hidden cameras.

Ten minutes later, when they peeled off the white wax, to my surprise my feet weren't in need of urgent skin-grafts but were soft and petal-like. Then they painted all twenty of my nails in a pretty ice-cream pink – they'd laughed indulgently but shaken their heads when I'd asked for the stars and stripes – and sent me on my way. Already I was a convert, promising myself that I'd definitely have it done once a week from now on. The way you do.

Back at home, Emily was hiding her worn-out pallor beneath a mask of make-up. I don't know how she does it, but when she'd finished she looked fantastic – radiant and shiny and not at all like a sleep-deprived, stressed wreck who'd been working flat-out and living on cigarettes and Lucky Charms.

My family were due to arrive at Emily's at seven, and when they hadn't arrived by twenty-five past, I was a ball of anxiety.

'They've got lost!'

'How could they get lost? It's six blocks, it's a straight line!'

'You know what they're like. They've probably ended up in South Central and are already in a street gang. Gold chains and uzis and bandannas.'

'Could you imagine your Dad in a bandanna?' Emily got sidetracked.

'Could you imagine Mum in one?' For some reason, we were suddenly snorting with uncontrollable laughter. 'An orange one.'

'She'd look like a space-hopper.' And we were off again, shaking with mirth. It was lovely.

'Oh God,' Emily sighed happily, scooping an expert finger under her eye and removing a little pool of mascara, 'that's fabulous. Hold on,' she cocked an ear. 'I hear them.'

The four of them burst into the house, bringing their collective bad humours with them.

'It's her fault we're late,' Mum glared at Helen.

'We're here now, that's the main thing,' Dad tried.

'And you all look lovely,' complimented Emily.

Indeed they did. We were a glitzy, perfumed lot (except for Dad), and it came as no surprise when, almost immediately, the Goatee Boys appeared at the door.

'We're just going out,' Emily said shortly, trying to bar them entrance.

'Hey, I'm Ethan.' Ethan bobbed up and down, trying to see around Emily and make eye contact with Helen and Anna.

'Oh, let them in for a second,' I said.

'Go on, then.' Emily stood by narkily as the three of them filed in and stood shyly in front of the girls. I did the introductions and for a few minutes left them to sniff around each other like dogs, then we really did have to go.

'What do those lads do?' Dad asked, as he hoisted himself up into Emily's jeep.

'Catch VD,' Emily muttered.

'They're students,' I said.

'Yeah,' Anna said, 'but Ethan, the one with the shaved head, he's going to be the new Messiah.'

Mum's lips tightened. 'Oh, he is, is he?'

38

The première of *Doves* was taking place off Doheny, in a wonderful old-fashioned movie theatre with red velvet seats and art deco mirrored walls, a throwback to a more glamorous age. I was glad we'd made an effort with our appearance, because everyone else looked fairly ritzy. There were even a few photographers hanging around. 'More likely to be from *Variety* than *People*,' Emily said, but all the same.

Emily went off to network – 'Just a quickie before the movie,' and I shepherded my charges to our allotted seats. I was just settling myself in comfortably when, a couple of rows ahead, I noticed Troy and Kirsty and instantly shrivelled. Seeing him – and worse still, seeing him with Kirsty – reminded me of my stupidity, of how naïve I'd been. But then I remembered what Emily had said: I wasn't the first woman who'd let herself be made a fool of and I wouldn't be the last, and all of a sudden I felt a bit lighter, freer. Perhaps I'd always nurse a desire to stick a fork in his leg, but that wasn't the worst way to feel about someone.

Troy turned around to check the place out and I lowered my eyes, but too late. He nodded coolly at me, I nodded even more coolly at him – I like to think my head didn't move at all, just some of my strands of hair – then his look slid over me and arrived at Helen, where it lingered speculatively. Brazenly, Helen winked at him and he grinned back. Kirsty, alerted by some sixth sense, also twisted around and when she saw who Troy was looking at, her whiny voice started up in some attempt to distract him. At least I wasn't like her, I thought – at least I no longer wanted him.

Then Emily took her seat, the lights went down and the movie began.

'What kind of film is it?' Dad whispered hopefully. 'A horse opera?'

'Is Harrison Ford in it?' Mum asked into my other ear.

Harrison Ford has cross-generational appeal in my family; Mum is as keen on him as the rest of us. In fact, even my niece Kate stops crying when Claire plays her the bit in *Working Girl* when he takes his shirt off – arguably his finest hour.

Well, I can tell you that *Doves* didn't star Harrison Ford and it wasn't a horse opera. I'm not quite sure what it was. It could have been a love story, except the hero kept murdering his girlfriends. It could have been a comedy, except it wasn't funny. It could have been a porn movie, except it was mostly filmed in black and white so that we'd know the sex wasn't gratuitous but was essential to the plot. (It really is intensely uncomfortable watching graphic sex scenes while sandwiched between your parents.)

It was the kind of film which makes me feel incredibly thick, which reminds me that I didn't go to university, that I haven't read any Simone de Beauvoir, that I thought Kieslowski's *Three Colours: Red* was complete tosh (and I'd only gone because *When a Man Loves a Woman* had been booked out). I spent most of it a) wishing the sex scenes would end and b) trying to think of things to say to Lara afterwards about it, other than 'pile of shite'. It took me the full 120 minutes of running time to decide that 'Interesting' was a good neutral phrase. After two dreadful hours – and seemingly midway through a scene – the credits began to roll, the lights went up and the clapping and whoops began. Mum turned, smiled brightly at me and declared, 'Marvellous!' Then muttered in an undertone, 'The oddest thing I ever saw. I thought *The English Patient* was bad, but it was nothing on this yoke.'

As everyone stood up to applaud the director, Dad remained sitting, staring straight ahead.

'It's not actually completed, is it? This isn't the actual thing people will pay money for into the cinema?' He was almost pleading. 'Maybe they've shown us the out-takes, the funnies that turn up on *It'll Be Alright on the Night*?'

'Where's the drink?' Helen demanded.

'I've to go to the loo, I'll investigate.' As I excuse-me-excuse-me'd through the audience out into the lobby, I over-heard someone describing the movie as 'very European'.

'Brave,' someone else said. 'Challenging,' yet another person said. I filed the phrases away, they'd come in very handy the next time I wanted a euphemism for 'pile of shite'.

'Maggie, Maggie!' Lara, luminous in a copper-coloured, floor-length, beaded sheath and big Barbarella hair, was beckoning me over. 'Thank you for coming. What did you think?'

'Yeah, great. Interesting, really interesting. Very European.'

'You think? You hated it!' She laughed with delight.

'No, I . . . oh OK, it wasn't really me. I'm more of a chick-flick kind of girl.'

'That's OK.' Then she noticed. 'Hey, *great* nails. You went to Nail Heaven? Who did you?'

'Mona.'

'Mona? Wow.'

'Why "wow"?'

'One of the greats but she's kinda in semi-retirement. Only does the special cases. I better go talk to some journalists, but I'll catch you later.'

She shimmied away and I felt happy – at least things were OK with Lara. I still wanted to keep her away from my parents, but there was no residue of awkwardness from our brief dalliance.

After I came out of the ladies', I found the glittering room where the hooley was being held, full of glinting trays of champagne and tables bearing finger food. I took a glass of champagne and made my way through the tanned, glam throng to Emily, who was standing in a little knot with Anna, Kirsty, Troy and – surprise, surprise – Helen.

'Weren't those old velvet seats like totally grungy?' Kirsty said.

'I loved them, it's a great theatre,' Emily said and we all made noises of agreement.

'Eeuw!' Kirsty exclaimed, in elaborate disgust. 'You're gross! Don't you think of all the butts that have been in them before you . . .'

I tuned out, and not just because I hated her; there was something weird going on with the food. The quantities were disappearing fast – each time I turned away from it, then looked again, it had diminished even further – but try as I might, I couldn't see anyone actually putting any of it in their mouths. *No one* was visibly eating – except for my Dad, who was leaning against one of the tables, going for it – but he wasn't eating it all. And turning around very fast gave me no clues, just got me a couple of funny looks. It was as if people were eating using something like the Vulcan mind-meld.

'So howja like the movie, Short Stuff?' Troy asked Helen, looking at her from under meaningfully lowered eyelids.

Christ, he already had a nickname for her! I almost felt sorry for Kirsty.

But was I jealous? I wondered anxiously. I so didn't want to be, I'd been doing well on the emotions front and didn't want a setback. So I had a good rummage through my feelings, and all I could find was a mild interest in what might happen. Perhaps I should have been protective of Helen, but I was sure she could take care of herself. I reckoned Troy was the one who'd want to watch out.

My pride in how well I was coping took a bit of a knock, though, when I saw who my mother had engaged in intense conversation – none other than Shay Delaney. That hadn't taken her long. He was leaning his dark-blond head down to her level and his tawny eyes were fastened so attentively on to hers that I had a strange urge to laugh.

As though he knew I was watching him, he suddenly looked up and gave me a stare that went straight to my stomach. Mum craned her neck to see who he was looking at and, when she saw me, beckoned me over – and of course I went. Out of obedience? Politeness? Curiosity? Who knows. But I found myself standing beside him where, big and kind of shaggy and smiling and charming, he was being *very* Shay Delaney.

'Look who I found!' Mum was skittish and over-excited. 'We were just reminiscing on old times. It only seems like yesterday that I had Shay Delaney sitting in my kitchen, eating . . . what were they again, Shay?'

'Bakewell tarts!' the pair of them said simultaneously.

'You were the only one who ate any. None of my lot would touch them.'

'I don't know why,' Shay's eyes twinkled. 'They were delicious.'

But he would have said that even if he'd gone home and promptly died of food-poisoning. He'd always been this way: full of compliments, and he went out of his way to make everyone feel good about themselves. Except for me. My look lingered on the golden stubble on his jawline and I swallowed a sigh.

'And you're married, I hear,' Mum probed.

'I am, six years ago, to a girl called Donna Higgins.'

'The Higgins family from Rockwell Park?'

'No, the Higgins from York Road.'

'Malachy Higgins or Bernard Higgins?'

'Neither, although she does have an Uncle Bernard . . .'

A brief detour to establish exactly which branch of the Higgins family Shay's wife hailed from, then Mum was off again. 'Margaret's marriage is after breaking up, but sure these things happen. You're no one these days if you don't get married more than once. We have to move with the times, isn't that right? What's the point in having divorce if we don't use it? Use it or lose it, as they say.'

With each passing sentence, my surprise stacked up until it became fully fledged shock. My mother is the woman who cried when divorce came to Ireland and said it was the end of civilization as we knew it. And how tactful it was of her to bring it up in front of Shay, considering his background.

'And your wife?' she asked Shay. 'Is she with you right now or back . . . Oh, back in Ireland. I see. And you're out here for work a lot? It must be tough when you don't see that much of each other. Well, who knows, you could be one of the fashionable types who have more than one marriage, if you're not careful!'

I thought I was too old to be embarrassed by my mother. Well, there's a turn-up for the books.

'It seems no length of time since you were teenagers,' Mum said wistfully. 'Where do the years go?'

Silently, Shay and I looked at each other and suddenly I was right back there, remembering one particular afternoon. Him lowering me into a patch of sunlight on his bedroom carpet. The heat, the light, the rare touch of his naked skin against mine. I'd been almost unable to bear the pleasure.

He remembered too, or something very similar, because the atmosphere thickened almost visibly.

I'd tried to keep my teenage romances secret from my parents. Naturally, they'd suspected when I first went out with Garv when I was seventeen. But at the time I never confirmed it – or that we'd split up. Nor did they ever know for sure that I went out with Shay, either. Not that I ever went *out* with Shay – all we did was have sex. What I remember of that time was the constant waiting and yearning for his mother to go out so I could slip into his house and out of my clothes. I was in a state of constant arousal and even when his mother and younger sisters were home, all we did was have sex, although a little more surreptitiously – we pretended to watch television while I had one hand in his jeans, one eye on the door handle and my pants under a cushion. Sometimes his nervy, beleaguered mother cracked under the constant badgering and let us go to his room to 'listen to music', where we had sex with most of our clothes still on: my skirt pulled up, his jeans pulled down, dreading the footfall on the stairs that had us leaping to our feet and hastily covering up our flushed skin. Even when we went to parties, it was just an excuse for him to lock me in a bedroom and screw my brains out on the pile of coats.

'I'll leave you two to catch up,' Mum said with a warm smile, and promptly turned on her heel, pushing through the crowds. I hadn't ever thought I'd see the day when my mother was pimping for me.

'When did she get so liberal about divorce?' Shay asked.

'In the last ten minutes.'

I hated the pause that followed. I couldn't think of anything to say. I was stripped of all conversational skills, which was a shame because there was so much I wanted to talk to him about.

'Right,' he said, and I knew what was coming next.

'Time up, is it?'

'What?'

'You've talked to me on my own for more than five seconds, so it's time you stuck out your hand and said, "Well, great to see you again." Isn't it?'

He didn't like that. He seemed startled – because he'd been caught out not being perfect? I was rather startled myself; I'm not normally so forthright. But we'd once been so close that maybe I still felt I had the right to say anything I wanted to him.

'It's not like that.' He stumbled over the words. 'It's . . . I mean . . .' He looked anxious, as if he was pleading to be understood.

But before we got any further, Dad spotted Shay and came running joyously. 'Shay Delaney, as I live and breathe! It's great to see someone from home!'

I swallowed another sigh. Dad had been away from Ireland less than two days. What is it with Irish people? Rachel, my sister, says we can't even go on a daytrip to Holyhead without singing maudlin songs about how we were forced to leave the

Emerald Isle and how much we wish we were back there. Do we share some sort of inherited memory, so that whenever we leave the country it triggers recollections of being deported to Van Diemen's Land for stealing a sheep?

'We're all heading back to the hotel now on account of the jet lag, but I'm taking everyone out for their dinner on Friday night,' Dad told Shay, 'and I'll take it as a personal insult if you won't join us.'

39

On Thursday evening, Mum, Dad, Helen and Anna arrived unexpectedly at Emily's. They'd gone to Disneyland for the day and I hadn't thought they'd be home till midnight. Right away, I knew it wasn't just a casual call because Mum had on her best cardigan and her 'going-out' lipstick, i.e. a ring of lipstick that was wider than her lips. She looked like a respectable clown.

'Come in, come in,' I said. 'How was Disneyland?'

Mum silently stood aside to reveal Dad. Wearing a neckbrace.

'Oh.'

'That's how Disneyland was,' Mum said. 'He stood up on that log thing again. He wouldn't listen. He never listens. He has to know it all.'

'It was worth it,' Dad said, having to turn his entire body to glare at her.

'Dad, when you came here with the other accountants, did you wear your suits?'

'Suits?' He sounded shocked. 'We were ambassadors for our country. Of course we did.'

'Did you have a good time at Disneyland?' I asked Helen.

'Yeah, because we didn't go. We went to Malibu looking for surf gods.'

'You've no car,' Emily said to Anna. 'How did you and Helen get to Malibu? Surely to God you didn't . . . get the *bus*?'

But Anna shook her head. 'No. Ethan and the other lads from next door drove us in their Dukes of Hazzardmobile.'

'But you only met them last night.'

'*Tempus fugit*,' Anna said knowingly. 'No time like the present.'

The whole room fell silent and stared, because Anna was the girl whose motto had always been, 'Don't do today what you can put off till tomorrow. Or preferably some time next year.'

'Anna fancies Ethan,' Helen said.

'No, I don't.'

'Yes, you do.'

'No, I don't.'

'Yes, you do.'

'Do you really?' Emily asked, agog.

'No!'

'She does,' Helen insisted. 'We'll just have to torture her to get her to admit it. Emily, have you anything we can give her an electric shock with?'

'Look in the kitchen. While you're at it, bring out some wine and glasses as well, would you?'

'Could you not just tell us, pet?' Mum asked. 'Electric shocks can really sting.'

'I don't fancy him!'

From the kitchen came the sound of rattling and rummaging in drawers. 'Emily, all I can find is an electric carving knife,' Helen called. 'We could cut off bits of her.'

'If you torture me, I'm going home,' Anna said.

'Leave it so. Just bring the wine.'

'And what did you do today?' Mum asked me.

I'd had a funny kind of a day, assailed by all manner of nostalgia, cast back in time to when I was seventeen and first involved with Shay. So much had come back to me, remembered with bitter-sweet pain . . .

Mum's voice cut across my thoughts, returning me with a jolt to present-day Los Angeles.

'Am I talking to the wall?' she said sharply. 'What did you do today?'

'Oh, sorry. I washed clothes. Went to the supermarket.' Got shouted at again by the raggedy man, something about a car chase with 'Lala' getting a bullet in the thigh. This time I didn't take it personally. Bought loads of lovely food, then wondered why it is, no matter whether it's in a supermarket in Ireland or one six thousand miles away in Los Angeles, that I always end up standing behind the Person Who Gets a Big Surprise When They Realise They Have to Pay. Their stuff is all packed in bags, which are sitting in their trolley to be pushed to the car, then when they get told the amount they act amazed, and only then do they begin patting their pockets or opening their handbag, looking for their wallet. Eventually paying either with a credit card whose swipe doesn't work or counting out the exact amount in small change.

Then I went next door to the drugstore, bought a tongue-scraper and waited hopefully for my life to change.

'And when I got home I helped Emily.' Well, I'd made her a blueberry smoothie, given her another word for 'growled', and answered the phone to Larry Savage and told him that Emily was at her colonic irrigation person when she was just lying on the couch smoking and crying.

'Last night was marvellous,' Mum said. 'Apart from the film. Shay Delaney hasn't changed a bit, it did me the power of good to see him. And he's going to come out with us all for dinner tomorrow night, Dad says.'

'He won't come,' I said. 'He was only being polite.'

'He will come,' Mum insisted. 'He said he would.'

Dad had practically held a knife to his throat, of course he'd said he'd come.

'I think he's a bit creepy,' Helen said. 'He was looking at you, Maggie.'

'He was looking at all of us,' Mum said smartly.

'No, I mean he was *looking* at her. *Looking*. With his *eyes*.'

'What else would he be looking at her with?' Mum snapped. 'His feet?'

Before I could separate and label the clump of feelings this engendered, Anna said something surprising. 'He wants everyone to like him.'

'What's wrong with that?' Mum asked. 'Anyway, everyone does like him.'

'I don't,' Helen said.

'You're just contrary.'

'Go home, old woman, I'm tired and you're annoying me.'

'I'm going, but only because I want to. C'mon, you!' Mum summoned Dad as though he was an obedient dog. 'Let's get this over with.'

'Where are you off to?'

'In next door to their fable-telling evening.'

When we'd all finished laughing, I said, 'Why are you going if you don't want to?'

'Sure, what could I say?' Mum said indignantly. 'That Mike put me right on the spot the other night.'

'Just don't go,' Helen suggested. 'Let him fuck off.'

'No.' Suddenly Mum was all hauteur. 'If I say I'll do something, I'll do it. I'm not the kind of woman who goes back on her word. We'll go for an hour to be polite, then we'll say we've another engagement.'

'Say you're going to the Viper Room,' Helen suggested. 'It's oldies' night.'

'The Viper Room,' Mum repeated. 'Right you are. And if we're not out in an hour and a half, come and get us.'

As soon as they'd gone, Helen said, all business-like, 'Now, the bloke with the big schnozz? Troy? I find him strangely attractive.'

'Take a number and get in line,' Emily said, just like she'd once said to me. 'Don't fall in love with me baby 'cos I'll only break your heart.'

'Fall in love,' Helen scoffed, highly amused. 'That's a good one. So who's slept with him?' She looked eagerly at Emily. 'Surely you have?'

'Ask Maggie.'

'OK. Who's slept with him?' I shrugged and Helen gave me a gimlet look. *'You?'*

'Yes, me.'

'But . . . you're a lickarse, a good girl.'

'Is that right?'

She gave me a mistrustful look, then pressed on, 'But you and this Troy, you're not an item?'

'No.'

'Well, do you mind if I have a go of him?'

'Nothing to do with me.'

'You might want to run it by his girlfriend.' Emily sounded unexpectedly sharp.

'Who? That ringlety one?' Helen laughed softly. 'I don't anticipate any problems with her. Now tell me all about Lara. The lads were saying she's a lesbo. I wonder what it's like to have sex with a girl,' she said dreamily – only because she wanted to cause a bit of a furore. 'I wonder what they get up to in bed.'

'Ask Maggie,' Emily said.

'HAHAHAHA!' went Helen. Then stopped as if she'd just driven into a granite wall. The colour vanished from her face. 'I don't believe you.'

I shrugged again. 'Up to you.' I was enjoying this.

'When?'

'Last week.'

'I don't believe you. I'm going to ask Lara.'

'Ask away,' I said equably.

Helen spent the next hour staring at me as though she'd never seen me before, then shaking her head and murmuring faintly, 'Jesus Christ. Jesus *Christ . . .*' She only stopped when Emily looked at her watch and exclaimed, 'What about your Mum and Dad? It's been nearly an hour and a half. Should we go and rescue them?'

'Right, come on.'

We filed out, stood on the street and looked through the window into Mike and Charmaine's front room. Mum was sitting majestically on a chair, while all the others were clustered at her feet. She was talking and smiling. Dad was propped on the couch, his head in his neckbrace, unnaturally still. He was smiling too.

I knocked on the glass of the front door and a slender, beardy type tiptoed over and held a finger to his lips. 'It's the story of Famous Seamus. How he won the love of the doctor's daughter.'

Emily, Helen, Anna and I exchanged baffled looks, followed him in and took our place on the floor. Straight away, I was worried. Mum's accent was more Irish than I'd ever heard it before and the 'Musha' and 'Wisha' hit rate per sentence was alarmingly high.

'. . . Wisha, me prime boy Seamus could do it all. Reversing tractors, making reeks, and as for the dancing! Musha, he was the tidiest dancer you ever saw, he could dance on a plate . . .'

I was mortified, she was making such a show of herself. But a glance at the assembled faces gave me pause for thought: they were spellbound. Every person there was angled towards her as though she was a magnet and they were iron filings. You could have heard a pin drop.

'He could jive, he could line dance, he could do an eight-hand reel. But he had brains too, musha, brains to burn! Great, he was, at the book-learning . . .'

'"*Book learning*"?' Emily whispered. 'What is she *like*?'

'Sshhh,' a poster girl for tie-dyeing hissed fiercely at her.

'. . . he'd the heart of every woman in Ireland broke. Every mother in the townland had her eye on him.' A professionally timed beat. 'And not just for their daughters!'

Much laughter ensued and I took advantage of the disturbance to make wind-it-up gestures at her. She saw and acknowledged. Mind you, she looked disappointed.

'Ladies and gentlemen,' she cut across the laughter, 'ladies and gentlemen. As you can see, my daughters have arrived and want to take me away to the Viper Room.'

Instantly, several heads snapped around and glowered.

'So reluctantly I have to take my leave of ye.'

'"Ye"?' Helen questioned. '"*Ye*"?'

'Couldn'tja wait five minutes?' a large pony-tailed man turned to us and asked aggressively. 'We wanna hear the end of the story.'

'Yeah,' someone else called. '*Let* Johnny Depp wait.'

How was it we were getting the blame? 'Fine,' I said. 'Makes no odds to us.'

'Wisha,' Mum acted coy. 'I'd no idea ye were enjoying it so much. Sure, if ye insist . . .'

'WE INSIST!' the room erupted, then one of her front-row acolytes touched her gently and said, 'Carry on, Mammy Walsh.'

Mammy Walsh carried on for quite some time, and by the time they finally let her go, she was floating on air and so was Dad. Unfortunately, things got a little ugly out on the street when she discovered that she wasn't really going to the Viper Room, that it had only been a ruse – agreed upon by herself, we had to remind her – to get her out.

'I want to go to the Viper Room.' She sounded like a spoilt child.

'You can't, you're too old!' Helen said.

'You said it was oldies' night.'

'It was a joke. And we're knackered, our jet lag has caught up with us, we're going home to bed.

Mum turned an Et Tu, Brute? look on Emily and me. 'I've a screenplay to write,' Emily said nervously. 'I need my zeds.'

'And I'm helping her. 'Night all, see you tomorrow.'

Emily and I hurried into the house and closed the door behind us, but from the street we could still hear her plaintively insisting, 'But I'm on my holidays. You lot are no fun.'

40

The holiday that was supposed to do Garv and me the world of good did the exact opposite. We returned frayed and shrouded in a dreadful suspicion that everything we did together would go wrong, that we were travelling on a non-stop, one-way ticket to disasterville, and that the more we struggled to extricate ourselves, the more trapped we'd become.

The atmosphere remained strained on our return and once or twice I caught Garv looking my way, with blame in his eyes. But about ten days after we got back, we had an appointment with Dr Collins, my gynaecologist, where we tried once again to find a reason why I'd miscarried twice. It was in that room that the final prop was removed for Garv and me. I can pinpoint, almost to the second, the exact moment that my marriage keeled over and died.

However, often when fatal things are happening, you don't know at the time that they're fatal. You get an inkling that they're Not Good, that they Haven't Helped, but only the passage of time will reveal just how bad they are.

I blame routines. Routines mask disaster. You think if you're getting up in the morning, putting on clean clothes, going to work, eating from time to time and watching *East-Enders* that everything's under control. And we were doing all that, but dragging the weight of our moribund relationship with us.

After the first miscarriage, we'd both been eager to try again immediately. We'd had a lot of hope that a new pregnancy would erase our sadness. This time was different. I think I was afraid of getting pregnant again, in case I miscarried once more. But nevertheless, I consulted my temperature thing daily, and Garv and I dutifully had sex if the signs were auspicious. Until one day something that had never before happened, happened. We were in bed and Garv was about to enter me, when I noticed that he was having trouble. His erection had gone a bit bendy and flippy.

'What's wrong?' I asked.

'It's just a bit . . .' he said, trying again to hit the target.

But he hadn't a hope, and before my eyes it got softer, softer, softer, shrinking in seconds from a hard baton to a shy marshmallow.

'Sorry,' he said, rolling away from me and staring at nothing. 'It must be the drink.'

'You only had two pints. It's me, you don't fancy me any more.'

'It's not you, of course I fancy you.'

He rolled back to me and we lay wrapped around each other, rigid in our separate miseries.

The next time we tried, it happened again and Garv was wretched. I knew, from *Cosmopolitan* and sessions with my girlfriends, that this was the worst thing that could happen to a man, that he felt his very manhood was failing him. But I didn't have what it took to provide comfort. I was wound too tightly around myself; sore that he'd rejected me and angry at his uselessness – how could we ever have a baby with this carry on?

We had one more disastrous attempt, before reaching a silent, mutual decision not to chance it again. From then on, we barely touched each other.

One Sunday night, we were watching a video – I think it was *Men in Black* – one about the world being about to end unless someone does something heroic very quickly. It was near the end of the film, time was running out, urgent music was playing, it was all very tense . . . And suddenly Garv says, 'Who cares?'

'Sorry?'

'Who cares? Let the world end. We'd all be better off.'

It was so unlike him that I took a good look to see if he was joking. But, of course, he wasn't. I watched this person slumped on the sofa, his hair flopping over his dark, mutinous face and I wondered who he was.

The following morning, I'd got up, had my shower, had my coffee and got dressed, and he was still in bed.

'Get up, you'll be late,' I said.

'I'm not getting up. I'm staying in bed.'

He'd never done that before.

'Why?'

He didn't reply and again I asked, 'Why?'

'For tax reasons,' he mumbled, turning his face to the wall.

For a short time I stood looking at the inert mound of him under the duvet, then I left the room and went to work. He wouldn't talk to me and I was barely even frustrated. Upsets no longer sent me plummeting with despair, they simply settled calmly on top of the others. Probably because there was no place left for me to plummet to – I was as low as it got.

Apart from the occasional day skipping work – but never together – our routines kept us running like rats in a wheel. We thought we were moving forward, but all that was happening was that we were marking time, getting nowhere. It was around then that I started drinking my contact lenses.

Click, click, click, the days passed. We paid our mortgage, we marvelled at how expensive our phone bill was, we discussed Donna's love life – all familiar stuff, the lifeblood of normality. We went to work, had the occasional night out with friends where the pretence was maintained, then went to bed without touching, and got a few hours' sleep before waking at four a.m. to worry. And yes, I did wonder when things were going to get better. I was still convinced that this horrible patch was temporary. Until the night, shortly before it all went pear-shaped, when I was afflicted with sudden x-ray vision. I could see straight through the padding of the daily routine, the private language and the shared past, right into the heart of me and Garv, into all that had happened. Everything was stripped away and I had a horrible, too-clear thought: *We're in big trouble here.*

Somehow, three months had passed since the holiday in St Lucia.

The day we were supposed to be going out with Liam and Elaine dawned no differently from any of the others. No one could have predicted that today was the day that the whole rickety structure would come crashing down. Then, inexorably, the series of events kicked off – the flat-screen telly falling on Liam's toe, the phone call where I said I'd pick up some food, the box of truffles in the chilled compartment – ending with the awful tableau of Garv lifting the chocolates out of the shopping bag and exclaiming, 'Hey, look! Those sweets again. Are they following us?'

Then I was looking at him, at the box, then back at him. Baffled.

'You *know*,' he insisted happily. 'The same ones we had when –'

And then it all went see-through and I *knew*. He was talking about someone else, another woman.

I felt that I was falling, that I would go on falling for ever. Abruptly, I made myself stop. The gig was up, the end had come and I just couldn't do it. I couldn't bear to watch the downward spiral of my marriage begin to catch other people and spin them into the vortex too.

41

On Friday, Dad went to the chiropractor and Mum, Helen and Anna went to Rodeo Drive. Mum had insisted on going, even though we'd told her it was very expensive. No doubt she'd enjoy it, or at the very least she'd enjoy tut-tutting about the outrageously high prices when she returned.

I couldn't go with them because, as Emily put it, I had to help her hammer the final few nails into the coffin of her rewritten script. Larry Savage wanted it by lunch-time and it was all hands on deck. We worked through the morning, reading aloud, looking for inconsistencies and checking for continuity. Then at midday – High Noon, Emily kept calling it – we printed it out, the courier came, and Emily kissed the bundle of pages goodbye, 'Good luck, you poor bastard.'

Straight away, an exhausted Emily went to bed. With Lou. I found myself at an unexpectedly loose end. It was too hot to sunbathe, there was nothing on telly and I was afraid to go shopping in case I bought stuff.

My thoughts turned to that night's dinner. I was pretty sure Shay wouldn't show; you'd want to have seen his face when Dad had strong-armed him with his invitation. Not keen – he'd just said yes so he wouldn't give offence, and it would come as no surprise to get a message saying he'd been unavoidably detained at a meeting or something.

But what if he did come? Then what?

In no time at all, I'd decided to get my hair blow-dried. My only real option was Reza; she was strange and narky, but she was only two minutes down the road and, apart from the way she'd gammied up my fringe the last time, she'd done a fine job. I'd just wear tights on my head for a couple of hours when I got home and I'd be grand.

I rang for an appointment, and when I showed up at the salon it was no surprise that Reza wasn't friendly – but she wasn't as brusque as she'd been the other time, either. In fact, she seemed a little subdued. A few times while she was lathering my hair she exhaled wearily on to my scalp, then as she started tugging the head off me with the blow-drying brush, she gave a big, heavy, despair-sodden sigh.

Seconds later came another huge sigh, gathered up from her toes and released like a hurricane all over me. Then another. Eventually I had to ask, 'Are you OK?'

'No,' she said.

'Er, what's wrong?'

Another sigh was on the way. I could feel it, being collected, climbing its way through her body, expanding her chest, then being exhaled. It took so long I thought she wasn't going to answer me. Then she found words. 'My kusband is cheeedink me.'

God, was I sorry I'd ever risen to the bait. 'Cheedink you? Out of money?' I asked hopefully.

'No!'

Oh dear, I didn't think so, and I simply couldn't bear to discuss unfaithful husbands.

'He has found another love.'

To my horror, a tear zoomed down her cheek, then another and another.

'I'm very sorry to hear that.'

'But still he sleeps in my house and eats my food and rings this *whore* on my phone bill!'

'That's really terrible.'

'Yes, my sorrow is great. But I am strong!'

'Good for you.'

Then she seemed to notice my hair for the first time in ages. 'Your bangs are too long,' she said mournfully.

'Ah, no they're fine!'

But it was too late. She was reaching for the scissors, then she was cutting and all the while tears filled her eyes, blinding her vision. *Blinding her vision.*

It only took two or three seconds for the terrible damage to be done. One second I had normal hair, the next my fringe was a pure diagonal, as if I was a New Romantic. At its shortest point it was less than an inch long. Appalled, I gazed into the mirror. Reza might as well have gone the whole hog and given me a Mohican. And what could I say? I could hardly berate her, a woman in her condition. (Not that I would anyway. Don't we all know that it's harder to be honest with hairdressers than it is to get a camel through the eye of a storm, or whatever it is.)

Feeling sick, I paid up. Then, my hand over my forehead, I hurried towards home. But as I passed the Goatee Boys' house, Ethan opened a window and yelled, 'Hey Maggie, your bangs look kinda weird.'

In no time, in a reprise of my last visit to Reza, the three lads were on the street examining me.

'I think it's cool,' Luis said.

'I don't. I'm too old for novelty hair-dos. Have you any suggestions for fixing it?'

Luis studied me thoughtfully. 'Yeah.'

'Great. Tell me.'

'Let it grow.'

At least the whooping noises from Emily's room had stopped. They must have gone to sleep. The sky had clouded over and it was fearfully hot, so I turned the air-con up full, watched telly and willed my hair to grow. This was like a sign: I'd never impress Shay Delaney. It just wasn't going to happen.

Around five, Emily emerged in her robe and wandered about yawning and smoking, then saw me and stumbled in fright. 'What happened to your HAIR?'

'Reza.'

'Why did you go back after the last time?'

'Because I'm a fucking eejit,' I said disconsolately. 'Is there anything you can do?'

She tried to pick up the shortest bit of the fringe. 'Hmmm,' she said speculatively. 'Let's see. I'll get some stuff.'

Minutes later, she emerged from the bathroom with a ton of gear for taming unruly hair – gels, wax and spray – and rummaged through them. 'I think we'll need warp factor ten. Class A. The hard stuff.' She showed me a tin of wax. 'They use this on horses, you know.'

While she was coaxing the lard-like horse wax through my butchered fringe, the phone rang and she said urgently, 'Don't answer. Let the machine get it. It'll be Larry the Savage, getting me to rewrite more of that fucking script and I'll lose my reason.'

We listened, but it was a hang-up. 'Another one,' frowned Emily. 'There's been a fair few over the last day or so. Don't tell me I've got a stalker, on top of all my other troubles. There now, how's that?'

I looked in the mirror. She'd done a very good job of sweeping the fringe over to one side and making it look almost normal.

'Great. Thanks.'

'You'll need a lot of wax and hairspray to keep it in place, but it should work. And don't go back to that woman *again*.'

'No, I won't. Sorry. Thanks.'

The dinner that evening was in some outdoor place in Topanga Canyon, and the cast of characters were me, Emily, Helen, Anna, Mum and Dad – proudly sporting his brand new clicked-back-into-place neck. ('I thought it was a gun shot but instead it was my own neck!')

We had all squashed into Emily's jeep and the restaurant, when we got there, was beautiful. Lanterns were strung through the trees, a rushing sound indicated a stream nearby, and it was mercifully cooler than it had been on lower ground.

No sign of Shay. We were herded into the bar to wait for him and I nervously went to the bathroom to check my fringe, but I shouldn't have gone because when I came out Emily and Dad were squaring up to each other and the atmosphere was tense.

'Mr Walsh,' Emily said, 'I really don't want us to fall out over this.'

My heart sank. What was happening?

'I have my pride,' Dad said.

'Let me make this very plain,' said Emily. 'I will buy the first round. I live here, you are the guests, it's appropriate that I buy the first round.'

Sulkily Dad said, 'And what about the second?'

'One of you can get it.'

'Which one?'

'I don't know. You can fight it out amongst yourselves.'

But as it happened, the first round was bought by Shay, who strolled in, blond and hunky, suavely flicked some sort of gold card at the bartender, then smilingly said hello to us all in turn.

'Hi, Maggie, you look beautiful. And so do you, Emily. And there's Claire. Oh, sorry, Mrs Walsh, I thought for a minute you were Claire.' Then he moved on to Helen, who was more beautiful than the lot of us put together, but she bared her teeth in a silent snarl and all his words disappeared. He never got to Anna. Instead Dad locked him into a conversation, proudly boasting about how loud his neck fixing had been. ('I thought a gun had gone off, so I did.')

After our drinks, we were led to a table beneath the stars and surrounded by rustling, fragrant trees. Our waiter was the usual full-on experience.

'Where you guys FROM?' he shrieked.

'Ireland.'

'Iowa? NEAT.'

'No – oh never mind.'

Then we had the performance about that day's specials. Vegan this, lactose-friendly that and zero per cent the other. The waiter addressed most of it to Shay, who made murmury, approving noises until the guy went away and then said, 'God, it'd wear you out. Why does it always have to be so complicated? But that's LA, I suppose.'

'Do you like it here?' Mum asked him.

'Yes,' he said thoughtfully. 'So long as you realize that this town is all about movies, nothing else matters. Like, remember when the American hostages were released from Iraq?'

Everyone nodded, though I'm sure they didn't.

'I was in the Grill Room that day for lunch with two agents

and one of them said, "Did you hear they released the hostages?" And the other guy says, "Released it? I didn't even know they'd started shooting it." It's that kind of place. Hey, Mr Walsh,' Shay urged, 'tell the snooker story.'

'Will I?' Dad asked shyly, acting like he had a crush on Shay.

'Ah, do,' we all urged, so Dad told the story of the only day in my entire life that he persuaded me to do something wrong – to take a day off school sick because he'd got tickets to the snooker final and no one to go with – and how it ended up being on the evening news. Really, it did; as the champion potted the winning shot, right behind him, clear as day, clapping like an eejity seal, is me. I am more in focus than the champ and the clip got shown on the six o'clock news, again during sports round-up, then a longer piece on the nine o'clock news, and even though I didn't see it myself, I'm told it was on the late news too. It got run on the following day's lunch-time news, then at the weekend when they were doing a review of the week. Even at the end of the year, when they were showing the year's sporting highlights, once again I could be seen. In fact, only about a year ago, when the player announced his retirement, they ran the clip again and there I was, the fifteen-year-old me, with my terrible fifteen-year-old hair, grinning and clapping happily. Everyone in the whole country saw me at least twice, and included in their number were my teachers. Some were sarcastic – 'Feeling better now, Maggie?' – but more of them were confused. 'I'm surprised at you,' several said. 'You're normally so good.'

Dad told the story so well that we were all crying with laughter.

'I'm terrible at being bad,' I agreed, wiping my face. 'Every time I do something dangerous I get caught.'

I couldn't help it. I looked at Shay and he was looking at me and our smiles kind of faded. I looked away, and the next thing there was a right kerfuffle as a cordon of people surrounding another person moved as one well-oiled machine between the tables.

'Celebrity alert,' Emily said.

The whole restaurant was trying to look without seeming as if that's what they were doing, then a word began to ripple, almost as if it was being carried on the wind. Faint and whispery at first, '. . . hurll . . . hurll . . . hurley . . . lishurley . . . lishurley . . . Liz Hurley.'

'It's Liz Hurley,' Emily hissed, and that was our cue to dislocate our necks looking. It was hard to see through the wall of minders, then one of them moved slightly, the light from a lantern caught her face and it was! It was Liz Hurley.

'Does anyone dare me to go over there and ask for her autograph?' Helen asked.

'Does anyone dare me to go over there and tell her to wear more clothes?' Mum asked skittishly.

Shay shook his head admiringly. 'I'm not daring you, Mrs Walsh, because I know you'll do it. You're a wild woman.'

'The nerve of you. I'm a respectable married Catholic.'

'You're a wild woman.'

As Shay and Mum twinkled at each other, I watched with bittersweet amusement. Mum and Dad were mad about Shay. What would my life have been like if I'd married him instead of Garv? A lot easier with my family, that was for sure. Mind you, Helen didn't seem to like him any more than she'd liked Garv.

'OK GUYS.' The waiter was back, doing his interpretation of the dessert list. 'Fat-free ice-cream, anyone?'

'Ice-cream?' Shay asked me softly.

Mutely I shook my head.

'Some other time,' he said. It sounded like a promise.

It was a nice night, apart from the row over the bill. Shay tried to pay it and Dad nearly had a fit, then Emily threw her oar in, insisting that the evening was on her. Eventually, some kind of compromise was reached and we made our way to the car valets.

They brought Shay's car around first, and next thing Mum piped up, 'We were very cramped in Emily's jeep coming up. Would you be able to drive one of us home?'

'Sure.' Shay offered her his arm. 'Shall we?'

But there was no fear of that.

'I'd better go with himself,' Mum nodded at Dad. 'Why don't you bring Margaret.'

'No, I –' I started.

'Ah, do.'

I was acutely embarrassed. Even more so when Helen said loudly, 'I was reading a thing in the paper about some country where mothers sell their daughters. Where was it again? It began with "I".'

'India?' Anna said.

'Yes! Or was it Ireland?'

I was perspiring from every pore. I wished the ground would open up and devour me whole, then Shay smiled at me, a smile packed with sympathy, understanding, even amusement. He knew exactly what was going on and he didn't seem to mind.

'OK,' I said. 'I'll go.'

As we drove away, I said, 'I'm sorry about Mum.'

'No problem.'

But he said nothing else, so eventually I asked, 'How long more are you in LA for?'

'Until Tuesday.'

'Long time. You must miss your wife.'

'Ah,' he shrugged easily, 'you get used to it.'

I didn't know what next to say, and we maintained silence – not entirely comfortable – until, in an astonishingly short space of time, he was pulling up outside Emily's, the engine still running.

'Thanks for the lift.' I reached for the door handle.

'You're welcome.'

I already had the door open when, out of the blue, Shay asked, 'Do you hate me?'

I was so shocked I gave a funny bark of laughter. 'Um, no.' I tried to recover myself. 'I don't hate you.' I couldn't have told you what I did feel, but it wasn't hate.

But if we were asking leading questions, I had one that I'd wanted the answer to for years.

'Do you ever think about him?'

Shay paused for such a long time, I thought he wasn't going to answer. 'Sometimes.'

'He'd be fourteen now.'

'Yeah.'

'Nearly the same age as when we first met.'

'Yeah. Look, Maggie,' he flashed me a quick smile. 'I've got to go. Early start in the morning.'

'Even on a Saturday? Tough schedule.'

He was handing me a business card. 'I'm staying at the Mondrian. Out of office hours,' he scribbled quickly on the card, 'you can get me at this number. 'Night.'

''Night.'

Then I was out of the car and standing in the humid, flower-scented night, listening to the screech of his tyres as he drove away.

42

I rang him in the morning, as soon as was civilized. I'd been awake since six, my arm itching like crazy, but made myself wait until five past nine before calling. Shay answered, sounding asleep.

'It's Maggie.'

Silence.

'Garv . . . Walsh,' I explained.

'Oh, hi,' he laughed. 'Sorry, I haven't had any coffee yet, brain not engaged. So, ah, last night was good fun.'

'Yeah, it was. Listen. Shay –' I said, at the same time as he said, 'Look Maggie –'

We managed a laugh and he said, 'You go first.'

'OK.' My blood was pounding in my ears and I plunged into what had to be said. 'I was wondering . . . can I see you? Just for an hour or so.'

'Today's not so good. Or tonight.'

'Tomorrow? Tomorrow night?'

'OK, tomorrow night. Call here around seven.'

'See you then. Thanks. And what were you going to say to me?'

'Oh, nothing, doesn't matter.'

My agitation calmed. I'd see him tomorrow night.

When Emily got up, we went to the supermarket for more supplies (mostly wine). As usual the raggedy man was in the parking lot, and when we abseiled down he yelled, 'Interior shot. Night. Jill takes a box from under her bed and opens it. Camera lingers on the gun inside . . .'

'Oh my God, Maggie,' Emily clutched my shoulder. 'Listen to him.'

'What?'

'Can't you hear it?'

'What?'

'He's doing a pitch. He's pitching a movie.' She was walking over to him and I was hurrying behind.

'Emily O'Keeffe,' she stuck her hand out.

'Raymond Jansson.' He extended his filthy hand with its long black fingernails and gave her a good firm shake. From a yard away I could smell him.

'Is that your movie you're pitching?'

'Yeah. *Starry, Starry Night.*' His eyes were bright in his smeared face.

'Has someone picked it up?'

'Yeah, Paramount, but the producer got fired, then Universal did but they closed that division down, then Working Title came on board but they couldn't get the financing.' Suddenly he didn't seem at all mad, until he said, 'But I've got some meetings set up and I think I'm gonna get another deal real soon.'

'Good luck with it,' Emily said, linking me and moving away.

'Jesus,' she muttered, tears filling her eyes and overflowing down her cheeks. 'This is an awful town. Is that what's going to become of me? Going loopy from disappointment and pitching to the fresh air. That poor man, that poor, poor man.' She wept all the way through fruit and veg, breakfast cereals, baked goods and dried pasta and didn't stop until we reached savoury snacks.

Back home, we were unpacking the groceries (mostly wine) when the phone rang.

Automatically I went to answer it and what happened next was like the bit in a film where a child is about to get run over by a car, and the hero flings himself, in tortuous slow motion, into the road and an echoey 'Nooooooo!' is heard. Emily threw herself bodily across the room and screamed, 'Noooo, don't answer it! I'm waiting for the other shoe to drop. It'll be Larry the Savage and I need the weekend off.'

But it was another hang-up. 'Definitely a stalker. I'm a fully fledged LA woman now.' Emily sounded cheered.

'We're wilting in this heat,' Mum gasped, flinging herself on to Emily's couch and waving her hand in front of her face.

Anna, Helen and Dad trooped in behind her, their faces pink from the five-minute walk from the hotel.

'It's very oppressive,' Emily agreed. 'I think we might be due a thunderstorm.'

'Rain?' Mum sounded alarmed. 'Oh God, no.'

'Sometimes in Los Angeles you can have a thunderstorm without any rain,' Helen said.

'Is that a fact?' Mum asked.

'No.'

Shopping at the Beverly Centre was on that afternoon's agenda.

'Let's get going.' Emily jingled her car keys.

'I've been practising my signature.' Helen flexed her hands. 'For all the credit-card slips I'll be signing.'

'Go fecking easy,' Dad barked. 'You're up to your neck in debt as it is.'

'I don't know why you're coming shopping,' Mum said to him. 'You'll have an awful time.'

'I won't.'

417

'Oh, but you will,' Helen promised. 'D'you know what I'm thinking?' she asked dreamily. 'I'm thinking underwear. Lots of revealing, lacy underwear. Half-cup bras and thongs and...'

'He doesn't know what a thong is,' Mum said. 'To be honest,' she admitted, 'neither do I.'

'Let me *explain*,' Helen said, and launched into an eager exposition. '... no VPL and though everyone says that they're like bum floss –'

'Oh, those ones,' Mum said sourly. 'I've washed plenty of them. When did they stop being g-strings?'

As it happened, the Beverly Centre lift disgorged us not at an underwear shop but at the next best thing – a swimwear shop. In we all tramped, Helen leading, Dad bringing up the reluctant rear.

It was a class act: not just swimming togs, but coordinating wraps, sarongs, overshirts, hats, bags, sandals, sunglasses ... Not cheap, mind. The bikinis cost more than the week in the sun they'd be bought for, the changing-rooms were bigger than my bedroom and the shop assistants were those determined, terrier-like helpful ones that you couldn't fob off by murmuring, 'Just looking.' The type that riposte, 'For what? An all-in-one? We have some great Lisa Bruce pieces that would be perfect on your figure.' And before you know it, they're frogmarching you to the changing-room, sixteen wooden hangers belonging to sixteen different pairs of togs clanking in their arms. These women were the type who'd squeeze in the door of the changing-room to get a gawk at you. The sort who'd double-bluff you by saying that one didn't suit you – so you thought they were honest – just to tell you that the next one (the more costly one, of course) was wonderfully flattering. And if they saw you were in any way unconvinced, they'd call five or six of their fragrant, Twiglet-thin colleagues to press the message home.

I knew this to my cost. There was a boutique in Dublin with the same air, where I'd ended up buying an expensive chiffon skirt – that I'd never once worn – just to get out of the place. And I wouldn't mind, but I'd only gone in because it had started to rain and I'd no umbrella/hood/hat/nice hair that looked better after it had been drenched in rainwater. I'd have been better off going to the small chemist's next door and buying thrush ointment (or something else that involved a time-wasting question-and-answer session).

However, despite all of this, I felt an adrenalin rush as soon as we entered the swimshop; everything was so beautiful. Helen, Anna, Emily, Mum and I instantly split up and spread out, alighting on our favourite colours like bees on flowers. Dad hovered by the door, staring at his feet.

Within seconds, I was well on my way to talking myself into a swimsuit-wraparound skirt-visor ensemble, when my attention was caught by an exchange at the cabana-hut-style changing-room. From the number of discarded bikinis and fluttering assistants in evidence, a choosy customer was within.

'Marla,' a laden assistant called over the straw door, 'is the DKNY totally great on you?'

'Totally great,' Marla's disembodied voice said. 'But my breasts are still too high.'

Too high? All of us out-of-towners ceased our browsing and turned, as one, to exchange what-on-earth? looks. What did she mean, 'too high'? Too big?

We regrouped in the centre of the room – even Dad – and Helen went to the cabana hut for a gawk. 'Too high,' she confirmed on her return. 'So lifted, her nipples are almost on her shoulders. A halter-neck is her only hope.'

'Ah here,' Dad murmured, squinting up from his feet, 'I think I'll just go to the pub and have a pint and read the paper.'

'There aren't any pubs round here,' Emily said. 'Just some strip joints.'

'Don't let any of the girls sit with you,' Anna advised. 'You'll be charged for it.'

'No,' Mum said firmly. 'Find a coffee shop, that's good enough for you.'

'It's Saturday night tonight. I'd love a bit of glamour, girls,' Mum sighed. 'Where's a good place to go?'

'There's the Bilderberg Room,' Emily said doubtfully, but I shook my head. I knew where to bring Mum. I'd known it was her sort of place the first (and only) time I'd gone there: the Four Seasons, Beverly Hills.

Dad refused to go. 'Feck this for a haircut, I'm sick of getting dickied up. I want to watch sport and eat peanuts.'

'Fine. Stay at home then, we don't care.'

I needed the horse-hair wax to fix my hair for the Four Seasons, so I picked my way through Emily's bomb-site bedroom.

'It's on the dressing table,' she said.

But the dressing table was crammed with stuff and when I lifted the wax, I dislodged a heap of photos, which slithered to the floor. 'Sorry.' As I gathered them up, I saw that they'd been taken at a party eighteen months before, when Emily had been home. Instantly intrigued – I love looking at photos – I shuffled through pictures of Emily and her friends in various states of disarray. One of her winking, another of me and her blowing kisses at the camera – 'The state of us,' I held it out to her. 'And we thought we were gorgeous' – Emily with Donna, Emily with Sinead. One of me, waving a bottle of Smirnoff Ice, my pink, shiny face and red, Satan eyes happy and carefree; me again, slightly more demure; then a picture of Emily with the cutest man. He had lovely cheekbones and shiny, dark hair flopping over his forehead and he was laughing mischievously into the camera.

'Christ, who's he?' I asked in admiration. 'He's yum!'

'Hahaha,' Emily deadpanned.

Before she'd even finished, I'd recognized the man – of course I'd recognized him – and I started to shake with reaction. Emily was staring carefully at me. 'Did you really not know who he was? Or were you joking?'

'Joking,' I said. 'Of course I knew who he was.'

It was Garv.

I was almost afraid to turn to the next photo, because I suspected I knew who it was of – and it was: Garv and me, head-to-head, together and happy. And for a second I could remember what that felt like.

'Come on, then,' I said, my heart rate returning to normal. 'Fix my hair.'

Mum loved the Four Seasons, fingering the swagged curtains and saying with respect, 'I'd say they didn't come cheap.' Next to be admired was the couch. 'Isn't it a bee-yoo-tiful shade?' Then she asked in awe, 'Would you say those statues are antiques?'

'Pretty old,' Helen said. 'Not as old as you, obviously, but good and old.'

When the waiter came, Emily, Helen, Anna and I ordered

Complicated Martinis and urged Mum to have one too. 'Should I?' Her eyes were alight at her daring. 'All right, so. Lord above!' Her attention had been hooked by a pair of high, enormous breasts, which had walked past attached to a child's body. 'She's very well developed.'

Maybe it was because it was Saturday night, but the breast-implant girls were out in force.

'It's as good as a cabaret,' Mum said, after a particularly ginormous pair passed us. 'Just as well your father didn't come. He'd probably banjax his neck again.'

'Look at her,' Emily said in an undertone, indicating a woman wearing HUGE big sunglasses.

What was it? Someone famous?

'Nah, that Jackie O look is so over. No, she's had her eyes done. Any time you see someone wearing those glasses indoors, they've just had their eyes lifted. Will we get another drink?'

We'd just embarked on our second round of Complicated Martinis when, across the room, I saw someone I recognized. 'Oh. My. God.'

'What? Who?' Emily asked.

'Look,' I nudged her. On a nearby couch, no more than twelve feet away from us, sat Mort Russell. He was on his own, ostentatiously reading a script, just so everyone would know he was in the Business. Gobshite. He hadn't noticed us.

'Who's he?' Mum, Anna and Helen clamoured.

Maybe we shouldn't have said anything but, like I said, we were garrulous to the tune of one and a half Complicated Martinis, so Emily and I spilled it all: the story of the pitch; the wild enthusiasm from Mort and his acolytes; the talk of Cameron Diaz and Julia Roberts; the possibility of opening on three thousand screens across America . . . and how it all came to nothing.

'But why?'

'Dunno. He might have meant it at the time.'

'Could have been he was just being cruel. Leading you on, like,' Helen posited, her eyes narrowed thoughtfully.

'That's no way to behave,' Mum scolded. 'And letting your poor mother buy that navy spangledy dress under false pretences. And it was a shocking price. Even though it was at –'

'– forty per cent off,' we all finished for her.

An attempt to explain that Mort Russell had had nothing to do with Mrs O'Keeffe's navy spangledy dress, that that was the fault of an entirely different and unrelated executive, was fruitless. All Mum cared about was that Mrs O'Keeffe had been swizzed into buying an expensive dress to wear to a film and that, as yet, no film had materialized.

'She's had to wear it to the Christmas party *and* the Lions' fundraising barbecue to try to get the wear out of it. And her manning the sausages.' Tight-lipped, Mum shook her head at the injustice, the downright *indignity* of it all. 'Getting it splashed with some honey marinade stuff. I've a good mind to go over there and tell that pup what's what.'

'Haven't we all?'

The five of us were looking at Mort Russell so hard I was surprised that he hadn't intuited it. Perhaps he was used to it. Maybe he thought our stares were admiring ones.

'Do you know what? I will go over to him!'

We tried to talk her out of it. 'No, Mum, don't. It'll only make things worse for Emily.'

'How could it make things worse for Emily?' she asked with irrefutable logic. 'Didn't he waste her time, lead her up the

423

garden path with false promises, then turn her down? And hasn't she a contract with someone else now?'

She had a point.

'Listen to me,' Emily said quietly. 'Just don't humble him in front of anyone else.'

My head snapped back to Emily. She was giving the OK!

'They can live with humiliation so long as none of the people they want to impress know about it,' she explained to Mum. 'Try and find out why he passed on my script. And Mrs Walsh, if you can make him cry, I'll make it worth your while.'

'You're on!'

And without further ado, she was up and off! Appalled and thrilled, we watched her go.

'It's the Martinis,' Anna muttered. 'It was too much for her delicate, two-spritzers-a-month constitution.'

My mother isn't a small woman, and I almost felt sorry for Mort Russell as this Irish battle-axe descended upon him, bristling with righteousness.

'Mr Russell?' we saw her mouth.

Mort assented, his face withholding friendliness. Then Mum must have explained who she was, because Mort twisted his head to have a look at us, and when he registered Emily his tan retreated by a couple of shades. Emily wiggled her fingers at him in a travesty of sociability and then the berating began: a wagging finger, a voice high with indignation.

'Oh God,' I whispered faintly.

We followed the action closely and our anxiety was tempered with glee. Mort's face was sullen and hostile. I'm sure they never have to deal with the consequences of their wild promises, these Hollywood types.

We could hear most of what Mum was saying. 'There's a

name for people like you,' she scolded – then abruptly faltered. 'Except it's usually for girls . . . But never mind!' Back on track, the dressing-down resumed. 'A tease, that's what you are. You should be ashamed of yourself, getting the poor girl's hopes up like that.' Then she told him about Mrs O'Keeffe's navy spangledy dress, with no mention that it had been at forty per cent off.

Mort Russell mumbled something and Mum said, 'So you should be,' then she was back.

'What did he say?' we clamoured. 'Why did he make all those promises and not follow up?'

'That's just his way, he said. But he said he was very sorry and he won't do it again.'

'Did he cry?'

'His eyes were wet.'

I didn't really believe her, but so what?

'I think this merits another round of Complicated Martinis,' Emily said gaily.

43

I was already awake when the doorbell rang at eight-thirty on Sunday morning. I went to answer it but Emily was ahead of me, pulling up her pyjama bottoms and complaining about the earliness of the hour.

'Why are we both awake?'

'Worry?' I suggested.

'Guilty conscience?'

I didn't answer.

Mum and Dad were at the door. 'We're going to Mass,' they chorused cheerfully. 'We wondered if you'd like to come.'

I waited for Emily to hastily assemble an excuse, but instead she hitched her pyjamas even higher – so that she looked like a fifty-four-year-old psycho man who lives with his mother and wears his waistband up around his chest – and said, 'Mass? Why not? Maggie, how about it?'

And then *I* thought, why not?

I hadn't been to Mass for so long I couldn't remember the last time – perhaps when Claire had got married? I was a foul-weather Christian, and only prayed when I was afraid or when I desperately wanted something. Same with Emily. Seemed like we were both afraid – or desperately wanted something. So we pulled on some clothes, stepped out into the butter-yellow day and walked the four short blocks to the church.

Mass, LA style wasn't how I remembered it from home. The young, handsome priest was standing outside making people shake hands with him on the way in, and the pleasantly cool church was packed with good-looking – and here's the weird bit – *young* parishioners. As we squeezed into a polished pew, someone was intoning, 'Testing, testing,' into the altar microphone, then a manic woman shrieked, 'Gooood Mor-naane! Welcome to our celebration.'

A bell jingled and a girl with swishy hair and Miu Miu shoes walked slowly up the aisle, holding a huge Bible above her head like someone about to do an exorcism. Following her dramatic lead came the priest and a coterie of the handsomest altar boys I'd ever seen. They climbed the marble steps and suddenly it was SHOWTIME!

Were there any visitors to Santa Monica, the padre asked, or anyone who'd been *away*? The *away* was said meaningfully, so I took it not to mean 'away' in the geographical sense. Someone stood up, then everyone started to clap, so several more stood up. 'Out-of-work actors,' Emily murmured. 'Their only chance of applause.'

Mum, who'd stretched up like a cobra, checking out the standers, turned to me – to cuff me for talking, so I thought – but she whispered, 'That last fella was in *Twenty-One Jump Street*. Got taken out by the mob.'

Another few people stood up and got clapped. Beside me, I felt Mum get twitchy. 'No,' I begged. 'No.'

'We're visitors,' she hissed. 'Why shouldn't we?'

'No,' I repeated.

But, dragging Dad and me with her, she was rising to her feet and smiling around graciously. 'We're from Ireland,' she told the congregation, meaning: *We're REAL Catholics*.

Everyone put their hands together for the über-Catholics from Ireland and then I was allowed to sit down again, my face burning.

Next we had to turn to the person on our right and greet them. Dad turned to Mum, Mum turned to me, I turned to Emily, and Emily, who was at the end of the row, refused to look across the aisle.

Then it started. My clearest memory of Mass in Ireland was of a miserable priest droning at a quarter-full church, 'Blah blah blah, sinners, blah blah blah, soul black with sin, blah blah blah, burn in hell . . .' But this was more like *Mass: the Musical*. Lots of singing and melodramatic acting-out of the readings – I suppose you never knew when a hot-shot producer might be in the audience – sorry, I mean congregation.

I wasn't exactly comfortable with so much unbridled zeal, and Emily and I nudged each other and sniggered a fair bit, as if we were nine years old. The upbeat and celebratory mood reached its cringy zenith in the Lord's Prayer, where the people in each row held hands and sang. Emily smiled smugly, letting her end-of-aisle hand swing emptily. But her smirk turned sickly as the man across the way stretched out his hand and clasped hers, pulling her out of her seat and me with her. In the row in front of me, a slender young man with a dispro-portionately large bottom sang the whole thing into his girl-friend's avid eyes. It was creepy.

At a certain sentence ('And lead us not into temptation,' if I remember correctly), we had to raise our joined hands above our heads. I couldn't help thinking that if you'd had a camera on a pulley above the crowds it would've been a really good shot, like a Busby Berkeley musical. Maybe.

No sooner was the mortification of the Lord's Prayer over

than the padre uttered words that struck new dread into my heart. 'Let us offer each other the sign of peace.' All of a sudden, I remembered that this was the main reason I'd stopped going to Mass. It's an awful thing to do to people, make them be affectionate, especially on a Sunday morning. In Ireland we do the bare minimum – touch paws, mutter 'Peace be with you,' and defiantly refuse to make eye contact. But I suspected we wouldn't get away with that here, and sure enough, we ended up practically having sex with the people around us. People were stepping out of their pews, confidently crossing the aisle and giving bear hugs all round. It was horrific. I got smothered into the shoulder of the boy with the big arse who'd sung to his girlfriend.

But then the priest invited us to bow our heads and pray for our 'special intentions', and the we're-only-here-for-the-laugh air abruptly lifted from Emily and me. Emily buried her face in her hands; no prizes for guessing what she was praying for. And me? I knew what I wanted, but I was afraid to pray for it.

The comfort I'd hoped to get from going to Mass evaded me, and for the rest of the day a nervy excitement hummed within me. When the Goatee Boys invited everyone over for an evening barbecue, I had to take Emily aside. 'This barbecue tonight,' I said, flooded with anxiety in case it scuppered my plans, 'I can't go, I'm sorry.'

'Why, what are you doing?' Emily was alert – and alarmed.

'I'm going to see Shay.'

'On your own?'

I assented.

'But Maggie, he's married! What are you at?'

'I just want to talk to him. I want . . .' I picked a word I'd heard on Oprah, '. . . closure.'

In exasperation she said, 'We all have ex-boyfriends – it's called life. We can't go tracking them down and getting closure off every one of them. We just live with it. If you'd had more boyfriends in your time you'd know all this.'

'He's not just an ex-boyfriend,' I said. 'And you know it.'

She nodded. I had her there. 'But I still don't think you should see him,' she said. 'It's not going to help.'

'We'll see about that,' I said, then went to my bedroom to try on everything I owned several times.

The Mondrian is another of those hotels where you'd get snow-blindness; any colour so long as it's white. The lobby was overrun with chiselled, bronzed men in Armani suits, and they were just the staff. Kitchen porters, probably. I jostled my way through them to the desk clerk and asked him to call Shay's room.

'Your name, please?'

'Maggie . . . um . . . Walsh.'

'I have a message for you.' He handed me an envelope.

I tore it open. It was a slip of paper, with a typewritten message. 'Had to go out. Sorry. Shay.'

He wasn't there. The fucker. My tense anticipation flipped into hollowed-out let-down and I was so disappointed I wanted to kick something. I'd dressed so carefully, I'd spent so long taming my hair, I'd been so buzzy and hopeful. All for nothing.

Well, what did you expect? I asked myself bitterly. What did you expect after the last time?

I am bad at being bad. Terrible, actually. The one time I tried shoplifting, I got caught. The one time I sneaked in Shay

Delaney when I was babysitting for Damien, I got caught. The day I bunked off school to go to the snooker with Dad, I got caught. The time I threw the snail at the Nissan Micra packed with nuns, they pulled over, got out and told me off. So you'd think that that would have taught me that I couldn't get away with stepping out of line. But it didn't, and the one time I had unprotected sex with Shay Delaney, I got pregnant.

Perhaps it wasn't the only time it was unprotected – the way we had sex was often so fraught and hurried that slips and spills might have happened anyway. But there was one definite occasion when we didn't have a condom and we couldn't help ourselves. Shay had promised that he'd pull out in time, but he didn't and somehow I ended up assuring him that we'd be OK, as if my love for him was so powerful I could tame my body into obedience.

When the time for my period arrived without anything happening, I told myself that it was study stress that was keeping it away – I was due to sit my Leaving Cert in less than three months. Then I tried the trick of telling myself that my period wouldn't come until I stopped worrying about it not coming. But I couldn't stop fretting – every twenty minutes I ran to the bathroom to check if it had arrived yet, and I analysed everything I wanted to eat to see if it could be classed as a 'craving'. But that I might be pregnant was literally almost unimaginable.

I couldn't bear the not knowing, I had to find out that I wasn't pregnant, so when I was three weeks late I went into town and – anonymously, I hoped – bought a pregnancy kit, and while Shay's mum was out, we did the test in the Delaneys' bathroom.

We grasped sweaty hands and watched the stick, willing it to stay white, but when the end of it went pink I lapsed into deep shock. The kind of shock that people end up going to hospital and getting sedation for. I couldn't speak, I could barely breathe, and when I looked at Shay, he was almost as bad. We were terrified children, the pair of us. Sweat broke out on my forehead and gaps began to break up my vision.

'I'll do whatever you want,' Shay said dully, and I knew he was just acting a part. He was petrified as he watched the bright star of his future implode. A father at eighteen? 'I'll stand by you,' he said, like he was reading from a crappy script.

'I don't think I can have it,' I heard myself say.

'What do you mean?' He tried to hide his relief, but already it had transformed him.

'I mean . . . I don't think I can have it.'

The only thing I could think of was that it didn't happen to girls like me. I know unplanned pregnancies happen to lots of women; even then I knew it. And I'm certain most people are distraught and wish it hadn't happened. But I felt – and maybe everyone feels this – that it was somehow *worse for me*.

I suspected that if someone wild and breezy like Claire had got pregnant at seventeen, it would be as if everyone had almost expected it from her, and would just sigh a little and shake their heads, 'Oh, Claire . . .'

But I was the well-behaved one, my parent's comfort, the one daughter they could look at and not have to say, 'Where did I go wrong?' The idea of having to break this news to my mother was unimaginable. But then I thought of having to tell Dad and I shrivelled entirely. It would kill him, I felt.

I was gripped by intense panic. Being pregnant felt like one of the most frightening things that could ever happen to anyone.

Within the boundaries of my middle-class world, it was as bad as it got. I thrashed around like an animal in a trap, torn asunder and trapped ever deeper by the ugly realization that no matter what choice I made, it would have terrible implications that I'd have to live with for the rest of my life. There was no way out – every one of my options was terrible. How could I have a child and give it away to someone else? It would break my heart wondering how it was getting on, if it was happy, if the new people were looking after it and if my rejection had scarred it. But I was also terrified of having a baby and keeping it. How would I take care of it? I was only a schoolgirl and felt young and incapable, barely mature enough to take care of myself, never mind a helpless scrap of life. Like Shay, I too felt my life would be over. And everyone would judge me: the neighbours, my classmates, my extended family. They'd talk about me and scorn my stupidity, and they'd say I'd got what I deserved.

Fifteen years later, I can see that it wouldn't have been that much of a disaster. It was all survivable – I could have had the baby, taken care of him, eventually sorted out a career for myself. And of course, while my parents wouldn't have hung out the flags, they would have got over it. More than that, they would have loved him, their first grandchild. In fact, as the years passed I saw people live with far worse stuff than being presented with an illegitimate child by their best-behaved daughter. Keiron Boylan, a boy from our road a few years younger than me, got killed in a motorbike accident when he was eighteen. I went to his funeral and his parents were beyond recognition. His father was, quite literally, wild with grief.

But back then, I was seventeen and knew none of that. I was inexperienced at life, at standing up to people, at going against

433

expectations. I had no capacity to be rational and I was in the grip of extreme fear, which woke me on the hour every hour through the night and turned my days into lucid nightmares.

I dreamt about babies. In one dream I was trying to carry a baby, but it was made of something like lead so it was far too heavy to carry, but I still struggled. In another, I'd had my baby but it had an adult's head and kept talking to me, challenging me, exhausting me with the strength of its personality. I was constantly nauseous, but I'll never be sure if it was because of the pregnancy or the accompanying terror.

Shay kept parroting that he'd stand by me, no matter what I decided, but I knew what he wanted me to do. The thing was he'd never say it straight out, and though I wasn't able to put words on it, I hated feeling that I alone was responsible for the dreadful decision. I'd have preferred him to yell at me that I'd better go to England and get myself sorted out pronto, instead of him acting all caring and 'mature'. Even though he looked like a man and was the head of the Delaney household, it began to dawn on me that perhaps he *wasn't* as mature as he seemed; that it was merely role play. And despite us being inseparable, I felt oddly abandoned by him.

Three days after I'd done the test, I broke the news to Emily and Sinead, who were appalled. 'I knew something was up with you,' Emily said, her face white. 'But I thought it was exam worry.'

They kept shaking their heads and breathing, 'Jesus!' and 'I can't believe it!', until I had to tell them to shut up and advise me on what to do. Neither of them tried to convince me to have the baby, they both thought that not having it was the best – or least bad – option. Their eyes were so full of pity and relief that it wasn't them, that once again I yearned for all this to be a terrible dream, for me to wake up, shaky with relief that I'd imagined it all.

They decided my best option was to go to Claire, who was in her final year at university and very vocal about women's rights and what bastards the priests were. In fact, she used to go on so much about the right to abortion that Mum often sighed, 'That one'll get up the pole and have an abortion just to prove a point.'

So I told Claire about my condition and she was staggered. In other circumstances it might have been funny, but at the time nobody was finding anything amusing. Claire actually cried and, peculiarly, I ended up comforting her. 'It's very sad,' she wept unconsolably. 'You're so young.'

Through her welfare officer, Claire was able to get information for me and Shay, and with unexpected ease the arrangements were made. A load lifted off me – I wouldn't have to have the baby and face the consequences – and then a whole host of new, horrific worries bobbed to the surface. I'd been brought up as a Catholic, but somehow I'd managed to avoid a lot of the accompanying fear and guilt. I'd always thought God must be a decent kind of bloke and I'd only suffered mild agonies of guilt about having sex with Shay because I figured He wouldn't have given us an appetite if He didn't want us to use it. It had been a long time since I'd believed in Hell, but all of a sudden I started to wonder, and reactions that I didn't recognize as mine began to play out.

'Am I doing something terrible?' I asked Claire, dreading the answer. 'Am I . . . a murderer?'

'No,' she reassured me. 'It's not a baby yet. It's only a bunch of cells.'

I clung uneasily to that thought as Shay and I got the money together. It wasn't hard for me because I was a saver, and it wasn't hard for him because he was a charmer. And on a Friday evening in April – my parents under the impression that I was on a study weekend with Emily – Shay and I left for London.

Plane fares were out of our price range, so we went by ferry. It was a long journey – four hours on the boat, then six on the bus – and I sat bolt upright for most of the way, convinced I'd never sleep again. Somewhere outside Birmingham I nodded off on Shay's shoulder and I remember waking up as the bus was driving past red-bricked mansion blocks in a London suburb. It was spring and the trees were startlingly green and the tulips were out. Even to this day, I shy away from London. Whenever I have to go there, I relive those feelings, my first glimpse of the place. Those red-bricked mansion blocks are ubiquitous and I always wonder, *Were these the ones I saw?*

I rose back into consciousness, like swimming to the surface, and I heard myself crying. A noise that I'd never before made was tearing itself from my gut. Stunned and still part-anaesthetized, I lay and listened to myself. I'd stop soon.

And pain. Was there pain? I checked, and yes, there was, a low-down, pulling cramp. When I'd finished letting these yelps come out of me, I'd do something about the pain. Or maybe someone would come. In this hospital that wasn't a hospital, surely a nurse who wasn't a nurse would hear me and come.

But no one came. And almost dreamily, as if someone else was making those sounds, I lay and listened. I must have fallen back to sleep, and the next time I woke I was silent. Bizarrely, I felt almost OK.

*

On Saturday evening, when Shay collected me and brought me to the B&B where we were spending the night, he was immensely tender. I was relieved, yet I cried – only when it was all over and safe could I afford to let myself get sentimental about the baby. For some reason I'd decided that the baby had been a boy, and as I wondered out loud if he would have looked like me or him, Shay was clearly uncomfortable.

We left for Ireland on Sunday morning, arriving back that evening. Unbelievably, less than two days since I'd left, I was back in my bedroom, where everything looked deceptively – almost bafflingly – normal. My little desk was piled high with textbooks requiring my urgent attention. This was my future, it had never gone away, all I had to do now was re-embrace it. Immediately, in fact that very night, I knuckled down and threw myself into my work, it was only six weeks to my exams. But over the following days, weird stuff began to happen. I could hear babies crying everywhere – when I was in the shower, when the bus was moving – but when the water stopped running or the bus came to a halt, the faint wailing stopped too.

I tried to tell Shay, but he didn't want to know. 'Forget it,' he urged. 'You feel guilty but don't let it beat you. Think about the exams instead. Just a few weeks to go.'

So I swallowed my need to talk about it, to convince myself I'd done the right thing, and instead forced myself to list how many hours of study I'd managed. When the urge to talk about our baby got very bad, I'd ask Shay something about *Hamlet* or the early poetry of Yeats and he'd earnestly explain, mostly regurgitating study guides.

I got through the suspended animation of exam time and then it was all over. I'd left school, I was an adult, my life was about to begin. While we waited for our results, Shay and I were almost never apart. We watched a lot of telly together – even on the warm, sunny days when the celebratory sunshine made the corduroy couch and brown carpet look ridiculous, we stayed inside and watched the box.

We never had sex again.

Mid-summer, we got the results of our Leaving Cert – Shay did brilliantly and I did badly. Not disastrously, but I'd worked so hard that everyone's hopes for me had been high. My parents were confused and immediately set about reducing my failure into something unimportant. How were they to know that I'd spent the last six weeks before the exams sitting in my room straining to hear imaginary babies crying behind the ring of a burglar alarm?

The aftermath lingered for a very long time. Almost from the moment I was no longer pregnant, guilt and regret arrived and I began to think that having the baby wouldn't have been so bad. (Although I was just about together enough to understand that if I was still pregnant, I'd be yearning not to be.)

Contradictions pulled me this way and that. I felt I'd had the right to have an abortion – but I was still bothered by horrible uneasiness. No matter how cleanly I lived the rest of my life, till the day I died this would always be with me. I couldn't exactly find the right description: 'sin' was the wrong word, because that was about breaking someone else's laws. But a part of me would always be broken and I would always be a person who'd had an abortion.

I felt so trapped by this irreversibility that I thought about killing myself. Only for a few seconds, but for that short time I sincerely wanted to. It was like being shackled to something shameful and painful for ever. Not like having points on your licence or a criminal record that lapses after five years or ten. It could never be fixed. It would never be fixable.

And yet . . . I was relieved that I didn't have a child to bring up. What I really wished was that I'd never had to make the decision to begin with. And of course it was my fault, I should have kept my legs closed in the first place, but life isn't like that – even then I knew it – and it's easy to be wise after the fact.

Occasionally, anti-abortionists paraded through the streets of Dublin, campaigning to make abortion in Ireland more illegal than it already was, carrying rosary beads and waving placards with pictures of unborn foetuses. I had to look away. But when I listened to them condemning abortion so vehemently, I wanted to ask if any of them had ever been in my situation. I would've bet money that they hadn't. And that if they had, their commitment to high-minded principle might have wavered.

What bothered me most were the men – men protesting against abortion! Men! What did they know, what *could* they ever know, of the terror I'd felt. They couldn't get pregnant. But I never voiced any of it at home, because I didn't want to draw attention to the issue. And – at least when I was there – Claire never said anything either.

At the end of September, Shay went to London to do his degree in Media Studies. That had always been his plan, because Irish universities didn't offer such imaginative courses.

'This changes nothing,' he promised me, as we said goodbye at the ferry port. 'I'll write lots and see you at Christmas.'

But he never wrote. I'd had a premonition this might happen – I'd already started having dreams about trying to catch him even before he'd left – but when it did, I refused to believe it. I watched the post every day and after seven wretched weeks I took my pride in my hands, visited his mother and gave her a letter to give to him. 'Maybe I've been sending them to the wrong address,' I said. But she checked and the address I had was the right one.

'Have you heard from him?' I asked, and flinched when she said, in surprise, that of course she had, that he was getting on great.

I regrouped my hopes and instead hung everything on him coming home at Christmas. From the twentieth of December onwards I was a ball of adrenalin, waiting for the phone or the doorbell to ring. But when they didn't I began walking past his house, up the hill, down the hill, shaking with cold and nerves, desperate for a sighting of him. When I saw Fee, one of his sisters, emerge, I nabbed her and in a high, wobbly pretence of unconcern said, 'What day is Shay coming?'

Looking confused, she broke the news. He wasn't coming, he'd got a holiday job. 'I thought you'd know,' she said.

'Oh, I thought there was still a chance he might get here for a couple of days.' My humiliation had me stuttering.

Easter, I thought, he'll come home at Easter. But he didn't. Or for the summer. I waited for him long after most people would have given up hope.

In the meantime I'd got a job, where I'd made a new friend, Donna. Like my other friends, Sinead and Emily, she went out a lot, on the hunt for men and good times. I used to tag along and, with them urging me on, if some decentish bloke asked me out I'd say yes; nothing much came of any of them. There was someone called Colm who gave me an engraved lighter for my birthday, even though I didn't smoke. Then, for about six weeks, I saw a DSS worker who kept coming across his dole claimants working in the pubs he took me to; he ditched me when I wouldn't sleep with him. After him was a cuteish one called Anton, even though he wasn't foreign. I towered a good three inches over him and he kept wanting us to go for walks. I actually went to bed with him – probably, I later suspected, because I found it so embarrassing to be upright with him.

But no matter how I tried, I just couldn't get worked up about any of them.

The current of life was trying to drag me forward, but I resisted. I preferred the past, not yet convinced that that's what it was – the past. And I would never have believed when I'd said goodbye to Shay at the ferry port that it would be fifteen years before I saw him again.

44

I drove from the Mondrian back to Emily's. Roars of laughter and a smell of burning were coming from the Goatee Boys' back garden. Ignoring it all, I let myself into the mercifully empty house, and made straight for the couch. I didn't even turn on the lights, I just lay in the dark, feeling flattened, soulless, lost to myself.

As time passed after Shay's departure for London, occasional news reached me of him: he was spending the summer working in Cape Cod; he'd graduated; he'd got a job in Seattle. At some stage I understood that it was over, that he wasn't coming back to me. I tried my best with the other men I met, but I couldn't move forward. Then one night when I was twenty-one I bumped into Garv in a pub in town. It had been more than three years since I'd seen him. Like Shay, he'd gone away to college – Edinburgh for him. Now he was back, working in Dublin, and as we swapped autobiographical details, I felt so guilty about the way I'd treated him that I could barely look his way. Mid-small-talk I blurted out a shamefaced apology and, to my relief, he began to laugh. 'It's all right, Maggie, take it easy. It was a lifetime ago.' And he looked so cute that for the first time in a long, long time, I got a *feeling*.

It was a great surprise to find myself going out with him again, the boyfriend I'd had when I was seventeen, my first-ever boyfriend. I was wildly entertained by the novelty of it, as indeed was everyone else. But then it stopped being funny the day I lifted a snail off his windscreen and threw it at a passing car of nuns – because I realized I'd fallen in love with him.

I loved him so much – he was such a good man. Though he didn't have Shay's quicksilver charm, he enchanted me nevertheless. And I thought he was gorgeous. Again he didn't have Shay's full-on hunkiness, but he had subtler good looks that had worked their way under my skin, so that whenever I looked at him I got a rush. His eyes, his silky hair, his height, his big hands, the way he smelt of ironed cotton – I was mad about him. Above all, we were mates – I could tell him anything. He even got chapter and verse on myself and Shay and was nothing other than entirely sympathetic. Not even a flicker of judgement came from him.

'I'm not a murderer who's going to burn in hell, am I?' I asked anxiously.

'Of course you're not, but no one's saying it was an easy decision.'

And I felt so, so relieved to have met a man as benevolent as Garv was.

But some people went a bit weird when we got engaged. Emily, in particular. 'I'm afraid you're playing it safe by marrying him,' she said.

'I thought you liked him!' I said, wounded.

'I love him. But you got so badly burned by Delaney, and Garv is so cracked about you . . . Look, I just want you to be sure. Just think about it.'

I promised I would, but I didn't because I knew what I wanted.

So we got married, moved to Chicago, moved back to Dublin, got the rabbits, started trying for a baby, had one miscarriage, had a second miscarriage, then watched my past come back to haunt us.

For a long time, I was the only person I knew who'd had an abortion. Then, when she was twenty-five, Donna had one and Sinead's sister had one when she was thirty-one. Both times I was called on to relate how it was for me and I told them honestly what I thought: it was their body and they had the right to choose. They shouldn't give any credence to those pro-life bullies. But – at least if they were anything like me – they shouldn't expect to emerge unscathed from the experience, but should brace themselves for fall-out. Every emotion from guilt to curiosity, shock to regret, self-hatred to wretched relief.

Though I was glad no longer to be the only one, both those terminations churned up memories, so I almost felt as if I'd gone through it all again. But it passed and, mostly, I lived with being someone who'd had an abortion. As the years went by, I thought about it less. Except for every anniversary, when I felt awful, sometimes without even realizing why, at least not immediately. Then I'd remember the date and understand, and wonder what the baby would be like now, aged three, six, eight, eleven . . .

But I thought it had been absorbed safely into my past – until that last visit to Dr Collins, the day of reckoning, when I had to vent the worry that had been gnawing away at me.

'Could I keep miscarrying because . . . because . . . I've damaged myself?'

'In what way, damaged yourself?'

'By an operation?'

'What kind of operation? A termination?'

I flinched at his bluntness. 'Yes,' I mumbled.

'Unlikely. Very unlikely. We can check but it's highly unlikely.'

But I didn't believe him and I knew Garv didn't either, and though we never discussed it, that was the very moment our marriage keeled over and died.

Some time later – I don't know how long – the phone rang in the darkness of Emily's front room; I had no intention of getting it. I let it ring, waiting for the machine to pick up, but someone had switched it off so, cursing, I dragged myself over to the phone.

The second I answered, I remembered Emily's ban and said a silent prayer that it wouldn't be Larry the Savage. But it was Shay.

'Oh, hi.' He sounded surprised. 'I thought I'd get the machine.'

'Well, you got me instead.'

'I'm real sorry about tonight.' He sounded so contrite that my bitterness began to melt. 'It was a work thing, it came up suddenly.'

'You could have rung me.'

'Too late,' he said easily. 'You would have already left.'

'You're going back on Tuesday?'

'Yeah, so we're out of time.'

'But there's tomorrow. Or tomorrow night?'

'Bu –'

'Just for an hour or so.'

He was silent and I was holding my breath. 'OK,' he finally said. 'Tomorrow night, then. Same arrangement.'

I put down the phone feeling marginally better and decided

to pop next door and see how the barbecue was going. To my great pleasure, I was given a hero's welcome, as though it was years since they'd seen me, instead of a few short hours. Then it dawned on me that they were all scuttered; red-faced and rowdy, exhibiting the kind of aggressive drunkenness engendered by drinking tequila on an empty stomach. The smouldering grill was abandoned and a dozen shrunken, blackened things that might once have been burgers lay upon it. When Dad sidled up and asked if I'd any chocolate in my handbag, it transpired that no one had been fed.

Troy and Helen were curled up on the flowery couch, looking very cosy; there was no sign of Kirsty. Either Troy hadn't brought her, or she'd refused to enter the house on the grounds that it was a health hazard. Anna, Lara, Luis, Curtis and Emily were ensnared in a hard-to-follow discussion on the merits of brunch over TV. I would have liked to join in but I was so patently on a different wavelength to everyone else, i.e. not psychotic drunk, that it was pointless.

'You get freshly squeezed orange juice with brunch,' Lara said hotly. 'When has your TV ever done that for you?'

'But you can watch *The Simpsons* on TV. Gimme that over French toast any day,' Curtis retorted.

I wandered away, over to Mum and Ethan, but they were toe-to-toe in a barney.

'Who died for our sins?' Mum asked shrilly.

'But –'

'Who died for our sins?'

'Hey –'

'Tell me, come on, tell me. Who died for our sins? Just give me the name.' It was like being in an interrogation cell. 'His name, please!'

446

Ethan hung his head and mumbled, 'Jesus.'

'Who? Louder, I can't hear you.'

'Jesus,' Ethan said angrily.

'That's right, Jesus.' Mum almost smacked her lips with satisfaction. 'Did you die for anyone's sins? Well, did you?'

'No, but –'

'So you can hardly go around being the new Messiah, can you?'

After a pause, Ethan admitted, 'No, I suppose not.'

'You suppose right. Carry on with your computer studies, like a good lad, and less of the blasphemy, if you don't mind.' Then she turned the force of her personality on to me and slurred, 'Where's Shay?'

'Working.'

'Ah, feck,' she said moodily, lurching away.

I went and sat with the others, and then we noticed that Troy and Helen had disappeared.

'Where are they?' Emily clutched me.

'I don't know. Gone, it looks like.'

'Gone,' she wailed, clapping a hand over her mouth. 'Gone! He's going to fall in love with her.' Her face crumpled with sudden, drunken tears and she was snorting and coughing from crying. When she hadn't stopped a full five minutes later I said, 'C'mon, I'll take you home,' and led her, bent almost double from hopeless sobbing, back to her own house.

'I'm just very tired,' she kept saying. 'I've been working very hard and I'm very tired.'

I put her to bed, but before I put her light out she said, 'Wait Maggie, I want to talk to you.'

'What?' I asked defensively. She was going to tell me off again about Shay Delaney and I so wasn't in the mood.

'I'm going to ask Lou to marry me and have my babies.'
'Oh. Oh. Why?'
'Because I don't want to see him ever again.'

45

Conchita was due to come on Monday morning, so as soon as I awoke, I began a hurried clean-up. But then she rang to say she was sick and not coming and instantly I abandoned the housework. Only to recommence it about an hour later out of boredom – Emily was still sounders and there had been no visits or calls from any of my family. So when someone knocked on the door at ten past twelve, I nearly wrenched it off its hinges, so delighted was I to have company. It was Anna.

'Come in, come in,' I said. 'Tell us, did Helen come home?'

'Yeah, about half an hour ago.'

'Oh my God, she must have slept with Troy.'

'She did. Do you mind?'

'No, not a bit.' Although Emily clearly did; what was going on there? 'Sit down,' I urged Anna. 'What did she say about it?'

'He tied her up, it was great. Um, listen, I've got to talk to you about something.'

'Oh.' I'd got a bad feeling.

'You've to promise not to kill me.'

'I promise.' I didn't mean it, I only said it, so she'd tell me whatever she had to tell me.

'I've got a job.'

'And?'

'In Dublin.'

'Good for you.'

449

'In Garv's firm.'

Ah.

'Well, Dublin's a small town, coincidences happen.'

'It wasn't a coincidence,' she said in a little voice. 'He got me the job.'

'*What*? When?'

'After I crashed your car – sorry, sorry, sorry! – I couldn't find anything about insurance in your room, so I rang Garv and he told me to come over to get the stuff from him.' She looked at me almost questioningly. 'He was asking me how I was getting on without Shane and I told him how poxy it was and how I felt left behind by everyone and he was really, really kind.'

'Was he?' I was tight-lipped. So Garv managed to stop riding Truffle Woman for long enough to be nice to Anna?

'Really kind. He said that if I'd like to get a proper job he'd try and help me – he wasn't being, like, manipulative or anything, I promise. You know him, he's not like that. He was just being decent. So I got my hair cut and he set up an interview.'

'Big of him,' I muttered. I was suddenly very bitter.

'Yes, it was,' she said gently. 'That's exactly what it was. So they've offered me a job in their post room.'

That Garv was being so nice to one of my family while at the same time doing the dirty on me filled me with hot fury. I had to wait for the bad feelings to pass before I could speak.

'Congratulations.'

'Thank you,' she said with dignity. 'And I'm sorry.'

'Ah, it's OK,' I said, as the poisonous rage began to drain from me. 'And if you're really that sorry, you can do something for me.'

'What's that?'

'Tell me if you fancy Ethan.'

She thought about it. 'Kind of. But I'm not going after it. He's too young and flaky. There'd be no future in it.'

'It never stopped you before.'

'I know. Well . . . I'm different now.'

'Jesus Christ.'

'People can change,' she said, with most un-Anna-like defiance.

'Did I hear right?' Emily emerged from her bedroom, mascara crumbling from her lashes and her hair like a fur ball. 'She fancies Ethan? Oh God, it's all too much.' Banging around the room, making coffee, she muttered something that sounded like, 'They come over HERE.' Bang! 'They take our JOBS.' Bang! 'They steal our MEN.' Bang! Then a violent coughing fit overtook her and she inhaled deeply on her cigarette. 'I'm not long for this world. Thank God.'

Before I could explore her bad humour – which I was pretty sure had something to do with Troy – Mum and Helen arrived. I was dying to ask Helen all about Troy, but couldn't with Mum there. Instead I had to make sympathetic noises as everyone compared hangover symptoms.

The atmosphere was tense. Emily was smoking heavily and saying very little, just flicking Helen narrow-eyed looks from time to time. 'OK,' she uncurled herself with a sigh from the sofa, 'I'm going to call Lou.'

'Are you really going to tell him you want to marry him and have his children?'

'Yes,' she said shortly. 'If that doesn't scare him away, I don't know what will.'

She went into her bedroom and closed the door a little too loudly for comfort.

'What's up with her?' Helen snapped. 'Narky bitch.

'Oh Jesus!' She suddenly remembered something. 'You'll never fecking guess who rang last night for you.'

'Who?'

'Slimebucket. Creephead. Gobshite of the year.' At my puzzled face she shrieked, '*Garv!* Do I have to spell it out for you?'

'Garv rang? Here?' I knew I sounded stupid, but I couldn't help it.

'Yeah. I told him you were out with ridey Shay Delaney. Even though I don't think he's ridey, of course, but there's no need for Garv to know that. He sounded good and pissed off,' she said with relish. 'It was three o'clock in the morning in Ireland when he rang. He's obviously having trouble sleeping. Good enough for him!'

'What were you doing answering the phone? Didn't Emily say we weren't to?'

'Red rag to a bull, I'm afraid,' she said regretfully.

Emily came back out of her bedroom.

'Well?'

'He said yes,' she said faintly. 'Oh my God, now what am I going to do?'

'In my day,' Mum said, 'if you broke off an engagement you were sued for breach of promise.'

'Thanks a bunch.'

Various unspoken hostilities filled up the room and when Mum decided to go to the bathroom, they spilled over into an actual row. All of a sudden, Helen and Emily were leaning into each other, trading clipped barbs – concerning Troy.

'If you like him that much, why don't you do something about it?' Helen scorned. 'Like, if you don't stake your claim on him, you can't blame anyone else if they do.'

'It's too late,' Emily muttered. 'Now that he's met you.'

'Don't be so stupid, I'm leaving in a week.'

'I bet you'll decide to stay for him.'

Helen barked with laughter. 'Are you joking me? I'm going back to Ireland to set up my detective agency. Why would I bother staying here?'

'Because of Troy.'

'He's not that special.'

'Emily,' I had to cut in, 'what do you care about Troy? You're just friends with him. Aren't you?'

She shrugged sullenly and I had my answer: she was in love with him. I'd suspected the previous night and now I knew for sure.

I withered with shame; I'd been so wrapped up in my own problems I hadn't seen what was under my nose. I'd been so dense. Worse, I'd been so selfish.

'Well, why didn't you say before now?' I pleaded. 'Then we mightn't all have slept with him.'

'I haven't,' Anna said.

'I'd get in there fast,' Helen said.

Mum had come back from the bathroom but the argument was too advanced to knock it on the head. She picked up on it immediately. 'What did I miss?'

We all lapsed into tight-lipped silence.

'Margaret?' she demanded. 'What's going on?'

'Ah, um . . .'

'It's about Troy,' Helen supplied. 'Emily's mad about him.'

'And he's mad about her,' Mum said. 'So what's the problem?'

'No, you stupid old woman,' Helen said. 'He's mad about *me*.'

'Troy?' Mum confirmed. 'The one with the nose? That one? Yes, he's mad about Emily.'

'No, he's not,' Helen repeated. 'Just because the crowd of nutters next door think you're some sort of wise-woman-guru type doesn't mean you actually are.'

'Helen, you were just a diversion to the chap. And I suppose he thought it was no harm to make Emily jealous.'

'But –'

'Am I right, Emily?' Mum asked. 'He's got his eye on you?'

'Well, once he had,' she conceded, then coyly went further. 'He said he was in love with me.'

'When?'

'About a year ago.'

'And were you mad about him then?'

'Yes, probably.'

'So what,' Mum demanded in exasperation, 'in the name of GOD was stopping you?'

'He was too into his work,' Emily mumbled. 'I'd always be second. I thought it wouldn't work, then we wouldn't even be friends.'

'And now?'

A head-bowed reluctant mumble. 'I've changed my mind.'

'But in the meanwhile he started "getting off" – is that the phrase? – with all of your friends?'

'Yeah, except Lara.'

'Why not Lara?'

'I'll tell you some other time.'

'And you were jealous of these other girls?'

''Course.'

I closed my eyes at the memory of Emily realizing I'd slept with Troy, of her in convulsions when I asked if anything had ever happened between them. God, it must have been horrible for her.

'But I didn't totally mind, because I knew he liked me more than any of them and that his work was still his main love. But . . . but . . . I was worried about Helen.'

'Don't be,' Helen said. Not exactly pleasantly. 'You can have him.'

'He mightn't want me any more.'

'Only one way to find out,' Mum said.

'You mean ring him and ask him?'

'I do not!' Mum was appalled. 'I never rang anyone and told them I fancied them and I had my pick of the men. No, flirt with him, wear perfume, maybe cook him his favourite meal . . .'

'Ring him and ask him,' Helen, Anna and I chorused.

'OK,' Emily said thoughtfully, lighting another cigarette. 'I will.' She took the phone and the ashtray into her bedroom and closed the door, and ten minutes later she came out again. She was dressed, made-up and happier looking. 'I'm going out to meet him,' she said.

'Act coy,' Mum advised.

'Be straight,' I urged.

'Be straight yourself, Maggie,' Helen said slyly.

Mum darted me a suspicious look.

'Now what'll we do?' Mum asked, when Emily's block of flats had screeched away. 'Tell a joke, someone.'

We were all a little too fragile to want to do much else. Helen told a joke, Anna told one too but got the ending wrong, and I was garnering laughs by making my fringe stand out at right angles from my head when there was a knock on the door.

'The Goatee Boys, I suppose,' I said. 'Coming to apologize for not feeding you all last night.'

I opened the door, and there, standing outside, was someone I recognized but who didn't belong here. Garv.

Words deserted me.

'Hi,' he said.

'What the hell are you doing here?'

'You said if you weren't home in a month to come and get you. It's a month.'

It was actually only four weeks, not a full calendar month, and I knew that the real reason he was here was because he'd heard I'd been out with Shay Delaney. The bloody cheek of him, after his carry-on with Truffle Woman.

He looked the way people do when they've been trapped on a desert island for a while. His hair was longer than I'd ever seen it and was sticking up in tufts, three-day beard growth shaded his chin and jaw and, in the harsh glare of the sun, his eyes were lit blue – at least the bits that weren't bloodshot were. Even his jeans and T-shirt looked like he'd slept in them, and if he'd just got in on a flight from Ireland, I suppose he probably had.

'Who is it?' Helen asked.

'It's the adulterer,' I heard Mum say.

'Before they stone me,' Garv said, 'could we talk?'

'Come on,' I said wearily. 'We'll go for a walk on the beach.'

46

I was looking forward to this encounter with Garv about as much as a repeat of the time when I was sixteen and having hundreds of glass slivers removed from the tattered flesh of my knee. Nevertheless, we managed to maintain cordial chat while walking the six blocks to the beach.

'You cut your hair,' he said. 'It's nice.'

'Ah, you hate it really, admit it.'

'No, I like it. It's very . . . groovy. Especially the fringe.'

'Oh, please, don't mention the fringe. Have you somewhere to stay?'

'Yeah, it's near here. I rang Mrs Emily and she recommended the place she'd stayed in –'

I stopped him. 'The Ocean View. My family are staying there too.'

'Ohh-kaay. So I'd better have my breakfast in my room if I don't want to be pelted with rotten eggs in the dining room.'

'It might be for the best. So tell me, why didn't you just ring instead of coming all this way?'

'I did ring, loads of times, but the machine was always on and I felt weird about leaving a message . . .'

'Oh, so you're Emily's stalker.'

'Am I? God, my secret double life, I never knew. Anyway, I thought that some stuff is better said face-to-face.'

Up till then I'd assumed that Garv's appearance was in

response to Helen telling him I was out with Shay Delaney. But all of a sudden I was wondering what Garv had to say that merited a face-to-face visit? Could there be any further bad stuff to discover? Yes, actually, there could be: his new girl could be pregnant. The thought was such a shock that, as I stepped on to the beach, I stumbled.

'Are you still going out with that girl?' I asked.

To his credit, he didn't give me any wide-eyed 'What girl?' crap. He just waited a while, obviously weighing up what to say, then exhaled.

'No, I'm not.'

Relief was the first thing to hit, but immediately after, a wave of jealousy slapped me. So it was real. Really real. I forgot all about the two flings I'd had in the past month and I felt hollow and betrayed. A gathering sense of unreality surrounded me.

'Who was she?'

'Someone from work.'

'What was her name?'

'Karen.'

'Karen what?'

'Parsons.'

Driven by a self-destructive prurience, I wanted to know everything about her. What did she look like? Was she younger than me? Where had they done it? How many times? What kind of underwear had she? 'Was it serious?'

'No, not a bit. It lasted no length.' His every word hit me like a dart.

'Did you sleep with her?' I desperately wanted him to say no, that it had only been hand-holding and flirting. But, after a tense pause where I held my breath, he said, 'Yes, twice. I'm sorry, I'm sorry. I so wish I hadn't but I was off the wall.'

'Why's that, then?' I asked stiffly, jealous bile sickening my stomach.

'I was very depressed. They were my babies, too. But no one was interested in what I felt. I know it was harder for you, but it was killing me too. Then you and me stopped talking and the loneliness was unbearable, and then,' his voice dropped so low I could hardly hear him, 'when I couldn't get it up with you, I felt such a failure.'

'You'd no bother with her, I suppose. Your fancy woman. And look at what you've turned me into,' I cried. 'Someone who says things like "fancy woman".'

'I'm sorry,' he whispered.

'When did it start?'

'Not until you'd gone. Left for LA.'

I had a good snort at that. 'Something was going on long before then.'

'No, we were just . . . friends. I swear to God.'

'"Just friends." I can imagine. Flirting and sharing fucking truffles. You don't have to sleep with someone to be unfaithful, you know! You can be unfaithful with your emotions.'

He bowed his head.

'Was it the first time you did this to me?'

'Of course!' He sounded shocked.

'Your only fancy woman?'

'My only fancy woman.'

'But one too many.'

'I know, I know. I wish I hadn't. I'd give my left arm to go back in time and change things,' he muttered feverishly.

'You blamed me, didn't you? For the miscarriages?'

'How? It was hardly your fault.'

'It was. Maybe I'd . . . damaged myself . . . when I'd had the

459

abortion. That day in Doctor Collins's office, I knew you blamed me. But that was OK, because I blamed me too.'

'I didn't blame you. You were the one who was angry with me.'

'I was not.'

'You felt I'd forced you into trying for a baby. And if we'd never tried, we'd never have had all that misery with the miscarriages.'

I clamped my lips together, unwilling to admit anything, but the feelings were too big.

'OK, I was angry.' Still was. Furious, actually, I'd just discovered. Our life together had been fine until he'd opened that can of worms. 'But I wasn't the one who had an affair,' I said, consumed with bitterness.

'No, you just came to Los Angeles because of Shay Delaney.'

'What –? I did fucking not,' I stuttered indignantly.

'Yes, you did. You could have gone to London to Claire or New York to Rachel or you could have stayed in Dublin, but you came here.'

'Because of Emily.'

'*Not* because of Emily. Or not just because of Emily. There was that thing in the paper about Dark Star Productions and the work they were doing in Hollywood. You could have guessed he'd be here. I've been honest with you, why won't you be honest with me?'

We marched on in angry silence. The bloody audacity of him trying to shift the blame for *his* affair on to *me*. Somewhere in the recesses of my brain, a thought began to swim upwards, reaching to break the surface. Before it did, I turned on Garv. 'Why do you still hate Shay Delaney so much?'

He stopped, sat on a rock, put his head in his cupped hands, breathed deeply a couple of times, then looked up. 'Surely it's obvious?'

'Tell me.'

'Right, this is why. You are the most precious person in the world to me and Shay Delaney treated you like muck. When you told me about the abortion and all, I wanted to kill him. Then we got married, and it was fine when we were in Chicago, but then we moved home . . . every time Delaney's name got mentioned you went white.'

Really? I hadn't realized his effect on me was that evident.

'Yes, really.' Garv confirmed my unspoken query. 'And any time we drove past his mother's house, you turned and looked.'

Really? I had no knowledge of that either. Well, now that he mentioned it, maybe I did sometimes. Not every time, just sometimes.

'I used to go the long way round just so we wouldn't pass his old house. I felt like we were never going to be free of the fucker. Please try and imagine it the other way round – if every time some old girlfriend of mine was mentioned, one I'd ditched you for, I went funny. You wouldn't like it, would you?'

'Stop trying to blame me.'

'Then there's a thing in the paper about Dark Star Productions, then four days later you leave me, and the next time I hear from you, you're on your way to Los Angeles.'

'I didn't leave you because of reading anything about Dark Star Productions,' I said furiously. 'I left you because you were having a fucking AFFAIR. And you didn't even try to stop me –'

'Well, I'm doing it now,' he said grimly.

'All you did was say you'd pay the mortgage, then you helped me PACK, for God's sake.'

'I did try to stop you. I'd been trying to talk to you for days, but you ignored me or came home too drunk for there to be any point. The day you left I was all out of fight and I'd figured that you were going to leave me anyway.'

'How d'you reach that conclusion?'

'I suppose things had been desperate for so long. And you wouldn't talk to me.'

'*You* wouldn't talk to *me*! It was your fault.'

'I was hoping we could try and get beyond all that. Could we not just say that neither of us were perfect . . .'

'Speak for yourself. I didn't do anything wrong.' I was shaking with anger. 'So let me sum up what you've told me – you had an affair, but it was OK because it was all my fault.'

Then Garv did something he didn't do often – he lost his temper. He seemed to swell with it. His muscles were taut and his eyes were livid blue as he brought his face close to mine.

'That's not what I said.' He bit the words out. 'You KNOW what I said. But you don't want to hear it, do you?'

I looked at my watch and said coldly, 'I have to go.'

'Why?'

A pause. 'I have to meet someone.'

'Who? Shay Delaney?'

'Yeah.'

Garv went the colour of chalk and my anger got wiped away, to be replaced with the deadness I remembered from the first weeks of separation.

'Garv, why did you come here?'

'To try to persuade you to come home in the hope that we might rebuild us.' He smiled a little twist of a smile. 'Looks like I've had a wasted journey.'

462

'You were unfaithful to me. How could I ever forgive you? Or trust you again?'

'Oh, God.' He rubbed his hand over his eyes. I thought for a moment he was going to cry.

'Tell me one thing,' I said. 'Was she beautiful, this Karen?'

'Maggie, it wasn't like that, it wasn't about that . . .' He was in agony.

'Just a simple yes or no,' I cut in. 'Was she beautiful?'

'She was attractive, I suppose,' he admitted miserably.

'Oh yeah?' I grinned and he watched me warily. 'Well, I bet she wasn't as attractive as the girl I got off with.'

It took a moment. I could almost see the words being processed, then understanding dawn and when it did, he laughed out loud. 'Really?'

Garv was the only person – other than Emily – who knew how the girls in the porn films had affected me.

'Good for you,' he said. Then a little more sadly, 'Good for you.'

In a gesture that belonged to another life, he touched my head and hooked my hair behind my ears, first one, then the other. Then he noticed my red, flaking arm. 'Christ, your poor arm,' he said unhappily. Surprisingly, it seemed natural to hug one another and as I turned my face into his shoulder, he smelt of something that I couldn't identify. A huge sadness was mushrooming inside me, filling me up so I couldn't breathe.

'We really messed things up,' I choked into his T-shirt.

'No,' he said. 'No. We were just unlucky.'

47

This time Shay was waiting for me, smiling a slow, lazy smile as he watched me walk across the lobby. When I saw him, a thought flickered just beneath the surface, but I pushed it away and smiled back at him.

'Let's have a drink at the bar,' he said.

But the bar at the Mondrian was no ordinary hotel bar, devoid of character and atmosphere. It was the Sky Bar, hang-out of celebrities and beautiful people. Open to the warm, night sky and set around a luminous, turquoise swimming pool, a sexy decadent atmosphere was created by the scattering of huge silk cushions and low-slung day beds. The only lighting was from flame torches, which cast a mysterious glow and made everyone dewily beautiful.

FBI types in shades and walkie-talkies manned the reception desk – Fort Knox probably has less security – and only when Shay had produced his room key were the pearly gates opened.

We wandered amongst the silver, six-foot-high pot-plants looking for a seat, but all that was left was an enormous, white, satin mattress. Gingerly we placed ourselves upon it and one of the most beautiful girls I've ever seen took our drinks order.

Then Shay and I were alone, sitting on a mattress, looking at each other.

'I was afraid you were going to cancel me again tonight,' I blurted, out of need to say something.

'Look, I told you, last night was work, I couldn't help it,' he said, so defensively that for the first time I wondered if he was lying. And he'd tried to get out of meeting me tonight. And when he'd rung last night he'd been hoping to get the answering machine . . .

'I make you uncomfortable,' I said sadly.

'Not a bit of it.' Accompanied by a gorgeous smile.

'Ah, I do,' I teased. 'All that shaking hands with me, then running away.'

He half-laughed, 'Maybe I feel guilty.'

'For what?'

'For, you know, when we were teenagers. But it's all in the past and you don't hate me, right?'

'I don't hate you.'

He smiled with relief.

'But when you went away and never wrote to me,' I surprised myself by saying, 'I nearly lost my reason.'

He looked like I'd slapped him. 'I'm sorry, I thought it would be better that way. Less painful, to just let it all fade away.'

'Well, it wasn't, not for me. I spent years waiting for you.'

'I'm sorry, Maggie. I was only eighteen, young and stupid. I hadn't a clue. If there's anything I can do to make it up to you . . .' He stretched out, lay on his elbow, and placed his hand over mine. We sat in silence.

'Shay, tell me, are you happily married? Do you love your wife?'

'Yes and yes.'

'Are you faithful to her?'

'Yes.' Then a beat later, 'Mostly.'

'Mostly? What does that mean?'

'I am in Ireland,' he said awkwardly. 'But, like . . . when I'm working here . . .'

'I seeee . . .' I said speculatively, letting it hang in the air.

'Maggie, I want to tell you something.'

There was something about his tone that had me on the alert. His tawny eyes were on mine. 'Maggie, I want you to know . . .'

That he'd always loved me? That every day since he'd said goodbye to me at the ferry port, he'd yearned for me?

'Maggie, I'll never leave my wife.'

'Um . . .'

'My own dad left us and I saw what it did to the family.'

'Ah . . .'

'But you and I . . . I come to LA a lot – if you're still here, maybe we could . . .'

I understood what was happening: I was being offered a part-share in Shay Delaney. A consolation prize: *We apologize that your life was damaged by the abrupt withdrawal of Shay Delaney, but please accept this voucher to be redeemed by Shay Delaney at your convenience.*

Unexpectedly, I started to laugh. 'You're one of the good guys, aren't you, Shay?'

'I try. It matters.'

'Your wife is so lucky, having a husband who'll always stay with her.'

He nodded.

'Even though he rides rings around himself on his business trips.'

His face darkened and he half-sat up. 'Hey, there's no need to be like that. I'm just trying to . . .'

'What? Please everyone?' That started me laughing again.

'Trying to be fair.'

'Fair. Like you're a prize.'

He stared at me. He looked surprised, and I realized how very glad I was that I wasn't his wife, waiting at home six thousand miles away, taking care of three children and wondering anxiously what her handsome, charming husband was up to. And I knew something else – I wouldn't take a snail off his windscreen.

'You try to be everything to everyone; you can't say no. Don't you get tired?'

He wasn't happy. Not one bit.

'I thought this was what you wanted,' he sounded confused. 'You know, all that ringing me, insisting on seeing me. You knew I was married . . .'

Oh Christ, when he put it like that. He was right: I'd almost stalked him over the past couple of days.

'Why did you come here?' he asked. 'What did you want from me?'

Good question. Very good question. Being around him was like staring at the sun for too long: it temporarily blinded me. I'd gravitated to him, like a moth to a light, but with only the vaguest idea of what I'd hoped to get.

'I wanted to know why you never wrote to me.' But I already knew that, it was hardly rocket science: he'd outgrown me and didn't have the guts to tell me. No biggie, it happens all the time, especially at that age.

'And that's all?'

'Yes.'

'Sure,' he said, slightly scornfully. 'You wanted a lot more than that from me.'

I hadn't. I hadn't known what I'd wanted, but now I was certain of what I didn't want. I didn't want a relationship with him, part-time or otherwise.

'Honest to God, I just wanted closure.'

'Well, you've got it,' he snapped.

'I have, haven't I?' I grinned.

'You're in great form all of a sudden.'

'I am.' I felt light and free. Shay Delaney was just a guy from another life, the repository of hopes that were years past their use-by date.

Suddenly I found myself thinking about those people who break into the pyramids looking for treasure, but when they get there the tomb is empty because someone had got there long before them.

'Did you ever see *Raiders of the Lost Ark*?' I murmured.

He looked at me as if I'd cracked up completely. 'Of course I did.'

And the thought that had been striving to make itself known broke the surface, ready to be claimed – Garv had been right when he'd said that Shay was one of my reasons for coming to LA. It hadn't been a conscious decision, it had definitely been decided lower down in the sneakier part of my brain. But my first night in Los Angeles, when Emily had told me that Shay spent a lot of time there, I already half-knew – and even then I'd wondered if that was why I'd been so keen to respond to the invitation to stay with Emily.

You don't have to sleep with someone, you can be unfaithful with your emotions – and I was the one who'd said it.

Poor Garv. And what about the dreams I'd occasionally had about Shay? Garv didn't know about them – unless he did. He seemed to be several steps ahead of me.

Poor Garv, I thought again. What must it have been like, knowing that his wife still held a pocket of love for someone else? How lonely he must have been through the miscarriages, mutely carrying his grief and partaking in all the fuss around me. How humiliated he must have been when he became impotent. How frustrated when I wouldn't talk to him – because he was right, I had stopped talking to him.

Then I thought about him and Truffle Woman and a lick of anger touched me; I'd been adamant that I'd never forgive him. But what mattered more – my self-righteousness, or the truth? And I had to admit that I hadn't been perfect either.

That's the thing with relationships, I understood. It doesn't mean we don't hurt one another; how can we help it sometimes, we're only human? But if you love someone, you get hurt and you manage to forgive. And be forgiven. Garv had come to forgive me and I'd given him the bum's rush.

I rolled on to my back and stared up at the purplish night sky. Then I realized what Garv had smelt of when I'd hugged him goodbye earlier. He'd smelt of home.

'No stars tonight,' I said.

But the stars are always there, even in the daytime. Sometimes we just can't see them.

I sprang up. 'I've got to go.'

48

I drove fast, but all the stoplights were against me and it took nearly an hour to get to the Ocean View. I did one of my worst pieces of parking ever on the sidewalk outside and hurried into the tile-floored lobby. And who should I meet? Only Mum, Dad, Helen and Anna. I later discovered they'd been to the cinema.

'I thought you were out with Shay Delaney,' Mum said in surprise.

'I was.'

'Then what are you doing here?'

'Looking for Garv.'

'What for?' Her face was suddenly mutinous.

I didn't answer and she said hotly, 'If he can be unfaithful once, he'll do it again.'

The desk clerk followed this exchange with great interest. 'Hi,' I said. 'Can you ring Paul Garvan's room for me, please?'

'He checked out.'

My heart thumped hard. 'When?'

'About an hour ago.'

'Where was he going?'

'Home to Iowa.'

'Right, thanks, I'll get him at the airport.'

But when I turned around, Mum was blocking me. She drew herself up to her full height. 'You are not to go after him!'

'Don't, pet, for me,' Dad beseeched.

'Margaret, you're not to go!'

I stared at the two of them, stared long and confused, then said, 'My name is Maggie and just watch me.'

As I raced back to the car, there was the clatter of feet running after me. It was Anna. 'I'll come with you,' she said breathlessly. She jumped in beside me, slammed the car door shut and pulled on her seatbelt. 'Hit it!'

The journey seemed to take for ever, the traffic was very heavy for that time of night and, despite the spells Anna muttered, the stoplights were still against me.

'What airline do you think he flew?' I asked Anna, hoping for some sixth-sense action.

'American Airlines?'

'Maybe, unless he came through London, like I did.'

'Maggie, what about the other girl?'

'Gone.'

'But will you be able to forgive him for it?'

'Yeah, I think so. I hope so. The thing is, I wasn't without fault either.'

'And that makes it easier?'

'Yes, I love him, we'll work it out.' Then I added, 'Mind you, if he ever does it again, he is so dead.'

'Good for you. I always thought you and him were perfect for each other.'

'Did you?'

'Didn't you?'

'I have to say,' I admitted, 'there were times I had my doubts. I sometimes wondered if I was a wild girl who'd settled for a safe marriage.'

Anna sniggered and I gave an inquiring look. 'Sorry,' she said. 'It's just you . . . wild. Sorry.'

After a few seconds I said, 'It's OK. Because while I've been here I've tried being a bit wild and I just couldn't take to it.'

'Did you really get off with Lara or were you just winding Helen up?'

'I really did.'

'God Almighty.'

'But the point I'm making is I wasn't playing it safe when I married Garv. This is the way I really am!'

'Plain yoghurt at room temperature?'

'Um . . .'

'Plain yoghurt at room temperature and *proud of it*?'

I thought about it. 'How about plain yoghurt with raspberry puree at the bottom? I'd settle for that.'

'More interesting than you initially seem?'

'Exactly.'

'Has hidden depths.'

'Yes! I might even get a T-shirt saying it.'

'Two. One for Garv as well.'

'If we find him,' I said, my stomach tightening with fear. 'And if he doesn't tell me to fuck off.'

We finally reached LAX, and after some more truly atrocious parking, we ran into Departures. But when I asked the American Airlines check-in girl if she could tell me if Garv was on the flight, she said, 'I can't give out that information.'

'I'm his wife,' I begged.

'I don't care if you're the Dalai Lama.'

'It's urgent.'

'So is my need to use the bathroom, but there's nothing I can do about that either.'

'Come on,' Anna pulled me. 'We'll see if we can get him at the gate.'

LAX is huge and always crowded, no matter what time of the day or night it is. Panting, Anna and I ran through the throng, bouncing off people like pinballs. For a few frustrating minutes we got entangled in a flock of Hare Krishnas, and had to slow down to their pace, as they hopped and chanted. One of them even tried to give me a tambourine, before we managed to break free and begin sprinting again.

'What's he wearing?' Anna gasped.

'Jeans and a T-shirt. At least, that's what he was wearing earlier – he might have changed.'

'Is that him?' Anna said and my heart nearly jumped out of my mouth. But the man she was pointing at was an African-American.

'Sorry,' she said. 'I just saw jeans and T-shirt and jumped to conclusions.'

We raced in and out of all the shops and bars in Departures, and Garv was nowhere to be seen. The only place left to check was his actual gate, but without boarding cards we couldn't get past the barrier and the woman official was so not interested in our story.

'Security. You could be terrorists.'

'Do we look like terrorists?' I pleaded, hoping she'd see reason.

She snapped her gum a few times and drawled, 'Yeah, you do.'

I stared at her, trying to psych her into giving in. She stared back, bland and unaffected, and with each empty second my hope dwindled away. But I wouldn't give up.

'Let's check the shops and bars one more time.' But there was no sign of him. Sweating, my heart pounding, my blood fizzing with awful hope, I skidded back and forth like a headless chicken, Anna doing her best to keep up, and I only stopped when I ran myself into exhaustion. Still I didn't want to leave. 'Let's just hang around a bit and see if he comes.'

'OK,' Anna said, stretching and scanning like a meerkat on guard.

But when time passed and passed, I filled up with despair.

'Come on,' I eventually said. 'We're not going to find him. We might as well go.'

I drove home feeling like a waxwork model of myself. The streets and houses of Los Angeles disappeared and I was driving through a wasteland.

'You can call him,' Anna encouraged. 'The minute he gets back to Ireland.'

'Yeah,' I mumbled, but a lump of cold terror was lodged in my stomach. I knew I'd left it too late. He'd come, I'd chosen Shay, he'd gone. I'd had my chance and blown it. The realization was like that moment on a plane when your ears pop and everything is clear again.

'It was silly thinking I'd catch him at the airport,' I said wretchedly. 'That sort of thing only happens in movies.'

'Starring Meg Ryan,' Anna nodded gloomily.

'He would have vaulted over the barrier.'

'And everyone would have clapped and cheered.'

We both sighed and, in silence, continued the drive to nowhere.

For a long time I'd thought of my marriage as a horrible, dark place where I didn't want to go. I hadn't been able to remember anything good about it – but all of a sudden I could think of loads. Like, when we used to get ready to go out for the evening, Garv would appear before me in his Calvins and an ancient pair of cowboy boots and say, 'I'm ready!' And I'd frown and say, 'You can't go out like that. It's cold, you need a jacket.' Then I'd dot my foundation all over my face but not rub it in and he'd say, 'Exquisite, my dear, you're like a flower. But might I suggest a soupçon of lipstick.' So I'd put a streak of red on my chin or forehead and he'd declare, 'Perfecto!' Then hand me the cotton wool to rub it off.

And Friday nights used to be lovely – we'd get a video and a takeaway (no change there) and lie on the couch and unwind after the week. And before the second miscarriage, Friday night had always been sex night too – that's not to say we didn't sometimes do it at other times, Sunday mornings could be nice – but Friday night was always a given. And even though, like I said, it was a long time since we'd had sex on the kitchen table, I'd had no complaints. It had been wonderful being with someone who knew my body almost as well as I did.

Then I remembered the way we used to do each other's toothpaste. And how, whenever we went to the local Tex-Mex place, we used to share a basket of chicken wings as our starter, a basket of chicken wings for our main course and a basket of chicken wings for dessert. And the time . . .

Memories, each one happier than the next, tumbled into my head and presented themselves for inspection and I had to put my fist into my mouth to stop myself bawling with loss. I'd often heard it said, but never thought it would apply to me – you never know what you have until it's gone.

When we arrived back in Santa Monica, I'd no real idea of how I'd got us there.

'Do you want to be dropped at the Ocean View?' I asked Anna.

'No, I'll come to Emily's with you.'

I shoved my key into the lock and half-fell into Emily's front room – where so many people were sitting quietly that my first thought was, 'Who's dead?' In a second I'd taken in Emily, Troy, Mike, Charmaine, Luis, Curtis, Ethan . . .

'You got a guest, man,' Ethan said coldly, indicating the person beside him. Who happened to be Garv.

'I thought you'd gone back to Iowa.' Surprise made me sound stupid.

'Couldn't get on the plane. I only had a stand-by ticket. How was your date?'

'Short. Ludicrous. I went to the airport to try and catch you.'

My face was burning with emotion and everyone was staring, boring holes into me with their eyes. And was it my imagination or were they all clustered protectively around Garv – and sending me hostile vibes?

Emily stood up. 'How about we give them some space?' And after a brief, reluctant pause, everyone trotted meekly behind her towards the front door. As Curtis passed, he pointed to Garv and said angrily, 'This guy's a way better man than the jazzy dude with the toney wheels who gave you a ride home Friday night!'

'How do you know about that?' Emily asked.

'He's got a telescope,' Luis said.

'Ugh,' Emily groaned.

'This love thing, it's not like a haircut,' Luis leaned into me, as he left. 'You fuck it up, it's not going to grow back, right?'

'Er, right.'

'If it don't come back, it was never yours,' was Ethan's contribution. 'If it comes back, it's yours to keep.'

'Be careful what you wish for,' Mike nodded meaningfully. He was right there – I'd wished for Shay.

'Think of the snail,' Charmaine said.

'Huh?!' several of them exclaimed.

'The *snail*?' I heard Emily query. 'What's that all about?'

Then everyone had left and Garv and I were alone.

'What's going on?' he asked wearily.

'You were right. I'm sorry.'

'Right about what?'

'Shay Delaney. I was still sort of hung up on him – but I didn't know about it, I swear. Not really.'

Garv rubbed his eyes – he looked exhausted. 'This is one time I'd have been happy to be wrong.'

'I'm sorry. I'm so, so sorry.'

'I'm sorry too.'

The way he said it started alarm bells ringing; it was the wrong sort of 'sorry'. It sounded final and defeated. 'What for?' I asked, too quickly.

'Everything. For Karen. The awful months when we didn't properly talk. For keeping my mouth shut about Delaney and hoping it would go away.'

'It has gone way.' My breath was short. 'I swear.'

'Why did you come to the airport?'

'Because . . .' How did I say it? How to encapsulate the shift where everything came into focus and Garv was centre? 'I'd thought it was over with us, I really thought it was gone for ever. Then after seeing you today it all flared up again and every feeling was still there and I knew I'd always take the snail off your windscreen. And not off anyone else's.'

I finished on a gasp and, as Garv said nothing, my nerves stretched to the limit. I felt like a prisoner waiting to hear the verdict of the jury.

'Let me put it another way,' I tried. 'I love you.'

'Do you?'

'Yes, honestly. I mean, of *course* – would I have gone to the airport and tried to be Meg Ryan otherwise?'

And he surprised me by saying, 'The flight wasn't really full – I just said it to try to hold on to the last shred of my self-respect. I got to the airport and thought it was stupid to come all this way and give up so soon.' He shrugged. 'I came back to give it one more go with you.'

'Oh. Oh. Well. Great! Why?'

He looked away to one side as he thought about it, then laughed softly and faced me. 'Because you're my favourite.'

'Well, you're *my* favourite.'

'Make up your own compliments.'

'Sorry. OK. I love you.'

'I love you.'

'Now you're at it.'

'That's because I've very little imagination.'

'That makes two of us. We've a lot in common.'

'Yeah.'

'What would you have done,' I asked cautiously, 'if I hadn't come home? If I had . . . you know . . . stayed with Shay?'

'Dunno. Gone mad. Started eating lightbulbs.'

'Well I didn't, so the lightbulbs are safe.'

'Yeah.'

'Yeah,' I swallowed. And all of a sudden, the way he was looking at me made me nervous and shy. 'So . . . um . . . what happens now?'

'Well, we're in Hollywood,' he said, taking a step closer to me, 'So . . . ah . . . we could drive a car off a cliff?'

'Or run down a hill in slow motion?' I shifted nearer until I was close enough to get his delicious Garv smell.

'Or I could take you in my arms and kiss you until the room starts spinning around.'

'I like the sound of the kissing,' I said, barely above a whisper.

'Me too.'

So we did.

Epilogue

A week later, Larry Savage got the sack from Empire – just came in one morning and without explanation was told to clear his desk, then was escorted off the lot. Par for the course if you're a movie executive, they say. Emily's script is languishing on a shelf at Empire and the story of Chip the wonder dog looks likely never to be told. Which would have been a blessing, Emily said, except it also meant she only got paid half of her fee. So great was her fear of turning into the man shouting outside the supermarket that she resolved to get out of the scriptwriting game altogether. But Troy put an end to that by getting financing for an independent production of her newest script. Apparently, it's brilliant, really dark – Emily says it's thanks to the fact that she was so depressed and scared while writing it. Some producer from another small studio is interested in reviving *Hostage!* And one way and another, the wolf is being kept from the door, even if Mrs Emily still hasn't had a chance to wear her navy, spangledy dress to a première. However, she might get a chance to wear it in the near future. Not to a film première, but to a wedding – Emily and Troy's. I will admit to having had my doubts over Troy's fidelity, but since Emily hooked up with him, he's been a model of good behaviour.

Lou half-heartedly stalked Emily for a couple of weeks, then gave up, but when Kirsty heard about Troy and Emily, she turned to food. Apparently she put on fifteen pounds in as many days. I'd laugh, except it would be mean.

Lara continues to be a great big golden ball of fun. She hasn't yet found the right girl, but is having a fantastic time looking. Justin is still living a shut-down life with Desiree, but things picked up recently for him when the other expendable fat guy contracted glandular fever and lost a ton of weight.

Reza kicked her husband out and told him to go and live with 'his whore'. He was back within the week, prostrating himself with contrition.

The poor mad scriptwriter is still hanging around the supermarket shouting set directions at the people buying their groceries.

Luis's little problem cleared up on the second lot of antibiotics. Himself, Ethan and Curtis finished college, shaved off their goatees, grew their hair (those who were in the habit of shaving their heads) and got respectable. The Dukes of Hazzardmobile was sent to the wrecker's yard.

Charmaine and Mike are still Charmaine and Mike. Before I left, Charmaine told me my aura wasn't as toxic as it had been. Occasionally the fable-telling group ring Mum and ask her to come back. She sent them a copy of *The Tales of Finn McCool* and hopes that they'll now leave her in peace.

Connie got married and didn't get kidnapped on honeymoon.

Helen, to everyone's astonishment, really did set up a private-detective agency when she returned to Ireland. She specializes in 'domestics' – i.e., she traps cheating spouses – and she's kept busy. Anna got on so well in her new job that they promoted her from the bowels of the post room to the bright lights of the front desk. She no longer mentions Shane and apparently she gets the occasional e-mail from Ethan. Sometimes, to upset Mum, she says he's going to come and visit as soon as he gets time off.

Dad's neck is better now. So are my relations with him. It took a while, and even longer with my mother.

Dark Star Productions went to the wall, but Shay already has a high-flying new job in another film company. As Claire said – almost admiringly – when she heard, 'There he goes again. Falling into a pit of shite and coming out smelling of Paloma Picasso.'

I was watching telly the other day and it was previewing a glossy new drama series from America, when I saw someone who looked familiar. It took me a moment; he was a lot more shiny and packaged than the last time I'd seen him. 'It's Rudy!' I yelped. 'It's the ice-cream seller from the beach in Santa Monica. I used to buy Klondike bars off him.' No one believed me, of course.

Is that everyone? Oh, me. I'm in bed, unable to move, on account of being eight months pregnant and huge. I haven't seen my toes for weeks and once I lie on my back, I can't turn over or get up without Garv sliding a stick in under me and leaning on it. I've promised Helen that I'll tell her how agonizing the birth is and that I won't fob her off with any talk of miracles.

Garv and I are very together. It hasn't always been easy; we've had the occasional shout at each other as we've ironed everything out, but, at this stage, we're sure our bond is strong enough to survive the blips. Even though we were separated and angry with one another, we were still linked.

As he says himself, the stars are always there, even in the daylight. Sometimes we just can't see them.

Publishing in **September 2012**

The Mystery of Mercy Close

Enjoy the first chapter now . . .

I wouldn't mind – I mean, this is the sheer irony of the thing – but I'm the only person I know who *doesn't* think it would be delicious to go into 'someplace' for 'a rest'. You'd want to hear my sister Claire going on about it, as if waking up one morning and finding herself in a mental hospital would be the most delightful experience imaginable.

'I've a great idea,' she declared to her friend, Judy. 'Let's have our nervous breakdowns at the same time.'

'Brilliant!' Judy said.

'We'll get a double room. It'll be gorgeous.'

'Paint me a picture.'

'Weeeeell. Kind people ... soft, welcoming hands ... whispering voices ... white bed-linen, white sofas, white orchids, everything white ...'

'Like in heaven,' Judy said.

'Just like in heaven!'

Not just like in heaven! I opened my mouth to protest, but there was no stopping them.

'... the sound of tinkling water ...'

'... the smell of jasmine ...'

'... a clock ticking in the near distance ...'

'... the plangent chime of a bell ...'

'... and us lying in bed off our heads on Xanax.'

'Dreamily gazing at dust motes ...'

'... or reading *Grazia*.'

'... or buying Magnum Golds from the man who goes from ward to ward selling ice cream ...'

But there would be no man selling Magnum Golds. Or any of the other nice things either.

'A wise voice will say –' Judy paused for effect: '"Lay down your burdens, Judy."'

'And some lovely wafty nurse will cancel all our appointments,' Claire said. 'She'll tell everyone to leave us alone. She'll tell all the ungrateful bastards that we're having a nervous breakdown and it was their fault and they'll have to be a lot nicer to us if we ever come out again.'

Both Claire and Judy had savagely busy lives – kids, dogs, husbands, jobs and an onerous, time-consuming dedication to looking ten years younger than their actual age. They were perpetually whizzing around in people carriers, dropping sons to rugby practice, picking daughters up from the dentist, racing across town to get to a meeting. Multitasking was an art form for them – they used the dead seconds stuck at traffic lights to rub their calves with fake-tan wipes, they answered emails from their seat at the cinema and they baked red velvet cupcakes at midnight while simultaneously being mocked by their teenage daughters as 'a pitiful fat old cow'. Not a moment was wasted.

'They'll give us Xanax.' Claire was back in her reverie.

'Oh lovvvvely.'

'As much as we want. The second the bliss starts to wear off, we'll ring a bell and a nurse will come and give us a top-up.'

'We'll never have to get dressed. Every morning they'll bring us new cotton pyjamas, brand new, out of the packet. And we'll sleep sixteen hours a day.'

'Oh sleep . . .'

'It'll be like being wrapped up in a big marshmallow cocoon; we'll feel all floaty and happy and dreamy . . .'

It was time to point out the one big nasty flaw in their delicious vision. 'But you'd be in a psychiatric hospital.'

Both Claire and Judy looked wildly startled.

Eventually Claire said, 'I'm not talking about a psychiatric hospital. Just a place you'd go for . . . a rest.'

'The place people go for "a rest" *is* a psychiatric hospital.'

They fell silent. Judy chewed her bottom lip. They were obviously thinking about this.

'What did you think it was?' I asked.

'Well . . . sort of like a spa,' Claire said. 'With, you know . . . prescription drugs.'

'They have mad people in there,' I said. 'Proper mad people. Ill people.'

More silence followed, then Claire looked up at me, her face bright red. '*God*, Helen,' she exclaimed. 'You're such a cow. Can't you ever let anyone have anything nice?'

Thursday

I

I was thinking about food. Stuck in traffic, it's what I do. What any normal person does, of course, but now that I thought about it, I hadn't had anything to eat since seven o'clock this morning, about ten hours ago. A Laddz song came on the radio for the second time that day – how about that for bad luck? – and as the maudlin syrupy harmonies filled the car I had a brief but powerful urge to drive into a pole.

There was a petrol station coming up on the left, the red sign of refreshment hanging invitingly in the sky. I could extricate myself from this gridlock and go in and buy a doughnut. But the doughnuts they sold in those places were as tasteless as the sponges you find at the bottom of the ocean; I'd be better off just washing myself with one. Besides, a swarm of huge black vultures was circling over the petrol pumps and they were kind of putting me off. No, I decided, I'd hang on and –

Wait a minute! *Vultures?*

In a city?

At a petrol station?

I took a second look and they weren't vultures. Just seagulls. Ordinary Irish seagulls.

Then I thought: Ah no, not again.

Fifteen minutes later I pulled up outside my parents' house, took a moment to gather myself, then started rummaging for a key to let myself in. They'd tried to make me give it back when I moved out three years ago but – thinking strategically – I'd hung on to it. Mum had made noises about changing the locks but seeing as she and Dad took eight years to decide to buy a yellow bucket, what were the chances that they'd manage something as complicated as getting a new lock?

I found them in the kitchen, sitting at the table drinking tea and eating cake. Old people. What a great life they had. Even those who don't do t'ai chi. (Which I'll get to.)

They looked up and stared at me with barely concealed resentment.

'I've news,' I said.

Mum found her voice. 'What are you doing here?'

'I live here.'

'You don't. We got rid of you. We painted your room. We've never been happier.'

'I said I've news. That's my news. I live here.'

The fear was starting to creep into her face now. 'You have your own place.' She was blustering but she was losing conviction. After all, she must have been expecting this.

'I don't,' I said. 'Not as of this morning. I've nowhere to live.'

'The mortgage people?' She was ashen. (Beneath her regulation-issue Irish-Mammy orange foundation.)

'What's going on?' Dad was deaf. Also frequently confused. It was hard to know which disability was in the driving seat at any particular time.

'She didn't pay her MORTGAGE,' Mum said, into his good ear. 'Her flat's been RECLAIMED.'

'I couldn't *afford* to pay the mortgage. You're making it sound like it's my fault. Anyway, it's more complicated than that.'

'You have a boyfriend,' Mum said hopefully. 'Can't you live with him?'

'You've changed your tune, you rampant Catholic.'

'We have to keep up with the times.'

I shook my head. 'I can't move in with Artie. His kids won't let me.' Not exactly. Only Bruno. He absolutely hated me but Iona was pleasant enough and Bella positively adored me. 'You're my parents. Unconditional love, might I remind you. My stuff is in the car.'

'What! All of it?'

'No.' I'd spent the day with two cash-in-hand blokes. The last few sticks of furniture I owned were now stashed in a massive self-storage place out past the airport, waiting for the good times to come again. 'Just my clothes and work stuff.' Quite a lot of work stuff, actually, seeing as I'd had to let my office go over a year ago. And quite a lot of clothes too, even though I'd thrown out tons and tons while I'd been packing.

'But when will it end?' Mum said querulously. 'When do we get our golden years?'

'Never.' Dad spoke with sudden confidence. 'She's part of a syndrome. Generation Boomerang. Adult children coming back to live in the family home. I read about it in *Grazia*.'

There was no disagreeing with *Grazia*.

'You can stay for a few days,' Mum conceded. 'But be warned. We might want to sell this house and go on a Caribbean cruise.'

Property prices being as low as they were, the sale of this house probably wouldn't fetch enough money to send them on a cruise of the Arran Islands. But, as I made my way out to the car to start lugging in my boxes of stuff, I decided not to rub it in. After all, they were giving me a roof over my head.

'What time is dinner?' I wasn't hungry but I wanted to know the drill.

'Dinner?'

There was no dinner.

'We don't really bother any more,' Mum confessed. 'Not now it's just the two of us.'

This was distressing news. I was feeling bad enough, without my parents suddenly behaving like they were in death's waiting room. 'But what do you eat?'

They looked at each other in surprise, then at the cake on the table. 'Well . . . cake, I suppose.'

Back in the day this arrangement couldn't have suited me better – all through my childhood my four sisters and I considered it a high-risk activity to eat anything that Mum had cooked – but I wasn't myself.

'So what time is cake?'

'Whatever time you like.'

That wouldn't do. 'I need a time.'

'Seven, then.'

'Okay. Listen . . . I saw a swarm of vultures over the petrol station.'

Mum tightened her lips.

'There are no vultures in Ireland,' Dad said. 'Saint Patrick drove them out.'

'He's right,' Mum said forcefully. 'You didn't see any vultures.'

'But –' I stopped. What was the point? I opened my mouth to suck in some air.

'What are you doing?' Mum sounded alarmed.

'I'm . . .' What was I doing? 'I'm trying to breathe. My chest is stuck. There isn't enough room to let the air in.'

'Of course there's room. Breathing is the most natural thing in the world.'

'I think my ribs have shrunk. You know the way your bones shrink when you get old.'

'You're only thirty-three. Wait till you get to my age and then you'll know all about shrunken bones.'

Even though I didn't know what age Mum was – she lied about it constantly and elaborately, sometimes making reference to the vital part she played in the 1916 Rising ('I helped type up the Declaration of Independence for young Padraig to read on the steps of the GPO'), other times waxing lyrical on the teenage years she spent jiving to 'The Hucklebuck' the time Elvis came to Ireland (Elvis never came to Ireland and never sang 'The Hucklebuck', but if you try telling her that, she just gets worse, insisting that Elvis made a secret visit on his way to Germany and that he sang 'The Hucklebuck' specifically because she asked him to) – she seemed bigger and more robust than ever.

'Catch your breath there, come on, come on, anyone can do it,' she urged. 'A small child can do it. So what are you doing this evening? After your . . . cake? Will we watch telly? We've got twenty-nine episodes of *Come Dine With Me* recorded.'

'Ah . . .' I didn't want to watch *Come Dine With Me*. Normally I watched at least two shows a day, but suddenly I was sick of it.

I had an open invitation to Artie's. His kids would be there tonight and I wasn't sure I had the strength for talking to them; also their presence interfered with my full and free sexual access to him. But he'd been working in Belfast all week and I'd . . . yes, spit it out, might as well admit it . . . I'd missed him.

'I'll probably go to Artie's,' I said.

Mum lit up. 'Can I come?'

'Of course you can't! I've warned you!'

Mum had a thing for Artie's house. You've probably seen the type, if you read interiors magazines. From the outside it looks like a salt-of-the-earth working-class cottage, crouched right on the pavement, doffing its cap and knowing its place. The slate roof is crooked and the front door is so low that the only person who could sail through with full confidence that they wouldn't crack their skull would be a certified midget.

But when you actually get into the house you find that someone has knocked off the entire back wall and replaced it with a glassy futuristic wonderland of floating staircases and suspended bird's-nest bedrooms and faraway skylights.

Mum had been there only once, by accident – I had warned her not to get out of the car but she had blatantly disobeyed me – and it had made such a big impression on her that she had caused me considerable embarrassment. I would not permit it to happen again.

'All right, I won't come,' she said. 'But I've a favour to ask.'

'What?'

'Would you come to the Laddz reunion concert with me?'

'Are you out of your mind?'

'Out of *my* mind? You're a fine one to talk, you and your vultures.'

about marian

Marian Keyes is one of the most successful Irish novelists of all time. Though she was brought up in a home where a lot of storytelling went on, it never occurred to her that she could write. Instead she studied law and accountancy, and finally started writing short stories in 1993 'out of the blue'. Though she had no intention of ever writing a novel ('It would take too long') she sent her short stories to a publisher, with a letter saying she'd started work on a novel. The publishers replied, asking to see it, and once her panic had subsided she began to write what subsequently became her first book, *Watermelon*.

It was published in Ireland in 1995, where it was an immediate, runaway success. Its chatty, conversational style and whimsical Irish humour appealed to all age groups, and this appeal spread to Britain when *Watermelon* was picked as a Fresh Talent book. Other countries followed (most notably the US in 1997), and Marian is now published in thirty-three languages.

To date, the woman who said she'd never write a novel has published eleven of them: *Watermelon, Lucy Sullivan is Getting Married, Rachel's Holiday, Last Chance Saloon, Sushi for Beginners, Angels, The Other Side of the Story, Anybody Out There, This Charming Man* and *The Brightest Star in the Sky*, all bestsellers around the world.

Anybody Out There won the British Book Award for popular fiction and the inaugural Melissa Nathan Prize for comedy romance. *This Charming Man* won the Irish Book Award for popular fiction and was the biggest-selling novel of 2009.

The books deal variously with modern ailments including addiction, depression, domestic violence, the glass ceiling and serious illness, but are always written with compassion, humour and hope.

As well as novels, Marian writes short stories and articles for magazines and other publications. She is also involved with various charities – she contributed to a multi-authored book, *Yeats is Dead!*, where all the royalties were donated to Amnesty International. She has published two collections of her journalism, titled *Under the Duvet* and *Further Under the Duvet*, and donated all royalties from Irish sales to the Simon Community, a charity which works with the homeless. More recently, Marian wrote a beginner's baking book, *Saved by Cake*, which gave an extremely honest account of her battle with depression.

She was born in Limerick in 1963 and brought up in Cavan, Cork, Galway and Dublin; she spent her twenties in London, but is now living in Dún Laoghaire with her husband Tony. She includes among her hobbies: reading, movies, shoes, handbags and feminism.

Find out
more about

marian
at
www.mariankeyes.com

Q&A with
marian

Q: On average, how long does it take you to write a book?

A: I'll tell you how long! A couple of years ago on a book tour in Australia, I had the great privilege of sitting next to a woman at lunch who asked me how many books I 'churned out' a year. 'Three?' She suggested. 'Four?' 'Oh God no,' sez I. 'Twelve. One a month. Only it doesn't take me the whole month to churn it, it only takes about a week and I spend the other three weeks at a top-notch spa having lymphatic drainage on my thighs.'

No, sadly, *mes amis*, I said no such thing. I only thought of that fabulous reply several sleepless nights later. Nor did I enact scenario number two and tell her to 'fuck off'. No, what I did was stammer apologetically that actually it took a full two years for me to 'churn out' a single book.

Q: Do you ever base your characters on real people?

A: Christ alive, are you mad! No. No, no, no. That would be so cruel — and I'd end up with no friends. But that doesn't stop people assuming that I've stuck them in a book. I was told a great story about an ex-boyfriend who, when he heard I'd written my first book, leapt up from the pub where he'd heard the news, abandoning his pint, ran down the street to the nearest bookshop, rattled the shut door and begged the security guard to let him in so that he could get his hands on the book because he was convinced I'd written all about him and his unusually small mickey. Which of course I hadn't (his mickey wasn't even that small, certainly no worse than average). But really, it's far more fun to just make people up.

Q: Do you have a particular method or approach to writing?

A: I always start with a character and really work on them until I know them: as I said, they're never based on real people but maybe have attributes of a number of different people. And I generally have a subject I'm thinking about – and then I put the two together. That sounds so simple, but it isn't.

I used up my own life in the first three books (although they weren't autobiographical), and I've had to do research since. I find research very difficult as I have to ask people impertinent questions, which makes me very uncomfortable.

I never have the whole book planned out – I feel I'd lose interest if I did.

Q: Who or what was your biggest influence in deciding to become a writer?

A: I'm not sure I did decide to become a writer. I started writing short stories as an escape, and to entertain myself and my friends. I would have been terrified to call myself a writer – it was only a couple of years later when I gave up my day job that I realized that that was what I was. In terms of storytelling, my mother was a big influence, her family had a great oral storytelling tradition.

Q: Do you have any tips for aspiring writers?

A: Keep backups. Also: firstly, stop talking about it and start writing it word by word. Formally set aside time to write – respect your book enough not to try to fit it in, in bitty gaps, around the rest of your life. Better still, try to write at the same time every day; this seems to trigger the subconscious into readiness.

Don't be surprised if your first efforts are shockingly bad — indeed, expect to marvel at the gap between what you want to say in your head and how it appears on the page. But persevere: chances are it will improve.

Beware of setting yourself up as the 'new' Maeve Binchy or the 'new' someone else; it's always cringingly obvious. Instead, write in your own unique voice and be proud of it.

Write what you know — and if you don't know it, be prepared to research it.

Finally — enjoy it! If you enjoy writing it, chances are that people will enjoy reading it.

Q: **What are your favourite books?**

A: I read quite widely, but thrillers are always a favourite. Sometimes I get fixated by writers — I had a spell when I read everything Alexander McCall Smith has written, and wondered how he would take it if I called round to his house and asked if I could move in, and live with him like a household pet. At the moment I'm mildly obsessed with Michael Connelly. I also had a Dennis Lehane spell. I'm also very fond of non-fiction, especially any accounts of those who have suffered 'My drink and drugs hell'. The gorier the better.

I'm also trying to educate myself about — God, I'm not sure of the right word — feminism? 'Women's issues?' Anyway, whatever it's called, I've been trying to read seminal feminist books because my generation were never encouraged to do so — we were told that the battles of the sexes was over and we were all equal now. But I sort of couldn't help noticing that women are still second-class citizens and, you know, it really annoyed me but I didn't have the language to articulate how I felt, so I decided to educate myself in the subject.

Q: **When you're not writing, how do you pass the time with your family?**

A: Doing good works amongst the deserving poor.
Also, lying on the couch watching *Big Brother*, and if not available counting the days until it comes back.
Hanging around shoe shops.
Looking at *net-a-porter* on the internet and complaining about the prices.
Wondering why my fingernails always split when they reach their optimum length.
Sometimes I make curries and buy socks.

rachel's holiday

How did it end up like this? Twenty-seven, unemployed, mistaken for a drug addict, the back arse of nowhere with an empty Valium bottle in my knickers . . .

Meet Rachel Walsh. She has a pair of size eight feet and such a fondness for recreational drugs that her family has forked out the cash for a spell in Cloisters – Dublin's answer to the Betty Ford Clinic. She's only agreed to her incarceration because she's heard that rehab is wall-to-wall jacuzzis, gymnasiums and rock stars going tepid turkey – and it's about time she had a holiday.

But what Rachel doesn't count on are the toe-curling embarrassments heaped on her by family and group therapy, the dearth of sex, drugs and rock'n'roll – and missing Luke, her ex. What kind of a new start in life is this?

'Both hilarious and heartbreaking'
Daily Express

THE NUMBER ONE BESTSELLER

marian keyes

'The voice of a generation'
Daily Mirror

rachel's holiday

A Walsh Family Novel

I'm in the Last Chance Saloon. In my decrepit, thirty-one-year-old state, I'd probably never get another man . . .

Tara, Katherine and Fenton have been best friends since they were teenagers. Now in their early thirties, they've been living it up in London for ten years. But what have they got to show for it?

Sure, Tara's got her boyfriend — but she loves food, shopping and her lipstick so much more. Katherine, on the other hand, is a serial singleton whose neatness fetish won't let a man mess up her life. And Fenton? Well, Fenton has everything. Until he gets ill and he has to ask himself: what have you got if you haven't got your health?

All three are drinking in the last chance saloon and they're about to discover that if you don't change your life, life has a way of changing you . . .

'A comforting doorstopper of a read that's as addictive as solitaire'
Sunday Times

'Dammit',
she realized.
'I think I'm having
a nervous breakdown.'

sushi for beginners

Hot-shot magazine editor Lisa Edwards's career is destined for high-rise New York when suddenly she's diverted to low-rise Dublin. But what can she do about it?

Ashling Kennedy, Lisa's super-organized assistant, worries about everything from her lack of waist to the lack of men in her life. She's even anxious about a little bit of raw fish . . .

Clodagh Kelly is Ashling's best friend and has her prince, her beautiful kids and a lovely house — everything in fact that Ashling ever wanted. And yet, she's still not satisfied.

Three women on the verge of happiness and even closer to complete breakdown. Which way will they fall?

'Laden with plot twists,
joke asides and
nicely turned bits
of zeitgeisty humour'
Guardian

THE NUMBER ONE BESTSELLER

marian keyes

'Should come with a health warning.
It's totally addictive . . . a real page turner'
Sunday Express

sushi for beginners

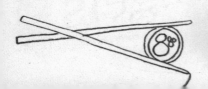

I'd always lived a fairly blameless life . . .
So when, out of the blue, everything
just disintegrated like wet paper,
I couldn't shake a wormy suspicion
that this was long overdue.
All that clean living simply
isn't natural.

angels

Unlike the rest of her family, Maggie Walsh has always done everything right. At thirty-three she has a proper job, is happily married to Garv and never puts a foot wrong. So why does she make a bolt for Hollywood and her best friend, Emily?

In the City of Angels, Maggie gets to do things she's never done before: mixing with film stars, pitching scripts, partying non-stop. But is this really a once-in-a-lifetime journey of self-discovery, or is she simply running away from married life?

'Funny, compassionate, well-observed and irreverent, this is a romp of a read'
Time Out

THE NUMBER ONE BESTSELLER

marian keyes

'An outstanding writer and chronicler of our times'
Independent on Sunday

angels

A Walsh Family Novel

The answering machine was hopping; it looked like it was going at triple speed, like it was furious. (Could that actually happen? Does it speed up if you've got a lot of unlistened to messages on it?)

the other side of the story

The agent: Jojo, a high-flying literary agent on the up, has just made a very bad career move: she's jumped into bed with her married boss Mark . . .

The bestseller: Jojo's sweet-natured client Lily's first novel is a roaring success. She and lover Anton celebrate by spending the advance for her second book. Then she gets writer's block . . .

The unknown: Gemma used to be Lily's best friend — until Lily 'stole' Anton. Now she's writing her own story — painfully and hilariously — when supershark agent Jojo stumbles across it . . .

When their fortunes become entangled, it seems too much to hope that they'll all find a happy ending. But maybe they'll each discover that there's more than one side to every story . . .

'Wildly funny, romantic and nearly impossible to put down. Elbow your way to the front of the queue to get a copy'
Daily Mail

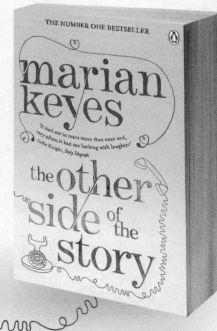

THE NUMBER ONE BESTSELLER

marian keyes

'It had me in tears more than once and, very often, it had me barking with laughter'
India Knight, Daily Telegraph

the other side of the story

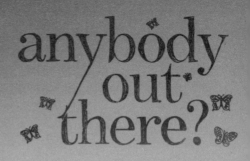

I had to go back to New York and try to find him. There was a chance he mightn't be there but I had to give it a go because there was one thing I was certain of: he wasn't here.

anybody out there?

Anna Walsh is officially a wreck. She's covered in bandages and she's lying in her parents' Good Front Room dreaming of leaving Dublin and getting back to New York. To her friends. To The Most Fabulous Job in the World™. And most of all, back to Aiden.

But her family has other ideas (not to mention headaches of their own). And Aiden, for some reason, seems unwilling to get in touch.

What could possibly have shattered the world that Anna loved so much? And is Aiden the only one who can put it all back together again?

'An inspirational tale of one woman's triumph over despair'
Daily Telegraph

THE NUMBER ONE BESTSELLER

marian keyes

'Hilarious, heartbreaking fiction'
Cosmopolitan

anybody out there?

A Walsh Family Novel

WINNER of the Popular Fiction Prize

The worst day of my life . . .
I was his girlfriend,
the media was going wild
that he was getting married
to another woman,
and he hadn't called me.
Bad sign.

this charming man

'Everybody remembers where they were the day they heard that Paddy de Courcy was getting married.'

But for four women in particular, the big news about the charismatic politician is especially momentous . . .

Stylist Lola has every reason to be interested in who Paddy's marrying – because she's his girlfriend, yet she definitely isn't the bride-to-be . . . Journalist Grace wants the inside story on the de Courcy engagement and thinks Lola holds the key . . . while Grace's sister, Marnie, still can't forget her first love: a certain Paddy de Courcy. And what of the soon-to-be Mrs de Courcy? Alicia will do anything for her fiancé and is determined to be the perfect wife. But does she know the real Paddy?

Four very different women.
One awfully charming man.
And the dark secret
that binds them all . . .

'Gripping from the start . . .
the master at her best'
Daily Telegraph

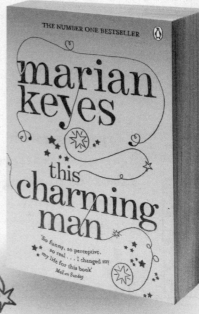

marian keyes

this charming man

'So funny, so perceptive, so real . . . I changed my life for this book'
Mail on Sunday

June the first,
a bright
summer's evening,
a Monday . . .

The brightest star in the sky

At 66 Star Street in Dublin, someone is watching over the lives of the people living in its flats. But no one is aware of it — yet . . .

One of them is ready to take the plunge and fall in love; another is torn between two very different lovers. For some, secrets they want to stay buried will come to light and for others, the unveiling of those secrets will have tragic consequences.

Fate is on its way to Star Street, bringing with it love and tragedy, friendship and heartbreak, and the power to change their lives in the most unexpected of ways.

As the couples, flatmates and repentant singletons of No 66 fall in and out of love, clutch at and drop secrets, laugh, cry and simply try to live, no one suspects the visitor patiently waiting in the wings. For soon, really very soon, everything is going to change . . .

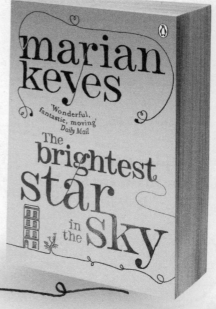

'Wonderful, fantastic, moving'
Daily Mail

marian keyes

The brightest star in the sky

'Zips along with engaging characters, fabulous plotting and spot-on dialogue'
Daily Mail

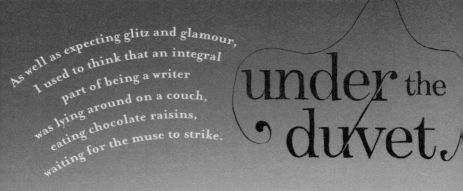

As well as expecting glitz and glamour, I used to think that an integral part of being a writer was lying around on a couch, eating chocolate raisins, waiting for the muse to strike.

under the duvet

Her novels are adored by millions around the world — now read Marian Keyes's collected journalism and exclusive, previously unpublished material in *Under the Duvet*.

Bursting with her hilarious observations — on life, in-laws, weight loss and parties; her love of shoes and her LTFs (Long-Term Friends); the horrors of estate agents and lost luggage; and how she once had an office Christmas party that involved roasting two sheep on a spit, Moroccan style — it's the perfect bedtime companion, and will have you wincing with recognition or roaring with laughter.

'A great book to dip into'
Company

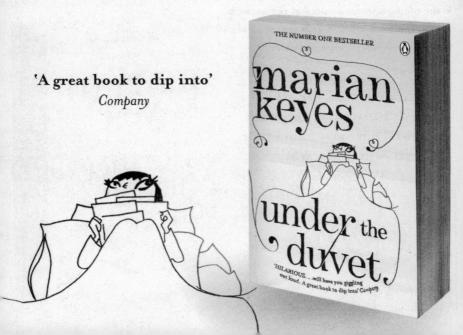

THE NUMBER ONE BESTSELLER

marian keyes

under the duvet

'HILARIOUS. . . .will have you giggling out loud. A great book to dip into' *Company*

Let's get one thing straight: I'm not an outdoorsy type. If I was offered the choice between white-water rafting and being savaged by a rabid dog, I'd be likely to tick the box marked 'dog'.

further under the duvet

Slide further under the duvet, get yourself comfortable and let Marian take you places you've never been before . . .

Places like the Irish air-guitar championships, a shopping trip to Bloomingdale's with a difference and Cannes with a chronic case of Villaitis. Along the way you'll encounter knicker-politics, fake tans, sticky-out ears and passionate love affairs both with make-up and Toblerones. And of course, agony aunt Mammy Walsh is on hand to solve all your problems.

Hilarious and poignant, down-to-earth and moving, Marian's long-awaited second volume of journalism and previously unpublished writing is the modern woman's perfect companion. So put the kettle on and grab that KitKat Chunky – everything else will wait.

'A must read for all. Keyes's funny and poignant tales will have you chuckling in your train seat'
Heat

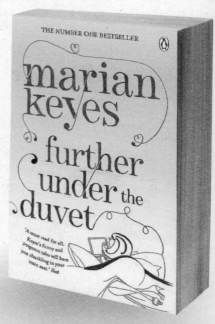

So I baked a cake – a chocolate cheesecake, as it happens.
And I enjoyed making it so much that I baked another. And another . . .

Saved by Cake

Learn to bake
with Britain and Ireland's
favourite women's fiction author, Marian Keyes

Saved by Cake gives an extremely honest account of Marian Keyes's recent battle with depression, and how baking has helped her. A complete novice in the kitchen, Marian decided to bake a cake for a friend and that was it – she realized that baking was what she needed to do in order to get her through each day. And so she baked, and she wrote her recipes down, and little by little the depression has started to lift, along with her sponges . . .

With chapters on cupcakes, cheesecakes, meringues and macaroons, chocolate cakes, fruit cakes and favourite classics, Marian's recipes are aimed firmly at beginner bakers, offering hints and tips to help along the way. Never patronizing, always honest and witty, accessible and full of fun, the bakes and cakes that Marian serves up in this cookbook will put a smile on your face and make you happy. From her Consistently Reliable Cupcakes and Very Chocolately Macaroons, to the ease of her Fridge-set Honeycomb Cheesecake, you will want to have a go at making all of Marian's recipes.
The shoe and handbag biscuits particularly.
Very covetable. Very Marian.

'Wonderfully presented and with an incredibly honest, moving introduction this book is a treat that should lift anyone's spirits . . . and appetites'
The Sun

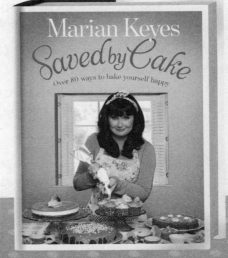

marian keyes books

DIRECT TO YOUR DOOR

9780241958438 **RACHEL'S HOLIDAY** £7.99
'A gloriously funny book' *Sunday Times*

9780241958452 **LAST CHANCE SALOON** £7.99
'A comforting doorstopper of a read' *Daily Mail*

9780241958476 **SUSHI FOR BEGINNERS** £7.99
'It's totally addictive…a real page turner' *Sunday Express*

9780241958421 **ANGELS** £7.99
'Brilliantly satisfying, unputdownable' *Company*

9780241958445 **THE OTHER SIDE OF THE STORY** £7.99
'Another chart-topping blockbuster' *Guardian*

9780241958469 **ANYBODY OUT THERE** £7.99
'Another beautifully written triumph' *Heat*

9780241958483 **THIS CHARMING MAN** £7.99
'Compulsively readable' *Daily Express*

9780141028675 **THE BRIGHTEST STAR IN THE SKY** £7.99
'The master at her best' *Daily Telegraph*

9780241959107 **UNDER THE DUVET** £7.99
'Her honesty and humour can have you laughing out loud' *Heat*

9780241959121 **FURTHER UNDER THE DUVET** £7.99
'A must read for all' *Heat*

9780718158897 **SAVED BY CAKE** £16.99
'A book that will put a smile on your face and banish the blues'
Daily Express

Simply call Penguin c/o Bookpost on **01624 677237** and have
your credit/debit card ready. Alternatively e-mail your order
to **bookshop@enterprise.net**. Postage and packaging is free in
mainland UK. Overseas customers must add £2 per book.
Prices and availability subject to change without notice.

Psst

want the latest gossip on all your favourite writers?

Then come and join us in . . .

THE BOOK BOUTIQUE

. . . the **exclusive club** for anyone who loves to curl up with the latest reads in women's fiction.

- All the latest news on the best authors.
- Early copies of the latest reads months before they're out.
- Chat with like-minded readers as well as bestselling writers.
- Excellent recommendations for new books to read.
- Exclusive competitions to get your hands on stylish prizes.

SIGN UP for our regular newsletter by emailing
thebookboutique@uk.penguingroup.com

or if you really can't wait, get over to

www.facebook.com/TheBookBoutique

He just wanted a decent book to read ...

Not too much to ask, is it? It was in 1935 when Allen Lane, Managing Director of Bodley Head Publishers, stood on a platform at Exeter railway station looking for something good to read on his journey back to London. His choice was limited to popular magazines and poor-quality paperbacks – the same choice faced every day by the vast majority of readers, few of whom could afford hardbacks. Lane's disappointment and subsequent anger at the range of books generally available led him to found a company – and change the world.

'We believed in the existence in this country of a vast reading public for intelligent books at a low price, and staked everything on it'
Sir Allen Lane, 1902–1970, founder of Penguin Books

The quality paperback had arrived – and not just in bookshops. Lane was adamant that his Penguins should appear in chain stores and tobacconists, and should cost no more than a packet of cigarettes.

Reading habits (and cigarette prices) have changed since 1935, but Penguin still believes in publishing the best books for everybody to enjoy. We still believe that good design costs no more than bad design, and we still believe that quality books published passionately and responsibly make the world a better place.

So wherever you see the little bird – whether it's on a piece of prize-winning literary fiction or a celebrity autobiography, political tour de force or historical masterpiece, a serial-killer thriller, reference book, world classic or a piece of pure escapism – you can bet that it represents the very best that the genre has to offer.

Whatever you like to read – trust Penguin.